Work
has never b

THE DARE
by Barb... ....

Fasten your seatbelt for the hot air balloon
ride of your life in sunny Spain—this intense
rollercoaster of emotional excitement will
leave your romance senses tingling!

HIRED: SASSY ASSISTANT
by Nina Harrington

When your feet are firmly back on the ground,
curl up in an English mansion with this warm,
witty and wildly romantic story by sparkling
new British talent Nina Harrington.

Dear Reader

What if…? This is the way I start a lot of stories. What if a young woman is rather conservative, has the care of her teenage brother, and needs to earn a living to support them both? What if she's paired with a daredevil sportsman in a hot air balloon race? Can you imagine how you'd feel if to keep your job you needed to fly for a week in a balloon with some sexy guy who doesn't even know the meaning of 'afraid of heights'?

That's the beginning of Amalia Catalon's great adventure.

Ever since I was in Reno, Nevada, during its hot air balloon event, I've dreamed of a story that captured the excitement and uncertainty of hot air balloons. From the ground, ballooning looks effortless as the balloons quietly sail overhead. Only when researching the various aspects of the sport did I learn how skilled the pilots must be, and how important the ground crews are to the sport.

Come fly away with Amalia and Rafael Sandoval as they explore each other's lives, hopes and fears, and end up with a most unexpected ending—one where love soars above all.

My heartfelt thanks to Diana Dempsey and John Wright for their help with the technical aspects and flying experiences.

I hope you enjoy Amalia's and Rafael's journey, soaring over Spain in a red and black hot air balloon. And I hope that their ending makes you long for your own adventure.

All the best

Barbara

THE DAREDEVIL TYCOON

BY
BARBARA McMAHON

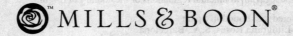

MILLS & BOON®

All the characters in this book have no existence outside the imagination of the author, and have no relation whatsoever to anyone bearing the same name or names. They are not even distantly inspired by any individual known or unknown to the author, and all the incidents are pure invention.

First published in Great Britain 2009
Paperback edition 2010
Harlequin Mills & Boon Limited,
Eton House, 18-24 Paradise Road, Richmond, Surrey TW9 1SR

© Barbara McMahon 2009

ISBN: 978 0 263 86963 7

Harlequin Mills & Boon policy is to use papers that are natural, renewable and recyclable products and made from wood grown in sustainable forests. The logging and manufacturing process conform to the legal environmental regulations of the country of origin.

Printed and bound in Spain
by Litografia Rosés, S.A., Barcelona

Barbara McMahon was born and raised in the south USA, but settled in California after spending a year flying around the world for an international airline. After settling down to raise a family and work for a computer firm, she began writing when her children started school. Now, feeling fortunate in being able to realise a long-held dream of quitting her 'day job' and writing full time, she and her husband have moved to the Sierra Nevada mountains of California, where she finds her desire to write is stronger than ever. With the beauty of the mountains visible from her windows, and the pace of life slower than the hectic San Francisco Bay Area where they previously resided, she finds more time than ever to think up stories and characters and share them with others through writing. Barbara loves to hear from readers. You can reach her at PO Box 977, Pioneer, CA 95666-0977, USA. Readers can also contact Barbara at her website: www.barbaramcmahon.com

**Barbara's next destination
is the desert kingdom of Quishari. Don't miss
her sparkling new duet** *Jewels of the Desert:*

**ACCIDENTALLY THE SHEIKH'S WIFE
and
MARRYING THE SCARRED SHEIKH
April 2010**

To John Wright, who shared so much about
hot air ballooning it makes me want to take a ride.
Thank you!

CHAPTER ONE

AMALIA Catalon set the coffee tray down on the low table between the sofa and the visitor chairs. The two men were in deep discussion, hardly noticing her. She stepped back, wondering if her boss needed anything else. A quick glance out the window showed the storm that had been threatening had arrived. Sheets of rain slid down the windows. It was so overcast it looked like dusk, though it was only late afternoon. She could hardly see the sea. Sighing softly, she regretted the wet walk she would have to take to get the bus and then again after her stop for the three blocks to the flat. She'd be soaked and cold by the time she reached home tonight.

Still, it couldn't be helped. She had an umbrella, but the way the wind was driving the rain, she knew it would offer little shelter.

"Ha, in your dreams," Stefano Vicente said,

laughing sardonically at something his business rival had said.

Amalia turned to look at Rafael Sandoval. What had he said to cause her boss's outburst? Not that Stefano Vicente was the most complacent man. She'd worked for his firm more than seven years, and the last three of those for the head man himself. She knew how quickly he flew off the handle if aggravated.

"Care to wager fifty grand on it?" Rafael asked easily. He leaned back casually in the chair, watching his rival with calculating eyes. Amalia moved back a bit, preparing to leave, watching Rafael Sandoval warily. Despite being a trust-fund baby, Rafael had developed a thriving import-export business that was a major player in the Mediterranean area and was now moving globally, with offices around the world. He worked hard and played hard. Young to have achieved so much, he had the arrogance that went with amazing success. When he walked into the office, she always felt a bit in awe. He wasted no time with chitchat with a lowly employee. He knew his worth, and his time was valuable. Still, twice over the past several months she'd caught him studying her. When she'd met his gaze, he'd winked and looked away.

She watched him every chance she got—he

was mesmerizing, fascinating. But if ever he caught her staring at him, she would be mortified.

"You're on. And I'll delight in taking your check," Stefano replied with an arrogance equal to Rafael's. Amalia shifted her gaze to her boss. In his late fifties, he was always looking for new challenges to prove to the world he was still in top form. What was it about men that they had to constantly be in competition with each other?

"You're mistaken, it's I who will delight in taking yours," Rafael retorted. Mid thirties, and gorgeous to boot, Rafael Sandoval had risen in the ranks of important men in Barcelona with meteoric speed, which was why she'd seen him numerous times over the last three years. The only men her boss dealt with were the city's high rollers. She would also bet her last Euro that Rafael had never paid enough attention to her to recognize her on the street. A quick glance, eyes trailing over her trim figure, and then he'd move on.

Stefano picked up a cup of the hot coffee and poured cream in it, stirring gently. When the small ritual was complete, he looked at Rafael.

"You have only been ballooning a couple of years. You're a fool to think you can outrace me. I've been doing it for more than a decade."

"I'm a quick learner," Rafael said.

His easy grin captivated Amalia's attention. What would it be like to have him smile at her that way?

"Or is that your way of trying to get out of the wager we just made?" Rafael taunted.

"I'm not trying to get out of anything," Stefano protested. "It'll be easy money."

"As will the deal we're about to sign. You are signing, are you not?"

Stefano looked at the contract that lay on the low table in front of him. "Should I have my attorneys review it once more?"

"They've had it for a week. Nothing's changed."

"So you say."

Rafael's easy manner dropped in a heartbeat. He narrowed his eyes as he studied Stefano. He said slowly, "So I do say. Do you doubt my word?" The silky tone of his voice belied the anger that showed in the clenched jaw, the flashing dark eyes. He would not be an adversary Amalia would want.

Stefano shrugged and sipped his coffee. After a swallow that had Amalia wondering if he was playing with fire to delay his answer, he deliberately put the cup back on the saucer.

"I do not doubt your word. It's not a small deal that can be brushed away if it fails," Stefano explained.

"It will not fail," Rafael replied.

Stefano stared at Rafael for a long moment, then nodded. He took his pen and signed both sets of papers with a flourish.

Rafael wasn't quick to relax. Amalia almost held her breath as the drama played out before her. Both men had forgotten she was in the room. She dare not move for worry of drawing their attention. She wished she could just ease out the door and be gone.

Tossing his pen on the table, Stefano leaned back in his chair. "How about we make the challenge a bit more interesting," he said.

"By?" Rafael asked, calmly reaching for the pen to sign his own name to the contracts.

"We'll limit people on board to ourselves and one guest—a nonballooner—chosen by the opposition. I choose who rides with you, you choose for me. We each have a man on the chase team to keep the records in conjunction with the chase team. We compete in the daily events at the festival and then begin our long jump."

Rafael considered the suggestion for a moment, then with an obvious change in demeanor, relaxed, leaned back and smiled. "That works for me. You'll be so far behind by the fourth day of the festival you'll concede without the long jump."

Stefano looked at Amalia. "What do you think?"

She glanced at her boss's longtime rival and regretfully shook her head. Stefano wasn't one to concede defeat in anything. "It'll never happen."

"Spoken like a true PA, loyal to the end," Stefano said with a grin. "You're my choice."

Amalia stared at him in shock. "I know nothing about hot air balloons!" Only that they looked lovely when quietly sailing by, far overhead. And that it made her sick to even think about being so high above the ground.

"The purpose of the bet is to pit Rafael's skill, such as it may be, against mine. By each having a novice, we'll equalize the competition. One on one, so to speak," Stefano said.

"The Barcelona Balloon Festival will be four days of races and events. For us after day four we make a long jump and see who can get the farthest in a week. Are you up to that?" Rafael asked her.

She looked at him, feeling the full force of those dark eyes as he regarded her. She shivered. Spend eleven days with him in the confines of those little baskets that dangled beneath the balloons? Not likely.

"No. I can't do that. Pick someone else," she said to her boss. She knew nothing about the sport, but she knew she feared heights. To spend days in the air was more than she could deal with. Not to mention spending that time with Rafael Sandoval.

The man was beyond gorgeous—tall and masculine, his dark hair shone beneath the artificial light. At thirty-four he had no gray marring the rich mahogany color. His dark eyes mirrored his emotions—when he wanted them to. Moving from amusement to anger in a split second, he fascinated her when she was around him—which wasn't often, thank goodness. He drew her involuntary interest like a flame drew a moth. And she would expect the same results if she let herself be drawn in—instant annihilation.

He was one of the best-looking men she'd ever seen, everyone thought so. Especially the society photographers who loved to have him on their pages—usually escorting a beautiful woman to some high-society event. Of course they also captured him racing his yacht last summer and when he won the single-engine airplane race from Cadiz to Barcelona two years ago. He participated in a wide and wild range of sports. She had seen the spreads in the Sunday newspapers and read with fascinated interest, since she could claim a brief acquaintance with him because of his dealings with her boss.

But she had no desire to spend even an hour in his company. He was far too dynamic and flamboyant to have anything in common with her. He'd find her boring and predictable and probably amusing.

With all the adulation he received, he was undoubtedly self-centered and self-focused. Did he ever approach life like a normal person—with worries and concerns? Probably not. Having the Sandoval fortune behind him didn't hurt, either.

"Yes, Vicente, pick someone else," Rafael agreed, turning away from Amalia.

"Like the woman you're dating now?" Stefano asked sardonically. "Maybe I should. You'd lose track of even the basics with the charm Teresa offers and I'd win easily. But I'd rather have a challenge."

"Teresa would dislike the early hours and the discomfort when it's cold. How do I know a person of your choice wouldn't sabotage the race?"

"I would never do such a thing!" Amalia exclaimed, incensed. How dare he impugn her integrity!

He shrugged and took one of the contracts, putting it into his briefcase. "Second choice?" he asked Vicente.

"I'll get back to you."

"I think I'll ask my PA to join you. Helena at

least follows the sport, though she has never participated in any events. I gave her a ride last year and she liked it."

"Send me her name and phone number and I'll talk to her," Stefano said. "And I'll have one of my chase crew contact yours. There will be no sabotage. He'll help as a regular crew member— only be there to verify the times and distances."

"Do we get rights of refusal?" Rafael asked.

"If both agree," Stefano replied.

"Then start writing your check," Rafael said, deliberately goading the other man.

Amalia thought about the report that still needed finishing. She didn't have time to stand around and listen to two very wealthy men talk about a silly hot air balloon race. The fifty thousand Euros they bandied around so easily would make a world of difference in her life. To most people's lives. To these men it was chump change. Betting on a balloon race seemed frivolous in the extreme.

"Maybe we should sweeten the pot a bit. Loser has to present to winner in front of the Barcelona Business Alliance at the next quarterly meeting," Rafael suggested.

Amalia looked at Rafael, seeing the devilment in his eyes. He was wild and daring, and she strongly suspected he loved every moment of this.

It was obvious he never expected to lose; he rarely did. Not only did he have pots of money, he had the best luck in the world, if the newspapers could be believed. From learning to fly a few years ago, to deep sea diving, to this newest hobby of hot air ballooning, he loved to challenge himself—and anyone involved in the sport with him.

Stefano gathered his copy of the contract and held it out for Amalia. She stepped closer to take it and then retreated to the door of his office.

Standing, Stefano held out his hand to Rafael. "May the best man win, and I intend to!"

Rafael stood, as well, and shook his hand. "Prepare your presentation speech for the BBA's meeting. It had better be good, to wipe out the sting of humiliation."

Amalia opened the door for the departing man. When Rafael drew level with her, he looked at her again. "It's not too late to change your mind," he said. "Find out what working with a winner is like."

"My boss will win," she said loyally.

He shook his head and winked at her before walking past. She could smell the expensive after-shave lotion he used—something fresh and woodsy. Perfect for him. She felt the attraction that seemed like an invisible aura around him and for a split second she wished that wink had meant something special.

When Rafael Sandoval left her anteroom and walked toward the elevators, she turned and looked at her boss. While not as notorious as his competitor, he could still claim outrageous behavior and daring escapades that made the papers. How his wife stood it all these years was a mystery to Amalia.

She looked at her boss. "Can you win?" she asked.

"Of course," he said easily. Walking back to his desk, he looked at her. "But I need your help. I want you to go with Sandoval."

She shook her head. "I'm afraid of heights. Besides, what would I talk to the man about?"

He laughed. "No need to worry about that. He'll be too busy trying to outmaneuver me. Don't worry about receiving a pass from the man, you aren't his type. He likes luscious, sophisticated prima donnas, not hardworking businesswomen. The intent is to make sure he isn't getting help from a ringer."

Amalia shook her head again. She couldn't go off on a hot air balloon ride. Even if she didn't have a phobia about heights, she had work to do. Her brother to take care of. She'd have to find a way to convince Stefano it would be a mistake. He was too focused on the need to one-up Rafael Sandoval to worry about a mere personal assistant's reasons for refusing.

"I need to get the Tunisia report finished. And you need to think of another choice. I really can't do it." Turning, she headed for the door.

"Then call Teresa Valesquez for me, will you?" he asked. "I might get her interested. Maybe she would distract Rafael long enough for me to have an easy triumph."

Amalia nodded and kept walking. Teresa Valesquez was Rafael's latest girlfriend. Amalia had recently read about them attending a reception together. The accompanying picture had captured the worldly look of his latest. Her sleek, short blond hair contrasted so well with her dark eyes. The gown she'd worn was the latest fashion and had looked fabulous on her figure.

Except, would she still be around by the time the balloon race began? The one thing Amalia had noticed was how frequently Rafael changed companions. The balloon race was still a couple of weeks away—plenty of time for him to find a new woman and for Teresa to be old news.

She sat at her desk and looked up the phone number for Ms. Valesquez. When she was on the line, Amalia clicked her over to Stefano's phone. She could finish the report if she had no more interruptions before close of business.

Just before five, she finished the last set and put them in the envelopes for different staff members.

That was a major project completed. The rest of the week should be a breeze—or as much as it ever was working for Stefano Vicente. She liked her job well enough; she found it interesting and fulfilling. Which was good, since she'd likely be at it for another four or five years. Once her brother was out of college and on his own, she'd give a thought to returning to school to work for her own degree—interrupted barely months after she'd started university by the death of her parents.

Amalia's goal remained to become a graphic designer—working with multinational corporations to develop and maintain Web pages. She loved playing around on computers. She'd streamlined many of the office functions through technology. But it wasn't enough to satisfy her. She wanted new horizons. She dabbled in Web design for friends, but looked for more challenges and a monetary reward for her work.

When she'd expressed that interest to Stefano a couple of years ago, asking if she could switch divisions, he'd refused. He hadn't wanted to break in another new PA. Maybe she did her job too well, but it wasn't in her to do less than her best.

At least she had a good position that enabled them to live in a modest flat. After their parents were killed, there had been more debt than assets. Once everything had been sold, there was nothing left for extras. Amalia could still remember the panic she felt knowing that Jose depended entirely on her. She'd only been nineteen, Jose a mere eight. She'd floundered those first couple of years until she began to work for this firm.

Promotions had moved her up, and her current job now paid enough to save a bit for college for her younger brother. One more year of public school and he'd be off to university. He wanted to be a physicist. He'd probably be over the moon with a chance to ride in a hot air balloon. She dare not tell him; he'd badger her forever to take advantage of the opportunity.

She shut off her computer, tidied her desk and donned her serviceable raincoat. She was already planning the evening meal she'd prepare for herself and Jose.

Stefano stepped into her office.

"I need you to renew my order of weather schedules first thing in the morning." He handed her a piece of paper on which he'd written down the Internet addresses. One was from a local weather forecasting service in Barcelona. The other two covered other areas, including the eastern part of Spain and parts of southern France.

She nodded. "Anything else?"

"Not right now. I've got to prepare for the flight, though. There's more to it this time than casual fun. I can't wait to see Rafael's face in front of the BBA giving me the winning check."

"The entire plan sounds scary," she murmured. She had gone to the Barcelona Balloon Festival the first time it had been held after she joined the firm. She hadn't stayed after the first wave of balloons lifted into the air. The small wicker baskets were dwarfed by the huge balloons, dangling by incredibly thin ropes that connected the basket to the balloon. Imagine rising above the earth dependent solely on hot air in a large nylon bag. She shuddered just thinking about it. The entire venture looked precarious and dangerous. She preferred to keep her feet on terra firma.

"It's perfectly safe and a lot of fun. There's nothing like soaring a couple of thousand feet above the earth. Watching the landscape drift by below, going where the wind takes you."

"Unless you get tangled in power lines and get zapped, or go down in the Med and drown before rescue, or—" Or just fall from the basket and splat on the ground. She shook her head at the horrible image that popped into her mind.

"That happens, like, once in a lifetime." Stefano laughed.

"It could be *your* lifetime, or the end of it!"

"No, I don't think so. I haven't had even so much as a near miss in all the years I've been doing this. Anyway, you're off the hook. Teresa Valesquez is delighted to be going with Rafael. I think she expects a ring on her finger by the end of the trip. Doubt he'll ask, though, because he hasn't so far. He strikes me as the perpetual playboy bachelor who's having far too much fun to get tied down. See you in the morning," he added, turning and reentering his office.

She grabbed her umbrella, wondering if that or her raincoat would be much protection against the deluge that continued.

Stepping outside a few moments later, Amalia paused beneath the building's portico debating whether or not to dash to the bus stop without her umbrella raised and hope she didn't become soaked, or give in to the inevitable and use the umbrella until the wind turned it inside out.

A sleek black sports car drew to a stop at the curb in front of her. The passenger window slid down.

"Need a lift?"

She leaned over a bit to peer in. Rafael Sandoval looked back at her.

"Get in, I'll drive you home," he ordered.

Normally Amalia would object to his imperious tone, but she was pragmatic enough to appreciate a ride in the storm. She quickly got into the car as the window slid up.

"Why?" she asked as she fastened her seat belt.

"To get to know you, of course."

As the car pulled back into traffic, Amalia sighed softly. The luxurious leather interior even smelled like wealth. The seat cushioned her lovingly, and she surreptitiously rubbed her fingers against its softness. "There's no need. Stefano got Teresa Valesquez to agree to accompany you on the balloon race. I won't be going."

Would he let her off at the next corner now that there was no need to become better acquainted?

"Damn, I don't know which is worse, you or Teresa," he said, moving to another lane as traffic began to get heavy.

"Thanks a lot," she murmured, not feeling kindly toward the man. She fervently hoped he lost the race to her boss just to take him down a peg or two!

"They say 'better the devil you know,' but I'm not so sure. I do know Teresa and the spin she's sure to put on this. You're an unknown, but at least I know you have no ulterior motive."

"I'm not going, so there's no more to say," Amalia said firmly.

"Still, I'm not dumping you in the rain. Where to?"

She lived in an older section of town, with lots of flats and small markets, winding streets and little parking. Nothing like the palatial home he must live in surrounded by gardens and giving a stupendous view of the city and the Med.

"It's off Via Estrada," she said.

"So what's Vicente's game plan?" he asked a moment later, easily driving in the rainy evening twilight.

"He wants to win," Amalia pointed out dryly.

"So do I," Rafael said.

"He thinks you'll be distracted by Ms. Valesquez and that will give him the edge," she said, hoping to startle him.

Rafael glanced at her a second. "Honest. Hmm…unusual."

"Then you must hang out with the wrong people," she snapped. First he considered she would sabotage his race, now he seemed surprised to find her an honest person. The nerve of the man! She clutched her purse tighter, hoping she could hold on to her temper until she reached home.

"Touchy, too. I bet there's temper in there somewhere," he mocked. "But being the perfect little personal assistant to Vicente, I'm sure you've damped that down a lot."

She wanted to say something pithy to knock

him off his high horse, but nothing came to mind. She hated that!

"Do *you* think Teresa would distract me?" he asked, turning onto Via Estrada.

"I have no idea," she replied stiffly. His affair with the beautiful woman was none of her business. She refused to speculate based on the innuendos of the press. "If you and my boss have to have a stupid race, I suspect one distraction would be equal to another."

"So maybe I should find a beautiful woman to ride with him."

Amalia said nothing. Rafael had to know Stefano was married. Did he think Stefano would be unfaithful to his wife for a balloon race?

"No thoughts?" he pressed.

"None you want to hear," she murmured. "Turn at the second traffic signal, right. Then three blocks to Via Escondito."

"Maybe I do want to hear," he said.

She hesitated a moment, but knowing she was almost home, she felt reckless. "It's that stupid bet. Don't you think the two of you could find better use for that much money than betting it against each other? There are hungry children, sick people, homeless in the world who could benefit."

"I give to charity," he protested.

He couldn't see it; his type never would. She shook her head. He lived so differently from the masses.

"Tell you what," he said. "I'll turn over my winnings to your favorite charity. You just name it and I'll sign the check right over."

She looked at him in astonishment. "Why would you do such a thing?"

"Why not? The money isn't the important part of the wager, the winning is."

Amalia turned to look out at the street. She couldn't imagine carelessly dismissing fifty thousand Euros.

When he reached her apartment building a few minutes later, he stopped in front and looked up through the windshield. The building was old, but still interesting, with stonework embellishments and tall windows.

"Is the inside also old, or has it been renovated?"

"The building is almost a hundred years old, so of course the inside has been renovated." About fifty years ago, but Amalia saw no need to tell him that.

He looked at her. "I'm sorry you won't be going with me. I love a challenge."

Amalia frowned. "I'd be no challenge."

"Getting you on my side would be the challenge. Teammates should share the goal. Would you throw your heart into my race, or hamper it at every turn?"

"We'll never know, will we?" she asked. He was so close she could see the faint lines radiating from the corners of his eyes. See the deep-brown irises that almost melded into the black pupils.

He rubbed a finger lightly down her cheek. "Seems a shame."

She jerked back. "Thank you for the ride," she said hastily, throwing open the door and scrambling from the car. She made a quick dash to the front door and hardly felt the rain. She was churning with the emotional onslaught of his touch that had her insides turning to mush. He was wrong—she'd be no challenge to him at all if he ever turned his attentions on her!

She turned and watched as he tooted the horn and drove away, puddles splashing from the wheels. Long after the taillights had merged into traffic, she gazed after the sleek black dream machine. She didn't even own a car. Not that she needed the expense as the bus served her perfectly well. She and Jose had a nice flat, nothing like the home she'd grown up in, but the best she could afford. Her job was good, and in only a few years she'd be able to return to her own education.

Opening the door to the flat, she saw she'd beaten Jose home, probably because of the ride Rafael had given her. She'd start dinner then change. Afterward, she would read up on what she could find on the Internet about hot air balloons. She knew only the rudimentary facts about the sport, which she'd gleaned from Stefano's enthusiastic discussion when he returned from some ballooning event.

She did know long jumps meant trips beyond the one- to three-hour ones near a festival site. They were rarer than the gathering of balloonists in favorite spots like Barcelona or London or Albuquerque, New Mexico, in America. Those races followed some prescribed activities, like waves of balloons in the morning flights or just before sunset. They also required a chase crew to pick them up when they came down. If there were competitions, it was usually dropping beanbags in target sites. Points went to those who dropped the closest to the center or who dropped earlier rather than later.

Once in comfortable and warm sweats, Amalia turned on her computer. She told herself she was learning about the sport to talk more knowledgeably with her boss. But she also searched for what would fascinate a dynamic man like Rafael Sandoval. Doing a search on his name, she began to read about his life. Some aspects she knew, other items were new. A complete dossier online. Did he know people could find out so much merely by tapping a few keys on a computer?

Despite her own reservations about flight, she wondered a bit wistfully what it would be like to sail soundlessly over the countryside, going where the wind blew, seeing farms and towns from the air with a man who made life seem more exciting than anything she'd experienced.

His own parents were divorced. According to one source, he maintained "cordial relationships" with both, whatever that meant. She missed her parents all the time. She couldn't imagine having mere "cordial relationships" with them.

"Hola, I'm home," Jose called.

So much for dreaming about hot air balloon rides and sexy millionaires who took to the air! Reality returned: she had dinner to finish.

Rafael let himself into the empty house from the garage. It was raining like a monsoon outside. The house was dark and a bit chilled. He flipped on the switch to illuminate the mudroom, then stepped into the hall. Turning on lights as he walked back to the kitchen, he considered the bet he'd made. Then he almost laughed remember-

ing the outrage of Vicente's prim PA when he'd
suggested she might sabotage his flight.

He didn't know what had made him drive back
by Vicente's office building at the end of the
working day. He had wanted to talk to Amalia to
see if he could glean any information to explain
why Vicente had suggested she be part of his
crew. It made even less sense now that he knew
Teresa was going with him. What was Vicente's
thinking? He couldn't seriously suppose that
Teresa would distract Rafael from his goal of
winning the race?

The short car ride with Amalia hadn't given
him much insight except he now knew she
deplored the bet for altruistic financial reasons.
But she didn't seem to have a special interest in
Vicente's winning. Or his losing.

But she intrigued Rafael for other reasons. She
seemed as jumpy as a cat with dogs baying. He'd
caught her watching him the few times he'd
actually gone to Vicente's office. Rafael was used
to that from women, but she never flirted with
him, never acknowledged any interest besides the
looks he'd feel from time to time. If he glanced
her way, her eyes would already be moving away.

What made her tick? He'd given her even more
reason for Vicente to lose by promising his
winnings to her favorite charity. An offer which

she had not jumped on. That puzzled him as well. Most people he knew would instantly come up with a name or cause to gain that much money.

Stefano Vicente had long been a thorn in his side, ever since he'd made a rather underhanded maneuver five years ago that had cost Rafael time and money. Rafael would delight in showing up the man in front of the Business Alliance. Stefano had been the only ballooner in the group until Rafael took up the sport. Vicente liked to brag, but those bragging rights would be curtailed when Rafael beat him—especially since he was the newcomer to the sport.

The bet presented a new personal challenge as well—piloting a balloon farther afield. The trick would be with the weather and getting an ongoing reliable way to indicate the wind factor. How much fuel could he carry to keep airborne longer, without being too much weight for lift? The logistics suddenly seemed daunting enough to fire up his determination not only to beat Vicente, but to try for a new record.

Rafael smiled. He loved pitting his own resources against others. He could already see himself standing in front of the BBA and accepting Stefano's check. That he'd now promised to turn it over to charity didn't bother him. The entire bet was not about the money, but about proving to Stefano Vicente that he wasn't the only one in Barcelona with the *cojones* to venture into the unknown. Their balloons could end up over the Pyrenees, or over the Med. He briefly wondered if they could get to Africa. No, that was unlikely, as this time of year the prevailing winds blew north and west.

Opening the oven, he savored the aroma of the casserole his housekeeper had prepared and set in the oven before she left for home. It wouldn't be done for another half hour. He was home earlier than usual, having left work to get to Vicente's building early enough to catch Amalia.

The phone rang and Rafael picked up the kitchen extension.

"Sandoval," he said.

"Hola," Teresa said in her sultry voice.

"Teresa," he acknowledged. He wasn't expecting to hear from her tonight. Was she calling about the race?

"It's raining and I'm bored," she said. "It's too wet to go out, and there's nothing on television. No friends want to venture forth to visit me."

He could hear the pout in her voice. Picture her lush red lips in a moue that invited kissing.

"Unless you do," she finished.

He liked Teresa. They had fun together when they went out. But he did not relish becoming a frequent visitor at her home. That led to ideas that he was definitely not pursuing. She knew that.

"Not tonight. It's pouring and I just got home. Besides, I need to start planning for the race. I heard Vicente called you and you're going with me."

"Won't that be delightful, just the two of us in the gondola of the balloon, riding high above the crowds?"

"Delightful," he replied sardonically. Did she have any idea what was involved? If she thought they'd enjoy a tryst, he had better explain the facts of balloon racing.

"Ohhh, I could come there and plan the race with you," she said, as if it were a sudden idea.

"I thought you didn't want to go out into the rain," he said, loosening his tie. He wanted to look at maps covering all the possible directions the balloon might go on the long jump, get a head start on preparing for the event. He didn't have time to entertain anyone.

"If I get a taxi there, I won't get very wet," she almost purred.

"Not tonight, babe. I've got work to do."

"Honestly, Rafael, you need to slow down a bit and enjoy all that money you make."

Or let you enjoy it, he thought cynically. He knew the women he dated were attracted to his money and his notoriety. Normally it didn't bother him but tonight it did. If he were a pauper, would Teresa even look at him? Not in a million years. Much less invite him to her home.

Unexpectedly the image of Vicente's PA flashed into his mind. Amalia would probably do more than look at him if he were a pauper, she'd try to help him find a job and a place to live. Get money from the rich to help out the poor.

Great, he was either a charity case or a meal ticket, which didn't paint a very complimentary picture of him either way. Had that been what his father faced? He hadn't stuck with marriage for long. Unlike his mother who reveled in the state, if five husbands to date were any indication.

Rafael didn't like the way he was thinking. Reminders of his parents always fed his frustration. He had felt the odd man out in his family from the first time he'd been sent away to boarding school. His father was too busy to care for a child, and his mother was always concentrating on attracting her next husband to devote much time to her two sons. They would have done better not to have had children in the first place.

But then he wouldn't be here, nor his brother, so maybe it hadn't been all bad. But he had no plans for marriage for a long time—if ever.

"I've got to go. How about dinner tomorrow night?" he offered, to placate her.

There was a pause, then Teresa accepted. She wanted to talk longer, but he soon ended the conversation.

He had time to change into casual clothes before the casserole would be ready. He wanted to begin his study of the weather patterns and wind flows he might expect to find when making the long balloon trip. He liked planning strategy almost as much as implementation. But he did enjoy the flights he made with the balloon. Work kept him busier than he might like during the summer months, yet when time permitted, he'd take a sail in the balloon. He had several friends who volunteered for the chase team, in exchange for rides.

It occurred to him as he climbed the stairs that spending every day for a week or longer with Teresa might be more than he could take. She was fun an evening at a time, but how would she hold up to hours in the basket with the harsh sound of the burners going on and off? Or with the unexpected accommodations they'd have to make for the nights when they touched down who knew where? It wasn't like a normal holiday trip where they could phone ahead for reservations. Or festivals, where they knew where they were to put down each day, with the chase team already on-site.

They'd have to bed down wherever the balloon landed and be up early to get the dawn sky. He planned to beat Vicente, and there would be no time to look for the amenities she was used to.

He couldn't picture Teresa lasting. Was that Vicente's hope—rather than Teresa distracting him, she might abandon him? What would Rafael do if Teresa didn't stay the course? He would not forfeit, that he knew, even if he had to tie her to the gondola for the race. Or take Vicente's PA as a substitute.

As he changed into dark jeans and a dark sweater, Rafael thought about Amalia. She lived in an old building in an older section of town. She hadn't gushed about him giving her a ride. He almost smiled. Instead she'd berated him for squandering all that money on a bet.

And she'd looked outraged when he touched her cheek. The skin had felt warm and soft, and he bet she was warm and soft all over. Though she hid it behind a prickly exterior, she was a very feminine woman.

She still hadn't said which charity she'd like the payment to go to. He'd have to contact her again to find out. Not that he needed an excuse to call most women, but with this one…it would probably be wiser.

CHAPTER TWO

As THE day of the Barcelona Balloon Festival drew closer, work became totally chaotic for Amalia. She had a dozen things to do each day in preparing for her boss's part in the event. In addition to the normal business of the company, she had to line up the chase team, verify that the balloon was in top shape, work out various logistical scenarios to try to anticipate where the winds would drive the balloon each day on the long jump and field a dozen calls from Mrs. Vicente, who was enjoying all the social activity associated with the Balloon Festival.

She was tired each night but, oddly enough, also exhilarated. For once all aspects of the race were of interest. She listened more than she had for other events, soaking up every bit of information. That she knew two of the participants spurred her on.

"Amalia, where are today's weather reports?" Stefano called out, two days before the festival started.

"I put them on your desk, left-hand side," she yelled back, not leaving her desk as she tried to finish the last of the meal planning. The four members of the chase team would require a lot of food as they followed the balloon from the ground. No time to stop for meals or they'd lose sight of it and then have to rely on communications from Stefano in the balloon to find it again before it touched down.

She knew her boss would want some snacks to eat while airborne each day and bottles of water to drink. She hadn't met Helena Marisol, but the two of them had spoken on the phone several times. She seemed excited about the trip and talked glowingly of her boss. A couple of times during the week, Amalia almost regretted she wouldn't be going with him. But the mere thought of being that high with nothing but air beneath her had her nerves fluttering.

The trick was to get good food that required little preparation. The only fire on the balloon would be the burners. Suddenly she stifled a giggle imagining the immaculate Ms. Valesquez toasting a hot dog in the flames of Rafael Sandoval's balloon burners.

It was far more likely he'd arrange for caviar and champagne for a snack.

She stopped for a moment, trying to picture

Teresa even in the balloon. It was mind-boggling. From what Stefano said, the balloonist had to pay attention to the wind to get the maximum speed. Adjusting the height of the balloon to take advantage of different wind speeds took concentration. Stefano's rival would not be available to flirt with Teresa. Not if he was serious about winning. Did she realize that? Amalia knew Rafael would focus absolutely on winning the race rather than on the dubious delights of his passenger.

Amalia shook her head. That was not her problem.

It was Thursday. Saturday morning was the first event of the festival. Even as early as Tuesday, she'd begun seeing hot air balloons drifting by as balloonists from all over the world came to compete, show off and enjoy themselves. Foreigners were trying to get a feel for the locale and the winds before the festival officially opened.

Twice she'd stood at her window for long moments watching balloons drift lazily over the sea. If she didn't have a fear of heights, would she enjoy taking a ride in one?

"They're pretty, aren't they?" Stefano asked, joining her at the window late in the afternoon. "You'll have to come to see us off."

"Helena called a little while ago. She wanted to know if she should line up anything special for the long jump."

"I think I'll thank Rafael's PA at my acceptance speech when I get his check," Stefano said thoughtfully. "She's committed to being the perfect passenger. I wonder how Sandoval is faring with Teresa Valesquez?" He laughed at the thought.

"You're pretty sure you're going to win. What if you don't?" She would not relish working the week or so after such a loss. Her boss was not fun to be around when in a bad temper.

"I will. I never even consider defeat."

"Helena says Rafael is saying the same thing."

"Ha, he'll eat my dust."

Amalia didn't operate that way. She always had a plan B in case plan A didn't work.

"You and Jose come to the field on Saturday to see us off. Check in at the gate to find out where we'll be," her boss said.

She looked up at that. "Do you need me there?"

"No, but I thought you might like to see us fill the envelope and lift off. Marguerite says that's her favorite part," he said, mentioning his wife.

"The envelope," she repeated, remembering the explanation she had read on the Internet.

"The balloon. The nylon part is called the

envelope. Then there's the basket or gondola and the burners. It's not rocket science, but I enjoy it."

"If the weather's nice, we might come. I know Jose would love it. Of course, he'll be explaining to me all about the physics that makes the lighter-than-air balloon fly with the added weight in the basket." She loved her younger brother, but sometimes he left her in bewilderment discussing how things worked.

Saturday was a beautiful day. A bit on the cool side but perfect, as there were no clouds and only a brisk cool breeze blowing in from the Mediterranean Sea. Jose had been talking about the balloon festival ever since Amalia had told him they would attend. Stefano had instructed her to arrive at dawn as the balloons would be taking off very early. There were special buses from Barcelona to the festival, running on a frequent schedule.

Once she got to the large field a few miles outside of Barcelona, Amalia was caught up in the excitement. She and Jose checked in at the gate and received a map of the field, and the grid where her boss had his balloon. She and her brother set off down the area between the balloons. There were well over a hundred, all in various stages of being inflated. Fans pumped air in the inflation process. Once the balloon was more than half full, the burners began. The noise from the burners was surprisingly loud as they were fired up to heat the air in the envelope. Men and women were working, talking, laughing.

"Come to see me off?"

Amalia looked to her left and saw Rafael Sandoval. His balloon was halfway inflated, the bright red and stark black striking in the early-morning light. The basket lay on its side, two people at the opening of the envelope holding it wide for the fan to pump in air.

His attire matched the balloon, an all-black jumpsuit with a splash of red traversing his chest on the jacket. The colors suited him. The suit would keep him comfortable at the higher elevations and he could shed the jacket as the day warmed.

"Actually I came to see my boss off," she said, her eyes taking in all the activity around his balloon.

"A man can pretend," he said, flashing a smile at Jose. "I'm Rafael Sandoval," he said, extending his hand.

Jose shook it, introducing himself. "This is great. Can I see your balloon and watch how it inflates? I read up about the entire process."

"Sure, come on over."

Amalia stared after the two as they walked away. Jose should not be asking Rafael a dozen questions, the man was the competition. Stefano would surely be glad to give Jose answers to anything he could come up with.

She started after them to rein in her brother, but they quickly outdistanced her, and before she caught up, Jose was actually at the side of the gondola, studying the burner apparatus with Rafael right at his side instructing. Members of his chase team joked back and forth, the atmosphere growing more festive.

She watched, glad, despite her misgivings, that Rafael was taking time to explain everything so thoroughly. Stefano would have probably glossed over the details. Jose missed their dad more than anything. He had been a wonderful father, and the wound his loss had created would never be completely healed. With work and keeping their apartment and all, Amalia didn't date seriously. She had to wait for any permanent commitment until her brother was no longer her responsibility. So there was not a steady male influence in Jose's life. Had that been a mistake? Should she have tried to get married earlier to provide him with that adult male exposure?

She looked around her. The noise level was growing. There were five long rows of balloons all being inflated, and the roaring sound the burners made filled the air. The bright colors were highlighted slightly by the flames, appearing to glow in the early dawn light.

Looking back, she drew on her patience to wait until Jose had enough information so they could continue to Stefano's balloon, still another half dozen farther along.

Suddenly a long flame shot out of the burners of Rafael's balloon, the noise startling. Jose was grinning, Rafael by his side, watching as the flame shot into the balloon, the two helpers holding the mouth of the balloon wide. As she watched, the envelope began to tilt upward.

Rafael carried on pointing out things to Jose. Her brother looked as if he was in heaven. Amalia studied Rafael. He showed no impatience with the teenager. In fact, she thought it was a great kindness he let Jose even be there, much less try the burners.

Glancing around, she didn't see anyone looking like the picture she'd seen of Teresa Valesquez. Hadn't she arrived yet? There was still time, as the balloon was only half-inflated. But Amalia would have thought the woman would have been there first thing.

Amalia wondered what it would be like to be Rafael's girlfriend. She suspected he was lavish in his gifts when first squiring someone around. Did he send flowers, chocolates, gifts of jewelry? She'd love to be wined and dined as he did it—always the best places in town. The theater, opera, sailing—all gave the women in his life a wonderful glimpse into his world. Those relationships always ended, but until they did, Amalia thought it must be magical.

Feeling awkward and in the way, Amalia stayed to one side, watching the activity going on around her. As the balloon rose, the basket was gradually tipped up until it sat square on the ground, the fire now shooting up into the envelope that soared overhead. The flame looked to be twice as long as Amalia was tall. Jose and Rafael stood in the basket. It wasn't that large—four or five people might be able to travel in it—if they stood. The sides were high, made entirely of wicker. How safe was that?

The balloon looked fully inflated to her when Teresa sauntered into the area. One of the chase crew replaced Rafael in the basket and he walked toward his passenger. She was wearing high heels! Amalia wondered what Rafael would do. Anyone would know high heels were not suitable for a wicker basket. The skintight pants and open top looked stylish and more suitable for a walk along the beach than the early-morning chill.

As Rafael realized what the other woman wore, he took a second look. Amalia laughed at his stunned expression. He swung around and narrowed his gaze on her. She shrugged her shoulders and looked back at his girlfriend. A second later he stormed over to Teresa, his hands on his hips.

"What the hell are you made up as?" he asked.

Teresa was made of sterner stuff than Amalia expected. She merely smiled and trailed one finger down his cheek.

"I'm ready for our ride. Your assistant told me to dress warmly and in layers. This top comes off."

The men in the crew stopped their work and stared. Amalia noticed several men from other balloons were watching, as well. Teresa didn't seem to care.

"It should, it's hardly there to begin with. What were you thinking? It's cold at the higher elevations. We'll be going up a couple of thousand feet or more!" Rafael snarled.

"You can keep me warm."

He turned away in disgust. "I don't have time for this. Julio, give me your jacket."

The slender young man on the chase crew shrugged out of his jacket and tossed it to Rafael. He in turn threw it to Teresa, who barely caught it in her surprise.

"Put that on and find some suitable shoes. We will be lifting off in less than twenty minutes. I'm not missing my time slot for you." Rafael stormed off, leaving Teresa looking after him with a suddenly angry expression.

Jose came over to Amalia. "Wow, do you see? I got to fire up the burners. That was awesome. I want to go up in one of them someday." He looked at Teresa, still standing with the jacket in her hand, glaring after Rafael. "Do you believe that woman? She's supposed to go with Rafe today, but if I were him, I'd find someone else."

"Rafe?" Amalia echoed in surprise.

"He said I could call him that. It's what the men on the crew call him. Come on, let's go find your boss's balloon. I want to compare the two. If Mr. Vicente can give me the specs, I might be able to calculate who really has the better chance of more distance given the wind velocity and direction. If I factor in the air volume and guesstimate the weight each would be carrying, with passengers and propane canisters and…"

He continued talking but Amalia had lost the thread. She looked back once, wondering how the situation was going to play out. Teresa had shrugged into Julio's jacket, but she had made no move to find other shoes.

Stefano Vicente's balloon was fully inflated and straining the ropes that held it to the earth. Her boss and his wife were sharing a cup of coffee. Helena must be the woman standing with them. Amalia crossed over to greet them.

"Have you met Helena yet?" her boss asked.

"Only on the phone. Nice to meet you in person," Amalia said, noting the practical attire the woman wore. Her salt-and-pepper hair was tied back. Her fleece jacket covered a warm shirt. The jeans and rubber-soled shoes would be perfect for the flight.

Amalia almost told Stefano about Teresa, but thought it would just go to his head. He must know her. Surely the Vicentes went to the same functions as Sandoval. She suspected Teresa would prove a lot more distraction than even Stefano had hoped for—not all in a positive manner.

"Exciting, isn't it?" Marguerite Vicente said. She also was dressed warmly. Her hair was blowing in the breeze, but she didn't care.

Jose greeted everyone, then went to the gondola and began talking with one of the men.

"We lift off in ten," Stefano said, checking his watch once more. "Last chance for a pit stop for a few hours. I'd better take advantage."

Helena agreed and both hurried away.

"Do you usually go with him?" Amalia asked Mrs. Vicente.

"Often, not always. There are always friends who like the flights. He hasn't taken you yet. After the festival, maybe he can give you and your brother a ride. Jose looks enthralled—I hope he doesn't get bitten by the bug."

Amalia smiled and said nothing. She couldn't imagine anything compelling enough to have her get in one of those things. And they could never in a million years afford a hot air balloon, even if Jose did become smitten.

When Stefano and Helena returned, they went straight to the basket and climbed in using the step halfway up the wicker side. Testing the burners once, Stefano gave the thumbs-up to his ground crew.

A cheer was heard from the beginning of the row. Amalia turned and saw the first balloon slowly ascend. Two minutes later the next in line began to rise. In no time she saw the black-and-red one belonging to Rafael rise. Moments later the official walked to their site and gave the release order. Slowly Stefano's balloon began moving upward.

Jose came over. "I calculate the chances are even. The balloons are matched in size and weight carried. Though Rafael has one extra canister, Stefano is heavier than he is and has more stuff on the side pockets."

"So the race will depend on the pilot's skill," Amalia said.

"Yeah, and if he has a competent helper—but I think Rafe got shafted with that woman." Jose shook his head. "Why didn't he get someone else?"

"It was part of the bet." She did not tell her brother she'd been first choice. Or that Rafael had offered to donate the money to charity if he won. Jose would have loved to crew for one of the balloons. And loved to go up in one. Maybe she'd ask her boss if there was a place for him with the chase crew at the next outing. She wasn't as complacent about asking for a ride for her brother. What if Jose fell out?

"I'm returning home. Can I give you two a lift?" Mrs. Vicente said.

"You're not staying?"

"The second wave will begin soon, then the third. Once all the balloons are gone, this is just an empty field. There'll be more fun at the end. But that won't be for a couple of hours, so I'll go home and await the chase team's call."

Amalia accepted. It was much easier getting home by car than bus. Walking back to the parking lot, she looked at the balloons, the black-and-red one standing out against the more colorful ones drifting away. She wished she could at least hear how Rafael was coping with his passenger. She grinned at the thought of what was going on. She almost felt sorry for the man.

The rest of the weekend, Amalia was kept up to speed on how the races were going by Jose's involvement. He scoured every Web site and local newspaper for updates on the events and reported every fact at dinner each night.

Stefano was ahead the first two days in two drop events. Rafael surged ahead on the third day. Had Rafael been able to do all he wanted with his teammate? Or had Stefano suspected it wouldn't work out and deliberately chosen her? Would Rafael do better if he had competent help?

Amalia thought that perhaps she could be doing Teresa a disservice. Maybe she'd caught on instantly and was of immense help. After all, she was dating Rafael, surely she'd want to do all she could to help him win.

Amalia didn't expect her boss back in the office for more than a week. Once the festival ended on Tuesday, he and Rafael would begin the long jump to see who could go farther in their own private race. It was quiet at the office, and she relished the lack of distractions to get caught up on nonpriority tasks.

* * *

But on Tuesday afternoon Amalia got a call at work from Rafael Sandoval.

Without any greeting, he spoke in clipped words. "You have to fly with me starting in the morning. We leave at dawn. Pack light, and for heaven's sake bring *sensible* clothes."

"What are you talking about?" Amalia squeaked.

"The bet, what else? The festival ended at noon today. Vicente and I are almost equal in points. The rest will be decided on the long jump."

"I'm not going. You have your teammate," she protested.

"It's you or Teresa, and she's made it clear she won't step foot inside the basket again. I'm not forfeiting this bet because of some collusion between you and Vicente. You're the other candidate Vicente allowed me, so I say you will come. Be here no later than five-thirty. Your bag goes with the chase team and you come with me."

"No!" Amalia exclaimed.

"I'm in no mood to argue. Be there!" He hung up before she could respond.

She quickly called her boss's cell phone. He answered on the second ring.

"Amalia, is there an emergency? Have Benito handle anything that comes up."

"Rafael Sandoval just called and said I have to

go with him for the next stage because Teresa won't. I can't go, Stefano. I have Jose to think about and work to do here and—" She hated to harp on her fear of heights, because that would make her seem foolish. But it was real.

Stefano laughed. "Hot damn, I may win after all. Either you go or he has no assistant in the basket. Automatic forfeiture. Man, I can't wait to have him give me that check at the BBA."

"Find someone else to pair him up with."

"Hey, I did. Teresa Valesquez. If she can't stay the course he's out of luck. He had two choices, and I only got one. He can't complain."

"Just so you know, I'm *not* going."

"If you say no, so be it. It's good news for me." He rang off, leaving Amalia feeling odd. He didn't care how he won, as long as he did. It seemed unfair that if Teresa refused to go, Rafael would have to forfeit the race—and the money for a charity of her choice.

Amalia felt restless all evening. Even Jose picked up on her fidgeting and challenged her to a video game. She agreed, mostly to take her mind off Rafael's reaction tomorrow when she didn't show up in time for the liftoff. He'd be mad. She shivered. Furious, more like it. Still, what could he do to her? She didn't work for him. If her boss hadn't suggested the insane idea, Rafael Sandoval would probably not even know her name or be able to recognize her on the street.

It wasn't her fault. She had never agreed to the stupid plan her boss had devised. Rafael couldn't expect a stranger to drop everything just to accompany him. She had her own responsibilities.

Still, it was hard to fall asleep. Finally dropping off, she felt she slept for ten minutes before there was a banging on the front door to the flat.

She sprang out of bed and raced down the hall, almost colliding with her brother when he came from his room, both scrambling to don robes.

"Is it a fire?" he asked, following her to the door.

"I don't know. Maybe a neighbor needs help."

Throwing open the door, Amalia stared in astonishment at Rafael Sandoval. He appeared to loom over her, dressed in the black-and-red jumpsuit, his hair tousled and his eyes flashing.

"You're not dressed and, I expect, not packed. The shuttle buses stopped running now that the festival is over. I came to get you."

Jose greeted Rafael as if his awakening them in the middle of the night was a normal occurrence.

"I told you I'm not going," Amalia reiterated stubbornly.

"Going where?" her brother asked.

"Ballooning—on the long jump," Rafael said. "And yes you are. I'm not losing this race on a technicality. Get your stuff."

"Wow, how cool. You get to go with Rafe in the hot air balloon?" Jose said, turning a beaming face to Amalia. "You're so lucky."

"I'm. Not. Going," she repeated slowly. Were they both deaf?

"Amalia, you have to. What a great chance this is. Tell me all about it when you get back. How many people get this chance? You have to go." Jose was clearly excited. Why couldn't he be the one to go, instead of her? Perhaps she could suggest that to her boss?

"Yes she does have to go. If you convince her, I'll give you a ride when we get back," Rafael said, checking his watch. "You have ten minutes before we leave. Unless you want to travel the next few days in your pajamas, you'd better get going."

Amalia studied his implacable expression for ten seconds, then turned and walked back to her room. She was *not* going! Slamming the door behind her, she switched on her light and sat hard on the edge of her bed. If her boss and Rafael Sandoval thought she could be ordered about to fit into their feud, they were wrong.

"I can't leave Jose," she yelled.

She could hear the two of them talking in the living room. Didn't her brother think it totally crazy that a man would show up in the middle of the night to abduct his sister? She looked at her clock. It was almost five. Rafael had better get to the launch site or he'd miss takeoff himself.

She crossed her arms over her chest. Dare she go back to bed with him still in the flat? Not that she could sleep. Her blood pounded. Her heart raced. For one insane moment she actually considered going off for a week with Rafael Sandoval. Ha. It was likely, if she didn't die of fright on ascension, she'd deck him the first chance she got. She was amazed Teresa had lasted all four days without injuring him!

Jose knocked on her door. "I brought you one of my duffel bags and a backpack," he said. "And I can manage myself while you're gone. I'm almost eighteen. Besides, Rafe said he'd have his housekeeper come to cook my meals. How cool is that!"

"I can cook your meals," she said, annoyed Rafael seemed to think he could get everyone to jump to his commands by a snap of his fingers.

The door banged open and Rafael stood in the opening, seeming to fill the space. Jose stood beside him. Both looked at Amalia.

"I'm serious. If you don't come willingly, I'll

bring you however I can. You will be on that balloon for the next seven days," Rafael said levelly.

She glared at him. "I'm afraid of heights."

"Oh, yeah, I forgot about that," Jose said.

"So sit in the bottom of the basket and keep your eyes shut. You now have five minutes left until we leave."

CHAPTER THREE

AMALIA fumed as she sat in the passenger seat of the sports car. Rafael ignored her as he quickly sped through the almost empty streets. She wasn't at all happy—with either Rafael or Jose. Why did men band together whenever it suited them? She'd expected better of her brother.

"There will be coffee and food at the launch site. I don't want to stop before that," he said at one point.

She ignored him. Hunger was the least of her worries. The closer they drew to the field, the more anxious she became. He could not be seriously planning on her joining him.

Of course he was. She wouldn't be in the car if he weren't.

"What happened to your girlfriend?" she asked, surreptitiously wiping her palms against her pants. Her fear increased. She could not go up in a balloon. For heaven's sake, she had trouble going above the fifth floor in high-rise buildings! And there she was encased in glass and steel. Yet Rafael expected her to dangle from a large balloon in a flimsy wicker basket high above the earth? She couldn't do it.

She glanced at him when he didn't answer right away and saw the anger simmering. With a flick of his eyes her way, he replied, "She wanted a golden band on her finger. That was not in the cards, so she bailed. Good riddance, I say. She complained more than anyone I know. I need someone I can count on. If she's that unreliable, what would happen if she ditched me halfway through? At least this way, I was able to get you." He glanced at her. "You don't have to do anything but go along for the ride. A lot of people would love the opportunity."

Amalia cleared her throat. "I can't go. Truly. I really am very afraid of heights. I'm likely to faint or throw up or something that would impede your flight. You have to explain that to Stefano and get someone else."

"If you faint, do it in a corner so you won't be in my way. If you throw up, do it over the side. I can think of nothing Vicente would love better than for me to have no one to accompany me. Instant forfeit."

She stared at him. He couldn't be so cold-hearted as to ignore a truly serious phobia!

"It's just a stupid bet," she muttered rebelliously.

"You wouldn't say that if it was *your* reputation and money on the line," he returned.

"I wouldn't have made the bet in the first place."

A flicker of amusement flashed on his face, replaced almost immediately by the fierce concentration she was growing to know.

"I bet there a lot of things I do that you wouldn't," he said.

A short time later Rafael turned into the road that led to the field. Dawn was just a lightening of the sky in the east. The sun wouldn't rise for another half hour or so. Amalia looked at the startling difference from when she was here before. There were only two balloons, both glowing from their burners in the darkened sky. As they were almost fully inflated, she knew she didn't have much time to convince this man she really couldn't go.

"You should have taken Jose," she said, staring in horror at the gleaming red-and-black balloon.

"Terms from your boss were clear. You're my fall-back choice. Though, if you'd just accepted in the first place, you'd already have four days of experience."

"I'll just hold you up." She was desperate. What could she say to convince him?

He stopped the car next to a small truck and two other cars. Turning to face her, he reached out and caught her chin, turning her face to his.

"Sabotage this race and you'll regret it."

She pulled away and glared at him. "I was insulted the first time you suggested such a thing. I don't need to sabotage anything. But I don't have to help. That'll be enough detriment to let my boss win."

"I doubt it. The balloon only needs one pilot. I'm it. Let's go."

She sat in the car when he got out, wondering if she could open her door and run down the road to escape. No, almost certainly he'd just follow and pull her back again. As she stared at the balloon, her heart pumped like a piston.

He opened her door and unfastened her seat belt. She slapped his hands away. "I'm not some child," she said, getting out and judging the chances of her getting away in the darkness, which was quickly fading into daylight. Not good.

He took her arm firmly in one hand and walked toward the group of people working around the balloon. Did he suspect her thoughts?

Two men near the balloon saw them and called a greeting.

The rest turned and also called out.

"I wasn't sure you'd make it back in time," one man said.

"Her case is in the back of the car. Get it. Amalia, this is Manuel. That's Julio and Maria and Paolo. Paolo is your boss's man. Amalia will take Teresa's place. Maria, do you have a jacket she can wear?"

She knew he suspected her frantic plan to escape when he didn't release her. In only a moment Maria returned with a black jacket slashed by the red band. Rafael handed it to Amalia, releasing her at last.

"Put it on, it'll be cooler the higher we go. You can take it off later when it grows warm."

Stefano Vicente came into the light. "Want to call it off?" he asked Rafael, grinning maliciously.

"No need, I have my passenger," Rafael said, nodding to Amalia.

Stefano turned and saw her. "Oh, you're kidding. Amalia?" He laughed.

The tone made her look at him. "What does that mean?" she asked angrily.

"Nothing, Amalia. Only that it's in the bag now." He lifted his hand in a half wave and turned to walk back to his own balloon. "Liftoff in fifteen minutes," he called back.

Maria walked to the gondola, carrying a couple

of soda cans and a small bag. Leaning over the side, she handed them in to Manuel, who was operating the burners. He stowed them in small pouches affixed to the side of the basket.

"You have two blankets in the large bag, water, snacks, and Julio double-checked the fuel supply, so you're good to go." She frowned at Amalia. "You don't look ready. Last chance for a toilet break for the next few hours. Come on, I'll show you the loo."

Amalia protested, but there was no help for it. Whether she liked it or not, and she did so *not*, it looked as if she was going up in a hot air balloon.

Fourteen minutes later Amalia placed her foot in the small step built into the side of the gondola and scrambled over into the basket feeling as if she would be physically sick. If she'd had anything to eat, she knew it would have come right back up.

The basket sat on solid ground, so it didn't move, but the loud noise of the burners and the ringing shouts of the ground crew fed her nervousness. A second later Rafael jumped in, exchanging places with Manuel. When Manuel climbed out of the gondola, they were ready to go.

"Keep up," he shouted as he fed the fire, and the flames leaped high into the large balloon overhead.

Amalia cringed and looked for a corner to sit in. The basket was not exactly spacious, and valuable space was taken up with large propane tanks, all connected to interconnecting hoses that fed the burners.

She backed to an area against the side next to one of the tanks and sat down. Keeping her knees bent, she stayed out of Rafael's way.

"There're blankets in that side pouch if you want to sit on them," he said, pointing to a flap covering a canvas basket affixed to the side. She pulled both out. Neither was large, but at least it beat sitting directly on the wicker. Wedging her back against the corner made by the basket and tank, she closed her eyes. When the basket lurched, she gripped the edge of the blankets and began praying. She knew her last moments on earth were about to end.

Another lurch, the burners roaring, and suddenly the sounds of voices faded. She could only hear the burners. Two minutes later there was silence.

Slowly she opened her eyes. Rafael stared down at her.

"You weren't kidding about being afraid of heights, were you?" he asked. He had one hand on the control knob of the burners, but they were not shooting flame up into the balloon. There was only silence. The basket was slowly swaying, almost like floating in a pool. Or a cloud. She unclenched her hands, flexing her stiff fingers. It was cool up here, but not unpleasantly so. The sky around her was growing lighter.

"We're floating?" she asked.

"Yes. If you're serious about getting sick, stay where you are. I don't want that." Then he opened the burners and a roar sounded as loud as a motorcycle as the flames leaped. Five seconds later he shut off the burners again.

Silence.

For a long moment Amalia sat where she was. She stretched her legs out in front of her. Rafael was less than six inches away. Glancing around she noted how cramped the basket seemed. Due, no doubt, to the large propane tanks. Several people could ride as long as they stood, as there was space at each side of the basket. Storage pouches lined the walls. The tubes from the tanks were tucked under the covering at the top edge of the basket. Looking up, she saw the burners above Rafael's head, still a good distance from the huge balloon that filled her sight.

Curiosity flickered. "How high up are we?" she asked.

He looked over the edge of the basket and her heart skipped a beat. What if he fell out? She'd be alone in the sky. She caught her breath.

"Don't do that!" she said sharply.

"Do what?" he asked.

"Lean over the edge like that. What if you fall out?"

He laughed, looking around and then up at the balloon. "I'm not going to fall out. I'd have to climb up on the side to do so. But you'd feel better if you know how to operate the balloon. Come and I'll show you."

"I'm not moving," she vowed. He was right, it was unlikely anyone would fall out. The high sides were almost chest high for her. Still, freak accidents could happen.

"You're missing a great sight, Barcelona from the air. No truck or car noises. No pollution. Only the beauty of the city as it wakens against the blue of the Med. You may never have this opportunity again."

She definitely would not do this again! She was tempted to peek. But the thought of looking down from so high caused a wave of nausea to sweep over her. She dropped her gaze to Rafael's feet. She could do this as long as she didn't move. She drew a deep, slow breath.

The basket swayed and she grabbed the edge of the blankets. Looking up, she saw Rafael right over her.

"Get back in the middle, you'll dump us both out!" she yelled.

"It'll never happen. Really, come see this view. You'll regret it forever if you don't."

"I can't."

"Stretch yourself, you'll be amazed what you can do if you just try." He almost lifted her to her feet by his grip on one arm. Once standing, she pressed closer to him, her theory being he'd done this before and was less likely to fall than she was.

"Look." He stretched out his right hand, his left still holding on to her. "See Vicente's balloon? It's lower than ours, he's following a different air current. Still going pretty much the same direction, but not moving as fast as we are."

Slowly she moved her gaze across the edge of the basket and looked. She could see her boss's balloon, not too far distant, but definitely lower. She swallowed hard. How high were they?

"Now, look over there, you see the Serra de Collserola?" he asked, pointing to the high ridge that enclosed Barcelona on the northwest. "Beautiful."

She jumped a second later when he casually reached up and depressed the lever to the burners. Flame shot up. A few seconds later he glanced at one of the gauges near the burners and released the lever.

Silence once again. Peaceful and amazing.

The sun had risen enough to illuminate the top edge of the ridge. Slowly the light moved down the slopes and toward the city. Amalia watched, moving her gaze slowly down until she saw some of the spires and buildings lighted by the rising sun. Forgetting her fear of heights, she leaned against Rafael's solid strength and watched mesmerized as the city she'd lived in all her life was wakened with light from the sun. The white buildings began to gleam in the early light. Windows looked as if they were on fire as they reflected the early rays. She could see the grid pattern of the streets and the large yachts and boats in the harbor. It was breathtaking.

She looked around, still feeling as if any movement beyond her eyes would plunge her over the side and several thousand feet to the earth below. But she couldn't resist. The sea was a dark blue, stretching to the curvature of the earth.

It was hard to tell in which direction they were traveling. In fact, there was no sensation of movement at all except for the gentle swaying of the basket.

"Are we still rising?" she asked.

"We've leveled off a bit. I'll need to heat the air soon to stay with this current."

"But we're moving?"

"Sure. When the sun is higher, you can watch our shadow move across the land, judge how fast we're traveling."

"How fast?"

"Depends on the air current. We're just along for the ride." He let her go and depressed the burner lever again. The roar of the flame startled her. She was afraid to move a fraction. She had her balance, but could she drop to the floor and crawl back to her corner without making the basket tip?

"Relax, Amalia, you won't fall out." His voice was warm, right beside her ear.

"Don't we have to balance the weight or something?" she asked, slowly turning to face him. He was so close she blinked. Granted, the basket wasn't that large, but he didn't need to be so close. She felt her nerves tighten with an emotion other than fear.

"The ropes holding the basket to the balloon are evenly spaced. They support the weight. Even if we are both on one side, the basket is not going to tip."

She nodded, trying to calm her nerves with the rational tone of his voice. Trying to ignore the attraction that flared, and remember she was on this ride under protest.

She could do this. She had to, what choice did she have?

Slowly taking a deep breath, she looked out again. She might as well savor every experience to tell Jose. He'd certainly pepper her with questions the next time he talked to her.

There was no feeling of movement, but the competing balloon seemed to drop away. Amalia knew they had to be rising, but she had nothing to gauge their height. Not as high as an airplane, she knew that. But higher than she'd ever been.

She looked at Rafael. He was studying her.

"Shouldn't you be watching where we're going? What if we crash into a plane or something?"

"I hope that won't happen," he said easily. "Want a turn with the burners?" He shut them down and the silence again enveloped them.

"It's weird. One moment I can hardly think because of the noise, then there's that blissful silence."

"Combined with the floating sensation, it's a high, isn't it?" he added. "That's why I love it. Silently drifting over the earth, seeing things from a new perspective."

She shrugged. She was glad the experience wasn't turning out to be as bad as she'd anticipated. No thanks to the man who had practically forced her out of her home and into this flimsy wicker basket!

"Come." He reached out his hand. She took it and let him pull her even closer. With his firm grip she felt safe. How odd was that? She didn't even like the man. He had practically kidnapped her and put her in mortal danger. Yet who else was she going to trust at this moment? She wasn't sure her boss warranted her trust anymore. How dare he make her a condition of the bet!

Once she stood next to Rafael, she could smell the unique scent that was his. She wanted to close her eyes and savor the tangy aroma. It was totally masculine and had her heart beating faster.

The other problem—staying immune to this man for a week. Now, *that* she wasn't sure she was capable of doing.

"I'll explain," he said.

She had loved his voice from the first moment she'd heard it. Now she watched as his lips moved forming the sounds that produced speech. She savored how deep and melodious it sounded, the smooth way he pronounced his words, how the resonance gave her goose bumps along her skin. If she closed her eyes, would he continue talking?

"Got it?" he asked.

"No." She blinked. She'd been enjoying the sound, not paying attention to the explanation.

He lifted her hand and placed it on the grip. The burners themselves were above passengers.

No fire danger, at least, or bumping heads by walking into them.

"Now," he said, letting go.

She pulled and let go immediately when the roar of the fire startled her.

He reached out and grabbed the grip with one hand, pulling her hand back with the other.

"Try again," he said. There was no censure in his tone, which surprised her. She'd have thought him too impatient to let such a blunder pass without a scathing complaint.

She gripped hard and pulled steadily until she felt the grip stop, holding on while the flames soared into the balloon, the roar almost deafening.

"Won't it catch fire?" she asked, venturing a look up at the huge canopy above them. The opening was a wide circle. She couldn't judge how high the top was, but it looked a long way up. The fire rose ten feet or so, yet didn't come close to the balloon material.

"Check the gauge there." He pointed. "That tells us the temperature at the top. Let go."

The burners went silent.

"I keep it around that temperature. When it drops we fire up again. We stop the flame when it gets there. The material surrounding the opening is fire retardant and the flame is far enough away not to ignite. Of course, the rest of the balloon is too far from the flame to burn, either, as long as we don't get it too hot inside."

She gazed up into the balloon for a moment, then looked at him. His dark eyes watched her, narrowed as if in speculation. For a fleeting second, Amalia wished she were a beautiful blonde with the figure of a model. Would he want to take her places, spend time with her? Feeling foolish, she looked away as reason returned. She didn't have what it took to captivate a man like Rafael Sandoval. He was used to the most beautiful women in Europe. Women who weren't afraid of heights, or who owned more than one basic black cocktail dress to wear to office parties. Women who knew what to say to him when stranded in a basket hundreds of feet in the air.

"Better?" he asked.

She nodded. Bravely she looked around. Then down. Not being near the edge, she could only see the earth at a distance. Like from the lookout point at the top of the Collserola. She could do this! For a moment she felt giddy with relief.

"How far will we travel today?" she asked.

"I have no idea. That's what makes it an adventure. The wind is the sole factor in determining that. Currently we are moving about fifteen miles an hour."

"And when we land?"

"Actually, we'll sail until we run low on fuel. Then we hope to find a field large enough to hold the balloon when it's deflated."

"What if crops are growing in the field? Or it has cattle or something?"

"We hope they'll still accommodate the balloon. We communicate with the chase team from here." He pointed to a handheld radio on top of the cooler. "They move a lot faster than we do. If we locate a place, they'll negotiate with the owners when we think we'll be setting down. Except to flatten things temporarily, there is no lasting damage."

"Can the chase team keep up?" she asked.

"They always have," he replied. "We aren't moving as fast as they are, so even though the roads won't necessarily go the same direction we're going, they'll have plenty of time to circle round and be waiting when we come down."

"So we don't know where we're going. Don't know where we're spending the night. Don't know what we'll have for dinner," she murmured. It sounded awfully unsettling.

"Pretty much," he said. Firing up the burners again, he turned his attention to altitude and wind direction.

Amalia grew brave enough to approach the

side of the basket on her own. Reaching out, she grabbed on to the top and, staying an arm's distance away, looked around. As long as she didn't look down, she thought she'd be okay. It actually was tolerable. She knew Jose would love it. Would she get used to it by the end of the week? Would she even grow to enjoy it, perhaps?

Stefano Vicente's balloon was rising. Soon it was as high as theirs, though still some distance away. She could barely make out Stefano and Helena. The other woman waved and Amalia lifted her hand in return.

She turned, still holding on to the edge with one hand. "How did you get into hot air ballooning? I'd think you'd prefer race cars or flying airplanes or something," she asked Rafael.

"This is more subtle. Pitting skill and knowledge of topography and air currents and thermal patterns to find the level that offers the best speed and in a direction I wish to go. Auto racing is fun, but once I've mastered a track, it's just a question of speed."

"But in this, don't you just go where the air blows? There's no control."

"There is. There are different air currents at different levels, light nuances if you like. Finding the right levels is what makes it challenging. Balloons are maneuverable to a certain extent if you know where the air is blowing."

"And, of course, the biggest challenge is winning," she said.

"There is that," he replied. When he shut down the burners, he picked up the radio mike and called the chase crew. They had the balloon in sight, Manuel reported. They were almost directly beneath them but the road veered in the opposite direction soon according to their map, so they might have to find an alternate route. If it looked as if Rafael would drift out of range, they'd let him know.

Amalia looked over the side to see if she could find the chase vehicle and felt a wave of nausea overtake her. She closed her eyes and sank to her knees. Heart pounding, she thought she would be sick. Slowly drawing in deep breaths, she tried to quell the sensation. No more of that. She'd had a false sense of security, but one look at how far down the ground was and she felt scared to death.

Taking a couple more deep breaths helped, then she scooted over to the corner with the blankets and sat on them again. She hated this feeling. And she hated that she acted like this in front of Rafael Sandoval. He feared nothing. How silly she must seem.

Rafael finished talking and then took a bottle of water from one of the storage pouches. "Want something?" he asked.

Amalia shook her head. If he hadn't burst into her apartment and forced her on this stupid trip, she'd be having a nice breakfast with Jose instead of being terrified out of her wits, cold, and uncomfortable sitting on the floor of a flimsy basket dangling from a balloon by only a few thin ropes. What if one broke?

She glared at Rafael, wondering how anyone found this fun. He was clearly enjoying himself. His dark hair was tousled, unlike the sleek look when he was at work. He had unzipped his jacket and it revealed a tight black T-shirt beneath, lovingly sculpting his muscular chest. Tantalized, she stared, wondering what he'd look like wearing only a bathing suit, or nothing at all.

Shocked at her thoughts, she looked away, but not far in the small basket. And if she looked up, it would be to see Rafael or the balloon.

Endless minutes passed as slowly as any Amalia had lived through. For the most part Rafael ignored her. She didn't care; she wasn't out to be his friend. She just wanted to get on the ground and never leave it again. She drew her knees up and wrapped her arms around her legs. She was getting used to the cool air, feeling it warm as the sun rose higher.

When Rafael switched the valve on the propane tanks, she watched. There were six large tanks taking up a lot of room in the basket. How far would they get on those tanks? She surmised the chase team had extras to install when they landed. Could she hitch a ride back with them? Only if she could convince Rafael that she couldn't go on. Or maybe it was Stefano she had to convince. She would ask her boss to let Rafael find someone else to continue the race. She wanted to go home.

"What happens when we run out of gas?" she asked. There would be no midair refueling.

"We'll put down. When we reach halfway on the last tank, we'll start looking for a landing site. I don't want to run totally out of propane, it's what keeps us maneuverable."

"Up and down, maybe, but not in any other direction."

"That's enough to get us where we want. The closer to earth, the more we'll rely on reading the wind from the plants and trees on the ground."

Rafe looked at Amalia and almost felt sorry for her. She was not having the time of her life. Too bad her boss had made her a part of the bet. Or too bad Teresa got greedy and wanted more than the good times they'd enjoyed together. Her ultimatum had been unexpected. He thought she enjoyed what they had as much as he did. But the lure of riches and a lasting place in Barcelona society proved too much. Demanding he commit to more than he wanted had been the last straw. She'd left yesterday in a huff and he didn't expect to see her again anytime soon. He certainly wasn't going to ask her to marry him.

He himself didn't hold much stock in marriage—not with his own parents as examples. Granted, his father and grandfather had made a lot of money for the family. He was doing as well with his own company. But he wasn't some royal who had to ensure continuation of the family. He had a brother who was married and already had two children. He and his wife were talking about a third. Those grandchildren would satisfy any errant grandparent genes his parents might discover at some future date. He was content to do what he wanted, when he wanted—without some wife in the background.

Teresa had seemed to enjoy the ballooning at the festival. At least she hadn't huddled in a corner, looking white and scared. How could anyone not love the freedom rising above the earth brought? He flew airplanes, with a different feeling. This was quiet, peaceful and beautiful. Slow and leisurely. The views were amazing. The sense of tranquility an unexpected bonus.

They were drifting over the countryside north

and a bit west of Barcelona. The winds from the Med would continue in this direction for another month before shifting. He enjoyed watching the mountainous terrain, with the tree-covered valleys and canyons. Here and there a road wound through the open land. A reservoir sparkled in the sunshine. A small village opened in another valley. He studied the earth as if it was a living map. He knew the chase car would have a hard time following if the balloon continued in the mountainous terrain. Could he get over this range before having to set down?

He carried more fuel than usual, but he was not going to risk the safety of the balloon or his passenger by pushing to the extreme limit. He was determined to win the bet, but not if it put Amalia in real danger.

If Manuel or Maria had been his crew, they'd have plenty to talk about. The silence when the burners were off was beginning to wear on his nerves. Amalia could at least talk to him while sitting where she was with her eyes closed!

"How old is your brother?" he asked at the next quiet time.

"He'll be eighteen soon."

"So, still in school? How is it he lives with you? Are your parents divorced?"

"No, they died."

"I'm sorry."

She shrugged. "It was nine years ago. Jose was only eight when they died."

"You couldn't have been that much older yourself."

She flashed him a look. "I was nineteen. I had just started university."

"So you had to care for him—there were no other relatives to help?"

She shook her head.

"Future plans?"

She leaned back against the side of the basket to look up at him. "He's going to university," she said with pride. "He plans to study physics. I think that's why he was so interested in the how-to of flying this thing. He should be here, not me. He'd love it."

"I can see Stefano's rationale in having you partner me. If he knew me better, he'd know I'll put up with almost anything to win. I'm sorry you are not enjoying the ride. But blame him, not me," Rafael returned.

"Does that mean Teresa was a big help?" She was annoyed that even that society woman had outperformed her. At least Amalia felt she'd dressed more appropriately.

"Different situation, but she helped more than you're doing."

"So what do you need me for? You know how to fly this thing. I'd only be in the way."

"You could talk to me to make the time go faster."

"You want to hear about the exciting life of a personal assistant to a busy businessman? Somehow I doubt it."

"Why not? It'll be a novelty." He liked the flash of fire she displayed from time to time.

He could tell his cavalier attitude rubbed her the wrong way. He should stop, but he was intrigued by the bursts of emotions that were quickly damped down. What would she be like if she let herself go with no restraints?

In a monotone she recited, "We get up and eat. I go to work, Jose to school. I come home and prepare dinner and we eat. He studies, I clean, do laundry or shopping. We go to sleep. How's that for excitement?"

"You don't mention a special friend."

She shrugged. "Now is not the time to be dating. I have my brother to raise."

"What happened to your parents?"

"They died in a boating accident."

From what he could guess, money was an issue. Apparently the parents had not left their offspring comfortably covered in the financial realm.

"What would you do if you could do anything you wanted?" he asked.

She didn't hesitate. "Be a Web designer. I would love to study more about graphic design, learn more about all the aspects of Web design and work from home on projects that I selected. Working hours I choose."

He nodded slowly. He'd heard somewhere that a secretary's job was very stressful because they had so little control over it. They were at the beck and call of the boss they worked for. He glanced across to the other balloon, still some distance away. He couldn't see Helena clearly but wondered what she would do if she could do anything she wanted. He'd never asked. It probably would not be support all his endeavors.

The balloon spun around and began to waffle. Rafael quickly assessed the situation. There was an eddy of wind causing problems. Glancing around, he saw the other balloon also turning. Quickly opening the valve of the burners, he tried to rise above the turbulent air. Slowly the wild gyrations ceased.

Amalia had her eyes tightly closed and her hands clenched into fists, arms wrapped around her upbent legs.

"Are we going to crash?" she asked in a tight voice.

CHAPTER FOUR

"Not today," Rafael replied.

The balloon stabilized. Once the erratic motion ceased, Amalia opened her eyes. Rafael wished she could get over her fear and enjoy the trip. It would make it more pleasant for her, since she was essentially stuck with a week in the air. And easier on him as the hours stretched out.

Not that he should care. Stefano had known his PA wouldn't be an asset—while Helena was so efficient, she had probably mastered the controls and was offering Stefano streamlined ways to do things. Still, it was Rafael who maintained a slight lead. If he could increase it over the next few days, he'd win the bet.

Giving another blast, he shut down the burners and went to sit beside his unwilling crew. The space was tight and his leg brushed against hers.

She shifted a couple of inches away and the

action caused him to give way to the devilment that rose.

He reached for her hand, prying the fist open and interlacing his fingers with hers. She tugged, but he held firm.

"Let go," she said.

"We need to get some ground rules established," he said, ignoring her puny attempts to pull free. It gave him hope she really didn't want to. It was so much easier to get things he wanted if women met him halfway.

"Like what?" she asked. He could hear the reluctant curiosity in her tone.

"Like, you can't sit in this corner the entire seven days."

"I told you I have a fear of heights."

Slowly he traced the back of her hand with his thumb. Her skin was silky soft and cool.

"So don't look down. Look out. Forget the space beneath us and enjoy the beauty of the flight. Together we can win this race."

"You practically kidnapped me and now you expect me to help you?"

"I do. Make the most of the chance, as Jose said. And show your boss you don't answer to him outside of work. *He* put you in this situation, not I."

She thought it over a moment.

Rafael moved closer. He liked women, especially pretty ones with big brown eyes and wind-blown brown hair with streaks of gold. "Pretend—if only for a week—that this is what you want. If we win, the money goes to your favorite charity—which you have not yet told me. If Vicente wins, we get nothing and so all this effort would be in vain."

She studied him with those large eyes, questioning, weighing.

"Maybe."

Victory was close.

Leaning back, he continued to caress her hand, waiting. Maybe he needed to make the pot sweeter. "If we win, I'll treat you and your brother to a week at a place of your choice."

"Do you think you can *bribe* me, Señor Sandoval?' she immediately said hotly. "It is enough to have the money be put to use and not just exchanged from one rich man to another."

That response was not what he'd expected. "Do you have something against rich men?" he asked.

"Only when they are foolish in the extreme."

He smiled slowly. "Like this bet?"

"Exactly. You shouldn't have made the stupid wager."

"But I did, and here we are. He's the one who made the terms. You help me, I donate the winnings," he said.

"And if you don't win?"

"I won't even consider that. But if I lose, I'll still donate to your charity."

"It's a win-win for me then. So why would I help?" Amalia asked.

"For honor," he said slowly. He knew more about this woman than she suspected. He was good at judging character and knew integrity was important to her.

She watched his thumb rubbing her hand for a long moment. He wondered if she would capitulate or continue to defy him. It would prove a long week if they were not pulling together.

"Agreed. Either way I win, but I'll do what I can to make sure we both win," she said slowly. Tugging her hand again, she watched as he slowly released her. Was that disappointment in her eyes?

"But you needn't try your blandishments on me," she continued. "I know you were voted Barcelona's most eligible bachelor last year, but I'm not one of your society women to date for a couple of months before moving on. This is strictly business. Agreed?"

"Most certainly not. You interest me, Amalia. You don't want me to grow bored on the flight, do you?" He loved being with her. She was so different from the other women he knew.

"I don't care much about what you do on the flight. Just win so the money goes to the Sisters of Charity Children's Home. That was my parents' favorite charity and I want you to donate in their names."

"And something for you?"

"Nothing for me."

Rafael studied her expression for a moment. She was serious. It threw his calculations off. How could she not want something for herself? Everyone did. He didn't mind, he had the money to indulge himself and his friends. He knew how life went. Those with money were targeted by those without. It wasn't good or bad, just the way things were.

Or the way he thought they were. What was Amalia's game?

"What?" Amalia asked. She found his stare unnerving, as if he were trying to dissect her or something.

"Just thinking," he replied, and looked away. For a moment she wanted to ask him about what, but thought it best to leave things alone. He had already unsettled her enough for one day. She tucked her hands against her chest, still feeling the warmth of his palm, the erotic rubbing of his thumb. She wished he'd held on a bit more. Getting hot and bothered by his presence sure beat being afraid for her life. Though, given the two choices, she suspected that riding in the wretched balloon was safer than getting caught up with Rafael Sandoval.

Yet she wouldn't be human, wouldn't be a woman if she wasn't intrigued by his sexy good looks and charming manner. She knew it had to be calculated, he'd been getting his own way for far too long to change his manner of operating. For a few seconds she'd let herself go, imagined he really cared for her. It would be beyond anything she'd ever experienced to have a fling with Rafael.

Her heart raced at the thought and she looked away lest he catch a glimmer of the awareness that rose every time she came near him. Actually, if she were honest with herself, every time she even thought about him.

"So what are the rules?" she asked a moment later.

He looked back and smiled. The light dancing in his eyes almost had her groaning with pleasure. He looked incredibly masculine with that devil-may-care look, and incredibly sexy with that smile.

"We pull together, all for one, one for all."

She laughed. "That's original."

He smiled again. "Agreed?"

"I'm not out to sabotage your race," she repeated.

"So there's no problem with that one."

"There're more rules?"

He leaned closer. "We spend time getting to know each other."

Her breath caught. He was close enough to her that she could feel his breath brush against her cheeks. Close enough that leaning forward only a few scant inches would put her mouth against his, her lips brushing his.

"We know each other quite well enough." Was that breathless voice hers? She wanted to jump up and run away. A quick flick around the gondola convinced her that was totally impossible.

"We could know each other even better," he said, his fingers brushing her hair lightly.

She jerked back as if stung, scooting away several inches and trying to show her displeasure. Only, she was afraid her reaction was a bit extreme.

"Didn't we just agree you are wasting your time trying to charm me?" she said.

"Ah, but it's so much fun," he said, watching her with those dark eyes.

"I don't think there's any point in it."

"It will make the journey more interesting. We can become friends."

She rolled her eyes at that notion.

"Or lovers."

She snapped her gaze right back at him. "You're crazy. We don't know each other enough to ever get to that level."

"It doesn't take long to get to know someone when confined to such a small space for endless hours," he said, his voice deliberately pitched low and sexy.

She raised her right hand, index finger shaking at him. "Stop right there. We are *not* going to become that close."

He leaned back and stretched out his long legs, taking up all the available floor space. "Maybe not. But it's worth thinking about."

"You need to think about this balloon and keeping us up in the air," she said, scarcely able to form two words together as the mere thought of them tangled together in lovemaking almost erased all her thought processes.

He touched her cheek lightly and then rose in one easy movement and glanced around at the gauge. A second later the jets roared to life.

Once her breathing was under control, Amalia stood and looked around. Looking out instead of down, she spotted the other balloon. It looked closer than before. Now it was slightly higher than they were.

"Clear sailing until the ambient air warms too much to make it easy to keep our altitude," he said.

She nodded, amazed he could switch off the charm and move to dedicated racer in a heartbeat. She was still reeling from their discussion.

And wondering what it would be like to be a close, very personal, friend of Rafael's.

Rafael switched to the last fuel canister later. He was not getting as much lift as earlier when the air temperature had been cooler. Time to begin looking for a place to stop and exchange these tanks for fresh ones. It was early afternoon. He'd already covered more distance than every day of the festival combined. The wind was steady and probably moving them more than twenty miles an hour. He estimated they'd covered more than a hundred miles.

The mountainous terrain below didn't offer many wide meadows where there would be room to set down and let the envelope deflate without becoming tangled with trees or ground growth.

The chase crew would have replacement tanks and plenty of food, as well as the tents and bedrolls he hoped they would not have to use. If he didn't have to rough it, he'd choose not to. On the other hand, dossing down on a sleeping bag beneath the stars was something he'd done more than once. Once they refueled they'd be off again. Long jumps were also an endurance event. He'd go for a few more miles before setting down for the night.

Amalia had not said a word for a while. She had gradually relaxed enough to doze for a few minutes but she hadn't offered to help in any way. So much for a truce. If Vicente thought that would slow him down, the man had rocks in his head.

"We'll be setting down soon," Rafael said to Julio when he'd reached the chase team on the radio. He scanned the terrain for a suitable place. "Where are you?"

"You are a bit behind us and farther north. Maria has you in our sights comparing it with the topographical map. Do you see any place to set down? How far ahead of Vicente are you?"

Rafael noticed Amalia was awake now and watching him.

"His balloon set down about twenty minutes ago. I'm riding at half tank on the last one right now and would prefer to come down soon. But all I see is tree-covered hills."

"Wait, Maria says there's a new reservoir north of your position. Any chance you could get near that? There should be plenty of cleared space. Just don't land in the water."

With that Amalia rose and clutched the side of

the basket, looking around. "We aren't going to land in water, are we?"

"Can't swim?" he asked.

"Of course I can swim, but I'm not dressed for it. What if the balloon comes down on top of us and drowns us?" she asked anxiously.

"Relax, we're not landing in water. Often reservoirs have a lot of cleared land surrounding them, to allow for water fluctuation." He spoke back into the radio, "I see a clearing, and a road leading to it. We're lined up for it, I'll try for that."

The balloon began descending.

"We're heading in that direction," Manuel said.

She looked around. "Where's the other balloon?"

"They put down already."

"Why would they do that?"

"If he found a meadow Stefano wanted to take advantage of, he'd land. He needs fuel. So do we. Once we switch out the tanks, we'll be good to go again."

"Why didn't we put down when he did?"

She'd wanted time to talk to Stefano, get him to agree to let someone else take her place. Maybe she could switch with Maria and be part of the ground crew.

He smiled at her tone. "Don't you like to win?" he asked.

"Not if we're risking our lives!" she snapped.

"We're not. Relax. I promise to get you home all in one piece," he said. He saw the reservoir. He wished he had some better way to gauge the wind rather than flying in it to see where he ended up. Experience told him if they continued at the current rate, they should reach ground about the time they reached the cleared area surrounding the water.

"When we get on the ground, one of us has to keep the envelope inflated enough to keep it from tangling with the trees. The other has to jump out with a rope and secure the basket to the ground. Which task do you want?" he asked.

"Neither," she said, glancing around as if looking for a third alternative.

"I need your help in this, Amalia," he said. "This is no time to argue. We'll be on the ground, so your phobia about height shouldn't get in the way."

She glanced up at the balloon overhead. "I can't keep it properly inflated. I'll try to tie the rope."

"Don't try, do."

She glared at him. "Just tell me how I'm supposed to do that and I'll do my best. I am not here to sabotage your blasted race. Though if something happened, I'd sure get home sooner."

"Don't even think it."

She looked away. Her anger seemed to drive away her fear.

He gave her directions, keeping an eye on the rapidly approaching clearing. It was going to be a bit more tricky than he liked—especially with a novice on board. But unexpected challenges were what made the race interesting.

In less than ten minutes he set the basket down right at the edge of the clearing at least a dozen feet or more from the water's edge. As soon as it hit the ground he yelled at Amalia to jump off and grab one of the tethering ropes. She used the step in the side to scramble over the edge and he heard her land, then jump to her feet and pull on the rope.

"There's nothing here to tie it to. If you lift off, I'm letting go," she called.

He could just see her over the edge of the basket. It skidded along the ground for a few feet. He glanced at the balloon. He wanted to keep it as inflated as possible for quick rising once the tanks were switched, but not so much it pulled against the basket while they were on the ground. He didn't want to skid across the ground, but couldn't let the envelope collapse all the way, or they'd take valuable minutes rein-flating it.

"Wait, there's a stump sticking up. It's a big one, maybe too big for the rope to go around." Her voice faded as she disappeared from view. He looked over the edge. She was winding the rope tightly around a stump. If she didn't secure it just right, it could slip off. Frustrated, Rafael wanted to jump off and do it himself, but it would be a stupid move to leave the balloon unmanned.

When she finished, she looked up and smiled. Standing, she did a little dance.

"I'm on the ground again!" she shouted, turning in a big circle, her arms outstretched.

"Take this rope and secure a second anchor," he called, tying another to the frame and tossing it to her.

She found another stump and quickly tied that rope then sat on the stump and looked up at the balloon, then around the clearing. The basket was anchored; now it was up to the chase crew to find them.

Rafael tried the radio again, but being lower than the surrounding hills, the signal wasn't reaching the rest of the team.

There was nothing to do but wait.

"How long do you need to keep the balloon inflated?" she called.

"Until the crew can switch out the empty tanks with full ones, or we run out of propane. If that happens, I'll need your help to keep the balloon away from the water and the trees."

"How long before they get here?"

"Whenever they get here."

Amalia went to the water's edge and gazed across the expanse. It was a large reservoir with wide cleared areas surrounding it. Obviously trees had been cut—stumps were scattered as far as she could see.

Amalia took a deep breath. She relished being back on the ground. Somehow she'd have to convince Stefano to renegotiate the bet. She did not want to go up again. Though all things considered, it hadn't been as bad as her imagination. No one had fallen out. The basket hadn't given way. And she had been held closely for a brief moment by one of Barcelona's most exciting bachelors. Not that she had bragging rights. But for those few moments she'd felt totally safe.

She refused to think about the moments he'd held her hand and tried to charm her into joining forces with him. Best left in the past. It wouldn't be repeated.

Sighing softly for what could never be, she looked around, spotting a road winding down through the trees. When the chase crew arrived it would be from that direction.

She walked back to the basket.

"Now I'd like some thing to drink, please," she said.

Rafael tossed a soda to her. "Something to eat, too?" he asked.

"In a little while. I'm hoping this will settle the butterflies in my stomach."

"You did fine, Amalia. No need to be afraid," he said gently, leaning against the side of the basket, taking a long drink from the can he held.

"Phobias aren't something that go away on your say-so," she said. She drank from the cold can, then looked around.

"No, I guess not." He was silent for a moment then turned toward her. "So why the Children's Home, to make the check out to?"

"You'll really do that?" she asked.

"I said so, didn't I?" There was a hint of steel in his tone.

She flashed back to the meeting in her boss's office. Rafael had become angry with the slightest hint from Stefano that he wasn't honorable. Obviously that meant a lot to him, which struck her as odd, given the ruthless nature of every successful businessman. Was Rafael a bit different? Unlikely.

Amalia had never had such a generous gesture made for her. "My parents were both orphans.

My mother actually lived in the Home for a few months when she was about eleven. It was a favored charity for them. Made in their name should bring hope to other children that when they grow up they'll be happy, too."

"And were your parents happy?" he asked.

"Yes. We did things together as a family. It wasn't perfect. My mother had a real temper and she would let it fly rather than bottle things up inside. But ten minutes later the storm was over and they were hugging and kissing." She smiled a bit at the memories. "I want a relationship like that if I ever get married," she said, looking at the water, remembering the sudden storm that had swamped the boat they'd been on, ending their happy family life forever.

She shivered.

"I shall be happy to make the donation in their name," Rafael said, watching her.

The minutes dragged by. By feeding the hot air into the balloon periodically, enough to keep it from fully deflating and drifting to the ground, Rafael watched the gas gauge. It was getting lower each time he fired the burners. If the propane gas ran out, the balloon would gradually sink to the ground. If that happened before the rest of the team arrived, he'd just have to hope he and Amalia could control the deflating envelope enough to keep it from catching in the trees.

Amalia drank her soda and ate one of the sandwiches Maria had prepared.

"How far to the nearest town?" she asked, looking around.

"I saw one toward the east before we came down. I don't know, maybe ten miles."

Ten miles. Was there any traffic where she could hitch a ride? Now she wished she'd spent some of her time up in the air studying the layout on the ground.

Just as she heard the burners fire up again, she heard the honking horn and turned to see the chase team racing down the narrow road, horn blaring.

"They're here!" Amalia said, jumping up from the stump she'd been sitting on for most of the afternoon. "We're rescued!"

Rafael laughed. "We didn't need rescue. We'll refuel and lift off again. This time you won't be so afraid. You know how it all works."

By the time the balloon lifted again, Amalia hoped she would discover a way to be far gone.

But she didn't. Working in perfect synchronization, the team swapped full propane tanks for the empties, keeping the envelope almost full. In less than thirty minutes one of the chase team called to Rafael that he saw the other balloon.

"Oops, time to go," Rafael said. "Come on, Amalia."

She wanted to argue, but the camaraderie of the ground crew and the pride she felt that she'd actually survived the morning mellowed her thinking. If all these people thought the event worth taking part in, maybe she needed to give it one more chance. And, truly, if she didn't look down, she had grown used to the gentle movement of the gondola and almost gotten used to the sudden noise when the burners were engaged.

She had not gotten used to Rafael, however. Still, she could do this, what choice did she have?

She looked up and saw the other hot air balloon almost overhead.

"They'll get ahead of us," she said as she grabbed the jacket she'd discarded and hurried to the gondola. By the time they rose enough to catch the current, Vicente's balloon would have a slight lead.

Rafael turned his head to smile at her. "We'll catch them if they get ahead. Fire up the fans," he called as he opened the burners and the roaring filled their ears. In only seconds the balloon began to rise rapidly.

Amalia watched, her attention torn between their own efforts and the balloon sailing silently overhead.

"They're getting ahead," she said. If her boss outdistanced Rafael the first day, would that settle the race? Glancing at the charged energy Rafael showed, she doubted it. He'd fight to the last second to gain even an inch of distance.

"You come and take the controls," Rafael said. "I need to consult the weather maps of the area. Keep the burners going until the temperature gets near the limit."

Amalia stepped closer to the center. She grabbed the lever and pulled down, feeling almost like a pro. They were gaining altitude rapidly now. Soon they were level with Stefano's balloon, though some distance behind.

Rafael glanced up from the charts and maps he was perusing and looked around. He jotted a note on the margin of the paper.

The trees had dropped away, the surrounding hills were left behind. The burners roared and Amalia laughed in sheer delight. She'd done it! She wasn't about to go near the edge of the basket, but she'd lifted the balloon from the ground. Looking at the other balloon, she saw they were rapidly passing it in elevation. Would a different air current sweep them past?

She glanced at Rafael and found him grinning at her. "Told you it would get better," he said.

The euphoria she experienced allowed her to incline her head regally and agree. "So you did. How long do we have to keep the burners on?"

"You judge. Keep an eye on the gauge."

Amalia watched, and when it got close to the high temperature, she closed the controls. The silence echoed in her ears, ringing from the sound of the burners.

She kept her hand on the lever for balance and looked triumphantly at Rafael.

"We're higher than Stefano's balloon."

"Well done. Come here and I'll show you the route I think the currents will take us."

She hesitated a moment, glancing straight out over the side of the basket. But they were so high, she could see little. Her heart lurched and she quickly sat down beside Rafael. He held out the edge of the paper and she drew it closer. Leaning near, Rafael pointed out the topography and explained how air currents rose and fell, some on different currents, some impacted by the terrain and the heat of the day. His shoulder brushed hers and Amalia caught her breath, forcing herself to concentrate on his words and following where his finger pointed.

Turning her head slightly, she saw the faint

lines radiating from the outer edges of his eyes, as if he squinted in the sunlight a lot. His skin was tanned and taut, covering high cheekbones. His dark eyes sparkled with the excitement of planning where he'd try to take their balloon.

He glanced at her, and Amalia quickly turned back to the map, trying to quell her rapid heart rate. Surely he could hear her blood pounding through her veins? Better if he thought she was suffering from fright than the true nature of her feelings. She was too much attracted to the man!

"Any questions?" he asked.

"How did you get involved in this?" she asked, daring to look at him again.

"This race or hot air ballooning?" he asked, standing and doing a 360-degree scan.

"I know how you got into this race, I meant the entire sport."

"It was something new to try and I liked it once I did."

"Flying airplanes and scuba diving isn't enough?" she asked.

He raised one eyebrow in silent question.

She refused to admit she'd been interested enough in him to look him up and find out about him before the race.

"I like challenging myself," he said at last. "And exploring unusual things. I'm thinking of taking part in an archaeological dig in the Holy Land next spring."

"At least that would be safer than depending on hot air to keep you above ground," she said. "Doesn't your family worry about your recklessness?"

He laughed. "No one worries about me," he said. "And I'm not sure they'd consider what I do reckless, anyway. I'm not, you know."

"Now, how would I know that? I scarcely know you."

"I've been doing business for Vicente since before you were hired."

"Maybe, maybe not. I've worked for the firm for more than seven years. It's only the last three I've been Stefano's PA."

"And before that?"

"I worked for another company. It didn't offer the chances for advancement that I needed. I do have my brother to care for, remember."

He nodded, his expression becoming thoughtful.

"What?" she asked as he kept quiet.

"I was wondering if my brother would have put his life on hold to watch out for me if we had been in your situation."

"Why wouldn't he?" she asked. "It's what families do."

"Not all families. Some families don't stick together."

"I know your parents are divorced," she said. "Your father's mentioned enough in the papers."

Rafael laughed. "And you don't approve." He knew that for a fact from her tone of voice. Her expression supported it, as well.

"His life has no bearing on mine. But don't you think it's not in good form for him to be dating women younger than you are?"

"As long as we don't get our wires crossed and date the same woman, then, no, I don't care."

"I would. Parents are supposed to be a good example to their children."

"I'm hardly a child," he said.

"You were at some point."

Not liking the trend of the conversation, Rafael rose and looked over the side of the basket. They were gradually losing altitude. Vicente's balloon was farther to the west, and it was difficult to gauge if he was ahead or behind, since Rafael had lost track of where they were by talking to Amalia.

"Bring the map and let's figure out where we are," he said, opening the burners and heating the air above them.

Amalia slowly got to her feet and stepped closer, holding it out for him.

"Can you check the terrain and see what you think?" he asked.

"No." She thrust the map at him and reached for the controls. "You figure that out, I'll keep us afloat."

She didn't trust the amusement in his eyes, but didn't try to figure out what she'd done. Reaching for the knob, her hand brushed his and she felt the touch as if it had been a caress. Oh, oh, bad, bad, bad. She drew a deep breath and looked everywhere but at Rafael. She was not going to get some stupid crush on the playboy. That would be the dumbest thing she could do. Her immediate goal was to get back to earth in one piece and have a good night's sleep. Maybe tomorrow something would happen to end the race and let her return home.

Rafael calculated where they were and called the chase team. When he'd notified them, he handed her the walkie-talkie. "Press this button to talk, release to listen," he said.

"What do I have to say?"

"Anything you want, I merely want you to know how to use it."

"Why?"

"In case something happens to me, of course."

Amalia felt a flare of panic. "What could happen?"

"Nothing, this is just in case."

She stared at him as she pressed the button. "This is Amalia. Will we stop near a town that has a good restaurant for dinner?" It was inane, but the only thing she came up with.

"We can hope, Amalia," Marie responded. "And we hope for a decent hotel with hot shower and comfortable beds. Over."

Rafael took it back. "We have air mattresses. No time to be locating five-star hotels. We have a long-distance race to win. Out."

He heard their laughter before the radio went silent.

"We're sleeping on the ground?" she asked.

"Not if I can help it. But it keeps them on their toes."

She nodded. He had a good relationship with his ground crew. Did he operate his business that way? It was far different from the way Stefano ran things. He was the boss and he wanted everyone to know that.

The other balloon remained in sight all afternoon. Amalia felt more courageous and, as long as she didn't look directly over the side, she was able to keep her fear of heights under control. She enjoyed the distant views, watched the other balloon when it would move up or down, trying to see if Stefano or Rafael's PA was at the controls. Most likely Stefano. He didn't like to share the spotlight and would want bragging rights if he won.

At one point Rafael peered over the edge and called the chase team. It was time to switch out the tanks again and there were several wide-open spaces he thought would work.

This time the team was waiting when the balloon settled to the earth. Once again Amalia was amazed at the precision exchange. They were airborne again within thirty minutes.

Late in the afternoon, Rafael called the ground crew.

"I see what I think is San Paolo up ahead. If so, there's a large soccer field on the outskirts. I'll see if we can touch down there."

There was momentary discussion among the ground crew, then Manuel came on and confirmed Rafael's estimation. The small resort town was in a valley between two mountain ranges. Amalia had heard about it, but never thought to visit. It looked as if Maria might get her five-star hotel after all. Surely they wouldn't camp out if a hotel was that close?

She looked at the other balloon.

"Do you think they'll keep going?" she asked. Already Rafael was descending.

"I have no idea, but this is the best landing area

around. I for one wouldn't take the chance on finding something else farther on before dark."

Even as he said that, she could tell the other balloon was beginning to descend.

"I'll be able to call my brother, right?" she asked.

"Yes. Are you worried about him? I assure you my housekeeper will take care of all his meals. Beyond that, he's well able to look after himself."

"I'm not worried, but I do want to check in with him. He is only seventeen. Besides, he'll have a million questions about today. I wish he had been able to go in my place."

"Suggest that to your boss. Do you mother Jose a lot? In another year he will be going off to university. Are you planning to accompany him?"

"Don't be absurd. Of course not." Intellectually she knew she had to let her brother go. He was almost a man, had his own way in life to make. But it had been just the two of them for so long. Was this how parents felt when their children left the home? "Didn't your parents worry about you and your brother when you left home?" she asked.

"I doubt it. We were sent to a boarding school from the age of eight. Neither seemed particularly concerned."

"I gather you aren't close."

He looked at her and slowly shook his head. "Not close at all. I've only met my mother's current husband once. I avoid my father's woman of the week. He changes them too frequently to keep track."

"That's sad," she murmured.

"It's reality. Not that you have such a great life in comparison. No parents, no other family apart from your brother, and you're obviously struggling with money issues."

"I make a good living and support us just fine. There's money for Jose's university fees and he can also work." She was insulted he thought her unable to provide.

"I only meant it must have been hard when your parents died and everything fell on you."

She hated to talk about that time. It still could cause nightmares. She'd been so scared of the future, so worried she'd not be able to take proper care of her younger brother.

"I managed," was all she said.

CHAPTER FIVE

SAN Paolo was designed as a full-service resort catering to the wealthy from all over Europe. It was a short trip by car from Barcelona. It had taken the entire day by lighter-than-air balloon. There were spas, swimming pools, golf courses, equestrian centers, a soccer field and a plethora of fine restaurants.

The chase team was on-site waiting for the balloon when Rafael gently set it down. Moving with well-rehearsed efficiency, the team tethered the basket, and began aiding in the collapsing of the balloon. They folded it lengthwise several times then rolled it toward the basket. Throwing a tarp over it to keep off the evening dew, they were done in record time.

"Who got the short straw?" Rafael asked as he watched the activity.

"Julio," Maria said. She was already disconnecting the on-board propane tanks, handing the empty ones to Paolo, who stored them in the back of the truck to be refilled.

"Which means?" Amalia asked.

"He'll stay with the balloon tonight—just to keep gawkers away. We can expect a crowd in the morning to watch us lift off."

"So he has to sleep on the ground, but we get the hotel?"

Rafael laughed. "Indeed we do—unless you want to stay out here to keep him company."

She shook her head, to the laughter of the others.

Thirty minutes later Amalia closed the door to the suite Rafael had assigned her. It was beautiful beyond belief. The sitting room was done in lovely shades of rose and lavender. The sofa was huge and comfortable, she realized when she sat on it. Bouncing once, she jumped up and headed for the bedroom. It was complete luxury. A white-on-white monochromatic theme had gauzy curtains flanking the floor-to-ceiling windows. A mock canopy over the head of the bed with matching gauzy material gave it a fairy-tale feeling. The duvet was white with a brocade motif. There had to be a dozen large decorative pillows. It was spectacular.

She went to the bathroom and stared in amazement. It was larger than her living room. There was a spa tub and a separate shower with six shower heads at various levels. The glittering glass tiles sparkled in the light. Thick, fluffy towels filled a bin and were also stacked in rolls on the wide counter. A thick terry robe was artfully draped over the wide bench in the center of the room.

Amalia kicked off her shoes and was unbuttoning her shirt when her phone rang. There was a receiver in the bathroom. She lifted it slowly. "This is Amalia," she said.

"I told you we wouldn't sleep on the ground." Rafael's voice came through loud and clear.

"So you did." She clutched the opened shirt together.

"Is your room okay?"

"It's lovely, thank you." She was glad he was footing the bill; it would have set her back two weeks' pay to stay one night in this place.

"We're getting together for dinner in an hour. We'll discuss tomorrow's ride and get an early night. Join us. Main lounge, one hour."

"Okay," she said. Before she could say anything else, he rang off.

An hour gave her plenty of time to shower and see what she had to wear to dinner. Nothing suitable, she was sure. She'd crammed in clothes every which way when she'd had less than five minutes to dress and pack that morning.

Entering the lobby a short time later, Amalia saw the rest of the crew assembled near the entry to one of the restaurants. She walked over, relieved to see everyone was dressed casually in clothes more suitable to outdoor activities than a luxury resort restaurant.

At least she wasn't odd man out.

"There will be a table for us in just a few moments," Maria said, when Amalia joined the group.

While they waited, Stefano Vicente and his crew came from the elevators. Amalia hadn't known her boss was staying there, as well.

"Did we beat their distance?" she asked.

"Hard to say. Still, it's close enough to make it exciting—they came down not far from us. This is the nearest place to stay," Manuel said.

Paolo excused himself and went to talk to Stefano.

In a moment Helena left that group and walked to her boss.

"How are things going?" Rafael asked his PA after she greeted everyone.

"Fine. I think I would enjoy it more in your balloon. Stefano insists on doing everything, and he's obsessed with winning," Helena said.

Rafael shrugged. "So am I. He won't, you know."

"He thinks Amalia will hold you up." Helena looked at Amalia. "But it doesn't seem like you are trailing."

Amalia frowned. "Why would I hold Rafael up?"

Helena glanced at Rafael then said in a soft voice, "Stefano's counting on your fear of heights to delay you. In fact, he said he was surprised you hadn't already bailed."

Amalia felt a flare of anger at her boss. Was that the reason Stefano had proposed her—not for her lack of experience but her fear of heights? Did he expect her to refuse to fly and force a win by Rafael's forfeiture?

A warm hand gently took her arm. Startled, she looked at Rafael.

"No need to tear his head off. The best revenge is to win and show him he misjudged you."

"I've worked for him for years and I'm annoyed he'd use me like that," she admitted.

"He wants to win."

"Are you afraid of heights?" she asked Helena. She wasn't sure she cared either way, the warmth of Rafael's hand seemed to infuse her entire body. Her temper cooled and once again she felt the odd tickle of awareness.

"I jumped at the chance to go when Rafael asked me," she replied. "It's turning out all right.

As long as I just enjoy the scenery, I'm fine. Maybe before we reach the end I'll get to do more. Your boss strikes me as a bit of a control freak."

"I didn't jump at the chance," Amalia murmured.

"But you haven't let me down. I won't forget that, Amalia," Rafael said softly. It sounded almost like a promise.

Helena turned back to Rafael and said, "I checked for messages when I got to my room, which, by the way, I'm sharing with one of the chase team members. Gina said Teresa called for you and then asked for me. She seemed miffed neither of us was there to talk to her. She wants you to call her when you get the opportunity."

"Duly noted."

Helena grinned. "So, no return call tonight, then."

Amalia listened, wondering if Teresa now regretted her decision to refuse to go on the week-long trip with Rafael. She also absorbed the fact that Stefano was having his crew members share quarters while she had a luxury suite all to herself. Should she be sharing with Maria? She knew if that was the way Rafael wanted it, he would have made it that way.

She was grateful for her room.

Amalia felt a bit bereft when Rafael released her arm after the maître d' announced their table was ready. Following them into the dining room, she sat between Manuel and Maria. Paolo rejoined their group and before long meals were ordered. Conversation at the table centered on the race.

Looking around the restaurant, she wished Jose could see it. They'd never eaten in a place so elegant. Many of those present were dressed up, although of course neither their group or Stefano's were. What would it be like to come alone with Rafael, dressed to the nines, fascinating him with her scintillating conversation? Just the two of them, maybe in that small alcove that seemed more private than the main dining area.

The dream popped when the waiter poured bubbly beverages and Rafael rose to offer a toast. "To winning the race and besting the competition—always!"

"Yea!"

They all raised their glasses and then drank. Amalia was surprised to realize it was sparkling apple cider. She blinked and took another sip.

Maria leaned closer. "We do not drink during the race. Nothing must hamper our abilities, you know." She laughed and took a long drink from her own glass.

Amalia enjoyed the lively discussion, analyzing the day's flight, making plans for tomorrow's leg. All the tanks would be refilled. New weather maps would be downloaded from the Internet and topographical maps reviewed. There seem to be constant work she never knew about when thinking about hot air ballooning.

"I checked the weather before coming down," Rafael said at one point. "We might have a problem in a day or two as there's a storm predicted."

"Will that hamper our flight?" she asked with concern.

"It could," Rafael answered. "The air becomes too turbulent to safely navigate. With downdrafts that could collapse a balloon, contradicting wind directions throwing the basket every which way, it's not safe to be airborne in a storm."

"Not to mention if you get zapped by lightning," Manuel murmured.

"Or getting rained on," Maria added.

"So we put down if it appears a storm is imminent," Rafael concluded. "Don't worry, I promised to get you home in one piece."

All the more reason for her not to be on this trip. Her visions of falling out and ending up a spot on the earth rose again. What if the storm came too fast, collapsed the balloon and they fell like a rock? She grew nervous just thinking about it.

"Have you called your brother yet?" Rafael asked as the meal was ending.

"I plan to do so when I get back to my room." After this sumptuous meal, she'd have even more to tell him. She'd make the event sound adventuresome. Jose probably wouldn't think about her fear of heights. He would be too caught up on the facts of the trip and on how far they'd come. She would have to tell him about firing the burners and could stretch reality a bit by telling him she was fine on the journey.

The group broke up once they finished eating. Most of them headed for the elevator, one or two going for a quick walk or to peruse the gift shops.

When they crossed the lobby, Amalia glanced around and stopped when she saw her boss holding court with several reporters.

Rafael stopped with her, following her line of sight.

"Couldn't stand not to be in the limelight," he murmured.

"You think he arranged this? We didn't know where we would be stopping for the night," she said, watching as her boss appeared in his element, fielding questions, giving a larger-than-life account of the day's events.

"It was pretty easy to predict by midafternoon how far we'd get. And there aren't a lot of places around here to stay. I think he would have traveled a lot farther this evening to have his moment in the limelight. I can't wait to see him at the end of the last day. He won't be so anxious to give press interviews. Did you want to join him?" Rafael asked.

"Good grief no."

He flung an arm casually across her shoulders and turned back to the elevators. While they waited, he leaned close and said, "Be sure to get enough rest tonight. We'll head out before dawn. Leave a wake-up call with the front desk so I don't have to come get you."

Like he had that morning.

Amalia nodded, feeling conflicted. She liked his arm across her shoulders. She didn't like his autocratic orders—she almost felt as if she should salute him. He must have caught a glimmer of annoyance in her eyes, because he leaned closer and said, for her ears only, "Think of it as besting your boss. You'd like that, wouldn't you?"

"It's a toss-up. By besting him, I'm aiding you." He was so close she was getting dizzy.

"And I'm the enemy?" His eyes sparkled with amusement.

Amalia felt herself grow deliciously warm. Her

heart rate increased. This man was dangerous to be around—at least for her sanity. They were cocooned in a world of their own. His body blocked the rest of the lobby. She could only feel her heart race and the weight of his arm. He'd moved slightly so she felt sheltered in his embrace.

"Perhaps not precisely an enemy, but certainly not a friend." She licked her lips and watched as his eyes followed the movement. He licked his lips in reflex and she could imagine feeling them pressed against her own.

"Maybe that will come. We have six more days," he said, his gaze holding hers.

Become involved with one of the wealthiest businessmen in Barcelona? Totally unlikely, especially if he truly wanted more than just friendship. But she smiled at the odd notion. Wouldn't that be something to tell her friends, casually mentioning Rafael Sandoval in conversation? She almost laughed aloud imagining her friends' reactions.

The bell announcing the elevator shattered her foolish thoughts.

It was dark when the wake-up call came. Amalia struggled with the desire to go back to sleep, but knew Rafael wasn't past demanding security open the door and admit him so he himself could drag her from bed, so she reluctantly got up and dressed as quickly as she could. Tossing everything back into her bag, she was ready five minutes ahead of time. Leaving the room, she rode an empty elevator to the lobby.

The lobby was quiet and subdued compared to last night. Even the lights were dimmed. She took her bag to the large entrance where a bellman took it and soon had it stored on the chase truck. Most of the crew was already standing by the truck talking and they greeted her cheerfully. When Rafael joined them a few seconds later, they took off for the field.

Amalia was better prepared for today's outing, though she constantly scanned the sky to see if there was any sign of the storms they talked about. The stars shone brightly everywhere. Not a cloud in the dark expanse.

Her anxiety rose as the balloon filled. She gratefully took the mug of coffee someone handed her, sipping the hot beverage and hoping she could cope again today. She was a bit proud of herself for sticking with it yesterday. Even though fleeing to a town would have been impossible, she was glad she hadn't tried. Even Jose had been encouraging during last night's phone call, after asking her for every detail. Telling her how lucky she was to be able to make the long jump.

"Ready?" Rafael asked.

She glanced at him, taking in the fact he looked wide-awake and excited. Obviously waiting in the dark didn't dampen his spirits at all.

"As I'll ever be," she said, holding out the cup to one of the crew as they walked by.

"I hope by the end of the trip you don't look as if you're going to the guillotine every time you approach the basket."

"Maybe if you had some phobia, you'd be more sympathetic," she replied smartly.

"Maybe my phobia is losing, something I don't intend to explore. Let's go. We can get an early start on Vicente today. They were still at the hotel when we left. If we ride the wind just right we can gain more ground."

"It's still dark," she said, once in the basket and watching as the team released the tether lines and slowly began to grow smaller beneath them.

The jets roared. The glow in the balloon was the only light around until they rose high enough to see the streetlights and windows of the resort.

"It'll be light soon enough. Watch the eastern horizon, you'll see it's lightening there now. No power lines around, nothing but clear skies and smooth sailing and, we hope, a fast wind," he called over the sound of the burners.

Standing near the side, still an arm's length

away, Amalia didn't feel the fear she normally did; instead she felt an odd sense of anticipation. It was odd to look out and see dark rolling hills silhouetted against a starry sky with few scattered lights on the ground below. There was no sense of height or distance in the diffused light of early dawn. She should enjoy what she could. She would never do something like this again.

Turning, she stepped next to Rafael.

"Tell me what I can do."

"About?" he asked.

"Winning this race."

That surprised him, she could tell.

"Interesting. Why the change of heart?"

"What, that I would want to win? I'm competitive, too."

"What happened to your calling it a stupid race?"

"Nothing, it still amazes me that two grown men would wager an extraordinary amount of money on a hot air balloon race, but after Stefano's comments last night, I'm definitely switching loyalties for the duration. Besides, you have a fan in my brother. He suggested I reconsider my stance and give my team my all."

Rafael said nothing, just studied the other balloon in the distance as it began to rise. "There's nothing to do now, but you can spell me later on the burners."

Could he trust her? Rafael wasn't one to give his trust easily. He'd learned as a child to guard that which was his and count on no one but himself. Still…how much damage could she do unless she deliberately sabotaged something? Which was unlikely, as afraid of falling as she was.

"Fine." She crossed to the corner, stacked the two blankets and sat down. As long as she was below the level of the basket she wasn't as scared, but he wished she could enjoy the ride. The sun was just peeking over the horizon, bathing the earth in pure light. It was one of the joys he found in the sport. Gliding silently above the world when the burners were off.

Amalia leaned back against the basket, confident today it wouldn't give way and let her fall. In fact, when she thought about things this morning, she realized she hadn't felt the body-numbing fear she had yesterday. The notion brightened her outlook. She felt almost in charity with Rafael, forgiving him for forcing her on this adventure. As Jose had said, there were lots of people who paid for balloon rides. She was getting one for free.

Once the balloon reached the height to satisfy Rafael, he shut down the burners.

"Want something to eat?"

"I thought we were skipping breakfast."

"We picked up some croissants before we left."

She happily unwrapped the food while Rafael poured hot coffee from a thermos. In only moments they were enjoying a high-altitude picnic. She watched as he stood and kept looking around.

"So what made you challenge Stefano to this bet?" she asked.

"For the chance to win."

"What if you can't?"

He laughed. "Of course I can. Today we outdistance him, and by day five he won't even see us we'll be so far ahead."

"How can you be so sure?"

He studied her for a moment, then shrugged. "Stefano's a show-off. He does spectacular stunts for notice. He's never done a long jump before. And we're away from crowds and media. Last night notwithstanding; those were local reporters, no one from Barcelona was there. Granted the news story would go out over the wires, but we're not going to find a luxury hotel to stop in every night. Once there's no one around to show off for, he'll grow bored, and I'm hoping, sloppy in his efforts."

"While you're as driven as if this really meant something. Which it must, but I can't figure out what. You don't want the money, you've already said you'd donate that. So what do you get out of winning?"

"The satisfaction of beating him, and ramming home the point in front of the entire Barcelona Business Alliance."

"Is this some kind of revenge?"

He hesitated a moment, then said, "Just a way to put a man in his place."

Amalia thought about that for a while. She knew the company had had dealings with Rafael's company since before she began to work for Stefano. But she'd seen no sign of bad feelings between the two men—if she discounted the tension surrounding their meetings. Was it pure competitiveness? Each wanting to be the alpha male? She experienced a bit of that with her brother and his friends. Always jockeying for leader position of their group, they were friends yet rivals.

Yet something more than that drove Rafael, she was sure of it. What was it?

"I can almost see the wheels spinning in your mind," he said. Taking a last swallow of coffee, he put the cup in the bag and fired the burners for a few seconds to maintain their altitude.

"I can't figure you out," she said with some vexation.

"And you need to because why?"

"I like things tidy." She scrambled to her feet, pitching her own empty cup into the small bag and then cautiously looking around. The other balloon was some distance away. Other than that one, the sky was empty. It was another lovely cloudless day. She wondered if there would be bad weather later.

"Let's just say it balances things out," Rafael said at last.

Sounded cryptic to her. She watched the horizon for a while, then went to sit back in her corner.

Amalia was getting used to the slight motion and the alternating noisy and then quiet times. She was also getting a bit bored, sitting where she could look up and see the balloon, or looking around and seeing the four sides of the wicker basket and the man who had brought her along.

"Tell me more about your family," she said after a long stretch of silence.

"What's to tell? I have a mother, a father and a brother. He's married and has two children."

"The end? That's all? I've read about your father, but I don't know much about your mother."

"There's no reason you should."

Feeling rebuffed, Amalia lapsed into silence.

She would go bonkers if something didn't liven up the day. Maybe she could call Maria on the radio and have a decent conversation. But not a private one, she knew. And she didn't quite see Rafael meekly allowing her to monopolize the airways.

In fact, she couldn't envision Rafael ever being meek.

"I had my parents until I was in university. Their death was unexpected, but we had a strong family bond until that moment," she said. Maybe if she started the conversation, he'd open up.

"Lucky you."

He stooped down beside her. Amalia glanced at him. "Shouldn't you be watching—where we're going or how close to the ground we're getting?"

"We're going where the wind takes us. We're high enough not to worry about obstacles, and when you think we need to rise some more, you can handle the burners."

She scooted a bit to the left, not wanting to be so close to him. It was uncomfortable that her body seemed to think Rafael was the greatest thing since sliced bread while she knew intellectually that he was far beyond her league. She was no comparison to the lovely Teresa Valesquez for instance. And she wasn't sure she ever wanted to be. The idea of being escorted around for a few weeks or months and then left behind when he moved to another woman was too uncomfortable to imagine.

Amalia waited a moment, then stood, keeping as close to the center of the basket as she could. They were quite high. Still, a check of the gauge showed the interior air had cooled and she daringly reached up and turned on the burners for a half-dozen seconds.

Rafael watched her but said nothing.

She felt quite competent!

They talked through the morning. Amalia couldn't help jumping up more frequently than Rafael did to check their height from the earth. And scan around for anything that could impede their trip. The other balloon seemed lower and was veering in a different direction. One time she ventured to look straight down. Her heart caught in her throat and she felt an impending urge to keep moving over the edge of the basket and fall to earth. She dropped to the floor and tried to catch her breath.

"You okay?"

"I looked down," she said, her eyes tightly closed. She was not going to fall out of this balloon. Patiently she waited for the waves of nausea to pass. She would not look down, she'd be okay if she didn't look straight down.

Rafael grasped her shoulder with one hand. "Amalia, you're perfectly safe here. I would never let you come to harm." His hand rubbed her gently. She opened her eyes. He was right smack in front of her. Close enough to give comfort and a feeling of security.

Close enough to kiss. The thought popped into her mind and she almost groaned with the temptation. His dark eyes watched her carefully, trying to calm her nervousness.

The fear of falling faded and another emotion took charge. One of tempting the attraction she felt to push the boundaries and see if Rafael had any interest in her. It wouldn't be the same as in Barcelona. No press was hounding them. They were alone for hours at a time. She could let down her guard a little and see what happened.

Which would be totally stupid. Sanity regained the upper hand.

"I thought you were doing better," he said.

"I was, then I looked straight down."

"So don't do that."

She nodded. "You'd think I'd remember that."

"Come on, have a drink and take the burner, take your mind off your phobia."

"Heights don't bother you?"

"No."

"Is it true you scaled Mont Blanc a few

summers ago?" she asked, reluctantly standing back in the center, hoping she could concentrate on other things besides the huge amount of empty space between her and the earth.

"I did."

She had read that recently in one of the reports on the Internet. "Wasn't that a bit scary?"

"I'd have called it exhilarating."

"Dangerous, rather. You could have fallen and been killed."

"Danger gave it an extra fillip of excitement. I never thought about dying on the mountain."

"But it *could* happen."

"Of course it could. But I could also be killed by a truck crossing a street in Barcelona," he replied, leaning casually against the side of the basket.

"I guess. But to deliberately put yourself in danger, that's just weird."

He laughed. Her heart skipped a beat.

"I like some excitement in life. No crime in that."

"Reckless," she commented.

He shrugged, his eyes dancing in amusement. "Maybe. But it's my life to do with as I will."

"Since you have no family to worry about."

"Families are overrated." The amusement vanished in an instant.

She blinked. "If I hadn't had my brother when my parents died, I don't know what I'd have done. We don't have any other family, just long-term family friends. Which in a way could be considered an extended family. You're lucky, you still have both your parents and your brother."

He took another swallow from his can, then studied it a moment before looking at Amalia.

"You were stuck raising a boy when your parents died. Where's the luck in that? You're still young. You should be out having fun. Doing a job you love instead of working for Vicente."

"How do you know I don't like that job?"

"You said you'd change it if you could."

"I love my brother. I told you, if not for him, I'd be alone in the world. Though I do hope to marry someday."

"Ah, the great panacea for life."

"What do you mean by that?" she asked curiously.

He crushed the empty soda can and put it into the small trash bag. Looking around, he made sure things were going according to plan and then looked back at Amalia. She looked around, trying to see what he did. Should they go up some more? She opened the throttle and the jets roared. The balloon rose.

He watched her, making her feel funny. When

she felt the balloon move, she realized they'd risen into another current. The basket actually swayed a moment, and she fought to keep her balance. Fear flashed. She took a deep breath, reassured by Rafael's casual pose. Once they stabilized, she grinned. She'd held her ground. Quite an accomplishment for her.

"Don't you believe in marriage?" she asked then.

"It seems to be all right for some, but not all. Look at my parents—they married in the heat of passion when young. Once the passion faded, they didn't even like each other much. Too bad they didn't think of that before having two children."

"Yet you wouldn't be here if they had," she murmured.

"Would the world be worse off because of that?" he asked.

She was shocked. It was not something she had ever considered—whether the world was better off because she lived.

"Maybe not, but you have the opportunity to do good."

"Oh, oh, Miss Crusader. Like what?"

"If nothing else, you'll donate a lot of money to a children's charity. And I know your company gives to various organizations in Barcelona," she ended triumphantly.

"So how does my father benefit mankind?"

She laughed. "I'm not saying everyone has to. Maybe his sole purpose was to produce you."

Rafael laughed at that. "Right. And my mother's sole purpose? Besides seeing how many men she can marry before she's too old to appeal to anyone."

"Oh, you are so cynical. Maybe she's searching for happiness and doesn't recognize it when she's got it."

"Pop Psychology 101," he retorted. "Maybe she's just a wealthy, bored woman looking for thrills. I like mine on the mountain side."

"Or in a hot air balloon," she answered.

He inclined his head in agreement. "It's a different kind of sport but satisfying all the same."

Rafael watched as Amalia assimilated his comments. He could tell she still had starry ideas about marriage, love and happy ever after. He wished her good luck with that. In his experience it was truly rare.

Maybe that was the problem. His experiences were limited. If Amalia were anything to go by, he'd missed an entire category of women. She was unlike anyone he'd dated in the last ten years—maybe ever.

Of course their circumstances were unlike any other. She didn't want to be with him. Was it the novelty of that idea that intrigued him? He'd become accustomed to the attention of beautiful women. Was he jaded? It would be unreasonable to expect all women to fall over themselves for a chance to be with him.

But it irked him that Amalia didn't. He could offer her so much more than anything she'd had so far in life yet she remained aloof and distant. He didn't understand her.

"I feel sorry for you, Rafael," she said slowly. Her eyes showed the sympathy.

He felt a flash of surprise. "Why?"

"Because you're missing out on the best part of life. Finding someone to share your joys and sorrows and to go through life together. My parents loved each other very much and my mother once said she could put up with anything as long as she had my dad in her corner. Who do you have in *your* corner?"

CHAPTER SIX

"Any one of a number of friends," Rafael said calmly.

But was it true? He had many business acquaintances, some casual friends to go to parties with or sail with. But except for Phillip Stanton and Marco Valdez from school days, he had a superficial relationship with most people. It had even been a number of months since he'd spoken to Phillip or Marco.

Or his brother.

For a moment he wondered what special tie connected Amalia and her brother. Banding together in the face of tragedy? Would he put his life on hold if Andreas needed him? Rafael liked to think so, but he began to wonder if Andreas would reciprocate.

"Good for you," she said, looking out at the other balloon. "How long before we stop again?"

"Another two hours, I hope. The air is cooler

today, meaning it's easier for us to get lift with the hot air. As long as the propane lasts, we're good to go."

She sighed.

"Hey, this is a perfect chance to see Spain from the air. You're missing a lot by not taking advantage."

"Like heart attack, nausea, fainting."

He laughed and crossed to her side. Taking her hand in his, he pulled her closer to the side. "I'll hold on to you to keep you safe," he said as he positioned her near the wicker, but not too close. Wrapping his arms around her, he pulled her back against his chest, leaning over slightly to rest his chin on her shoulder. "Look at that. It's hard to imagine all that open land when we live in such a crowded city."

Amalia slowly let her eyes drink in the view. It was breathtaking. Rafael had been right, it was lovely. Slowly she turned her head to see as much as she could. When she turned it the other way, she bumped into Rafael's face. His cheek was warm. She could feel him smile.

"Nice, huh?"

What, the view?

Or being held by him, feeling safe and secure and almost cherished? She savored the moment. His arms held her securely to his rock-solid body.

His feet were braced to balance them in the slight sway of the basket. She could let go of her fear and enjoy the spectacular vision spread out beneath them.

And her senses were far more attuned to the man holding her than to her fear of falling. It was a delight to savor the moment. She closed her eyes and tried to imprint every detail on her mind to remember through the rest of her life. Soaring over Spain, held by Rafael, her real life faded into the background. For these few moments, this was real.

By the time Rafael found a spot where he could safely put down the balloon, Amalia was more than ready to stop. A person could only stand being on edge for so long. She wanted to run on the ground, get away from his disturbing presence and touch base with reality.

Her boss's balloon had put down twenty minutes earlier. She was beginning to suspect he didn't carry as much fuel as they did. So they, once again, gained some distance, but Stefano could easily catch up and pass them while they exchanged tanks. They were still too close to predict any clear-cut winner.

The chase crew was already in the clearing, which Amalia found amazing.

Once the balloon was down and secured, a

festive picnic lunch was served and quickly eaten as everyone stood. Using a GPS indicator, Rafael calculated the distance they'd already gone.

"Think we can make another one hundred miles this afternoon?" Julio asked.

"If the wind holds. It kicked up once or twice."

"A problem?" Manuel asked.

"No."

Amalia finished her meal and jumped up. "I'm going for a quick walk. Being in that confined space gets to me," she said.

Maria offered to go with her.

"Thanks, but unless you really want to, I'm fine. I'll look at the scenery from ground level and relish not being airborne for a while." She flicked a glance at Rafael.

"We leave in ten," he said.

She started off along the road the truck was parked on. It was dirt, but packed hard and easy to walk on. It had grown warm and she left her jacket at the picnic area. There was plenty to do to ready the balloon for the next leg, but the others were far more competent than her.

And she needed some time to herself. Being with Rafael felt like a roller-coaster ride. She disliked being in the balloon yet she was captivated by her pilot. She resented his autocratic ways yet she yearned for a kiss.

That stopped her. She shook her head and started walking again. The very last thing in the world she needed was to be kissed by Rafael. She had a feeling it would spoil her for any man in the future.

And for him it would merely be another woman in a long line of women. He'd probably forget her name by Christmas.

Sighing softly, she tried to count her blessings and hope something would happen to speed up the race.

Amalia was just about to turn around when she heard a vehicle behind her. Stepping to the side of the road, she stopped. It was the chase truck. Rafael was driving. He stopped even with her and looked at her through the passenger side window.

"You walking home?" he asked easily.

She shook her head and opened the door. Climbing in, she looked at him.

"I was just walking. Has it been ten minutes?" She wasn't wearing a watch, but surely she hadn't been gone that long.

"Nine. We'll be back in a sec and take off again."

"Did you really think I'd try to walk away?" she asked. She hated being his partner, but she would not let him down, because she was starting to believe her boss needed taking down a peg or two.

"No. But if you twisted your ankle or something, it would have been hard for you to get back. Feeling better for the walk?"

"Yes," she said.

It took only a moment to return to the balloon. Maria had a phone to her ear. When she saw the truck, she said something to Paolo and then headed to meet Rafael.

Amalia hopped out of the truck and watched as Maria came up to Rafael.

"The office is trying to reach you," she said, holding out the phone.

Rafael took it. "Make it quick," he said. A moment later he bit out an epithet. "Under no circumstances tell her you've talked to me. If she calls again, tell her you'll relay the message and that's all. Put Jaime on the phone." Rafael walked away talking to the man on the other end.

Maria grinned at Amalia and said, "Girlfriend troubles."

"Teresa Valesquez?"

"Yes, she keeps calling. I think Sophie is getting fed up with all the messages she's left. Guess now Miss High and Mighty wishes she hadn't thrown away her chance for the long jump after all. Though she was not a ballooner—you never heard such complaining!"

Amalia vowed to keep her own thoughts about

ballooning to herself. She may not like it, but she wanted to give no cause for gossip.

Rafael was impatient to begin the ride. Amalia scanned the sky. There was no sign of the other balloon. Maybe they would maintain their lead.

Once in the basket and beginning to lift, she asked Rafael, "Do you think Stefano will have reporters there again tonight?"

"I wouldn't put it past him," Rafael said, eyeing the balloon. Amalia was not able to judge their rate of ascent since she kept her eyes inside the basket and had nothing to gauge it by. She enjoyed watching Rafael when he was concentrating on something else.

When he turned off the burners, she looked around. Still no sign of Stefano's balloon.

"So we got a jump on him this leg," she murmured.

"Enough to keep the lead, I hope."

Amalia stood in one corner and leaned against the propane tank.

Rafael took the map from one of the storage pockets and began to study it.

"Shouldn't you be watching?" she asked.

"I'll check it soon. You let me know if we're going to crash into anything."

She looked at the empty sky. They were far too high to worry about power lines, even if there had been any around. The other balloon was lifting in the distance.

"The scenery aside, there's not much to do, is there? Are the festivals like this, too?"

Rafael shook his head and began telling her about the ones he'd attended. She liked listening to him as he talked, closing her eyes to concentrate better.

"Am I putting you to sleep?" he asked.

"No, I listen better with my eyes closed," she said. The last thing she felt around him was tired. She could feel the heat from his body. She could smell the unique scent that would forever be imprinted in her mind as Rafael's. Wishing she could record his voice to listen to years down the road, she smiled as he told her of the antics and contests at the festival. His description was romantic and dramatic, and surprisingly the stories did not all feature him as the star.

He fired up the jets and she opened her eyes to watch him. He was tall and slender, with broad shoulders and a tapering waist. His hair had been permanently disheveled since they started. She liked it. It made him seem that much more approachable.

By the time he switched to the last propane tank, dusk was drawing near. Rafael constantly scanned the horizon, but there was no place in sight to set down. The last thing he wanted was to have to land in the dark. There was no telling what dangers there would be.

Maria called him on the radio, the signal poor and staticky. "Lost sight of you…different direction…we can find."

"Say again," he replied.

"You are going in a different direction from the road. We cannot find a way to cut over. Do you see a landing site?"

"Negative." He glanced behind him but did not see Vicente's balloon. The man had been behind all afternoon and had probably put down at the wide area Rafael had seen about a half hour ago. He looked ahead again. Still nothing suitable.

Static again. Then "…us your GPS coordinates. We'll find…"

Rafael glanced at the GPS device and then relayed the coordinates, saying them slowly and then repeating them.

"Got it."

Rafael clicked off the radio and glanced at Amalia. He expected to be reproached or have her complain or say again she was frightened.

But she watched him calmly. Was that trust he saw in her eyes?

"So I'll do the burners if you watch for a place to land," she said, stepping close to him.

He let her hand brush against his when she reached for the lever. He was playing with fire to entertain any thoughts of getting involved with Amalia. She was content in her life and had her brother to raise. Heck, she probably didn't even have a dress suitable for some of the places he liked to take women.

Though that would be no problem; he could buy her whatever she needed. He knew enough from the talk at social events who the leading designers were, where their gowns could be purchased. But maybe he'd take her for a weekend sail, just the two of them on the sea.

Frowning at the way his thoughts were going, he took advantage of her offer and rummaged in a side pocket for the binoculars he carried. Finding them, he began to scan the direction they were going. There had to be something opening up soon.

Had he been with one of his chase team who had experience in the balloon, he wouldn't be as concerned. Meeting all challenges was one of the things he liked best about the sport. One couldn't plan out as with plane flights, but meeting the unexpected and handling it was exhilarating. Or it would be, if he wasn't constantly aware of his passenger and her fear of heights. The last thing he wanted was to give her any reason to fear during the flight.

There, in the distance, he saw an opening in the trees. He lowered the binoculars and tried to gauge how far it was and when they should start down. They had far outdistanced Vicente today. Tomorrow he'd get even farther.

In less than twenty minutes they were on the ground. Amalia jumped over the side and grabbed a tether rope. There wasn't the need to find an anchor quickly this time, as the balloon was deflating, with nothing nearby to cause a problem.

Once the tug from the breeze died, he jumped over the side with her and took another rope, securing the basket.

"So we just stand here?" she asked.

"For a few minutes. The envelope is already almost down."

"It's not going to cover us, is it?"

"It won't hurt if it does, we can just crawl out. But, no, it'll go the other direction. There, it's almost down."

When the nylon was lying on the ground, Rafael dropped his rope and indicated Amalia could do the same.

She did so, hesitantly.

"Good job," he said, joining her.

"Now what?"

"We wait for the others."

She looked around. "I don't see a road."

"They'll come."

"We are not where we were when you gave them the GPS location."

"Manuel and Maria both know how to calculate distance and direction. And we have a beacon that I can start that gives off a signal. When they are close enough, they'll receive that. I haven't been wrong yet, have I?"

"Not that I know of, but that doesn't mean you can't be," she said, annoyed with him. He looked as fresh and energetic as he had that morning. She would love to sit somewhere and relish being on the earth again. She knew any hint of makeup she'd put on that morning was gone. Her hair had to be a mess. And she'd love to forget about everything and just veg out—preferably away from Rafael Sandoval.

He laughed. "True enough. But better for my image if every time I'm wrong, few people know about it." He looked around, fists on his hips.

Amalia thought he looked the way a conquistador probably looked when landing in the New World and thinking he'd conquered all he surveyed.

"We can wait in the basket if you like," he said.

"No, thanks, I've spent enough time there today."

"Then help me with the balloon."

They stretched it out, then began rolling it toward the basket. Once it was compacted, he reached in the basket for the blankets and a large plastic tarp.

"We cover the balloon, then we sit and wait."

"Why cover the balloon?"

"To keep it dry. Wet nylon doesn't inflate very well."

"Oh."

"I'll take a blanket to sit on," he said when the envelope was covered. He also took the last two sodas.

She handed him a blanket and then put hers down on the ground. Rafael sat opposite her.

"Will we have to spend the night here?" she asked as he tossed her one of the sodas and kept the other.

"Probably. I didn't see an when looking for this a lot of time travel could be airborne.

"I'm not much

"Ever been?"

She shook he

"Then how

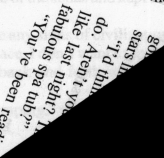

stars

do. Aren't yo

like last nig

fabulous spa tub?"

"You've been reading

"I like hot and cold running water too much."

"Look on this as a great adventure."

"Yeah, that's what my brother says. Who says I want adventure?"

Rafael laughed.

Amalia swallowed her drink wrong and ended up in a coughing fit. He pounded her on the back until she stopped.

"Thanks, I'm okay now."

She looked around. The clearing was several acres in size. There were a few scruffy trees here and there, but otherwise it was a rocky flat area on the dry side of the hills they'd been following all day. She was already feeling the hard unevenness of the ground beneath her. How could she sleep on it? How could she sleep alone with Rafael?

Were there wild animals? She looked around, realizing how fast the light was fading.

"It'll be dark soon," she said.

"We have a couple of flashlights in the ndola. At least when it's dark, you can see the ike never before. Each one is crystal clear."

k you'd dislike it even more than I

u missing the fancy restaurants

he luxurious hotel with the

too many newspaper

accounts. Sure I enjoy fine things. And I like eating good food. But I also enjoy climbing, hot air ballooning. Versatility is needed for both."

"So tell me about climbing. How did you get into that?"

"Friends from school and I first went on a trek in France when I was around eighteen. I was hooked. Talk about a challenge—finding my way up the face of a cliff that looked as if it had never been scaled. Reaching the summit and feeling like I was on the rim of the world. You should try it sometime."

Amalia shook her head in horror. "I can't imagine much worse—unless it's hot air ballooning."

"So your hobbies are needlepoint or knitting, safe and secure?"

"Don't turn your nose up at those kinds of hobbies. They're probably fun for many people. But not for me. I like computers."

"So you don't take your brother on camping trips?"

"Is that a guy thing? He does plenty outside. He's going on a science camp this week, with twenty other students. They'll be camping out and exploring geophysical phenomena. He'll love it, even if it rains."

"I do admit to preferring four walls and a roof in the rain," Rafael said.

He stretched out his single blanket, then lay down.

"Are you going to sleep?" Amalia asked. It was getting darker by the moment. She could already see a few stars in the sky.

"No, just wanting a good view of the sky. Once the crew gets here we'll have a fire and lights and miss some of the spectacle."

Rafael confused her. Every time she thought she understood him, he'd say or do something opposite to what she would expect. There was more to him than the playboy image he seemed to relish in Barcelona.

There was something rock solid about him. Even when he pushed for his own way, she knew she could count on him to keep his word and get her home safe.

She looked at the sky. If she sat looking up long enough, she'd get a terrible crick in her neck. Reluctantly she spread her own blanket and lay down. Shifting slightly to find a more comfortable spot she relaxed and enjoyed the starry sky. The darker it became, the more stars appeared. She could see the Milky Way.

"It is spectacular," she murmured.

"It always puts things into perspective," he said.

"Like?"

"Like work is not the be all and end all of life. That we are insignificant creatures in the great scheme of things. How many stars can you count?"

"I can't count them all!" She laughed.

"They say God knows the name of every star."

"I find that totally amazing." She was silent for a moment savoring the beauty above her.

"You could have asked for the fifty thousand Euros for yourself," he said.

"What?" She sat up. "Where did that come from?"

"I was thinking about your scathing comments about the bet. I'm sure you must have imagined what that kind of money could do for you and your brother."

"I provide just fine for me and my brother. Soon he'll be on his own and every penny I earn will be mine."

"A gift, then," he said.

"No, thank you. That's not my style."

He looked at her, silhouetted against the night sky. "So what is your style?"

"To earn my own way," she said.

He smiled, though she couldn't see in the dark. So idealistic. Refreshing after the women he usually dated. Then again, maybe the fault lay in his taste in women....

"After this balloon ride, maybe you'll feel you earned it. Or at least a bonus from Vicente for going above and beyond the duties of a PA."

"Are you giving Helena a bonus?" she asked.

"Yes." No need to tell her the thought had just come to him. Helena made a good salary, but this was certainly above and beyond.

"Money plays a big part of your life," she said slowly.

Her voice moved as she lay back down.

"It does in everyone's life," he replied.

"Not so much in ours, mainly because we don't have a lot. And we need to save for when Jose is at university. Besides, it mainly buys things. Not memories."

"Like?"

"Like the afternoons at the beach we used to enjoy with our parents. We'd spend all day playing in the water, picnicking, being together. I miss those times. And holidays, when we celebrated together."

"You paint an idyllic life. Real life doesn't follow that."

"Your parents didn't do right by you and your brother."

"So you're now an expert on my parents?" he asked. The old wound threatened to reopen. He knew she was right, but years of hiding the disappointment he'd felt at being shunted to school and holiday resorts while his parents went their separate ways resurfaced. He would never subject a child to that. Which was why he planned to stay single all his life.

"Money can buy memories," he argued, just for the hell of it. "Making enough to afford my interests is satisfying."

"So you try flying, either by plane or balloon, and scuba diving, racing. High-adrenaline sports," she said. "Sounds like something's missing."

"Nothing's missing. I do well in business and can indulge myself with any sport I want."

"If you were married, you'd have a family to build memories with. What happens when you're eighty and can't do all those sports?"

Rafael laughed. "I doubt I'll want to if I live to be eighty. And I will have the memories you put such store in."

"But who would you have to share them with?"

"Who do you have?" he countered.

"Jose for one. And I do hope to marry someday and have a family. Children to love and raise. A husband to grow old with, to share my life and his."

"I can't see my parents sitting on a veranda somewhere in thirty years swapping stories about the good old days."

"I bet my parents would have. With grandchildren around. That's sad your parents don't have family memories."

He sat up, not wanting to continue this topic. "Not sad, just fact. What about people who don't have a happy life, do you think they want to remember that when they get old?"

She fell silent.

Rafael stood and looked around. It was dark with no ambient light but that from the stars overhead. He could make out the silhouette of the rim of hills behind them. No roads, but plenty of open land for Manuel to drive over. He hoped the GPS locator was functioning.

"Hungry?" he asked.

"A little." She sat up, drawing the blanket over her shoulders. It was growing cooler.

"We have some snacks left. But dinner will have to wait on the crew."

"And that could be six hours away," she murmured.

"No, they'll be here before long."

"If not?"

"Then we bunk down here."

"Just the two of us," she said softly.

"Do you have a problem with that?"

"Should I?"

"Depends on what you consider a problem."

Amalia's heart rate sped up. She imagined a lot

of scenarios—none of which she'd classify as precisely a problem. Unless she considered being stranded with one of Barcelona's more infamous bachelors a problem.

"Look on it as a great adventure."

"I don't think I'm the adventurous type."

"Then it's time you break out of your mold and see what you find," he said. He sat beside her and nudged her slightly with his shoulder. "Live on the wild side for a while. Explore new things, push yourself. Find out who you really are."

"And who are you, Rafael?" she asked.

"Someone hoping to go through life experiencing many different facets. Like sailing, soaring, kissing beautiful women."

The low, sexy tone had her senses on full alert. What would it be like to be kissed by an adventurer?

She was about to find out, she thought, feeling giddy and breathless at the idea.

"Amalia?" he said softly, brushing back her hair from her face, turning toward her.

She saw his head blot the stars then felt his lips brush across hers.

Decision time. Should she scoot away and be outraged, or give in to rampant curiosity and indulge herself as he suggested?

He gathered her closer, blanket and all, and

moved past the mere brush of lips for a full-fledged kiss that had her blood pounding through her veins, her head spinning and her own hands reaching out to grasp his jacket and hold on.

The hard ground was forgotten. He shifted slightly, bringing her even closer in his embrace as his tongue teased her lips, dancing with her own when she opened to him. Amalia felt like a top spinning. It was glorious. No wonder women vied to date the man. He set a new standard in kissing.

Too soon he pulled back a bit, his breath fanning her cheeks. "Sorry, I couldn't resist."

Sorry! She pushed against that rock-solid chest and scooted back, suddenly feeling every pebble and rock beneath her. Disentangling herself from the blanket, she stood and moved even farther away.

"Try exercising more control next time you feel you can't resist," she snapped. She turned, tears of humiliation threatening.

"Hey, Amalia, it was only a kiss," he said, coming up behind her and putting his hands on her shoulders. "I didn't mean anything," he said.

That was the problem. It was the best kiss she'd ever had, and he didn't mean anything.

He stepped up and leaned his head next to hers. She felt the warmth from his cheek next to hers.

"I'm sorry if you're upset. I won't do it again."

Probably not. He was used to gorgeous sophisticated women, not some overworked PA who had to be forced to go on this race with him.

"I think we should keep this businesslike," she said stiffly. She really wanted him to turn her into his arms again and say nothing was more important to him than her. She almost laughed at the expression he'd have if she voiced that crazy idea.

"I agree. Friends?"

"I doubt we can ever be friends. Just let it drop," she said, shrugging out of his hold and stepping away. She dare not go too far, as she had no idea where anything was in the darkness.

Would they end up wrapped in the blankets, sleeping beneath the stars? At least the storms he mentioned hadn't materialized. That would really be horrid.

The silence grew awkward and she knew she hadn't handled things well. But she couldn't risk getting too comfortable with him or she'd make an idiot of herself over the man, and then where would she be? She had her brother to get off to university and her own dreams to pursue.

It was almost thirty minutes later that the first glimpse of the headlights shone through the trees.

"Is that them?" she asked, jumping up and trying to see more than flashes of lights at ground level.

"Probably." Rafael went to the basket and retrieved the radio. In seconds he was in contact with the crew and turned on both flashlights to show them where they were. In less than twenty minutes the truck arrived, lurching over the rough terrain, illuminating everything with its powerful headlights.

Amalia was so glad they'd arrived. She needed a buffer between her and Rafael.

Camping had never been high on her list of things to do, but with accomplished veterans, it turned out to be fun. The meal was cooked and shared by all. The crew and Rafael checked out the balloon, exchanged the propane tanks and made everything ready for the morning flight.

Then air mattresses were inflated, sleeping bags doled out and in less time than she'd expected, Amalia was warm and sleepy. She watched the sky for a few minutes, then closed her eyes and went to sleep—to dream about Rafael's amazing kisses.

Rafael lay in his bag, watching the sky, thinking of the earlier kiss. He'd done it as a lark; only, it had backfired. Amalia hadn't seemed to enjoy it, while he'd enjoyed it far too much. Who would have thought Vicente's PA could kiss like that? He wanted another taste, another kiss to see if what he'd felt had just been a rebound from Teresa or if there was a special spark there.

Unlikely, he thought sardonically. Amalia just

didn't approve of his lifestyle. And to top it off, she wanted marriage and children and memories.

He was making his own memories. Doing things most men only dreamed about.

He thought about the various things he'd tried over the past few years. Turned out this balloon race was the best of the lot, and it was all because of his reluctant passenger.

Rafael frowned. Amalia was no more special than any of the other women he'd seen over the past decade. She was pretty in a very nonpretentious way. Perhaps lacking the sophistication he was used to made her a novelty? Yet she was genuine. Like the woman his brother had married.

But that would change given half a chance. Amalia could be seduced by diamonds and couture clothing, embassy parties and luxurious cruises. He knew what women liked. It was all well and good to talk about family and memories. He'd like to see her dressed in a beautiful gown, jewels glowing around her neck, hair elaborately done. He could take her to a reception, or maybe a Christmas ball. Show her a different side of Barcelona than she knew.

And then what? Move on again? It was what he did.

* * *

They were airborne at first light. Amalia had been avoiding him while they prepared for liftoff. Yet she was friendly with the crew, joking and laughing. It was only with him she became distant. And Rafael knew the others had noticed.

The balloon filled and tugged at the land-tethered gondola.

"Turn us loose," he said. In seconds the ropes had been released and they began to soar. He kept the burners going full blast to heat the air to the maximum in the shortest time possible, and the balloon rose swiftly.

She sat in the corner, gazing up at the balloon. Without standing, there wasn't a lot to see.

The other balloon wasn't in sight. Satisfied he'd made a leap ahead of Vicente, he wanted to keep that lead. The farther ahead he got, the better he would like it.

By midmorning Rafael was tired of the silence. Amalia had dozed for a short time, and when she wakened, he beckoned her over.

She rose and glanced around. He could tell she was easier each day with the height. He felt a moment of regret that he'd forced someone so afraid to come up, but he'd honored the conditions of the bet.

"Take over. I'm getting a drink," he said.

She nodded and stepped in his place.

"Want something?"

"Sure," she said. Then she opened the throttle and the jets roared. The balloon rose even higher. Rafael smiled. She was getting used to it in a big way. Looking at a spot on the horizon, he estimated their air speed. They were being pushed by a current at a faster rate than he expected. Since the balloon gave little indication of movement, it was hard to gauge the exact air speed.

He searched for the other balloon. Taking the binoculars, he trained them behind them until he located the other balloon. It was quite a distance behind them.

"We're going to win this easier than I thought," he murmured.

"Great, my boss will be a bear in the office if he loses."

"Prepare yourself."

He raised the binoculars again and frowned.

"What?" Amalia asked.

He lowered them and looked at her. "Storm clouds on the horizon. That bad weather front they talked about might be coming."

Amalia held out her hand in silent request for the binoculars. When she lifted them to her eyes and trained them on the distant horizon, she could see clouds. They didn't look particularly threatening and were right at the edge of the horizon. How long before they'd catch up? Wouldn't the air current they were on keep them moving ahead of the storms?

She asked Rafael.

"They will to some extent, but it depends on if the storm front is moving faster than this current."

Rafael contacted the ground crew. They had refilled the propane tanks and were heading in his direction. Rafael gave their GPS coordinates and told them to contact him when they were below him, which Manuel said should be soon.

"Now what?" she asked.

"Now we see where to land to exchange tanks. And if we can outrun the storm," he said.

CHAPTER SEVEN

AMALIA relinquished the controls and went to stand on the side facing the clouds. Staying an arm's distance from the side, she watched as the sky gradually grew more and more cloudy, some fluffy white puffs, others long and dark. She could scarcely see Vicente's balloon, and shortly before lunch, she lost sight of it altogether.

"Are we stopping soon?" she asked.

"No. The temperature is cooling, we can stay up longer. We have propane, we'll go as far as we can."

She caught a glimpse of a town. Holding on to the side, she looked at it.

"There's a town down there."

"We'll push on a bit farther."

"Good grief, don't put down in the mountains. The chase team would never find us."

"Sure they would. But that's not my intent. If we can get another few dozen miles, there is an entire valley that would be perfect to set down in. And there's a nice-size town at the head of the valley. We could have a hot bath and comfortable bed tonight."

"That gets my vote," she said.

Turning, Amalia watched Rafael as he stood opposite her, leaning casually against the side. She no longer feared he'd fall out. In fact, thinking back over the last day or two, she realized she wasn't nearly as fearful as when they started, unless she looked directly down.

"Now what's going on in your mind?" he asked.

"Just thinking that maybe, *maybe* mind you, this isn't the worst that could happen to me."

He laughed. "It's exhilarating."

"I still can't look down, but I've stopped panicking every time the basket sways a little."

"We can make a ballooner out of you yet."

"I doubt that. Tomorrow will be the halfway day. After that, it's all downhill."

"Do you regret coming?" he asked.

"Not as much as I did," she replied.

He nodded. "I knew I could count on you to be honest about it."

She looked away. She hadn't been honest about her feelings for that kiss. If he wanted the truth, she'd be hardpressed to comply. Some things were too personal to share.

"Amalia, would you go out with me when we return to Barcelona?"

She turned back at that, stunned he'd ask.

"Where?" was the only thought that sprang to mind.

"Ballet, reception, dinner for two, dancing. Wherever you want."

For one breathless moment she wanted to say yes. Then she shook her head. "I'm so not your type."

"And what is my type?"

He had to ask? Lounging comfortably against the side, he personified gorgeous male. His body was trim and muscular, his skin tanned from so much time in the sun. His hair was thick and dark. Her fingers actually itched to brush through it, feel the texture, savor the right to do just that.

"From what I saw of Teresa Valesquez, about the opposite of me."

"Ah, a new dress, some strappy high heels and a diamond or two and you'd rival Teresa. Actually, your conversation far surpasses hers. She's more concerned with being seen in all the right places."

"You don't believe she cares for you?" she asked, startled at his comment. She knew she didn't measure up, but she didn't need him suggesting she get new clothes and jewelry. Which she wouldn't do, even if she had the money.

"She cares for me because of my money. If I were a cabana boy, she wouldn't even give me the time of day."

She blinked, wondering if Rafael had ever worked on the beaches around Barcelona. She'd love to see him in a swimsuit, all glorious tanned skin and sleek muscles.

"There is an even larger gap between me and you. What makes you think I wouldn't date you for your money?"

"So far you seem singularly unimpressed by it. When faced with fifty thousand Euros, you wanted it to go to charity and you asked for nothing for yourself. Think how that money could help Jose in university."

"We can manage on our own," she said. She was not some gold digger. If that was the type of woman he was used to, she felt even more sorry for him. But she was not joining the ranks of women he dated and discarded.

"So I buy you a pretty dress or two, a few baubles, and we go out," he said.

"No. Thank you for the invitation, but I buy my own clothes and I don't go out with you."

He tilted his head slightly. "Why not?" he asked softly.

She shook her head, not wanting to have to say anything more.

"Just no? There has to be a reason," he pressed.

"Just no."

He crossed the short distance and stood beside her, lifting her face to his with a finger beneath her chin. "Why?"

His gaze seemed to bore right into her mind. Fortunately, he couldn't see the jumble of emotions swirling around in there—exacerbated by his touch. She licked her lips and his eyes caught the movement.

"You're too dangerous," she said at last.

"Because?"

"Come off it, Rafael, you're just bored. You don't really want to date me—you've already made me over into a Teresa clone in your mind. If you wanted to take me someplace, you'd take me as I am, not try to make me into someone else."

He studied her for a few moments, then nodded and released her.

Amalia took in a deep breath. She clenched her fists and tried to casually turn away, lest she forget all reason and jump into his arms.

The balloon spun around, fast enough to catch their attention. The gondola swayed a bit with the sudden motion.

"What's wrong?" she asked, grabbing on to the side.

He leaned back to look at the envelope. Then, looking around, Rafael went to the burners and turned them on full blast.

Amalia turned and saw the clouds were closer—a lot closer. She cautiously made her way to where he was standing.

"I think we've hit the leading edge of the storm front."

The sky was growing gray behind them. Obviously the wind, which one couldn't see, had outpaced the clouds. It was more turbulent than any they'd experienced before.

It wouldn't take long for the sun to get behind the clouds. She looked for the other balloon, but couldn't find it.

"Do you think Stefano already put down?"

"Highly likely. Whatever else he is, he isn't a fool. Take the controls and keep the jets going until you reach the temperature." He picked up the radio to contact the ground crew. Manuel responded, but once again there was static on the connection. Rafael asked for an update to the weather, in which direction the wind would be blowing and how long before the storm mass would become critical.

The response wasn't reassuring. The front was moving faster than originally anticipated. But the leading winds should keep the balloon away from the rain and lightning for a while. His advice was for them to put down as soon as Rafael found a safe haven.

"How far away are you?" Rafael asked.

"We are tracking you by GPS now, but we haven't seen you in a while. I'd say you've picked up some speed with the storm front."

Rafe looked over the side, studying the ground. Hilly, no open meadows, and rocky in some places. He could set down if he needed, but the lack of roads made it highly unlikely his chase team would find them anytime soon. It had taken them hours last night. He'd rather set down near civilization.

"We're heading north-northwest. Anything on the map in that direction where we can put down near a town?"

"Checking."

Amalia watched with wide eyes. Rafael winked at her to keep her off balance. The last thing he needed was for a scared young woman to hamper the flight. She'd done well so far, despite her phobia about heights. He hoped she could hang on a bit longer.

If he were flying with Manuel or Maria, he'd be exhilarating in the speed, in racing the wind. The sky was clear ahead, there were no towns or airline flight paths or obstacles to hamper them.

But if the storm came faster than the wind pushed them, he'd have to put down, rugged terrain or not. Trees or not. Amalia's safety would come first. And second, the safety of his balloon.

But he wasn't conceding yet.

"If you keep on your course, there are some plateau lands in a few miles. But no paved roads lead to them and from your GPS position, you're about twenty miles west of us. There might be some sheep herders in the area. I don't know. We will keep on this direction. If you change directions, send the signal as arranged."

"Roger that. I'll let you know."

"What is an arranged signal?" Amalia asked when Rafael put the radio down.

"Every half hour. Saves batteries, and they'll be monitoring at the exact times."

"And that works? Did we do that last night?"

"No, I've never have had to use it. Don't plan to today, either."

Rafael could tell from the shadow racing across the landscape they were moving faster than before. Once or twice the balloon faltered, indicating traverse winds. He wasn't sure whether to rise or go lower to find steady winds. One last look around convinced him he was ahead on this leg of the trip.

Carefully watching the balloon, Rafael kept

busy trying to gauge the speed and pressure on the envelope. Amalia was proving to be more help than he'd expected. She kept the balloon elevated. The wind spun them around again and she gave a short gasp, but didn't desert her duty station.

She did look at him with those wide eyes, questioning silently.

"We'll look for a place to set down," he said at last. Watching in the direction they appeared to be going he searched for any open area. Snagging the balloon on tall trees on the way down could render it inoperable. Something he refused to do. There were several more days left on this flight and he planned to make the farthest distance when the week ended. He radioed his plans to the ground crew.

Amalia jumped. "Oh, lightning," she said.

He looked behind him. The storm was still miles away, but another flash of lightning demonstrated the strength and danger coming.

"We'll start dropping now," he said into the radio. "Find us." He tossed the radio down and turned to Amalia. "Don't fire the burners unless I tell you to."

Glancing behind him from time to time, he knew he was ahead of the rain. He wanted to be on the ground and erect some kind of shelter before the full force of the storm hit. They could not afford to get the envelope wet. It would take a day or more to dry out and that would definitely put them out of the running.

Amalia didn't say a word. She watched his every move. He wished he could reassure her, but only being safely on the ground would do that.

The basket swayed more strongly than before. He heard Amalia's gasp but was too intent on getting them down to do anything more than tell her to hold on and be ready to start the jets if he wanted more lift.

The balloon spun around, the basket swinging with the momentum. Even Rafael was having trouble holding his balance. The last sway had knocked Amalia off her feet. She scrambled up and held on to the frame, looking over the edge, her face white.

The gusts were stronger the lower he went.

"Are we going to crash?" Amalia asked.

"No."

And, surprisingly enough, they didn't. He reached a large plateau, pulled the emergency release cord and told Amalia to be ready to jump off the basket when he gave the word. "And take one of the ropes with you. I'll follow and pull on the other."

The basket hit hard, the balloon almost puddling

over them as it continued its waffling in the wind as it collapsed with lack of hot air.

Amalia jumped off and looked for something to tie the rope to. Rafael was beside her in a second, pulling on another rope. It was windy. Amalia could feel stinging from the sand particles in the air as the wind swept across the rocky plateau. The basket tugged against the rope. There didn't appear to be anything handy to anchor the rope.

Rafael strained against the pull even as Amalia ran a few steps to keep the rope from being pulled from her hands. She got a better grip and leaned back, throwing her entire weight against the pull of the wind.

The envelope settled into an uneven lump, ruffled by the wind, but no longer driven by it. The pull eased. Amalia was breathing hard, but held fast.

"Good going," Rafael called. He studied the terrain, and then moved to the left a bit, trying his rope to an outcropping of rock. Not a very substantial one, from Amalia's viewpoint, but she trusted Rafael knew what he was doing.

He crossed quickly to her side, taking the rope from her hands. He found another rock and made it fast.

"Let's do what we can before the rain comes,"

he said, already moving to the balloon. Before long he had it stretched out, flapping in the wind, but in the wind's direction, with the basket as anchor. He began folding it, first lengthways, then when it was as wide as the basket, began rolling it toward it.

As soon as Amalia realized what he was doing she went to help, keeping a wary eye on the clouds massing behind them. Before they'd finished, the first drops of rain began to fall.

"We'll turn the basket on the side, floor to the storm's direction and huddle inside to keep dry," Rafael said, using one of the lines to fasten the balloon, scrambling for the plastic tarp and stretching it over the balloon. He stood and looked around. There was no shelter in sight.

"Help me tip the basket on its side, it'll afford some shelter."

Once that was done, he sent Amalia to sit in it, while he double-checked the jets and then found a large rock and dug a shallow trench around the covered balloon.

In seconds he joined her in the makeshift shelter, the one side away from the wind open to the elements. The rest was cozy and so far dry.

"If the storm gets very bad, the wicker will leak," he said.

"But we stay with the balloon," she said.

"It's the best way for the crew to find us," he explained.

"How will they know where to look for us?"

"They'll find us."

They sat and waited.

"Is there a road to this plateau?" she asked.

"I saw a dirt one not too far away. Every half hour we'll use the radio and see if we can raise them. They'll get here, sooner or later."

She was quiet for a moment. "I think you liked our ride down," she mused.

He laughed, flinging an arm across her shoulders. "It's exhilarating, man against nature—especially when man wins this round. I didn't expect the storm to come so quickly or to be caught without adequate shelter, to be honest. But we'll manage."

"It wasn't so bad. It all happened so fast, I didn't have a chance to become afraid."

"You did well, Amalia. I'm glad you were with me instead—"

He cut himself off, but Amalia knew he was thinking of Teresa. For a moment she felt pleased she'd done better than the other woman would have. But only for a moment. Then the obstacles to getting safely to some hotel for the night made themselves felt. She had a feeling it would be a long time before his chase team located them.

"I've never been a big fan of camping out, as you know," she said. "So I really did get my fill last night."

"We have snacks, blankets, shelter. What more do we need?"

"I can think of several things, not the least of which is to be dry. This shelter may start to leak before long."

"We'll manage."

Amalia wished once again she wasn't on this expedition. But not one to bemoan things beyond her control, she gave in to the inevitable.

She studied her companion. "Do you camp often?" she asked.

He studied the rain as it began to come down. "Not if I can help it. I like my amenities too much. But now and then. Today is not good weather. But when it's clear, to be away from the city lights, to see the stars and feel the awesome vastness of space, it's well worth minor inconveniences. Admit it, once you had dinner, last night was not a total waste."

He puzzled her. She would expect him to rail against the weather, to vent frustration on the circumstances. Instead, he seemed to take the setback in stride—maybe even relish it a bit.

He reached for the radio and made a call. No one responded. He tried again, but again there came only static. Switching it off, he tossed it back on the pile they'd made on one side of the tipped basket.

"Might as well make ourselves as comfortable as possible," he said.

He stacked the blankets side by side and sat down. Patting the one beside him, he waited for her to join him.

Eyeing the dubious shelter they had, she wondered how much longer before the wicker began to leak. Even as the thought came to mind, a drop landed on her nose.

"I think our shelter is getting soggy," she said.

Rafael looked up and swore. He turned and rummaged through two of the pockets on the side, coming up with another plastic tarp, not as large as the one covering the balloon, but large enough. He went into the rain and tied it to the side of the basket now their roof, fighting it and the wind until he had it covered.

Crawling in, he brushed off his jacket, wet at the shoulders, and sat down.

"Won't the wind blow it off?" she asked, hearing the plastic snap as the wind slapped it against the basket.

"Might get some nicks and tears, but nothing major. I think it'll hold. I'm more worried that water will get on the balloon. We need it dry to fly."

The bright idea came that perhaps both balloons would be too wet to fly again and the men would call off the bet. Or decide on the result based on where they had landed today. Then she could get home.

"Cold?" he asked.

"Getting there," she said. She could sit on the blanket or wrap it around her. She wished they'd brought one of the sleeping bags.

He pulled her closer, next to him, and threw his blanket over their legs. "Combined body heat is better than both of us freezing. Later, you'll have to give up the comfort of sitting on that blanket for added warmth."

They sat in silence for a few more minutes.

"The interesting thing about you, Amalia," he said at last, "is that you rarely complain. This is not the way I envisioned the race. You'd have every reason to complain about the circumstances, the weather, everything."

"It's hardly your fault the rain came."

"Doesn't stop some people." He reached out and took her left hand. "You're cold." He engulfed both of hers with his own, which were much warmer.

"For the most part I'm comfortable," she said. Or as comfortable as she could be snuggled up to Rafael.

"Let's spread the other blanket."

"Then we'll be sitting on the cold ground, with only the wicker between us."

"Then, this is what we'll do." He encircled her shoulders again and pulled her partway across his chest, looping his other arm around her waist. "Better?" he asked.

He was like a warm furnace, generating enough heat to keep both of them warm all night long, she thought.

"Thanks."

The wind howled. The drumming of the rain on the plastic sounded unusually loud. Slowly Amalia began to relax. She was warm, dry and safe. Granted no one knew when the chase team would arrive, but they had showed up last night and would surely arrive before long today.

"So tell me about this family you hope to have one day," Rafael said just as Amalia was thinking about trying to sleep.

"And open myself up to sarcasm? You've made your position clear."

"Hey, just because marriage isn't for me doesn't mean it's not for other people. I do have a couple of friends who seem to be making their marriages work. So what's your timetable? Marry by thirty, have two point three kids and get a large flat with a roof garden or something?"

"I have no timetable. There's no guarantee I'll ever find a man to love. Or one who will love me. But if I do, I'd want a full family life. Wherever we could afford to live would be fine. Though I hope it's near the water, I love the beach."

"I could take you sailing one day," he murmured.

She ignored his comment.

"Then, when the time is right, we could have some children. I know I'd like a couple, I liked having a younger brother. But I'd have mine closer together than my folks did. There are almost eleven years between me and Jose."

"But lucky for him there was. You were able to raise him, keep your family intact."

"You're right. That's important."

"So what will this dream husband be like?" Rafael asked curiously.

She frowned. "Probably unlike anyone you know," she said. "Solid, down-to-earth, grounded. He'll have a good job, and like to spend time doing family things—even when it's just us before—and after the children arrive."

"No fancy parties, exotic vacations?"

"A week or two traveling each year might be nice. There are a lot of places in Europe I'd like to visit."

"But no camping," he said, his mouth right by her ear.

She shook her head. Though she'd never forget sleeping beneath the stars last night. Or the kiss they'd shared before the others arrived.

"So what do you see as your future? Dating different women every month, getting older while they get younger? Don't you get tired of such a superficial life?" she asked.

"You're more cynical than I thought," he said. Rafael didn't like the picture she painted. He had been going out less and less frequently in the last couple of years. He didn't mind spending time alone and it suited him to read a good book or watch something worthwhile on the television rather than a constant round of parties or social events.

"Like father, like son," she murmured.

Was that how others saw him, as careless and clueless as his father? The man couldn't settle on one woman, he was always dating new and even younger women.

"Do you ever wonder what older men trying to cling to their youth find to talk about with younger women? There have no shared histories of events. Music is probably different," she mused.

"Some women will say whatever a man wants to hear, just to keep him entertained."

"Good grief, that would drive me nuts. I want honesty in both parts," she said.

"I agree." One reason he dated and then moved on was the inane conversations he often ended up with. Yes, Rafael, of course you're right, Rafael. He could hear the echoes of their sultry voices. What he wanted was someone to stand up to him. Challenge his glib statements. Argue with him sometimes.

He suspected Amalia was exactly the kind of woman to challenge any statement she didn't agree with. He couldn't see her as a yes-woman even to her boss.

"How do you and Stefano get along?" he asked, testing his theory.

"Fine. He tries to get his own way in things, and succeeds for the most part, but not with my off hours. He's very controlling, but I draw the line sometimes."

It fit the image Rafael had of Stefano Vicente. The man was a control freak and driven, to boot. But not as much as Rafael was, which showed in their respective bottom lines.

Their talk during the afternoon ranged from mutual likes in music to differences in books they'd read. While coming from different backgrounds, they discovered they had similar ideas in entertainment—except for Rafael's extreme-sports bent.

When hunger drove them to raid the snacks, Amalia felt the chill of the day when Rafael no longer held her close. They ate quickly and then naturally moved back together as if they'd been a couple for a long time.

The afternoon passed slowly. The rain settled into a steady beat on the plastic roof.

"Tell me about your home," she said at one point, wishing to learn as much about him as she could. When would she ever have such a chance?

"It's up on the Via della Rosa, overlooking the city and the sea. It's primarily built from stone with lots of glass. I bought it about eight years ago. I have a housekeeper who keeps it in order for me."

"It's large, I suspect," she murmured.

"Too big for one man, but it's also an invest-ment for the future. I expect it will appreciate in value and then I'll sell it for a profit."

"Do you see everything in profit and loss instead of it being your home?"

"I'm not there that much." Rafael had no special attachment to his house. It pleased him to live there, but if he sold it tomorrow, he'd find something else just as suitable. "Besides, it's just stone, wood and glass."

"A home should be a special place—comfort-able to give you rest, secure to give you safety, a place to shut out the world."

"And your little apartment is that?" he asked. It had looked cramped to him.

"As close as Jose and I can make it. It was different when we lived at home with our parents." She fell silent for a moment.

Rafael felt a stirring of envy. She and her family obviously operated entirely differently from him and his. He tried to imagine what she described and felt a hint of frustration. Not everyone was cut out to find a special bond as her mother and father had. Look at his own parents.

"Will you stay there once Jose moves out?" he asked.

"I might. The rent is affordable, though I would love to have a place with a garden and perhaps a view of the sea."

He had acres of land, gardens galore and a sweeping view of the Mediterranean Sea. Would she like his house if she saw it? He frowned. He rarely invited women to his place, preferring to keep that part of his life his own. Yet he wished he could see Amalia's face when she saw the garden and the view. He bet she'd love it. And he'd love to show it to her.

Would the house appeal to a woman? Probably not as he had it decorated—with sleek modern furnishings. What he'd seen of her apartment was cozy, slightly cluttered and definitely not modern. Yet it had held a certain appeal even for the few moments he'd been there.

In fact, that was what made Amalia different from the other women he normally associated with. She was more old-fashioned—at least in family views and in decorating skills.

By the time it grew dark, Rafael had tried numerous times to reach Manuel, to no avail. Not having proper attire for the rain, the visits outside were brief and it took too long to warm up once back in the shelter. They ate more of the snacks before it got too dark to see. He wanted to use the flashlights sparingly to save the batteries. He had faith in his crew, but not knowing where the balloon had set down, it would be difficult to locate them in the weather.

"We're going to spend the night here, aren't we?" she asked.

"I didn't see any towns nearby," he said. The one thing about Amalia, she was easy to be around. She didn't rail against fate for things going the way they were. She didn't complain or voice her frustration with the circumstances. He couldn't imagine spending the night under these circumstances with anyone else.

"If the rain ends by morning, and the envelope didn't get wet, we can inflate the balloon ourselves. We have enough propane to get airborne and stay there for a little while. We'll plan to stop at the next town or field near a road so the others can locate us."

"I hope it's a town. I want to call home before Jose leaves on his school trip. If we don't make it early tomorrow, I'll miss him."

"He knows we don't always know where we'll set down for the night," Rafael said.

"He's the one who should have come on this trip, he would have loved it." She sighed.

"But you're getting used to it," Rafael commented. She had changed, whether she knew it or not. He enjoyed holding her against him. Her slight frame fit perfectly against his. They had to sit sideways, with the wicker behind him, his feet touching one of the propane tanks. It wouldn't be the best way to sleep, but they could manage.

"I am getting used to it, and that's astonishing. I can't believe I'm not sick at the mere thought of going so high each day. As long as I don't look down, I'm really okay." She looked over her shoulder at him. "But don't get ideas I want to do this again. If you hadn't forced me—"

"Hey, blame your boss. I was just making sure I got a fair shake at this bet."

"I plan to. We shall have words," she promised.

Rafael grinned. Anything to cause disruption with Stefano Vicente worked for him.

"You're not like I thought you'd be," she said slowly, tilting her head back down and wiggling slightly to get comfortable.

"And how was that?"

"Arrogant, self-centered, uncaring, riding over anyone and anything in your way. Not that you don't act that way sometimes—like forcing me on this trip. But I've watched you with the ground crew. You are not like that with them. You don't brag all the time or put on airs. Or boss people around. You treat them with respect. They know their jobs and you let them do it."

Rafael laughed aloud at that. "They'd put me in my place in a heartbeat if I tried to tell them what to do. They're my friends, Amalia. Not close, but we all share a mutual interest in ballooning. Manuel and Julio have taken the balloon up when I'm not around. I trust them implicitly."

Amalia nodded as if a question had been answered.

"Put on airs?" he said, amusement dancing in his eyes.

"Stefano does all the time, like he's king of the world or something. He really likes the attention, or adulation."

"Don't compare me to Vicente. He and I are totally different."

"I know. But on the surface, initially, you two seem a lot alike. Except—"

He waited, wondering what she would say next. She was very open, letting her emotions show every time—whether she was happy, sad or angry, there was no doubt. A person knew exactly what she was feeling just by looking at her.

"You have a stronger sense of ethics, I think," she said slowly. "I've noticed it more than once. If anyone challenges something you say, you get angry instantly. That old saying, a man's word is his bond—you take it seriously, don't you?"

"Of course."

She nodded. "Why? So many people today are more cavalier, not caring about others, or even what others think about them. Why is that so important to you?"

"To be different from my father," Rafael said. The words were out before he could think.

She frowned in confusion. "How so?"

Now he had to explain. Better if he'd kept his mouth shut. "As a child I heard endless times he would be taking me and Andreas out someplace special. Then something else would come up and he'd go off and leave us. Time and time again." The old anger brushed him. He had sworn as a young boy to never say anything he didn't mean or couldn't live up to. He knew what disappointment was.

"Your father is so different from mine. He loved spending time with his family. Why have kids if you aren't going to spend time with them?" she asked.

"I've often wondered that. Probably to leave the family fortune to."

"It could always be left to charity. Children deserve more than monetary inheritances, they need love and nurturing from their parents, grandparents, aunts and uncles. Everyone in their lives."

"Life isn't like that—it sounds like a fairy tale," he commented.

"It should be like that," she defended.

"So how long into your marriage do you think you'll make it before you change your mind?" Rafael wondered aloud.

"I wouldn't."

"People are basically selfish. My parents didn't like being tied down with the demands of children. They hired nannies to keep themselves free to do what they wanted. When we were old enough, we were shipped off to school."

She pulled away and turned to look at him. "That is selfish and self-centered. Once you have children, they should come first in your life until they are grown. It's not as though your parents' lives ended when you and your brother were born. Childhood is fleeting. Once you reached a certain age, they would have been free to do what they wanted. Would it have been too much trouble to put you two first for a few years?"

"For them, yes. Not for your parents, evidently." She felt passionate about this issue. For a moment Rafael wanted to say he shared her views. He knew his parents had been too extreme in denying their children. Yet it was the only way he knew—really knew. He didn't know them very well and they certainly didn't know him, though his father was pleased with the success Rafael had achieved—but merely as a reflection on him.

"I think they loved us enough to enjoy being with us. Maybe because neither had family of their own, they wanted that bond. Mama miscarried twice between me and my brother, yet they kept trying to have more children. They really wanted us," she said.

"And you'll be that kind of mother, too? Having children to complete your life, putting them first?" Dumb question, of course she would. She was doing it with her brother, so how much stronger the maternal bond would be with Amalia's own children.

She narrowed her eyes. "I plan to be the best parent I can be. As you will, as well, I expect."

That startled him. "I don't plan to marry," he said abruptly.

"What if you fall passionately in love with someone and want to spend your life with her?"

"I'm thirty-four years old. I haven't met anyone yet, and I don't expect to."

"You never know."

"Oh, so now you're the Delphic oracle?" he teased.

She shook her head in exasperation. "I'm trying to make a point here—that if you do get married and have children, you'll probably be a terrific father."

"Whoa, where do you get your ideas?"

"From you."

"I never plan to marry, so how would I have children?"

She looked smug. "Because you are one of the sexiest men on the planet, and women must fall over themselves to be with you. Sooner or later you'll find one you can't resist."

Rafael laughed. "What a picture you paint of me. I do not have women falling over themselves, though the notion has merit."

"Maybe you're just blind to what's going on," she suggested.

"You confuse people who want what they can get from me with people who want to be friends with me. There's a decided difference, you know."

Amalia was quiet for a moment. She hadn't thought about that.

"Is it horrible—never knowing if someone is with you because of your money?"

"Not horrible. But—" He bit off what he was going to say.

"But what?"

"Nothing. However, if I don't trust anyone, how could I marry?"

"You'll know. When you do marry, you'd cling to that with all you have. And you'd be the kind of father you wanted and didn't get. You don't need to devote every moment to business. You have enough money to support a family and spend time with them. Didn't you ever wish your dad would spend more time with you?"

"I am not getting married or having children," he repeated firmly. And he definitely wasn't sharing his feelings about his parents with her. He shared them with no one—not even his brother.

But for a flicker of a moment he wondered what having children with Amalia would be like. Laughing little boys or girls, happy, surrounded by love. Amalia's children would be lucky in having her for a mother. He almost envied her future.

"Say it enough and maybe you'll convince yourself," she said.

"I don't need to convince myself, just you."

The bubble popped and he was back in the rain wishing Manuel would find them so they'd have a dry and warm place to sleep.

She laughed. "I hardly factor in to any equations in your life. But when I read in the newspaper that you are engaged, I shall send you a note to say I told you so."

"Why do you think I would marry?"

"Because I hate to think of waste," she said.

"What does that mean?"

"Think what you can contribute to the gene pool when you have kids."

Rafael didn't know whether to laugh or not. She was teasing him. He did know he was fascinated by Amalia's thought processes. She was pretty in a low-key way, no makeup. And the clothes she wore were more serviceable than stylish. Still, there was something about her that had him looking at her more and more. So far she had not presumed on any kind of friendship, though he could think of several others who would have already tried.

He liked talking with her—really talking—about things like her philosophies on marriage. What would the man be like to attract her attention and keep her with him all her life? For the first time ever, Rafael felt the sting of regret for the way he foresaw his life unfolding.

"Getting cold?" he asked to squelch his thoughts.

"A little."

The rain had turned to drizzle, and the wind had finally died down. But the temperature had fallen even more.

"It'll be totally dark soon, we might as well resign ourselves to sleeping in the basket and hoping the morning brings the sun," he said.

"So we just sleep here? With only two blankets and no room to stretch out?"

"Do you have an alternate place in mind?" he asked, trying to get comfortable around the propane tanks.

Listening to the rain for a moment, Amalia knew there were no alternatives. She longed to hear the truck's horn alerting them it was almost upon them. Or at least catch a glimmer of headlights shining through the trees. Rafael had tried every half hour to raise someone and no one had responded. They were truly on their own for the night.

Amalia wasn't sure how she felt about that. In other circumstances, she might have been over the moon at the thought of spending the night with Rafael. But the longer she spent with him, the more she saw the difference between them. Would he be more inclined to see her as an available woman if she had her hair styled by some high-priced stylist and wore designer clothes? Unlikely.

She would not really want to base a relationship on such superficial artifice. She wanted to fall in love and find the happiness she remembered her parents having. What would it be like to be married to Rafael, to come home at the end of each day and prepare dinner together, talking over what they'd done since they'd last seen each other? Kissing between cutting vegetables and preparing the entrée? Discussing plans for a weekend or holiday? Really getting to know him and having him know her?

She longed for the kind of marriage that brought two people close, so they could essentially shut out the rest of the world and be happy together. Wouldn't it be even more special with Rafael? She closed her eyes and wished briefly for something that would never be. Then she made up her mind to enjoy their fleeting time together.

"So, what's the plan?" she asked.

CHAPTER EIGHT

"WE'LL put one of the blankets under us to protect us against heat loss as much as possible, then continue to share the second one together, capturing as much body heat as we can. At least the rain hasn't found its way inside."

Sleep together, that's what he was saying. Amalia's thoughts raced. Sure, they'd both be fully clothed, but to sleep with Rafael? She wasn't sure she could do that. What if during the night she gave herself away? What if he suspected the major crush she had on him? She'd be so embarrassed, she would have to walk back to Barcelona, that's what.

Yet the awkward position made it unlikely that he would guess her feelings for him. She'd practically been sitting in his lap all afternoon, so this would be just more of the same. She knew they'd doze, but it was too uncomfortable for a deep sleep.

"If we each wrapped up in one blanket, that would cover all sides."

"You forgot the shared body heat," he reminded her.

"Oh, yeah, that." She swallowed hard. So she wasn't the sophisticated kind of woman he normally saw. She could handle this. Camping wasn't like normal life, and the truth of the matter was that there was no risk. Rafael argued with her, even seemed annoyed with her sometimes, but he'd given no indication he'd like to do more with her than the light banter he'd indulged in from time to time.

"Okay," she said, scooting out of the way so he could lay out the first blanket. Then he sat down, pulling the blanket up to his shoulders against the side of the basket. She wedged herself in between the floor and him, half on the blanket, half on Rafael. A moment later the other blanket covered them both.

It was warmer being next to Rafael.

"Relax," he said softly, shifting to put his arm around her and drawing her closer.

Amalia couldn't relax. Every fiber of her being was attuned to him yet she dare not give way. "I'm fine," she said.

"You're stiff as a board. I'm not going to bite." She took a deep breath, which pressed her breasts against his arm. Letting it out in a gasp, she knew she would never sleep tonight. Every nerve tingled. Her blood pounded in her veins. She was aware of every inch of his body touching hers.

He brushed his lips against her cheek.

"What are you doing?" She jerked around to stare at him.

"Trying to warm you up," he said, trailing kisses down her cheek.

She wiggled, but he didn't give an inch.

"This is *so* not a good idea," she said, her heart racing.

"Why is that?" he asked, between feather-light kisses.

"We hardly know each other." Was her voice growing breathless?

"So we get to know each other better. If you tally the hours we've put in, we've already spent more time together than I can remember spending with anyone else in years."

"All the more reason to remember where we are. This is a false environment. We move in different circles. After this race we'll probably only see each other on the rare occasions when you come to our offices." She was babbling, but she couldn't stop. She tried to find every reason she could to keep her distance, when everything in her wanted to snuggle closer and feel the delight she knew Rafael would deliver.

"We're only trying to get some sleep here, Amalia, not making a life commitment."

"I know that," she said sharply, wishing she could regally take one blanket and move as far from Rafael as she could go. Which wouldn't be far with the limited shelter they had. One step outside and she'd be soaked in no time. She'd already had to go out a couple of times and she didn't want to be wet going to sleep. If she could even sleep so close to him! "I'm not your type," she added.

"Do I have a type?" he asked, drawing her even closer.

Amalia could feel the length of him against her. Heat soared. She would not be cold, at least—but she *was* totally wide-awake.

"Sophisticated, trendy, stylish." She tried to focus on the conversation and not the sensations racing through her.

"But maybe that's because I hadn't met you," he said, brushing another kiss against her cheek, dangerously close to her lips.

She caught her breath, feeling the pounding of her heart. It rocked her. He had to feel it, too.

"Don't mess with me, Rafael," she warned.

"Call me Rafe, my closest friends do. And they

don't ever get as close as this," he said before his lips found hers and he kissed her the way he had the other night. His hand threaded itself in her hair, holding her close as his mouth caused her to go into sensory overload. She was soaring higher and higher. In a split second she went from trying to push him away to turning to get as close as she could get, her own hands holding him tightly. It was glorious. Was forbidden fruit all the sweeter for being unattainable?

Time stood still. It might be dark outside but the kaleidoscope of colors in her mind lit up the night. The cold was left behind as heat spread to every inch. Engulfed in emotions, reveling in the exquisite sensations that roiled through her, she never wanted the moment to end. Forgotten was the weather and the tight quarters of the basket. She was soaring.

She didn't know how long they kissed, but when Rafael finally moved to her throat and the pulse point there, she tried to regain a modicum of control. His hands had moved from her head to her back, holding her close as they shared kiss after kiss. She felt she could conquer the world, if only he'd never let her go.

Finally the passion eased a bit and she could catch a random thought or two that reminded her they had no business doing this.

The chase team could arrive at any moment. She had her brother to look after.

Rafael was an avowed bachelor and notorious playboy.

She was the head of her family and had responsibilities.

He felt the change in her at once and pulled back to look at her, trying to read her emotions in the dark.

"What's wrong?"

"Is this your way of trying to seduce me?' she asked breathlessly.

He would do so in a heartbeat if he thought she was that kind of woman, but he knew she was not.

"No, it's my way of enjoying being with you. There is no seduction planned. This is hardly the setup for that."

"Darn," she said, surprising him.

"Unless you—"

"No. Just—never mind. This can't go anywhere."

"Because?"

"For tons of reasons, but mostly because I'm not the kind to do casual sex."

He hesitated a moment. If he tried hard, could he get her to change her mind? No, he wouldn't do that. Amalia was special.

"Then we stop now. But if you change your mind, you let me know, right?"

He could feel her smile. "You'll be the first to know," she said, tucking her head in against his cheek. In a few moments he felt her relax.

If any of his friends saw him now they'd laugh their heads off. He was not going to push the issue, much as he longed to do so. Holding Amalia, feeling her curled up against him, had him fantasizing about how fabulous it would be to make love to her. If he pushed it, however, he ran the risk of alienating her totally. And that was not something he planned to ever do.

She'd already turned him down for a date when they returned to Barcelona. Now that was something he'd try to change her mind about. Let her get to know him better, let him get to know her and see where it might lead.

He could start with insisting she accompany him to the Barcelona Business Alliance to see her boss present him—them—with the check. She deserved recognition for her part in the race. He could see her in a lovely burgundy gown, her cheeks tinged with pink, her eyes sparkling and happy. They would have dinner at the BBA meeting, but afterward, he'd take her dancing until the wee hours.

"Amalia?" He'd get her commitment now and have that date to look forward to.

She didn't answer. She'd already fallen asleep.

Rafael tucked the blanket around her and let himself relax toward sleep. He'd never spent the entire night with a woman before in such circumstances. Or with one who insisted they had nothing in common. Yet in the morning they'd waken together after being bundled close all night. Would it change her outlook? Would she immediately think about how to capitalize on the situation?

Old habits kicked in. He needed to make sure his defenses were in place. Escorting her to an event or two didn't mean a life-long commitment. She had him feeling vaguely dissatisfied with his life—which was going just the way he wanted. Not for him a family, children, shared experiences, activities and one woman for life.

The rain stopped sometime in the night. When Rafael woke before dawn, he heard only silence. Easing himself away from Amalia, he quickly tucked the blanket around her to keep her as warm as possible. He wanted to take a look outside. Finding a flashlight, he rose and stepped out.

The stars shone in the sky and all clouds had blown away. It was cool, but not too bad. Checking his watch, he saw dawn was still an hour away. Time they began to ready the balloon for liftoff as soon as it started growing light—if the envelope had not gotten wet. If it had, there was no telling how long they'd be stranded.

"Rafael?" He heard Amalia coming up to stand beside him. "Is it time to go?"

"We'll wait for light. I want to check the envelope but need to wait for daylight to do that. With luck, it'll be mostly dry.

"Can two of us get it ready to fly?"

"Of course." It wouldn't be easy, but he had to make it work. They couldn't afford the time to wait for other help. If Stefano got airborne before Rafael did, he could close the distance. Or maybe Stefano hadn't found shelter, either. Maybe his envelope had gotten wet and they could call a time-out or something until the balloons dried.

When dawn lightened the area enough, he went to the large tarp covering the balloon. The mound made sure the rain had run off, but it was where the envelope touched the ground he worried about. Had water seeped beneath the tarp?

Careful to lift the tarp so no water slid to the balloon, he was pleased to note the ground beneath was still dry. The makeshift ditch he'd carved out had done the job: the envelope was dry.

"Spread the tarp, dry side up, out this way. We'll roll the balloon out on it as far as we can to keep it dry."

In less than ten minutes Rafael fired up the fan using the auxiliary line from the propane tank to begin the inflation process. As the envelope filled, the top moved beyond the tarp and the plastic they'd also placed down. But not much of the envelope touched the ground. He hoped the light touch would keep it from absorbing mud and moisture.

Finally he fired the jets, and the envelope began to rise.

Amalia quickly folded the tarp and plastic sheet and brought them to the basket. Stepping in as if she'd done it all her life, she stowed them in the side pouches and glanced at Rafael.

"Will it fly?"

"Let's hope so." It was taking longer to fill, and one spot near the top seemed darker—damp or muddy, he didn't know. He hoped it was of a small enough size not to hamper lift.

Slowly the balloon began to rise off the ground.

Amalia watched the balloon, keeping her gaze firmly away from Rafael. She felt awkward and unsure after last night. His kisses had been the stuff of dreams. Was he astute enough to realize the kisses she gave in return were full of feelings she had no business having for him?

Closing her eyes for a moment, she was swept back to those heady moments. She couldn't help the smile that tugged at her lips. Her heart yearned for more. Snapping open her eyes, she tried to ignore the clamoring feelings. Finding him already up when she'd awakened had helped and hurt. There had been no lingering over a few kisses to get the day going.

By the time they were airborne, she hoped she would regain her equilibrium. Nothing had happened—except Amalia had fallen a bit more for the man. At least he didn't want to talk about it this morning. Then again, why would he? For him, she was just the latest one in a long line of women he'd romanced.

Slowly the basket rocked, then moved as it lifted from the ground. Amalia was used to feeling no speed or movement by now. Glancing at the horizon, she estimated they were rising quickly. The hot air was lighter than the colder air from the night.

She liked these times, she realized with surprise. Unable to tell how high they were, she didn't feel quite as nervous.

Rafael took the binoculars and scanned the sky. He paused a moment, and then gestured to Amalia. "Stefano is also getting an early start. Can you see his balloon over there?"

She looked in the direction he pointed. "Can he catch us?"

"Not likely as long as we stay up. But we don't have full tanks. We'll have to set down and replenish."

The radio crackled. Manuel came through and Rafael quickly answered.

"That's the plan," he concluded a short time later. If the balloon continued in the current direction, they'd find a small town before long. The chase team was racing there in hope of finding a field for the balloon so they could exchange tanks. They'd spent most of the night trying to find Rafael.

"Will our stopping give Stefano the edge?"

"Depends on if his chase team was able to get him full tanks yesterday," Rafael said.

Amalia exchanged places with him and looked at the distant balloon. She hoped Stefano needed fuel as much as they did. She wanted to keep their lead and maybe lengthen it. He had made her angry ordering her to participate. Now allegiance had been changed. She was crew for Rafael Sandoval and she would do all she could for this team to win!

She carefully turned around to watch the direction the balloon was traveling. In the distance she could see some rooftops. As they drifted closer, buildings in the town became visible. Manuel had found a soccer field on the map and that's what Rafael was heading for. They weren't very high, so she hoped they could line up with the soccer field and land there with no trouble.

It was on the far side of town. When Rafael spotted it he began his descent. The field was to the left, how was he going to get the balloon to change course?

Amalia watched. Caught up with trying to will the balloon to land in the field, she forgot to be afraid. Amazingly, Rafael landed right on the edge. As the balloon began to collapse, he fed it enough heat to keep it upright. The grass was glittering with raindrops.

"You did it!" she exclaimed. Excited, she threw her arms around him. He caught her up and turned her around in the narrow basket, ending with a kiss on her mouth.

"We need to get the ropes in place," he said, uncoiling them and quickly tying them to the basket cleats.

Amalia knew the routine and, using the step, quickly went over the side and was already looking for something to tether to. The grassy field offered nothing.

She told Rafael. He looked over the side and scanned the field.

"We're okay for now. When the truck gets here, we'll have stakes we can use."

"Can we walk back to the village? I'd love a

cup of hot chocolate," she said. Who knew how long it would be before the ground team arrived?

Of course. She still wasn't up to thinking in balloon terms.

"I'll wait with you, then," she said. Somewhere along the way something had changed. Had it been her? She wanted to spend time with Rafael now instead of avoiding him. She was not getting in over her head, she told herself. A few kisses, however passionate, meant nothing.

The radio crackled. Rafael got it and responded. The team wasn't far away. Amalia watched expectantly in the direction of the village. It would be good to get a hot meal and freshen up a bit before heading out again. She scanned the sky. No sign of her boss's balloon. Was he still moving or had he set down to refuel?

Once the chase truck came into view, things moved swiftly. Julio took Rafael and Amalia into town for some much-needed hot food. The others examined the balloon, checked all the ropes and connections, exchanged the tanks, pounded stakes into the ground to hold the tether ropes and, using the wind direction, tried to calculate where a good spot for landing would be for the next leg.

"No time for a room and shower," Rafael said as they reached the outskirts of the town. "Just a hot meal and time to wash and change clothes if you want."

"I do," Amalia said, grateful for that much at least.

One hour later they were back at the field. In the distance, Stefano Vicente's balloon was drifting by, a mile or more toward the west.

"He didn't stop," Amalia said.

"Apparently not. Ready to go?" Rafael asked the ground crew.

"He won't get ahead, will he?" she asked.

"Depends. Let's get up and going."

For the first time Amalia shared the excitement of the team, racing to get airborne again, hoping they could beat the other balloon. She watched as they rose from the ground, trying to figure out how far ahead Stefano might be and if they had a hope of catching up.

"Relax, we're loaded with fuel and will go as long as we can. Even if he filled up last night, he'll have to come down before us and we'll sail by. You can wave if you wish," he teased.

She laughed, feeling giddy with happiness. From stark fear to delight, she'd come a long way in a few days—mainly because of Rafael.

"Of course. And may the best team win—us!"

After the previous day and the storm, this day was clear and cooler, perfect for ballooning. The wind at the higher elevations was still brisk and when she ventured to look out, Amalia could tell they were moving faster than earlier in the race.

"This is fun," she said in surprise a little later. If she didn't look down, it was. She felt carefree and happy. And when she looked at Rafael and saw the gleam of interest in his eyes, she felt very feminine.

"You shouldn't be so surprised, why do you think so many people enjoy the sport? So maybe I'm not the big, bad guy for taking you from your home one morning?" he said whimsically.

She grinned at him. "Maybe not."

He laughed and she caught her breath. He had a day or two's growth of beard. His hair was not the neat cut she was used to seeing in the office, but tousled and windblown, and she wanted so much to run her fingers through it. To have the right to do that.

Looking away lest she reveal her thoughts, she watched as the other balloon also sailed silently on the wind.

"If the wind holds and keeps in this direction, we'll be close to another town when we stop tonight. We'll definitely get rooms and a good hot meal," Rafael said a short time after he'd made some calculations on the map.

"I'll look forward to that." But she would miss

the enforced intimacy they'd enjoyed last night. She would never have an occasion to spend the night with Rafael again. The thought put a damper on her delight. Every moment she spent learning about him was bittersweet. She relished the knowledge and the change in her viewpoint about him. But each moment also meant that the end of the race was that much closer. The end of their time together.

Next week she'd be back at work. The next time she saw Rafael Sandoval he would be in the society section of the newspaper—with some gorgeous woman accompanying him.

It was almost dusk when Rafael put down the balloon on a grassy meadow near the town of Santa Maria de las Montañas. Amalia had been quiet during the afternoon and he wondered what she was thinking. Last night had been unexpected—in many ways. Not the least was the way it changed how he saw her. She continued to intrigue him—primarily because she was so noticeably different from the women he normally associated with. He couldn't imagine his own mother taking last night in stride, much less the younger women he saw socially.

He wondered how she would fit into his social schedule. First the BBA dinner, then maybe a weekend in Madrid? The shopping there was amazing. Women were always telling him that. Would she like to sail the Med while the good weather continued? If he asked Jose to go, he knew she'd agree. That was the key, to make sure that he included her brother some of the time, until she grew used to seeing him.

He would start with the sailing…and work his way up to a weekend away together.

It was late by the time everyone reached the accommodations for the night, a small hotel in the center of Santa Maria. Once again Amalia had her own room, and as soon as she got her key, she headed for the elevator. Jose had left for his school trip, so there was no one to call. But the thought of a hot bath and then a comfortable bed held amazing appeal.

"Amalia." Rafael caught up with her at the elevator. The others were still by the front desk.

"Have dinner with me," he said.

"Aren't you tired of my company by now?" she asked, her heart fluttering. He didn't have to spend his time away from the balloon with her.

"No. We can eat in my suite if you like, and not have the bother of others around."

Her heart kicked into overdrive. Dinner alone in his suite? *Just* dinner?

"You don't want to discuss the race with the

others?" she said, stalling. Dare she take this chance?

"Not tonight. Maria and Manuel are plotting our most likely route for tomorrow. Tonight will be just for us."

"What time?" she asked, still uncertain.

"Say, eight?"

The elevator arrived, its doors opening.

"What room?" she asked, stepping inside. He remained in the lobby.

"Six eleven."

"See you at eight," she said as the doors slid shut.

Reaching her room, she quickly unpacked her nicest top and jeans. She had nothing suitable for a date with one of Barcelona's most eligible bachelors, but then, she reasoned, he would hardly be dressed up himself.

The room was spacious, with a small sitting area near the window and a huge bed dominating one wall. The ensuite bathroom contained a spa tub and a large shower. While not as luxurious as the one she'd had that first night, it was still more than she was used to. And it beat sleeping in the rain by a mile.

Her shower was quick, hot and delightful. With clean hair brushed until it gleamed, a light application of makeup and a freshly pressed cranberry-red top, she felt like a new woman. Staring at her reflection in the mirror she tried to look sophisticated and cool. Instead, her eyes sparkled and her cheeks were flushed with color in anticipation of spending a portion of the evening with Rafael. And that was all. Just dinner, some conversation and then she'd say good-night.

Just before eight there was a knock on her door. Opening it, Amalia saw Rafael standing there. He'd shaved, combed his hair and put on a dark shirt with dark slacks. With his tanned skin and dark eyes, he looked sexy and dangerous.

"I usually pick up my dates for the evening," he said lazily. His gaze traveled from her head to her toes and back up again. "You clean up nicely," he said, flashing a smile that threatened Amalia's good sense.

"Thank you, I might say the same."

"I looked like a pirate or something until I shaved," he said.

Maybe she had a thing for pirates—she thought he'd looked incredible. Even better now. "I'm ready. Let me get my room key," she said, retrieving it from the dresser.

"I could have made it to your room safely," she said as they took the elevator up two flights.

"I'm sure, but this is better," he said.

When they entered the suite, Amalia glanced

around. It was as luxurious as her suite had been that first night. Rafael obviously liked traveling first class. What would that be like? she wondered. But far better not to get too used to it—this was so temporary.

Dinner was delivered by room service just minutes later. She stood by the window looking at the lights of the small town as the waiter set up their table. "Very pretty," she said.

Turning, she looked at the feast Rafael had ordered. It seemed like enough food to feed the entire crew.

"I hope you like veal," he said.

"I do." Crossing to the table as the waiter prepared to place the first course in front of them, she felt like a princess or something. Usually she and Jose ate in the kitchen of their small apartment.

"Lovely," she said.

Rafael poured cider into the glasses and raised his in toast. "To our successful completion of the race."

"To winning," she replied touching her glass to his.

Once the waiter had been assured everything was to their liking, he withdrew.

"Alone at last," Rafael said.

Amalia laughed nervously. "We are alone together all day."

"But here we have nothing to do but concentrate on each other."

She sipped her sparkling beverage wondering what he meant by that. "And the delicious dinner," she said.

"True. We have the evening ahead of us."

"Actually, not a long one if we are getting up at five in the morning," she said, tasting the veal. It almost melted in her mouth it was so tender.

Amalia had no need to worry about conversation while they ate; Rafael was a skilled conversationalist and she enjoyed the banter they exchanged. After the crème brûlée dessert, he suggested they move to the sofa for after-dinner coffee.

"That'll keep me up forever," she said. "But I won't say no to a little."

He dimmed the lights and poured the hot coffee.

Amalia's heart pounded like a drum. Was this a setup for seduction? She would love some more kisses from the man, but knew her limitations. She was not getting intimately involved with Rafael Sandoval. The minute he returned to Barcelona, she'd be but a minuscule memory in his mind as he escorted some of the city's most glamorous women around.

"Did you call your brother?" he asked, sitting

beside her on the sofa and lifting his coffee cup in salute.

"Jose is on his school trip. He left this morning."

"Gone for how long?"

"Several days. He's one of the few students chosen for this trip. I know he'll have a million things to tell me when I'm back home."

"You'll have things to tell him, as well," Rafael said.

She took a sip of the coffee feeling its warmth spread. She did not plan to tell her brother everything.

The unexpected ring of the telephone startled Amalia and she jumped a bit.

Rafael rose and crossed the room to answer it.

"Helena, where are you?" he asked. Listening for a moment, he slowly smiled. "Sorry to hear that. Sounds like you are close enough to have come into Santa Maria."

Amalia glanced at her watch. It was getting late. She needed to get to sleep if she was getting up early again. Placing her cup back on the saucer, she rose. Crossing to the window, she tried to ignore the conversation behind her. It sounded as if Helena were reporting in to Rafael, and was not happy with where they were staying.

When he hung up, Amalia turned and raised her eyebrows in silent question.

"Your boss stopped for the night a few miles from here. There is cell service, but no hotels. Helena said after last night in the rain and tonight in a camping environment again, I owe her big-time."

Amalia grinned and nodded. "I'm sure she feels that way. While I'm living in the lap of luxury."

He crossed to her and brushed back her hair. "You look good in the lap of luxury," he said, and lowered his face to hers, his lips closing over hers.

Magical kisses were another perk of the race. Amalia reached up to encircle his neck when Rafael pulled her closer. Body pressed to body, mouth pressed to mouth, he deepened the kiss and Amalia responded like a flower to the sun. Desire rose. Time stood still.

His hands caressed her back, holding her against him as every nerve ending in her body craved a closer contact. This was the man who had practically kidnapped her for the race. Who had opened up to her as she had never expected. He'd been honest and forthright about not expecting anything more than a fling before moving on to another woman. He was not for marriage and children and growing old together.

But she was. Regretfully, she pulled her mouth back and looked at him. Rafael rested his forehead on hers and gazed into her eyes. She was slightly pleased he was breathing as hard as she was.

"I can't do this," she whispered.

"You seem to do it very well," he said softly.

"We have four more days of the race, then you'll go back to your life and I will go back to mine. We have nothing in common."

"Hey, it's just a few kisses," he said. "And we don't have to part after the race. I want you to come with me to the BBA dinner, when I accept your boss's check. You're helping me to win, so you should share the limelight."

"Don't count your chickens," she warned.

He laughed. "We will win. And Stefano will hate giving me that check."

"And am I part of the prize? Do you plan to lure his PA away from him?"

Rafael straightened and let her go. "If you think that of me, you don't know me at all. I have an excellent PA and I'm not looking for another."

Amalia felt suddenly cold when he stepped back. She should guard her tongue. She'd only been teasing. "I know. I'm sorry."

He relaxed. "No, I'm sure I overreacted. Say you'll go with me to the BBA dinner."

She considered and then nodded. "If we win, I'll go with you."

"We *will* win," he said again, absolutely sure of himself.

"Thank you for dinner," she said, walking to the door. He was there when she reached it.

"I'll escort you back to your room if you insist on returning there now," he said.

She regretted her hasty words about him luring her away from Stefano, as they had shattered the moment. But better, perhaps, to end any fantasies she had before she got in too deep. Fairy tales were well and good for children, but they were not for women who had responsibilities.

CHAPTER NINE

AMALIA had a quick breakfast in her room the next morning. She'd had trouble sleeping during the night and had woken early enough to indulge herself. When she joined the others in the lobby, her eyes went straight to Rafael. He'd obviously had no trouble during the night as he looked as fresh as ever. Just looking at him had her catching her breath.

When was she going to get over this stupid feeling? He was just another man—more gorgeous than most she knew—but just a man.

Maria came down last and hurried over to the group. "Sorry I'm late. I had the worst time getting up this morning."

Rafael glanced at Amalia. "No such trouble with you, I take it."

"I'm here, aren't I?"

When they piled into the truck, Amalia was pressed against Rafael. Had he deliberately arranged the seating? She looked straight ahead, not seeing much in the dark, and feeling every inch of him pressed against her.

They lifted off at dawn. Rafael kept to himself. Amalia still regretted her hasty outburst last night, but she'd been scared of the feelings for him that grew each day. She did not want to be attracted to him. Didn't want to admire him or feel he was becoming special to her. But a person didn't necessarily have control over the way they felt, just the way they acted. It would be better if they had a professional relationship—it would be easier for her to get over her feelings for him when they returned home.

"If we maintain our lead today, I think we'll be home free," Rafael said later in the morning, looking back at Stefano's balloon.

Amalia stood up and looked behind them. She couldn't judge distances, but from the small size of the balloon, the others were several miles behind.

"Good," she said. She was not feeling charitable toward her boss right now. He had put her in this situation. She would have been much better off not spending so much time with Rafael. Yet how could she regret even one second of it? When else in her life would she have such an adventure?

"The next BBA dinner meeting is in two weeks," Rafael said.

So he *had* meant what he said when he'd invited her as his date. She looked at him.

"I'll be delighted to attend," she said formally. She'd have to blow a week's salary on a suitable dress, but it would be worth it for one more evening in his company.

"Good," he said, looking satisfied.

Gradually they regained the camaraderie that had blossomed over the last few days and the time passed swiftly. They set down with the team waiting, and only thirty minutes later they were aloft again.

A late lunch, then they started up again and gained even more distance on Stefano's balloon. The storm had made the difference. Now they just had to maintain the gap between them and they'd win easily.

As shadows on the ground grew long, Rafael began searching for a place to put down. He ended up in a large field about a half hour's drive from a town behind them. Debating whether to camp out or seek a room in town, Rafael decided to go for town. They had a substantial lead and could afford the travel time to and from a hotel. He smiled when Maria danced in place.

"She's not much of a camper," he said to the group in general. The others gently teased her but Maria was made of strong stuff. She merely laughed and said the others could thank her when they got a good night's sleep.

To Amalia's surprise, when they reached town, Stefano and his group were already in the hotel Rafael chose. Of course the men had similar tastes in hotels, so that should be no surprise. What did astonish her was the fact that there were a couple of newspaper reporters interviewing Stefano.

"Where does he find them?" she murmured on their way to the registration desk. Rafael had his hand at the small of her back, and merely glanced over to the group congregated near the windows.

"He must have the best PR firm in the country," he murmured back.

Rafael checked them all in and turned to watch Stefano pontificate on his strategy for winning, despite being behind. He caught Rafael's eye and turned away quickly, making sure the reporters stayed with him and didn't go to Rafael for his side of the story.

"You should go tell them how far ahead we are," Amalia said as she watched.

"He knows," Rafael said.

"But the reporters don't."

"They will at the finish. That's all that counts."

As their group headed for the elevators, Helena crossed the lobby quickly, calling after Rafael.

"I need to talk to you," she said when she caught up, tugging him to one side.

Their conversation was hurried and quiet. Amalia wondered what emergency could have arisen to get his PA in a flap. From what she'd seen of Helena, the woman was used to dealing with difficult men and trying situations. She wouldn't be easily upset. Though dealing with Stefano Vicente could sometimes be extremely trying, as Amalia well knew.

An elevator arrived as Manuel was sorting out their bags. Amalia reached for hers just as the doors opened and Teresa Valesquez stepped out.

Amalia stared in disbelief. What was she doing here? How had she known they would be staying at this hotel? Turning slightly, Amalia sought Rafael. He and Helena were still talking.

"Rafael," Teresa called gaily.

Amalia watched as he looked up and saw Teresa. There was no expression on his face. Helena had obviously already told him.

The reporters turned and watched as the pretty blonde ran across the room and flung herself against Rafael. He caught her, and Amalia watched in dismay as she kissed him. He didn't seem to be protesting at all.

The pangs of jealousy and hurt hit her hard. She tried to tell herself she'd known all along nothing good would come of spending so much time with Rafael. But the reality still stung. She had thought—

Taking a breath, she pasted a smile on her face and started for the elevators.

She could hear the reporters behind her as they swarmed across the lobby and began to question Rafael.

Maria joined her in the elevator as they scooted in just before the doors closed.

"I'm on floor five," she said.

Amalia looked at her room key. "Me, too."

"As soon as I get to my room I'm calling Helena to get the story about the miraculous appearance of Ms. Valesquez. I bet Rafael is fit to be tied."

"Why?" Amalia looked at Maria. "I thought they were dating."

"Maybe." Maria shrugged. "But she was a pain from the get-go at the festival. You saw how she showed up that first day. Racing is serious to Rafael, and all she wanted was his total attention. Like that would happen."

"I think my boss was hoping for that," Amalia said, longing to ask more, but afraid of hearing the answers.

"Sure, if Rafael could be distracted, Vicente had a better shot at winning. But that would never happen. You know that. He's so focused."

Amalia nodded, remembering the picture she'd seen on the Internet with Rafael and Teresa attending some reception. He'd looked pretty focused on *her* that night.

"See you at eight," Maria said as the elevator reached their floor. Rafael had told the team they'd meet for dinner then.

"Okay," Amalia said. She did not want to spend the evening with the crew, trying to pretend everything was fine when she thought her heart was nicked a bit. But she liked even less the idea that in boycotting the meal she might give the impression that Teresa's arrival had somehow put her own nose out of joint. She'd *known* nothing would come of Rafael's attention. So why did it hurt that his flamboyant girlfriend had shown up? She did not expect more kisses from him and another night dining alone together, or the prospect of spending hours in his arms as she had in the storm.

Amalia went on a few more doors and reached her room. She was glad Rafael had arranged for each of them to have a private room. She could not share with another tonight.

Rafael watched as Amalia and Maria entered the elevator. He'd give her a minute to get to her room and then call her.

"You're ahead of Vicente. That is fabulous!" Teresa said, still clinging to his arm. Smiling prettily for the reporters, she made sure of her hold on him.

He pulled away and frowned. "I asked what you were doing here, Teresa." He ignored the men with notebooks and looked at her.

"Vicente called me and said his little secretary wasn't doing well on the balloon and would I consider returning. I have missed you. But now I can continue the race with you, and the secretary can return home. It worked out perfectly. He said he'd make sure I got a ride from here to your balloon no matter where you set down tonight. Aren't you the tiniest bit happy to see me?"

"You made your position clear. We have nothing further to talk about," he muttered. Checking to make sure everyone had their rooms assigned, he lifted his bag and headed for the elevators. Teresa walked right beside him.

"I think it was nice of her boss to think of her welfare," Teresa said.

"Maybe." Rafael knew what Teresa was saying was probably true. Amalia hated being in the air. He'd seen her pale in fear, grow sick in fright. Had she gone behind his back and asked her boss to help her out? Probably, since being altruistically concerned for one of his employees didn't sound very much like Vicente.

"So...I am on the fifth floor," Teresa said in her sultry voice.

Rafael merely looked at her.

"Where is your room?" she asked when he didn't volunteer the information.

"On one of the upper floors."

"I could go with you and wait while you change for dinner," she suggested.

"I'm meeting everyone in the lobby at eight. We'll decide where to eat then," he said, quickly changing his plans. His original thought had been to see if Amalia wanted another quiet dinner together. No way would he substitute Teresa for Amalia.

When he reached his room, sans Teresa, he tossed his bag on the bed and went to the phone asking for Amalia's room. The phone rang several times before he hung up. Was she already in the shower? Probably.

Once he finished his own shower and had shaved again, he tried her room once more. This time the line was busy. Rafael hung up feeling frustrated. Glancing at his watch, he noted it was close to eight. If he didn't make arrangements before then, she'd be downstairs with everyone else and he'd lose his chance to have dinner alone with her.

It was two minutes to eight when Rafael gave up trying to reach Amalia and headed downstairs.

The crew was congregated near the big glass doors leading outside. Teresa was flirting with Manuel. Maria and Amalia stood on the outskirts talking. Julio and Paolo were watching Teresa. Most people watched her, Rafael thought. She always looked stunning, and she did tonight in that clinging dress. She looked ready for dinner, and the rest of the crew looked as if they should be mopping floors somewhere. He was dressed as they were. Teresa was the one out of place.

Dinner at a nearby restaurant proved disastrous. Teresa sat right beside him and spoke to no one else. The crew tried to carry on a conversation about the race, how far they were ahead and the chances of Vicente conceding before the last day. Every time, Teresa tuned out their discussion and tried to engage him in an intimate topic excluding the rest.

Amalia watched them, her expression obviously one of disdain. Rafael had to admit that in comparing the two women, it was Teresa who came up short. She liked to go out to expensive restaurants or clubs and be seen. One of her favorite aspects was showing off her new clothes, and her escort. Flirting came naturally to her and she didn't limit herself to her date.

In the past that had been a normal date for him. Tonight he'd much rather sit beside Amalia and engage her in conversation. Listen to her views on things and have the give and take that normally only came with longtime friends. Ones who didn't feel the need to impress him.

With Amalia he was uncertain if she even liked him. And he wanted her to. For the first time he could remember, he cared what a woman thought about him. He was growing more and more fascinated with her. He'd like to explore all the avenues open to them. To take her back to her room and kiss her good-night. To share breakfast in the morning. He looked forward to their time alone in the gondola and felt she was opening up to him more and more each day. Wasn't that a good sign?

He had a sinking feeling that was not necessarily so.

"So if you are so far ahead, you don't need to push tomorrow, do you?" Teresa asked at one point, again changing the topic of discussion.

"It's always best to increase the lead," Rafael said. "Amalia and I have worked hard to gain the advantage. There's no telling what might happen to slow us down at some future time, so the wider the lead, the better."

Teresa smiled at Amalia. "And you so afraid of

heights. I think it's a real shame to coerce you into participating. I have no such fears." She turned back to Rafael. "We did well at the festival, didn't we?"

He shrugged, not wanting to dwell on how inappropriately she had dressed and behaved. Nor relive the constant complaints.

Manuel laughed. "You could have done better," he said bluntly.

Teresa flashed her biggest smile at him, but anger shone in her eyes.

Amalia watched, interested to see the interaction between Rafael and Teresa. It surprised her how much the rest of the crew disliked the other woman. There was nothing overt, but they didn't include her in the planning, didn't answer some of her questions—acting as if they hadn't heard. And each covered for the other. She looked at Rafael. Had he noticed?

She was flustered to find his gazed fixed on her.

"Amalia is to be commended for doing so well despite her fear." He raised his glass in silent toast.

She inclined her head slightly and made an effort not to glance at Teresa. She knew the woman would be furious, but so what? She felt on top of the world with Rafael's compliment.

Once dinner ended, Maria and Amalia excused

themselves and headed back to the hotel. "I'm not going to oversleep tomorrow," Maria declared as they bade the others good-night.

Rafael stood when they did, but made no move to detain them. Amalia wished he had. She would have stayed longer if he'd only asked. If she could have outlasted Teresa, the two of them could have had some quiet time together.

Which was silly, they had all day tomorrow to spend alone together. She knew she was hoarding the memories like a miser hoarded gold. Each one sparkling and special to her. At night, alone, her imagination soared. Sometimes she thought he looked at her in a particular way that suggested he was interested in her. She knew she was falling for him and was determined not to give way. Heartache was not something she wanted.

The walk back to the hotel was accomplished quickly. When they entered the lobby of the hotel, Helena was sitting in one of the chairs, reading a book. She glanced up and smiled when she saw Amalia and Maria.

"How's it going?" she called.

"I'm still alive," Amalia said, walking over to the other woman.

Maria continued to the elevator, calling out a good-night.

Amalia sat beside Helena. "How about you?"

For a moment Helena said nothing, then shrugged. "I don't envy you your job. I suspect your boss is a difficult man to work for."

"I've managed for the past three years."

"Then you are to be commended. Rafe is much easier to deal with."

"I wouldn't have thought so," Amalia said. "He's pretty driven to succeed." But he had shown a different side to his personality on the trip. He was more caring than most people thought.

"But not by trampling over the feelings of others. Stefano Vicente is a driving power and I believe an egomaniac."

Amalia laughed. Her boss did like to be the center of attention. Most of the time she didn't mind; she was content in her job. Until she could afford to move on.

"Are you waiting to see Rafael?" Amalia asked.

"No, I just wanted some quiet time to read. My roommate insists on talking on the phone until she's too tired to continue. She has an endless supply of friends."

"Rafael allocated us to individual rooms," Amalia said.

"Figures. He always does things top class. I think your boss is a penny-pincher. We're to get our own meals on this trip. But doubling up on rooms, when we find a hotel, is a pretty good way to shortchange the crew. I guess I'm lucky I don't have to pay for the room."

"How did he know we'd be here tonight?" she asked.

"A lucky guess on his part. We spend a lot of time in the balloon calculating rate of speed, direction, where we'll put down. He then has the ground crew radio ahead to any reporters who might be keeping tabs on the race. While it's not the Grand Prix, he's keeping the news alive in the Barcelona papers. I think he figures Teresa will be enough of a distraction to slow Rafael down, which shows he doesn't know my boss very well. Rafael is perfectly capable of separating work from play, and this race is too important to throw away at this point for some woman."

"Why is it so important to him to win?" Amalia asked softly.

"Did you ask Rafael?" Helena asked.

Amalia shrugged. "Once. He just said he wanted to show Stefano he wasn't the only one who could win at something."

"I probably should let him tell you. But it might help to know that Stefano pulled an underhanded deal about five years ago. It caused Rafael a huge loss and damaged his reputation slightly. Things have been smoothed over since, and I'm sure

Stefano has no idea Rafael still broods on that. This is merely one way to retaliate. And no one will ever know why, but I think it will soothe Rafael's ire a bit. Winning means a lot, but it's having Stefano present the check at the BBA that's the big thing. I think it'll take the sting out of the past a bit."

Amalia wondered how Rafael could still deal with her boss if he had been underhanded. Rafael had a strong sense of integrity and honor.

"I'll let you keep reading," Amalia said, rising. "See you at the finish."

Helena bade her good-night and returned to her book.

Upon reaching her room, Amalia called the front desk to leave a wake-up call, then prepared for bed. She'd take a clue from Maria and get to bed early to waken refreshed. She was tired. And a bit disappointed Teresa had found them. If she hadn't, would Rafael have wanted to spend more time alone with her as he had before?

The sun woke Amalia when its rays fell in her face. She frowned and rolled over, opening her eyes. She sat up in panic. It was full daylight! She checked the clock; it was after seven. Good grief, what had happened to her wake-up call? She dashed from bed and dressed in record time. Rafael would have a fit!

Suddenly she stopped. Had he changed the departure time? If not, surely he would have been pounding on her door by this time. There had been some talk last night about leaving later due to their lead, but she was sure she remembered him saying that he wanted to increase the lead, not tempt fate.

She finished dressing, then called Maria's room. No answer.

Packing her things, she left for the lobby. She'd be so embarrassed if everyone was waiting for her.

The lobby was empty. She went to the double doors leading to the street. No truck, no crew. No Rafael. Her trepidation increased. What was going on?

Turning, Amalia entered the lobby and approached the registration desk. "Did the balloon crew leave already?" she asked.

"I believe both groups left before five," the desk clerk said. He frowned and asked, "Were you supposed to go with them?"

"Yes. And I left a wake-up call for four-thirty. It never came." She could not have slept through the loud ring of the phone. How could they have left her? Was one of the crew already on the way back to get her?

The clerk frowned and clicked a few keys on

the computer. "Ah, that call was canceled shortly before midnight," he said.

"*I* didn't cancel it."

He frowned and clicked a few more keys. "I don't have the information on who canceled it, just that it was canceled. I apologize if that was in error."

She verified it was the call for her room, then turned, puzzled. Who would have canceled her wake-up call, and why hadn't Rafael come pounding on her door when she hadn't appeared with the rest of the crew?

"I don't understand. I'm part of the crew on that balloon. How could they leave me?"

"I'm sure I don't know, miss."

Amalia turned away. What was she going to do? She had no idea why they would have left her. Surely there was a logical explanation. Maybe Rafael was letting her sleep in and Manuel or Maria would be back to get her and she'd find the balloon was already inflated by the time she reached it?

She turned back. "Is there a message for me?"

"Let me check." He turned and looked into the box on the back wall that had her room number. "Indeed, there is." He handed her an envelope.

She crossed to the chairs where Helena had been reading the night before and sat to open the envelope.

"Your boss is a dear. Stefano suggested I take your place on Rafael's balloon so you can return home. No more fear of heights."

It was signed with Teresa's flamboyant signature.

Amalia stared at the paper. She didn't believe it. Rafael had taken Teresa and left her behind!

"What did you think, you stupid woman," she muttered. "That he'd favor you over the woman he's been seeing the last few months?" She'd thought he had liked her. Their discussions had grown more and more personal. She had learned more about him than anyone else she knew. She had revealed some of her uncertainties raising Jose, and her future, as she had never done before.

She thought they were growing close. But it had obviously only been on her side. She'd been falling in love, hoping against hope that he'd been feeling some kind of special attachment for her. But this—it proved the race was the only thing he was interested in. Now he had a willing passenger and Amalia was just so much excess baggage.

The enormity of the situation rose. She had virtually no money with her, no transportation, no brother at home to call on for help. She was truly stuck in this small town hundreds of miles from any place familiar. Just how was she going to get home?

Anger flared. How dare he bully her from her home, insist she accompany him when she was scared to death half the time, and then dump her the minute someone else showed up! He had assured her she'd get home safely. If he didn't want her on the trip, it was up to him to arrange transportation home.

Thankfully she had not yet checked out. She returned to her room and headed for the phone. She called her office. The temp who'd replaced her for the length of the race answered. Amalia asked for the number of Rafael's company.

She phoned there and talked to three different people, her ire rising at each brush-off. Finally she asked for Dominic. She remembered his name from a comment Rafael had made to Helena.

"Can I help you?" a masculine voice asked.

Amalia took a deep breath. It was not this person's fault his boss was a jerk.

"This is Amalia Catalon. Rafael has stranded me in some little town up near the French border, and I need to get back to Barcelona."

"I'm sorry, who did you say you were?"

"The woman he practically *kidnapped* to go on this stupid balloon race and then stranded with no way to get home. There might be some reporters still around who would love to hear that story," she finished. The thought had just occurred to her. Would they have left when her boss did? Or could she find one or two around to tell of the predicament Rafael had put her in? All sorts of fantasies played in her mind, but mostly she wanted to get home and put this behind her.

How dumb could one person be? A man like Rafael Sandoval would never truly fall in love with someone like her. She was a novelty. Someone so different from women he knew, he was temporarily intrigued. But that interest had vanished. Winning the race trumped everything else.

She could call the papers herself for that matter. Not that it would get her home. She was so angry!

And disappointed.

And hurt.

She had thought there was at least a tentative friendship developing. Did he think she willy-nilly kissed every man she spent some time with like she'd kissed him?

"I'm sorry, I don't recognize your name. I can get in touch with Rafael and get back to you," he said.

"Grrr." She hung up the phone and called her office again.

"This is Amalia, let me speak to Henrico, please." In a roundabout way it was her boss's fault she was in this predicament. She'd get home at the company's expense and let Stefano sort out the costs with Rafael later.

Rafael gazed in the direction they were moving. Teresa stood at the side, watching their shadow cross the earth. Her perfume was cloying. Why she even wore it on a balloon was beyond him. Firing up the jets again, he tried to quell his anger and, truth be known, his disappointment. He'd known from the beginning Amalia had been afraid of heights. That she hadn't wanted to make the trip. Still, the last few days she'd seemed to do fine on the flights. And the conversations they'd had held a lot of appeal to him.

Yet she had jumped at the offer of letting Teresa substitute for her when she'd arrived at the hotel last night.

He'd been furious when he arrived at the truck that morning and seen Teresa there instead of Amalia. He'd been on the point of going to her room and getting her when Teresa said Amalia had asked to switch.

To double-check, he'd asked the desk clerk to see if there was any message from Amalia. There had been none. So then he'd checked to see if she'd left a wake-up call for this morning. The clerk had confirmed one had been placed, but then canceled later in the evening.

Probably after she'd spoken to Teresa.

He vented his anger with the burners, firing them up for longer than the normal ten seconds. The balloon rose. He wished he could rise above the surprising letdown he was feeling from Amalia's defection.

At least Teresa appeared to be trying this time. She'd been the perfect passenger, except for the perfume. And the skintight T-shirt she wore. Her jacket opened to reveal as much as she could and still keep warm.

He was annoyed. Things had been going well and with the lead he had, he would easily beat Stefano Vicente.

But he'd pictured a totally different ending. He and Amalia celebrating at the finish. Riding home together with the crew. Sharing in the glory of winning. Him taking her out for a quiet celebration with just the two of them.

Her brother would still have been on his trip, so perhaps she would have invited him in. If she had, he would have accepted. Together they would have attended the BBA dinner. Together they could have received the check from her boss. He could have told her then how much he wanted to beat Stefano Vicente and why. She'd have understood.

The fantasy ended. The dinner was still on, but the ride home would certainly be different.

"I can hardly see Vicente's balloon," Teresa said smugly. "He is so far behind, he hasn't a chance to win."

Rafael nodded and fired up the burners. The noise gave a rest to Teresa's constant chatter. The morning was not soothing like other days had been. Amalia didn't speak a lot. He hadn't realized how much he'd enjoyed the silence, relished the challenge. Today he was just irritated.

Amalia could have at least told him to his face that she didn't want to continue now that Teresa had arrived. Women! He felt his anger rise. A courtesy call would have been nice. No—she should have verified with him whether the change was acceptable or not. Just because she wanted her own way didn't mean she got it. He wanted *her* on this flight.

He wanted *her* to be part of the win.

That took a moment to sink in. He cared about her. More than he should, obviously, given the way she'd bailed on him with no notice. But he could have sworn she was different from most of the people he saw socially.

She reminded him of Helena, solid, grounded, dependable.

He frowned. Amalia definitely had a sense of duty and integrity. She would have told him she was changing places with Teresa. If he hadn't been blindsided by her defection, he would have picked up on the sense of wrongness about all of this.

"Oooo, you look upset," Teresa said, coming to stand beside him, resting a hand on his arm. "You are winning, so what's wrong?"

"Nothing." But something was nagging at him. This morning's actions did not sound like the Amalia he had grown to know and care for.

"So tell me about this long jump. Do we fly all day?" she asked.

"We'll set down whenever we need fuel, then resume. We go as long as the propane lasts, or daylight ends, whichever comes first."

She glanced at the tanks. "Did you bring lunch?" she asked.

"The ground crew has it."

"They will be there?"

He nodded. "Who do you think has the tanks to change out?"

The radio crackled.

"Boss, you have a problem," Manuel said.

Rafael picked up the mike. "Go ahead." He looked back at the other balloon. It followed faithfully, maybe five miles behind. A comfortable distance given the steady winds and lack of radical weather change.

"Dominic called. He said some woman called him saying she was part of our crew and abandoned in some small town and demanded he get her home."

"She should have thought of that before backing out of the race," Rafael said. So she'd burned her bridges and hadn't thought about how she'd return home. Not his problem.

Yet he knew it was. He would never abandon anyone without a way for them to return home— especially Amalia.

Especially Amalia.

Rafael turned to see Teresa. She was not the woman he wanted with him; Amalia was. He had known that earlier—which was why it all felt wrong. He should have stormed up to her room and forced her to finish the race. He wanted her in on the victory!

"Actually she told him *you* had stranded her there and that she has no money."

Teresa was staring fixedly at the other balloon.

Suddenly everything became clear. He turned his head slowly and pierced her with a glare. "What have you done?"

CHAPTER TEN

AMALIA stood by the window in her room and waited. She'd done all she could. Henrico was checking on car services, air transportation from a private plane or bus transportation. She didn't care how she got there, she just wanted to go home.

Worst-case scenario, she'd stay in the hotel on Rafael's money until her brother returned home and could wire transfer her some money. But she hoped Henrico would manage to find a way for her to get home before then. She didn't want Jose to worry.

Her emotions went from anger to sadness at the way the race had ended—for her. She'd known nothing lasting would come of the time spent with Rafael, but had hoped for a few more days with him. Even her fear of heights had diminished. With other things to think about, she could push that away and deal with the soaring in the balloon.

For several wonderful days, she'd shared experiences with one of Barcelona's most eligible bachelors. Even dreamed that he'd fall for her. How absurd.

He was gorgeous; she was average. He was wealthy; she definitely was not. He liked dangerous sports; she liked sunning at the beach. He didn't want to marry; she wanted a marriage like her parents had. He didn't want children. Amalia thought about that. Eventually she'd like to have children. However, after the responsibility of raising her brother, she would like a few years to enjoy being a couple, able to take trips on the spur of the moment, plan events with friends, without the worry of child care.

Not that Rafael had given so much as a hint that he'd ever see himself in that role. Unsurprising really, when his style was much more of the no-ties, no-commitments variety. Was Rafael even now kissing Teresa? Was one woman so interchangeable with another?

She frowned and turned away from the window and those depressing thoughts. He'd never promised her anything. He had no obligation to her—except to get her home. And she'd make sure he never had a clue she'd fallen for him. Nor anyone else, either. It would be her secret forever.

Pacing her room, the luxury was wasted on her. The best aspect was that it was large enough so she had more steps to make before turning to retrace them. How dare he flit off without a word! Had he been afraid she would refuse to let Teresa take her place? Maybe cause a scene?

She doubted it. Rafael didn't appear afraid of anything—certainly not some heated words from a rival's irate PA.

Tears threatened. She shook her head. She was *not* going to cry over anyone or anything, especially Rafael Sandoval. She'd done her best, even when she hadn't wanted to be there. So now she'd gotten her wish—she was going home.

Be careful what you wish for… The old phrase came to mind.

Snatching up her bag, she left the room. She'd wait in the lobby. She was tired of her own company, tired of her thoughts, tired of waiting. She'd at least see some activity in the lobby.

Stopping at the desk to let them know she wasn't in her room and would take calls here, she went to sit down. There were magazines on the tables. She leafed through a couple, but the photographs and articles didn't hold her interest.

What was taking Henrico so long? Granted this small town was off the beaten path, but surely it had interaction with the rest of Spain. How much longer?

It was almost noon when Henrico called back.

"I have hired a private car from San Sebastian. The driver will be there in the early afternoon. You'll be back home late tonight. The costs will be paid on our account. You get to deal with Stefano on this one."

"Thank you. Stefano got me into this, so he can settle the accounts with Sandoval. I'll be back in the office tomorrow."

And give serious thought to changing jobs. She was not some pawn to be picked up and put down at the whim of hardheaded businessmen. For a moment she almost couldn't decide which one she was more angry with—Stefano or Rafael!

She left her bag with the bell captain and went to walk around the town and to get some lunch. It was early, but she didn't want to miss the car when it arrived. She'd given the doorman strict instructions about the car service. He was to make sure they waited for her if they came before she returned.

Since she hadn't eaten today, she ordered a large lunch at a sidewalk café and enjoyed the sunshine and the quiet little town. Then she walked back to the hotel.

To her surprise she saw the chase team truck parked in front. She quickened her pace. Maybe they had come back for her. Maybe she could still be part of the team and in on the finish. Maybe she'd misconstrued everything.

Amalia stopped dead upon entering the lobby. Rafael paced the area in front of the desk.

"Rafael?" she exclaimed. "What on earth are you doing here?"

He turned and crossed the lobby, taking her in his arms and hugging her tightly.

"You should be in the balloon. Did something happen?" she asked, muffled against his chest.

He put her at arm's length and looked at her. "Did you think I had deliberately left you behind?" he asked.

She blinked. That wasn't an answer to her question. "Well, here I am and everyone else is gone. What was I to think?"

"That I would never do such a thing."

This was wrong. He should be miles away, airborne, outdistancing her boss. What was he doing back here at the hotel?

"Why aren't you in the air?" she repeated.

"I was, until I found out Teresa had pulled that stunt. She told me when she came down to join the crew early this morning that you had convinced her to take your place. That you hated being in the balloon. It made sense. You've made no secret of the fact you don't like heights."

She drew herself up. "I would have told you myself if I weren't going today."

"Yeah, I got that about an hour ago. I wasn't

thinking straight. I was so mad you had backed out and sent Teresa in as a substitute."

"I did *not*," she said, outraged.

"I know that now. And I would have known it early this morning if I had been thinking sensibly. But I wasn't, only reacting."

"I don't understand. Rafe, where is the balloon?"

"In a field somewhere about an hour from here." He waved one hand.

"What are you *doing*? Stefano will get ahead! You have to get back!"

"He can win the damn race. It's you I'm worried about."

"Me?" Amalia didn't know what to do, how to react. Her heart was pounding so hard she couldn't even think.

"I would never leave you stranded, Amalia. Didn't I say I'd get you home safely?"

"Yes, but I thought that meant you wouldn't let me fall out of the balloon."

He brushed her hair from the side of her face. "I meant I'd take you home. You could have trusted me."

His touch felt heavenly. She tried to figure out what was going on. "And how would that have changed anything? I slept through until the sun woke me. You were gone. When I didn't come down to the lobby, why didn't you come get me? You had no qualms about doing that in Barcelona."

"I regret not coming to your room and demanding you get up and go with us. It was my first instinct and I should have followed through on it. But I didn't learn until a short time ago that Teresa had called down to cancel your wake-up call. You were still planning to go with me, weren't you? It was not your idea to send Teresa in your place."

"I would never have done such a thing!" she reiterated, hope finally blossoming. He hadn't abandoned her—not deliberately.

"It seemed logical—Teresa's taking your place. No more fear during the day. No more camping out or dealing with a storm. You'd return to your home and not care a bit about the outcome of the stupid race." He frowned. "Anyway, it all made sense at 5:00 a.m."

"It *is* a stupid race. And you're going to lose it if you don't get going," she urged.

"Not going to happen until we get this cleared up. You are more important than a hundred races. In fact, I think you are the most important thing I have in my life right now."

She blinked. "What do you mean?" She licked suddenly dry lips.

"I mean you're more important than besting Vicente. More important than finishing the race. I've fallen for you, Amalia. You're unlike any woman I know—in a very special way. Only, I didn't realize it until Teresa tried to explain why she'd pulled that stunt. All I could think of was you here alone. And that you might think I had left you. It doesn't take much to imagine what you must have been feeling. While I know you are capable, I feel responsible for you and I probably always will. I would do nothing to deliberately hurt you."

His hands cupped her face. The lobby faded. Amalia focused on the dark eyes that gazed so warmly down into hers.

"You hardly know me," she whispered. "I'm no one's responsibility."

"What I do know I love. And I hope the rest will follow as the years unfold. We've been together more in the last few days than many people are before they get engaged. I want that for us. I never thought I'd ask, but I want you to marry me, Amalia Catalon. Show me a family like I've never known. Take me into yours. I want to know Jose. Be included in family events. Learn what we can explore together, build a life that will give us all the happy memories we can want forever. As I drove like a madman to get back here before you could leave, I realized the crushing disappointment I felt this morning was because I thought you didn't want to be with me. But I remembered every moment we've been together on the drive back, and I'm hoping I saw signs that might mean you care for me as well."

"I'm not sophisticated or cosmopolitan," she protested, even though she wanted to bite her tongue. He knew that. If he was still asking her to marry him, she should ignore all the reasons why not and accept. Was there anything she wanted more?

"No, but I think you're perfect the way you are. You're honest, passionate about things you care about and have a strong sense of duty. I'm fascinated by the way your mind works, by the ideas you come up with. By how your eyes sparkle and your entire face seems to shine when you smile. I love you, Amalia. I didn't know the balloon trip would ever end up this way. Every spin of the tires had me remembering every second of our time together. The special bond that grew almost without my knowing it. Only when I thought you'd left did I realize how important it was for you to stay. Say you'll share your life with me for the next fifty or sixty years—or longer."

"I don't know, Rafael."

"We can have as long an engagement as you

want. Let you get to know me. Let me get to know you even more. But consider the time we've spent together. More than most couples who date a few hours one or two nights a week. I've seen how you handle adversity. How you're brave when needed. I know you stand up for your rights—I don't think Stefano will ever be quite the same again."

She laughed as the delight filled her heart. Dare she believe he meant it? Her heart swelled with love. "You do me great honor, Rafael Sandoval. I would love to be your wife! I love you. I—"

Her words were lost as his mouth covered hers when he pulled her into his embrace. The thrill of his kiss was only increased by the knowledge that she would have kisses like this for the rest of her life. Amalia felt as if she were soaring.

EPILOGUE

RAFAEL escorted Amalia to their table. He introduced her to the other members of the Barcelona Business Alliance seated at the table and met their guests in exchange. Seated, she smiled at him. He knew she would look beautiful in burgundy. The dress fit her trim figure perfectly, the long lines making her seem taller and even more slender. Her dark hair was done in some elaborate upswept design. One he would delight in taking down later when he escorted her home.

She leaned forward. "Nervous?" she asked.

"Not a bit. Should I be?"

She wrinkled her nose at him. "I did as you asked and did not say a word to Stefano. He's planning to gloat, you know. I still think we could have had a shot at the distance. He couldn't have been that far ahead if we'd dashed back to the balloon."

"Relax. The others had a great time taking rides

and there will be more opportunities to challenge your boss."

"Soon-to-be-former boss. Honestly, if I have another day like today, I'd likely deck him."

He laughed and Amalia smiled, happy every time she heard his deep laughter. The last two weeks had flown by. Jose had been over the top when he learned of his sister's engagement, corralling Rafael every time he came to the apartment to question him on everything from lighter-than-air travel, to scuba diving, to mountain climbing. She was almost afraid her studious brother might take a different turn in college!

They had dinner together every evening, but most of the time Rafael came to their flat and became engulfed in their lives. He seemed to enjoy every minute.

Amalia loved the evenings he insisted on taking her out. But unlike the past, Rafael kept their dating secret. There were no reporters with snippets in the newspaper, no photographs splashed across the society pages. They talked about everything under the sun, and she fell more and more in love.

Last weekend he'd taken her and Jose out on his sailboat. Heaven. She definitely preferred sailing on the sea than in the air.

Her only regret was he'd lost the race. Sure there would be other times, but she knew how much Rafael had wanted to beat Stefano. She wanted him to have everything. It seemed fair—he'd given her everything with his love.

After the sumptuous dinner, the president of the alliance rose to address those present. The speaker gave his speech. Applause was polite. Then the president introduced Stefano.

Rafael was sitting casually in his chair, watching with amused eyes. Amalia was nervous as she waited for her boss to begin his bragging winner's speech. She wished he'd just get it over with. She wanted to jump up and defend Rafe, to explain they'd been leading but he'd stopped for something he considered even more important.

Stefano rambled on for several minutes, ending with the announcement that he'd won and Rafael Sandoval owed him fifty thousand Euros.

Heads turned, smiled appeared. Rafael stood and reached for Amalia. "Come with me," he said.

The move surprised her and obviously Stefano. She hoped she didn't look as dumbfounded as she felt.

They climbed the few steps to the platform and walked to the center where the podium and microphone were.

Stefano smiled at Rafael, gloating every moment.

Rafael walked up to him and offered his hand. "Congratulations, Stefano, your balloon went the farthest." While not speaking into the mike, his voice carried.

Stefano faltered a moment and then nodded and shook his hand. He glanced at Amalia, puzzled.

Rafael took out a check from his pocket, looked at it and then turned to the audience. "As Stefano explained, we had a bet. He went the distance and I have a check for fifty thousand Euros to give to him." He handed Stefano the check. The audience applauded. Stefano beamed with satisfaction. He loved to be the center of attention.

Rafael pulled Amalia up beside him and turned back to the mike.

"But Stefano didn't win as much as I did. I found the love of my life on that balloon race and I'm delighted to share with each of you tonight that Amalia Catalon has promised to marry me. She thought the bet a stupid action between two wealthy men. There were many better uses for fifty thousand Euros, she insisted. I promised her I would turn over the winnings to her favorite charity if we won. Since I feel I won the biggest prize of all, I have a check for fifty thousand Euros made payable to The Sisters of Charity's Children's Home."

He pulled out the check and handed it to her. "In honor of her parents, who are unable to see the happiness their daughter has brought me because of their untimely deaths nine years ago. I thank them in absentia for giving me Amalia."

Amalia took the check, her eyes swimming with tears. "It's I who have won," she whispered as happiness bubbled over. She so loved this man.

The applause was heartfelt. But when Rafael took her into his arms to kiss her, the Barcelona Business Alliance went wild with a standing ovation. The first in the history of the organization.

Rafael hugged her close, saying over the sound of the crowd, for her alone, "We know the truth— Stefano loses. We win."

HIRED:
SASSY ASSISTANT

BY
NINA HARRINGTON

MILLS & BOON

All the characters in this book have no existence outside the imagination of the author, and have no relation whatsoever to anyone bearing the same name or names. They are not even distantly inspired by any individual known or unknown to the author, and all the incidents are pure invention.

First published in Great Britain 2009
Paperback edition 2010
Harlequin Mills & Boon Limited,
Eton House, 18-24 Paradise Road, Richmond, Surrey TW9 1SR

© Nina Harrington 2009

ISBN: 978 0 263 86963 7

Harlequin Mills & Boon policy is to use papers that are natural, renewable and recyclable products and made from wood grown in sustainable forests. The logging and manufacturing process conform to the legal environmental regulations of the country of origin.

Printed and bound in Spain
by Litografia Rosés, S.A., Barcelona

Dear Reader

I am a country girl at heart, and relish the delights of village life in my part of southern England. White-walled thatched cottages, historical manor houses and stately country homes are still very much part of our living heritage.

Lulu Hamilton was born and grew up in exactly this kind of tranquil English setting, complete with a rippling chalk stream and cosy open fires. Then emergency medic Kyle Munroe sweeps into her life like a tornado, and the village will never be the same again!

I do hope that you enjoy travelling with Lulu and Kyle on their journey to discover where they truly belong.

I love to hear from my readers, and you can get in touch by visiting www.ninaharrington.com

Nina

To Stephen. For everything.

CHAPTER ONE

IT WASN'T every day of the week that you saw a librarian carrying a package on her head that looked bigger than she was, struggling to get off a London tube train at eleven o'clock in the morning.

Especially when that librarian had sun-streaked blond corkscrew hair that fell around her shoulders in long, wavy tendrils.

As he stepped out onto the platform, Kyle Munroe glanced back to the next carriage just in time to see the librarian stretch up on tiptoes, lift the wide bag over the heads of her fellow passengers, then thrust it forward to use as a wedge through the crush of travellers rushing past her to board the train. They had little regard for anyone who might dare to get in their way.

Seconds before the train door beeped closed behind her, the blonde had to practically jump onto the platform, before snatching the package out of the jaws of the sliding doors with such force that she almost fell backwards as the tube sped away.

The librarian tried to restore her dignity by tugging the jacket of her dove-grey skirt suit a little lower, and lifting her cute, small nose a little higher, before hoisting the straps of what looked like an artist's portfolio case over her neck and shoulder. Only the bag was still dragging on the floor, so she forgot the straps and went for Plan B. This involved holding the edges of the case with her fingertips, arms at full stretch, while trying to hitch the wide strap around her neck with one shoulderblade and her chin.

After two trial steps in amazingly rickety-looking heels, she strode forward, the portfolio flapping against her chest, head high, eyes set on her goal—the escalator. Only Plan B let her down, and she was reduced to sliding, dragging and cajoling her oversized package towards the escalator.

Perhaps she was actually a schoolteacher, and any second now she would tell the unruly portfolio to go and sit in the naughty corner?

Nope—she was definitely a librarian. The only woman he had ever seen wearing that kind of dull grey skirt suit by choice had been the technical librarian at his medical school. That particular lady could dance a mean mambo, and was a world expert on parasitic diseases, but she still chose those hideous suits!

Then again, she had never, ever worn dove-grey mules below legs like the ones trying to walk ahead of him at that minute—the kind of legs that forced the first smile of the day from his lips.

So what if he was a leg man and proud of it?

This was turning out to be the high point of a journey that had started in squalor and sunshine a long way from London. Three hours across the mountains in a bone-shaking Jeep with bald tyres had been followed by a very long flight in economy class, surrounded by wonderful but exhausted screaming kids. Coming up with games and toys to amuse them had been fun—for the first couple of hours.

It had been a long day, and his body clock was starting to kick in. Perhaps it was time to show his appreciation for the lady who had finally given him something to smile about?

With his long athletic legs, and her shorter, high-heeled ones, it only took Kyle a few steps to catch up with her.

'Do you need any help with that?' he asked, trying to sound casual and non-threatening.

The librarian didn't break stride as she took a

sideways glance at his six feet one of athletic hunkiness—or at least that was how the TV company liked to describe him. From the stunned look in her pale blue eyes, she had decided that he was clearly not to be trusted.

He tried to act casual by running a few fingers through his shaggy, dark brown, now mostly dust encrusted hair. Hmm. Not his best look. Perhaps he should have made the time to take a shower and change his clothes at the airport?

'I'm fine, but thank you for offering.'

Except the words were barely out of her mouth before the portfolio slid off her shoulder and Kyle had to reach forward to stop it from being trampled underfoot by the crush of passengers trying to cram onto the escalator.

As they were swept along in the rush, the librarian took a sharp intake of breath and clutched onto the handrail. Her other hand was pressed to her throat, where a red welt showed that the weight of the bag was very far from being fine.

'It's okay—I've got it,' Kyle reassured her. 'Maybe I could carry it as far as the barrier? How about that?'

'Okay, just to the barrier.'

She half turned around to face him, and he was struck by her closed-mouth smile. His medical head noticed immediately that her right eye was flecked with deeper shades of blue than the other. Whatever she saw in his face he could only guess, but the half-smile creased the corner of a wide, plump mouth set in creamy skin sprinkled with freckles over her nose and cheeks. Like cinnamon powder on whipped cream.

Freckles. Why did she have to have freckles? He almost groaned. *Doomed.*

'I see that you've flown from Delhi. That's a long flight. Been there on holiday?' she asked, her dainty head tipped slightly in the cutest, loveliest, most freckly pose.

Drat! The airline tags were still attached to his old rucksack!

'Just passing through,' he replied, trying to sound flippant, before nodding over her shoulder. 'Here we go.'

The librarian suddenly realised that they were at the top of the escalator, and whipped around so that she could step to one side and stay within touching distance of her precious package.

He took a firmer grip on what felt like a thin wooden frame—not heavy, but an awkward size and shape—and casually swept the handles over one shoulder.

'What sort of picture is this?' he asked as he fumbled for his ticket, half expecting to hear that it was some Old Master bound for restoration by learned scholars in an ancient London guild.

'Orchids. Yellow orchids, to be exact.' She paused and nodded. 'I'm sure I can manage from here. It's only a short bus ride to the South Bank. Sorry to have been such a nuisance.'

'No apology necessary.' Kyle was just about to pass the portfolio over when he paused. 'Did you say the South Bank? That's where I'm headed. Why don't we share a cab?' He hoisted the bag a little higher. 'The bus could be a problem.'

Even though she had been the first to mention her destination, she hesitated, clearly weighing up the benefits of getting there in one piece against the danger from a scruffy potential stalker and orchid-picture thief. Kyle stared at her silence as she bit her lower lip before going for it.

'Um, okay. Yes, that would be great. Thank you. Normally I would walk along the Embankment—but not in these shoes, carrying that. And I am rather late.'

'Me too. Shall we risk it?'

That seemed to stun her for a few seconds, but with a gentle nod, the blonde climbed the steps out of the station. The crush of other pedestrians and the awkward shape of the portfolio conspired together to thwart most of Kyle's view of the spectacular legs in action on the stairs, but the little he did see was well worth the effort.

It took only minutes to clamber out into the noise and chaos of the city street. After eighteen months in the mountains he had forgotten what a physical assault on the senses it all was, and the girl in the grey suit had hailed a black cab before he'd pulled himself together.

Kyle made a point of swinging the package onto the backseat, then holding open the door for her before jumping in himself with his rucksack.

While he knew as much about London art galleries as she probably did about yaks, the name the librarian gave to their driver sounded familiar enough for him to be impressed.

As their cab took off into the traffic she collapsed back against her seat and slowly exhaled, her arm wrapped protectively around the edge of the portfolio.

'Are there a lot of career opportunities for art couriers these days?'

She looked across at him as though she had almost forgotten that he was there.

'Oh, this is only a sideline,' she replied in a matter-of-fact voice. 'My real job is in art forgery. That's where the real money is.' She leant closer and whispered, 'But I'm relying on you to keep my secret to yourself.'

'My lips are sealed. Best of luck in prison.'

The blue eyes crinkled up into a smile as she took in his filthy jacket, two-day stubble and the trousers that had last seen water two weeks earlier after an emergency Caesarean section on a riverbank.

'Passing through Delhi? That sounds like a lot of fun. Is it still warm and sunny there?' she asked in a light-hearted voice.

'Very,' he replied with a sigh. 'At this time of year they're getting ready for Diwali—the festival of lights. I'm sorry I'm missing that! It's a fantastic city. Do you know it?'

'Not personally,' she replied, then gave him a wistful smile. 'But people have told me about the wonderful colours and the atmosphere. I've always wanted to go there. Maybe one day,' she added, shrugging her shoulders. Then the blonde gestured towards his jacket with her head. 'I can see that you've spent time in the mountains. Let me guess. Have you been climbing or hiking?'

Wow. She really was observant. It was a pity that the truth was far too complicated, because ideally he would have loved to find the time to do precisely those things. But he had never got the chance.

'Not even close. What makes you think that I've been in the mountains?'

She grinned back before replying. 'I noticed

that you're wearing a white Buddhist scarf, and you have Hindi graffiti scribbled on your arm.'

Kyle stared down at the plaster cast encasing his left wrist, which was completely covered with colourful messages. Um. Perhaps some of them were a bit crude.

'You can read Nepali?' he asked, with genuine admiration in his voice.

'No, but I do recognise the Hindi characters,' she held up one hand, palm forward. 'And I don't need a translation, if it's all the same to you.'

'Probably just as well. I'm Kyle, by the way.'

He reached forward with his right hand, and she glanced at it for a second before giving it a firm, quick shake with small, thin, cool fingers. His rough fingertips rasped in contact with her delicate skin. Perhaps that was why she pulled back immediately, as the cab slowed for some lights, and started scrabbling about in her messenger bag?

'I could give you my name,' she replied, 'but I am on a very important mission where secrecy is vital. That sort of personal information is strictly on a need-to-know basis. This should cover my share of the cab fare.'

Kyle looked at the pile of coins she had passed him in bewilderment, and wondered if cab fares had increased at the same rate as female sass since he had been away.

'A mission at the art gallery? Ah. Of course. The old forgery trade.' He tapped his nose twice. 'Your secret is safe. What are you running late for?'

'I have to drop this off and then make a twelve-o'clock appointment. I'm cutting it fine.' She glanced at her watch, and noticed that he was not wearing one. 'How about you, Kyle? What are you late for? Oh, sorry—another time. This is the gallery.'

She flashed a beaming smile in his direction as the cab slowed in front of an elegant glass-fronted building. 'It's been a pleasure, and thanks again. I hope I haven't delayed you too much.'

'Wait,' Kyle replied, pushing the bag towards her. 'One question. Please? I have to know. Are you a librarian, by any chance?'

She stopped trying to drag the portfolio over her shoulder and looked at him wide-eyed for a second, before breaking into the kind of warm smile that stopped traffic and turned curly haired, blond librarians into supermodels.

'Not even close.' And with that she closed the cab door and gave him a regal wave, before striding away without looking back.

Twenty minutes later Lulu Hamilton sauntered down the wide South Bank pavement as best as she could in her godmother Emma's dove-grey mules, and revelled in the sights and smells of the crisp, late-October day.

As a beam of bright sunshine broke through the clouds she dropped her head back and closed her eyes to enjoy the moment.

Not bad, girl. Not bad at all. She had reached the gallery right on time. The job was done. It had meant sharing a taxi with a cheeky tourist with a killer smile, but for once her risky decision had paid off and she had delivered her painting in one piece.

The yellow orchid acrylic was destined for a luxury boutique in the city. The gallery was delighted, the client was thrilled, and best of all, she had been paid a bonus for delivering the piece in time for their grand opening. If she kept to a tight budget, the cheque in her pocket would see her through the first few months of art college. Her dream had just come one step closer.

She inhaled deeply, soaking in the sights and smells of the city. Ten years ago she had been a student here, before she'd left university to take care of her father after her mother was killed. She rarely came back. It was too painful to think about what could have been.

Not any longer. That was then and this was now.

For the first time in many years she was finally moving forward with her life and putting the past behind her. So what if it was a baby step, and she had a few steep hills head? Mountains, even? She was moving forward and she was doing it through her own hard work.

One thing was certain. She had forgotten how crowded the city was—and how noisy. The traffic din was worse than ever. The cacophony of mixed fragments of sound from buses, taxicabs, cars and people seemed to collide inside her brain.

Well, that was something she could control!

In one smooth, well-practised motion, her fingertips smoothed her shoulder-length hair down over her left ear and, oblivious to anyone else, she turned off the small digital hearing aid fitted behind it.

That was better. Much better.

Brightly coloured leaves in amazing shades of scarlet and russet, from the maples and London plane trees which lined the Embankment, blew against her legs in the fresh breeze from the Thames.

She loved autumn—it had always been her favourite season.

She couldn't imagine living in a tropical climate. Not when nature put on this glorious free display for people to enjoy.

The last few months had been tough, but the painting had been finished on time and it was as good as anything she had ever done. Perhaps her friends back home in Kingsmede were right, and she should take some time out to enjoy herself for a change and smell the rosebuds?

A half-smile creased her face as she glanced at her fellow pedestrians, crowding the pavement. Most of them either had their noses pressed into the pages of a tourist guidebook, or were chatting away on cellphone headsets while keying something desperately important into a personal organiser.

With a brisk shake of her head, Lulu twirled around a cluster of teenage tourists, then swallowed down hard as her gaze fixed straight ahead on the impressive entrance to the stylish media company offices, where the book launch event was being held.

It was still a total mystery why Mike Baxter had invited her to this book launch at all. Of course she had been thrilled to hear that he had been promoted to Clinical Director at the medical foundation where her mother had worked for the last eight years of her life, but his letter had certainly been intriguing.

They had kept in contact, but this was the first time that Mike had invited her to a press conference—so that he could talk to her about an 'exciting opportunity' over lunch. Mike was one of the few people who knew about her partial hearing, and that crowded public events were not her favourite places.

After almost twenty-nine years on the planet, the words *exciting* combined with *opportunity* usually meant a lot of work for her with all the kudos going to other people. Except that Mike had made it clear that this was going to be a great way to raise money for her local hospice, where her father had spent the last few weeks of his life.

And for that she was willing to face a crowded room full of chattering people, most of whom she would not be able to hear, and questions about a woman who had been dead ten years and yet still managed to control her life.

Ruth Taylor Hamilton. Her celebrity mother. The famous pioneering surgeon.

The very last person she wanted to talk about. Ever.

Kyle Monroe stared out of the office window at the overcast sky of central London in October. It was hard to believe that only eighteen hours earlier he had been trekking through sunlit forests in the foothills of Nepal.

His eyes felt heavy, gritty, ready to close, but

just as Kyle's head fell back onto the sofa cushion, Mike Baxter finished the call on his mobile phone.

'They're ready and waiting for us. Did you get any sleep at all on the flight? Eight hours, wasn't it? Nine?'

'More like twelve—and, no, not much. The flight was packed.' Kyle yawned. 'You forget what airport crowds are like. The noise. The stress. The smell.' He raised his right arm and sniffed. 'Speaking of which, is there any chance I can get a shave and a shower? I think I startled a pretty girl on the tube this morning.'

'Nope,' Mike replied. 'We're already late. Besides, you have the perfect image—the media company have been working on it. "Dedicated medic flies in straight from the clinic, still in his working clothes." Natural grunge. The press will love it.'

Then he looked more closely at something on Kyle's clothes and recoiled back. 'Are those bloodstains on your trousers?'

Kyle reached down and casually pulled up one leg of his cargo trousers, revealing a surprisingly white, muscular hairy leg. 'Ketchup. Or chilli sauce.' He nodded. 'Probably chilli sauce. The blood is on my jacket. Sorry about that, but we had to use the last of the soap powder to clean the sheets. TB clinics wash a lot of laundry.'

Mike gave a quick nod. 'No problem. Now, what's the story with your wrist?'

Kyle waggled the crusty filthy plaster cast which encased his lower left arm.

'Clean break. My own fault for sticking my arm out when I fell off a rope ladder. It was the only way across the ravine. I tried to do some sort of judo break-fall. And it worked. It broke. No problem.' He shrugged. 'The cast is coming off next week.'

'Any photographs from this ravine?' Mike asked, suddenly interested. 'They could always come in useful for the next book!'

'Next one?' Kyle laughed. 'I barely had time to write this one, Mike! Keep an online diary of your climbing and your medical life, you said. Take a few photos every now and then and post them on your blog, you said. Now look where it's got me!'

Mike lifted up his laptop computer and waved it in Kyle's direction. 'Over ten thousand hits a day. Online diaries are big business now. The income from your first book will pay for the entire Nepalese mission for the next few years. It's the best investment the foundation has ever seen!'

Mike came around to perch on the end of his desk.

'Look, Kyle, I need to talk business for a minute—so you can start groaning now. The way I see it, you're going to be out of action for at least another month. Am I right? Your wrist has not healed properly, and you need to get what's left of that chest infection out of your body.' Mike paused long enough to rub his hands along the edge of his desk in a nervous gesture. 'And then there is the real reason that I pulled you back from the mission. I know you don't want to talk about it, but from what your half-brother told me your family problems might take longer to resolve than you think.'

He was met with a shrug. 'That's not why I'm here,' Kyle replied. 'The rabies programme is behind schedule. That has to come before my personal issues. We need those vaccines, and we need them today. My job is to raise the money to make that happen.'

Mike looked hard into Kyle's face. 'Which is why I've been working with the TV company to pull together an amazing deal for your rabies project.'

Kyle sat up, his brows pulled together in concentration. 'What kind of deal? I don't know what else I can say about Nepal.'

Mike nodded. 'You're right. The film crew has already been to Nepal, and they have everything they need.' He paused and sat back. 'You might not have realised it, but you talked a lot over the past year about your very first mission. You went straight out of medical school into a war zone in Africa. I think you actually came out and stated on camera that it was a life-changing experience.'

There were a few seconds of silence before Kyle responded in a low voice, 'It *was* life-changing. For all of us.'

'That's why the producer wants to make a documentary about your first mission to Uganda. The problems you faced. How it inspired you. The film will probably be shown around March next year. If you could write a book about your diary from those days, and if it can be ready at the same time, it could be a top-seller.'

'Uganda?' Kyle breathed. 'That was ten long years ago, Mike, and I'm not sure I want to go back there. Even on paper.'

'They've offered to double your last advance to make it happen.'

There was another silence before Kyle coughed. 'Did you say double?'

Mike simply nodded. 'If you can force yourself to sit in one place long enough to finish this second book, you can be back in Nepal before the winter sets in—with enough cash to pay the drugs bill for at least the next five years, including all of the vaccines you've asked for.'

Kyle sat back and blew out hard, before shaking his head in resignation.

'You know me too well. When do they need the finished book?'

'The first draft is due in a month. But I know you like challenges,' Mike replied casually as he shrugged into his jacket.

'A month? You know what I'm like with paperwork! I haven't typed anything longer than a few paragraphs for my blog since university!'

Mike didn't even try to argue. 'We have a few suggestions on how we can help you with that—but later. Ready to rock and roll? All you have to do is enjoy the free beer, eat the snacks—and smile. Big smile. Use your charm. Think of the vaccines your book is going to bring into that clinic of yours. Leave me to make sure the press go away happy.'

Kyle grinned back. 'Free beer? What kind of beer?'

CHAPTER TWO

'DR BAXTER should be arriving with Dr Munroe any time now, Miss Hamilton,' the excited little secretary said, almost rocking in her seat behind the wide curved reception desk.

Lulu locked her smile firmly into place before replying in a sweet voice, 'You did say the same thing forty minutes ago, Marta. Are you sure this time?'

'Dr Munroe's flight was delayed, but they are on their way.' The young girl swallowed, smoothed down her mini skirt and gazed in wonder at the stack of books on the desk. 'Isn't Dr Munroe the dreamiest? Perhaps I could persuade him to sign my book for me?'

Each chair in the stylish reception area carried a copy of a paperback book with the words *Medicine Man* in large dark letters.

But it was the stunning cover that was designed to captivate and enthral.

It was an amateur photograph of a bearded young man, in brightly coloured clothing and large dark goggles, standing in deep white snow, with high mountain peaks behind him, reflecting bright sunshine. Buddhist prayer flags fluttered in the breeze above his head against a cobalt-blue sky.

He was grinning widely for the camera, clearly full of life.

According to the press release tucked into each book, K. B. Munroe was a British doctor doing pioneering work on disease control in the High Himalaya of Nepal.

From what Lulu could see, the photograph might just as well have been from a fashion shoot for an adventure sports magazine. Only there was something extra-special in the single image that shone from the man himself. She could not see his face behind the beard and the goggles, yet his energy leapt from the photograph. A life-force so powerful it was practically hypnotic.

The photograph was clearly of some sort of strange mythical creature—because this medic was one broad-shouldered, tanned, handsome and unshaven hunk. All in all, a tousle-haired, square-jawed dream of an emergency doctor and moun-taineer. Beyond rugged. Relaxed. In total control. Captured for ever in a moment. Frozen in time.

The creature in that photo could have been a

film actor playing the part. Maybe that was it? Maybe the real Dr Munroe was a wizened and cynical hard nut, still tramping through the ice and snow in Nepal, and the publisher had taken the easy way out with a gorgeous action-hero actor to play the role?

She smiled to herself. Doctors like K. B. Munroe did wonderful work in hard conditions. They deserved every scrap of praise and recognition. But she knew better than most people that the reality of that life was anything but attractive. Nobody should have to make those kinds of sacrifices.

As she picked up the book and looked more closely at the heroic figure on the cover, she could not help but wonder if this man had a wife and children back home. How did *they* feel when he left them for the mountains? Not knowing if they would ever see him again?

A cold shiver ran down her spine and she almost dropped the book back onto the chair. Too many memories. Too many ghosts.

Suddenly aware that Marta was still waiting for some kind of response from her, Lulu held back on her honest opinion and managed a polite, 'Oh, yes, he certainly is something. Do you think there is time for another tea before they get here?'

'Tea? Right, sure. Rush job. Don't want to miss

him,' the receptionist blurted out, and scurried off in the direction from where the previous two cups of tea had come in the forty minutes Lulu had been waiting, at about twice the speed she had before.

Lulu stood up and slipped the glossy style magazine back onto the flimsy black-and-red Japanese lacquer table beside a massive scarlet leather sofa.

Everything in the reception area shouted expensive, stylish—and in Lulu's eyes would be as long-lasting as the display of tall living white orchids which had been placed in the best position to catch the October blast from the Thames that blew in every time the doors slid open on the London street. Disaster!

She sauntered over as gracefully as she could in her borrowed shoes and fitted skirt, and checked the blossoms and leaves of the stunning blooms. If only the orchids in her conservatory back in Kingsmede were as lovely as these. They would look wonderful painted in a blue-and-white Delft porcelain bowl. Or perhaps against a backdrop of delicate foliage and lavender?

Lulu was so engrossed that she jumped back in surprise as she was suddenly jolted into the real world when the main street door was flung wide-open, sending it crashing against a chair. She turned back just in time to see a tall, gangly bundle of momentum and a flash of filthy stained khaki stride away from her towards the reception desk.

He had come 'In' through the 'Out' door.

A dark green, stained and heavy-looking military rucksack missed a stunned media company executive in a suit by inches as it swung out from one shoulder to the other. Judging from his back view, Lulu guessed this was a journalist who had just been involved in a street fight.

His stride was confident, powerful and energetic. Strong. Someone who knew exactly what he was doing and where he was going in life.

He had probably not even noticed her existence. Typical. Nothing new there.

She was glad when he pushed his way past the red sofa and dropped his heavy bag before the desk.

After looking from side to side a couple of times, he half turned, caught sight of her, and turned on a killer smile.

She had seen his back view a few minutes earlier.

Now Lulu got the full glory. And her mouth dropped open in surprise.

This man smiling across at her was the same tourist who had helped to carry her picture and shared her black cab not two hours earlier.

No doubt about it.

It was the crown prince of grunge.

As he strolled towards her, slowly this time, the confident swagger of his hips completing his hypnotic charm, Lulu could not look away from his face. In an instant she made the connection with the cover image on the book next to her.

He was *Medicine Man*.

K. B. Munroe. Kyle Munroe.

In one smooth movement she lifted her head, straightened her back and inhaled a fortifying breath. So what if she had always been attracted to the athletic type of man? She could handle this.

The adrenaline junkie sidled up to her with his best charm offensive. Lulu decided to take the initiative this time and stretched out her right hand. 'Hello, again. This is a pleasant surprise.'

Kyle stepped closer, but instead of releasing her fingers he raised the back of her hand to his lips, trying to avoid his sharp stubbly chin.

'The pleasure is all mine. It would seem that fate has had the good taste to put us in the same place at the same time. I had no idea that TV companies needed librarians.'

He slowly turned his head from side to side, looking around the echoing reception area before whispering, 'Or specialist art dealers…' And he gave her the kind of twinkly-eyed smile guaranteed to make any girl's heart beat a little faster.

And it was certainly effective! Lulu dragged her eyes away from his face as she slowly retrieved her fingers and casually picked up one of the books from the coffee table before waving it in his direction. 'Well, I wouldn't know about that. Seeing as I'm not a librarian. Dr Munroe, I presume?'

He shrugged. 'That's me. Did you make it to the gallery in time?' Then he leant closer. 'I don't know how undercover art forgers work, but if you have any influence around here at all, I shall have to throw myself on your mercy. If you can point me in the direction of a cold beer, I shall be your slave for a week.'

'Only a week?' Then her smile widened. 'I was right on time, so thanks for your help. You'll find the buffet and an open bar just through there— although…' She glanced down at her watch. 'You are running a little late. The presentation was due to start ten minutes ago.'

'No problem at all. You would be amazed at what I can achieve in ten minutes. Now, please allow me to do something to show my gratitude.'

He moved closer and leant his head towards her, and for a horrible, exciting, heart-thumping moment she thought he might kiss her. But as she leant back he simply laughed and gestured to the paperback with his photo on the cover, which she was still clutching to her side.

'Would you like me to sign your book for you?'

Lulu grinned back in relief, and possibly a touch of regret. He was good at this.

'Yes, please. If you could address it to my friend, Marta, that would be great.'

'No problem at all. I hope your *friend* likes it. Marta.'

Kyle squiggled a signature, then raised his eyebrows a few times before giving her another very saucy wink and a dazzling flash of white teeth, sweeping up his rucksack and striding over to the side entrance—just as Marta practically jogged up to the reception desk, splattering tea on the glossy black floor tiles before turning around to glare at Lulu in disgust.

Lulu was just about to explain when Marta stepped away to one side. 'Dr Baxter. You are running terribly late. Miss Hamilton has been waiting for ages!'

The next thing Lulu knew she was being crushed into a hug by a huge bear of a man with grey hair and wearing a smart business suit.

'Lulu—I am so sorry. But the Delhi flight was almost two hours late and the PR crew have tried to drink the bar dry. Let's get the launch out of the way so we can talk properly. Oh. Is that for me? Thanks, Marta. You're a star.'

And in one action Mike swallowed down what was left of Lulu's cup of tea, grabbed her arm, and almost dragged her towards the conference room, talking fast enough to stop her getting a word in edgeways. 'You look amazing, by the way. How have you been keeping?'

Five minutes of blurred, frantic activity later, Lulu was sitting in the second row in the conference room, watching Mike Baxter arrange his notes on the lectern. She was not entirely sure how she had come to be sitting there, in a crush of photographers, media company executives and journalists who all seemed to be talking non-stop.

She was starting to regret turning her hearing aid back on.

Mike waited patiently for the chatter and clatter to subside, before speaking into the microphone.

'Ladies and gentlemen. If you could take your seats? Thank you. My name is Mike Baxter, and it is my pleasure to welcome you all here today in my capacity as Medical Director of the Medical Foundation for Humanitarian Aid.'

He paused as the press settled into their chairs. 'As some of you will know, twelve months ago the foundation was asked by one of the largest television and multimedia companies in the western world to nominate three unique medical professionals working in hazardous conditions around the world who would be willing to be filmed as part of a TV series. Each mission would receive a charitable donation worth fifty thousand pounds. When that film was broadcast, earlier in the year, it soon became clear that one doctor in particular had touched the hearts of the viewers. Dr Kyle Munroe.'

Mike paused and looked around the room, making sure that he had the full attention of the audience before making his announcement.

'Ladies and gentlemen. What happened next has surprised us all. The programme made a bestseller of *Medicine Man* by Kyle Munroe. This book began as an online diary created during his first year spent working in the high Himalaya of Nepal. The diary is absolutely gripping from beginning to end, and has never been out of the top-ten list. I am pleased to announce that today marks publication of the paperback edition of the book, with a new introduction by the author.'

Mike Baxter glanced to someone at the back of the hall and nodded.

'I am delighted to tell you that the man himself has literally just got off a plane from Delhi, after travelling by foot, Jeep, and two international flights to be with us today. Ladies and gentlemen—Dr Kyle Balfour Munroe!'

The sandwich-chomping journo sitting in front of her, and everyone else around her, stood up to applaud, blocking Lulu's view and forcing her to step out into the side aisle just as Kyle stepped onto the podium from her side of the room. He was holding a pint glass of beer in his right hand, while trying to salute Mike with his plaster cast.

Only now he was wearing spectacles with thin metal rims, which instantly turned him into a younger and jaw-droppingly handsome version of Indiana Jones.

It might be sneaky, but it certainly was effective, and Lulu could not take her eyes from Kyle's face as he casually passed the beer glass to Mike Baxter so that he could raise up a copy of the paperback with his good right hand.

Turning to the microphone, Kyle cracked a beaming smile, displaying brilliant white teeth against his deeply tanned skin. She could see the corners of his mouth wrinkle up with the grin, the tiny pale lines radiating out from his full lips. The thin spectacles seemed to highlight his deep chocolate caramel hair and hazel green eyes. The kind of caramel a girl could savour and linger over for as long as possible, desperate to prolong the delicious pleasure.

Every eye in the room was focused on him long before he spoke.

'I am delighted to be here today to launch the new edition of *Medicine Man*. Every single person who bought the book has already made a huge difference to the lives of the people I work with on a daily basis. People who depend on you for the health of themselves and their families. On their behalf, I thank you all.'

And then he did it. He used the knuckle of his forefinger to just touch the end of his nose and push his spectacles higher. As though to conceal a glistening tear.

As the audience took a breath, Lulu stretched her head up over the reporter's heads as the scruffy Adonis stuffed the book casually into the front pocket of his cargo pants, retrieved his beer with a nod of thanks, and raised the glass to salute the rows of press and photographers, his face barely visible behind the flashguns and microphones.

Then he was swallowed up in the crush.

Mike paused for a few minutes for photographs, before valiantly making his way through the rugby scrum of press already six deep around the podium, each desperate to capture the human interest cover story for the next day. A few seconds later he came to stand next to Lulu. He didn't even try to lower his voice as they stood watching the scene.

'I know he's a bit rough around the edges, but that boy has raised more money for the foundation in the last twelve months than in the previous five years put together. We want Kyle to write a second book, about the time he spent with your mother in Uganda, and the foundation needs *you* to help him do that. What do you say?'

'Mike Baxter, you have an awful lot of explaining to do. And I think you had better start right now. You *know* how I feel about that subject. Please tell me why I shouldn't get the next train back to Kingsmede right now?'

'Well, I might do if you stopped pacing for five minutes. Did you read the dedication in Kyle's book?'

Lulu turned to face her mother's old friend and planted her hands on her hips before giving him a disbelieving look. 'That would be difficult, since I had never even heard of Kyle Munroe until today.'

Mike sighed and flicked to a specific page before passing the paperback over to her.

'Perhaps you should finally get around to buying a television some time soon? Anyhow, you might want to see this before we go any further.'

Lulu breathed out in exasperation and glared at him before accepting the open book and glancing down at the page.

This diary is humbly dedicated to Dr Ruth Taylor Hamilton, who started me on this crazy journey in the first place. The sacrifice and untimely death of this remarkable surgeon taught me what it means to be an emergency medic. Maybe one day I can come close to being that good. Thank you, Stitch. I owe you one.

Her balloon of annoyance popped into ragged shreds of flimsy plastic. Lulu sat down on the hard chair in the now-empty conference room and read it again. 'Oh.'

As she passed the book back to Mike, she felt sure that the thundering of her heart was loud enough for him to hear.

When she did force the air back into her frozen lungs, she saw that his eyes were still looking into her face. Intense.

Unlike the squeaky voice that emerged when she did try to speak through a bone-dry throat. 'Did they work together?'

'Uganda.'

She closed her eyes and tried to block out the horror of what that experience must have been like. 'Her last mission.'

'There's more. Kyle needs every penny we can raise to fund the infectious disease campaign. The TV company want to film a documentary about the Uganda mission and publish Kyle's diaries from that time. He needs help to make that happen.'

Lulu stood up and paced across to the podium in silence, before turning back to face her mother's friend. 'You don't need me! You need a professional editor.'

He nodded. 'Yes, I could hire someone. But they couldn't help Kyle like you can.'

There was something in his voice which caught Lulu's attention. 'What do you mean, like I can?'

'Do you remember the last time I came to Kingsmede? When Tom was still at home?'

'Of course.' She smiled back. 'Dad loved seeing you.'

'Tom made a point of showing me the work you had both done to organise the boxes of your mother's personal items we shipped back from Africa. You did a great job with sorting that lot out. I know he was proud of you for sticking with it and seeing it through. It must have been hard.'

Lulu swallowed down hard. 'Very. Where are you going with this, Mike?'

He lifted his head and looked her straight in the eyes.

'Kyle needs the letters and diaries your mother wrote from Uganda to help him write his book.'

Her face paled, and she had opened her mouth to tell him precisely what he could do with that idea when he raised one hand, palm up.

'Before you say no, please let me explain.'

Mike dropped his hands to his knees and spoke in a low voice.

'Kyle has already mentioned in interviews that Ruth Taylor Hamilton was the reason he got into emergency medicine. The media company have been inundated with requests for more information about this mysterious person, and they came to me.'

He waved his arms dramatically in the air while shrugging his shoulders. 'Things took off from there. I mentioned that your dad had collected together Ruth's letters and diaries from her time in Uganda, and the next thing I knew the publishing director wanted to know how soon they could have Kyle's manuscript about the time he spent in Africa! It's crazy, but they are serious. They want him to talk about Ruth and her work and how it inspired him.'

Lulu sucked in a breath and swallowed down the wave of nausea that swept through her. 'What? Not now!'

'Why not now? This is the perfect time! Kyle has already done the promotion work in advance! You couldn't ask for better publicity.'

'I think you might be forgetting something. My father and I didn't finish the work, and it would take months to pull everything together even if I wanted to do it. Which I don't.'

Mike held out a piece of paper with numbers written on it, and stretched it out in front of her eyes with a thumb and forefinger at each end.

Lulu inhaled sharply. Her eyes refused to take in the figure with several zeros at the end of it, and her brain stopped working as she blinked several times in rapid succession.

'They want this to be a very personal record. That was what made Kyle's first book so special. This would be one single payment. A consultancy fee, if you like.'

Lulu sat back in the chair and looked at the numbers again. 'You're serious about this, aren't you? '

'Very. The foundation gets a generous charitable donation, plus income from the film and the book, and this money is yours to do with as you will. And don't tell me that you couldn't put it to good use.'

Her brain went into overdrive.

Art college? Paid for by profits from her mother's sweat and ultimate self-sacrifice? No. She could never do that. However...

Lulu groaned out loud. 'Dad would want any money from the book to go to the hospice. It desperately needs a respite centre.'

'The hospice where Tom died?'

She nodded. 'They were brilliant. This money would probably pay for most of the work. I certainly don't have any spare cash to give them.'

Then the true impact of what he was talking about hit home.

'Wait a moment, Mike. This is going too fast. I need to think about this a lot more before agreeing to anything. You know that she wrote a letter home almost every week? I would have to read through all of her papers before Kyle could look at them. That could take weeks.' She sat back and shook her head. 'I'm not sure this could work. I'm only a bookkeeper and part-time artist from Kingsmede.'

'You're Ruth and Tom's daughter. They were two of the most extraordinary people I have ever met. And so are you. You can handle it. Besides, I have an idea about how I can help you pull it off.'

'I don't like the sound of that, but go on.'

Mike smiled and picked up Kyle's book. 'Kyle is a wonderful doctor and a good man, but he'd be the first to admit that paperwork is not one of his priorities. I paid two temporary secretaries to pull together his blog and the background material for this book, and they struggled with the technical details. The second book is going to be harder. He has already told me that his notes and diaries are scrappy at best. He needs help from someone who has done this before and can work with a field medic—otherwise he won't stand a chance of doing justice to the amazing work they did ten years ago.'

Lulu inhaled sharply. 'You can't be serious.'

'It's not as bad as it sounds. Kyle was only in Uganda for nine months. What he needs is help to put his boxes of personal notes into some sort of order so he can turn around the second book before he goes back to Nepal.'

'Just putting everything in order from those nine months? That's it? Simple admin and typing?'

'That's it. Kyle's notes will form the core of the book. Your mum's records covering those nine months will add the next level of detail.'

'And what does Boy Wonder think of this plan?'

'He doesn't know a thing. I thought I had better

discuss it with you first. Why don't we go and break the happy news over lunch?'

'So he *could* say no?'

Mike looked at her over the top of his spectacles in disbelief. 'He could. But then he would miss the chance of spending time with a lovely young lady such as yourself. Most unlikely.' He smiled as she groaned in horror, and linked her arm over his. 'Can I tempt you with food and wine, madam?'

'Lead the way. I feel like I'm going to need it.'

CHAPTER THREE

LULU sat alone in the far corner of the bar and watched as the media executives circled around Kyle like vultures flying above a prime piece of food.

Mike Baxter had been instantly snatched away by medical journalists, all desperate for an exclusive interview with the bestselling author and media star who was currently holding court from his bar stool. Kyle had made a joke of gobbling up most of the bacon and the prawn sandwiches from the luxurious buffet table, much to everyone's amusement.

He was so handsome it was unfair. When he turned that killer smile on a woman it was as though he could see her secrets and make her feel like the most stunning person in the room.

But he had not even noticed that she was there.

Kyle was so totally natural in these surroundings, while she…she could just about hear the person next to her against the furious hum of chatter—if she leant close enough…

Suddenly she needed air, and a chance to think away from the barrage of broken sounds.

By squeezing past the elegantly dressed media executives by the door, who looked at her as if she was a creature from another much less stylish planet, where couture did not exist, Lulu made her way onto the sheltered decking outside the bar. The view was amazing. She leant on the edge of a metalwork table and looked out across the cold width of the Thames to hotels and the financial heart of the City of London. So many people—and they all seemed to know where they were going and what they wanted in life.

What was she doing here?

Mike was way too good at sweeping her along with his ideas. Of course she could do the basic admin on a non-fiction book. That was not a problem. She sorted out other people's financial records to pay her bills. But her mother's diaries and letters? That was a different matter.

How could she read those letters her mother had sent from Uganda in the last few months before she was killed? There had been a time when she'd used to run home from school to see if there was an envelope covered in brightly coloured stamps in the post. Not at the end. In those cold, bleak winter days she'd simply left them unopened in her father's studio, where he could have the private joy of reading them first.

She would find them later on the kitchen table. Treasured words to be savoured in a safe and warm place, far away from fighting and danger and disease.

Everything had changed on that last mission. Ruth had changed. Her mother had made a choice. And left her for the final time.

Going back to revisit that pain was not just a step into her past—it was bigger than one of the mountains Kyle Munroe was used to.

She was not ready to climb that mountain. She hadn't even reached base camp.

A gust of cold wind eddied around the wall and she shivered inside her suit. The weather had changed. Grey skies. Grey river.

She had her own life now. And more than enough work to do back home in Kingsmede. It was madness to even think of accepting Mike's offer. That connection to her past life had died with her father, and she had to move forward.

Time to go in and tell Mike that the answer was no. Kyle would have to write his book as best he could without her help. Perhaps there was another way? Was it possible for Kyle to use the diaries without her involvement and pay the hospice a fee? That might work.

Encouraged by having an alternative suggestion, she had just slipped in through the side entrance to the bar when she heard a loud, 'Marta?'

Lulu whirled around in surprise at the man's voice, and stepped back so quickly that the heel of one of her mules got stuck in a gap between the wide strips of wooden decking. As she tried to slip it back onto her foot the mule flipped up and landed on a table, happily unoccupied, clattering against the crockery. Lulu hopped over to the table to rescue her shoe before it could be held to ransom—only to find that Kyle Munroe had saved the day and got there before her.

Responding to the yelps from the waiters, Kyle gave a sudden whoop and snatched up the shoe before it could do any more damage. He shook his head when he saw who the shoe belonged to. 'I thought I recognised this rampaging item of footwear. This is starting to become a habit, Marta. Are you a secret stalker? I am honoured, of course, but should I be worried?'

'Sorry to disappoint you, but I'm here with Mike Baxter.'

He gave her a slight bow from the waist. 'How intriguing. In that case, I believe this is your glass slipper, madam. May I have the honour?'

Before Lulu knew what was happening, Kyle had dropped to his knees and her shoe was on the decking. A rough skinned hand gently wrapped around her left ankle and as though by magic Lulu found herself holding her leg in position so that Kyle could slide her backless shoe onto her foot.

As she tried to pull away, his fingers brushed the back of her calf through her thin black stockings, sending the most delicious shivers up her leg. Lulu instantly tried to move backwards to pull away from his grasp.

With the predictable result.

She overbalanced and found herself having to jerk forward to support her weight by pressing one hand onto each of Kyle's shoulders.

'Whoa! Steady there.'

Kyle was still on his knees as he looked up into her face. Their eyes locked.

And Lulu's world turned over. It was as though time had stopped and they were the only people on the riverbank. No sound except her own rapid breathing and Kyle's heartbeat. A beat she could sense through the gentle rise and fall of the muscular shoulders under her fingers.

Something at the bottom of her stomach clenched so hard she inhaled deeply.

He opened his mouth to say something, and then closed it again before giving her a half-smile with his eyes and mouth. A knowing smile.

Idiot, Lulu thought. *He knows exactly what he*

is doing and I fell for it. So why did her stomach flip again when she looked at him?

It hit her with a very heavy thud that working close to this man every day could be *seriously* bad news. Yet another factor against the whole idea.

'Thank you. Again,' she managed to get out as Kyle stretched to his full height.

To her horror, Lulu realised that the whole sordid and humiliating scene had been acted out in full view of all the journalists and media company people, who were clearly sniggering behind their glasses of fizzy bottled water. And Mike Baxter. Whose lower lip was quivering so fast he had to be biting the inside of his cheek as he guided her inside, to a quiet table at the far end of the room.

Lulu narrowed her eyes, daring him to comment, but instead he pulled out her chair and waited until she was comfortable before going on.

'I'm sorry to have left you like that, Lulu, but the editors are pressing me for an answer about Ruth's diaries. This seems like as good time as any to get two of my favourite people together.'

'Then perhaps you ought to rescue your star?'

Lulu looked towards the bar, where Kyle was surrounded by a gaggle of tall leggy girls dressed in black and clearly revelling in the moment. As she turned away a beam of sunlight broke through the floor-to-ceiling glass windows, bringing his cheekbones and dark eye sockets into sharp focus. A little too sharply into focus.

'Has Kyle been ill, Mike?'

Mike nodded. 'Mmm. Not much misses you, does it?' He leant closer. 'The boy has lost weight. Chest infections are an occupational hazard, but this one is proving hard to treat. Oh, don't worry. He's responded well to the antibiotics, but it's going to take a while. Providing, of course…' he paused for a second and looked up as Kyle sauntered in with two large steaming beakers of what smelt like tea '…I can hold him down long enough to take some rest.'

'Rest? Are you talking about me?' Kyle responded with a chuckle, before placing one of the teas in front of Lulu. 'You should know better than that by now, Mike.' He glanced across at Lulu before sitting next to Mike. 'Thought you looked a bit chilly out there, Marta. This should warm you up.'

'That's very thoughtful, Kyle.'

Mike looked from Kyle back to Lulu in surprise. 'I didn't know that you two had met before? How did that happen?'

'Oh, Marta and I are old friends. I think I should warn you to watch your back, Mike. This lady is on a secret mission of her own! I hope you don't have any precious artwork lying around the place.'

Mike shook his head. 'Whatever you have been drinking, stop now. And why are you calling her Marta? Do you have the faintest idea what this idiot is talking about, Lulu?'

'Lulu?' Kyle burst out laughing. 'Now, please—I expected a more convincing alias cover name than that!'

While Mike stared, open-mouthed, the lady in question decided to take control and casually tried her tea. 'Oh, it's all quite simple, really. Kyle and I have not been properly introduced.'

She lifted the beaker towards Kyle before taking another sip. 'Congratulations on the book launch, Dr Munroe—it seems to have been a terrific success. And also thanks for the dedication. You see, my real name is Lulu Hamilton, and Ruth Taylor Hamilton was my mother. Apparently Lulu is an African word for *pearl*. Don't you think that's pretty?'

Kyle stared in mute horror at the extremely pretty blonde woman sitting across from him and was shocked into silence.

Never in his wildest dreams—and some of them could be pretty wild, even by his standards—had he imagined for one second that the inspirational surgeon he had worked with in Uganda could have another life as a wife and a mother.

Ruth Taylor Hamilton had been capable of it. He had no doubt about that. Except that she had never once ever mentioned she had a family back home. Not one word.

Other medics had had letters and photographs clipped to the walls of their tent, and he had envied them that many times, but not Ruth.

He glanced sideways at Mike Baxter, who simply nodded, and then dared to speak.

'I had no idea.'

'Ruth left her husband and daughter back in England, and that was the way she liked it. Two separate parts of her life. She never talked about Tom or Lulu when she was on a mission. That was her way of coping.'

Kyle took a couple of breaths before looking into the face of the girl who was apparently the daughter of the most amazing woman he had ever met.

He scanned her features. The lovely full bow of her upper lip, the high cheekbones sprinkled with freckles and the stunning blue eyes below fair eyebrows. And that hair!

But he couldn't see one single thing in her face that reminded him of Ruth.

'Kyle, mate. You're staring.'

Mike's voice startled him. He was right. He had been staring—and she knew it. His embarrassment was saved only by Lulu herself.

'It's okay, Kyle. I'm used to being compared to the famous Ruth Taylor Hamilton. It goes with the territory. I gave up on being upset about the disappointment in other people's eyes a long time ago. I know that I have my dad's colouring—and I'm definitely not the heroic type. In fact, didn't you think I was a librarian?'

Mike groaned and dropped his head into his hands.

'I'm very sorry for your loss, Miss Hamilton. Your mother was a remarkable woman. I apologise if I offended you, and... Is that your phone?'

Lulu dived into her messenger bag, where her cellphone was flashing away, and quickly checked the caller ID. *Drat*.

'Sorry, Mike, I have to take this. Why don't you tell Kyle about your crazy idea? I shouldn't be long.' She went outside again.

She'd lied. The text message was from an estate agent in the town closest to her home village of Kingsmede.

A month ago, after a hard look at her finances, she had taken the tough decision to tell the local agencies that she might be interested in renting out the huge family house she had lived in all of her life.

Big mistake. Since then she had been inundated with calls on a weekly basis. Now, apparently, a family with four small children were interested in renting the house for the next twelve months. Only there was a catch. They needed to move in six weeks. They were willing to pay the full rental rate and a cash deposit. Could she be out by then?

Her fingers hesitated on the keypad. She desperately needed that rental income if she had any chance of going to art college, but six weeks was not long to finish clearing the huge house. And it would mean leaving her home just before Christmas.

Lulu pressed her thumb and third finger hard against her eyebrows.

She wasn't ready. This was what she had planned—only she had not expected it to happen so quickly.

Before she changed her mind, she quickly created a message expressing her apologies and pressed the 'send' button. A few seconds later she received a text of thanks from the agent.

Next year. That was it. She would make a start in January. In the meantime she would have to sell more paintings and work longer hours as a bookkeeper. She could do it.

Someone came up alongside her and leant on the metal railing a few feet away.

It was Kyle.

She half turned, and was about to explain that she could not possibly work on his project when he started talking in the same voice he had used at the table when he'd discovered who she was. Serious. Sincere. Intense. Adorable. A voice she could not interrupt.

'Two months ago I lost a very special patient. A little girl. Lakshmi was the daughter of my friends who run the field clinic. Most of the community are Buddhists. They refuse to kill any living creature, including the packs of wild dogs that roam the villages looking for food. Lakshmi was a typical five-year-old—bright, always laughing, and she loved puppies.'

Kyle looked out across the river as he talked.

'We don't know when she was bitten by a rabid dog, but by the time the first symptoms appeared it was too late to save her. If she had been vaccinated she might have stood a small chance of lasting out long enough to survive the treatment. She hadn't.'

He turned sideways and looked at her directly. 'I have the job of choosing who gets the vaccines and who doesn't. There simply isn't enough for everyone.' He glanced back to the bar and all of the busy, healthy people going about their lives. 'That's why I'm here today. That's why I agreed to write this book. It's not about me; it's about the patients and what they need. Every penny goes to the foundation.'

Lulu lifted her head before replying. 'And this second book will pay for the vaccines you need?'

He nodded. 'The first book paid to build and equip a complete clinic, and the paperback should pay the wages for the next few years. I have Mike and the TV company to thank for that. I'm just a jobbing medic. I like to keep things simple.'

She was not ready for the feel of his cold, long rough-skinned working fingers that meshed with hers as she clasped hold of the railing.

'Mike thinks that you are the best person to help me. My patients need those drugs. If I have to get down on my knees and beg you to help, I will. Because I cannot go back to that clinic and tell them that other children could suffer like that little girl.'

He moved closer to her, face to face, and his fingers locked onto hers, leaving his thumb to move seductively across her wrist.

'I have the feeling that you might like to see a man beg. Am I right?'

She locked onto those hazel-green eyes with their tiny creases and her heart melted. She smiled when she didn't want to.

'That rather depends on what he's begging for.'

'Quite a lot, actually. Apparently I have three

weeks to produce this book if I want to have it ready for March publication. I need all the help I can get! Ruth's diaries would make a huge difference. Ten years is a long time ago. And did I mention that I am a two-finger typist?'

That knocked the wind out of her sails for a few moments, and he could almost see the cogs in her brain working overtime before she nodded. 'Before I agree to anything, I do have a couple of conditions.'

He tilted his head slightly to one side, his heavy brows coming together in concentration. 'Fire away.'

'First, I would prefer that the diaries did not leave my home. So if you want to read them, then you'll have to come to see *me* in Kingsmede. Not the other way around.'

'Done. Next?' His eyes had not broken focus.

She faltered slightly and fought to regain control of her voice. 'I work best on my own, so it would make sense if Mike could send me everything you have from that time, plus any official records. If you can give me a week to sort it all out the best I can, then you can decide whether there is enough material to write the book. Or not. How does that sound?'

Kyle pursed his lips tight together before replying. 'A week? That might work. I'll need to dig out what I have from Africa, and I have this book tour to take care of. There is also some…well, personal stuff— But, yes.' He nodded. 'A week could work out very well.'

Her eyes locked onto his eyes, and she kept them there until he sighed and nodded.

'Okay. It makes sense to sort through the bulk of the work in one session. I'll soon find out what I am missing.' His head lifted. 'I'll do my best.'

Lulu stared him down. 'Does that mean you'll do it? You'll come to Kingsmede and work with me—starting next Sunday for two weeks?'

'Absolutely. You help me with my book, and I'll make it the tribute that Ruth Taylor Hamilton deserves. I'll be happy to shout about it from the rooftops when the time is right. So, Miss Hamilton…' He paused and squeezed her right hand a little tighter. 'Do we have a deal?'

Lulu inhaled deeply, took in the unshaven upper lip and the solid square stubbly jawline of the smiling face in front of her, and closed her eyes for a second before nodding.

'I'm not sure if I can do this, and it is one huge risk, but, yes, Dr Munroe, we have a deal.'

He brought her fingers to his lips for a fleeting second before releasing her.

'In that case—' he shuffled his jacket closed

'—it's time to get down to the really important business of the day.'

Lulu held her breath, hardly daring to imagine what he had in mind.

'I have been dreaming about a huge British fry-up for the last six months. Care to join me?'

CHAPTER FOUR

LULU popped her pins and threads back inside her sewing kit and smoothed down the seam of the printed floor-length curtain so that the repair was invisible from inside the room.

Even in the faint autumn sunlight Lulu knew every pleat of the fabric where the sunshine had faded the pattern of bright yellow overblown roses to a dark cream. Her parents had never been able to afford to replace the curtains her grandmother had bought years earlier. Not with so many windows. Not in a house this size. Even her god-mother Emma Carmichael had mentioned that surely it was time to change them before the winter.

A cool draft swirled the curtains, and Lulu suppressed a shiver that ran across her shoulders and down her back.

The unused dining room had been the obvious place to spread out the boxes of documents that

Mike Baxter had sent over, but it was a cold, north-facing room and she had not lit the open fire in years. Time to change that.

Kyle might be used to the snows of Nepal, but she wasn't.

Lulu plumped up the cushions on the chesterfield sofa next to the fireplace, then turned to face the long, narrow antique dining table that ran the length of the room. The polished surface was hidden below neat parallel rows of folders.

One individual folder for each of the nine months that Kyle Munroe had spent in Uganda ten years earlier.

Mike had apologised in advance for the fact that the storage crates of records and files were 'a tad unorganised', but she had been unprepared for just how much of a mess they truly were.

It was only when the boxes of jumbled papers had arrived on the Tuesday morning following the book launch that the enormity of the task she was facing had begun to truly hit home.

It had taken her every spare minute for the last week, but she had done the best she could.

In a world and culture where computers had been a distant dream, the original records from Uganda were a jumble of single pages of handwritten notes, record cards with patient information, copies of invoices... In fact anything and everything that the foundation had saved from the Uganda mission for the last year or so before Kyle had been flown home.

Somehow all these simple pieces of paper seemed more intimate than an anonymous computer record or database. The hand that had created these marks on paper belonged to a living human being, and each piece seemed to have picked up some of the personality of the person who had created it.

Almost like the style of an artist, there was no mistaking who had written, or in many cases scribbled, the information. She had scanned through hundreds of separate pages over the last few days to check for dates, and some personalities shone through.

Kyle Munroe, for example.

Lulu picked up an undated but signed medical report from a crate of bits and pieces labelled *'Undated'* that only Kyle would be able to place. The handwriting was strong, direct and fervent, in long straight strokes and clear, concise language. Always in black ink. The man might have looked more than a little scruffy at the tube station, but the Kyle who had created these records was focused and organised. Professional.

Mike had already told her that Kyle would be bringing his personal diary with him in person, and yet there was so much of his personality in the box she was looking at now she felt that the diary would be almost too much.

She slipped the report back into the crate and her foot connected with a dilapidated old holdall with the letters KBM stencilled onto the cover.

It did not look too different from the rucksack she had seen Kyle carrying on the underground in London. And yet she had held back from opening up this bag.

It felt too private and too personal for anyone but Kyle to open.

Of course Emma had laughed at her, and accused her of simply being scared of what she might find inside. Frightened of the unknown. Right, as always.

Kyle Munroe remained an unknown entity.

She certainly did not recall hearing the name Kyle Munroe until Mike had told her about him. Perhaps her father had known about the new medics who had been recruited in that last year when she'd been away at university? It certainly wasn't something he would have talked to her about. Those last few months were a complete mystery. Just as much as Kyle himself.

Perhaps that was why she had taken the time to read *Medicine Man* and find out more about the work in Nepal. She had even visited his website.

The man in the book looked like the same man that she had met in London. There was no mistaking that.

Except that Kyle probably did not recognise how much of his personality came through the short posts he created every week on his blog. The humour. The dedication. The charm. She could well understand why the book and the TV documentary had become so popular. He was beguiling, and yet completely true to himself.

The thought of an emergency medic like Kyle sitting next to her at this table sent unfamiliar tremors of excitement direct to her cheeks, and instantly she felt the blood rush to skin. She had felt the fluttering sensation bubble up over the past few days, until the thought of actually seeing him again face to face was starting to make her nervous.

Skittery.

And she did not do skittery.

Not normally. Not ever. There was just something about this man. She actually *wanted* to see him again. Or was it the man in the book she wanted to meet? There was only one way to find out.

And he was due to arrive in—oh, a couple of hours.

A sudden flash of colour on the other side of

the glass broke her thoughts, and Lulu looked up to see a young red setter running around the lawn to the trees.

Belle—the red setter puppy that her godmother Emma had given her for a Christmas present. Belle was totally adorable, and her constant companion, but a boisterous dog and official paperwork were not a good combination, and Lulu was happy for her pet to exhaust herself in the huge garden instead of indoors.

Lulu smiled to herself and shook her head as she watched the madcap antics of the silly animal as Belle scampered and jumped around.

She was being an idiot. Mike Baxter had asked her to sort the files and paperwork into date order and she had done the best she could. Kyle should have no problem connecting his own diary pages with the records to create the background history for his book. And the sooner that was done, the sooner he would be out of Kingsmede and she could get back to her ordinary life.

This was simply a few days of work for both of them. Nothing more. And then the hospice would have the new respite unit they needed.

Tomorrow she would start reading through her mother's diaries. Tomorrow or the next day.

As for the personal letters? Well, that was a different matter.

Lulu turned her head away from the window and caught sight of her reflection in the silvered Venetian mirror above the fireplace. She stroked back her hair behind her left ear, so that her hearing aid was in full view.

She didn't need archived records to remind herself of what had happened in Africa. She saw the direct evidence every morning when she looked in the bathroom mirror, and every evening when she removed her hearing aid and reconciled herself to the fact that she would never hear again the things she'd once loved.

She lived with the memory every single day of her life.

The doctors had told her many times that she was very lucky to have survived the mysterious tropical infection that had robbed her of her hearing in that one ear. She still had her brain, and enough hearing in the other ear to enjoy life to the full.

Her father had brought her home and sat with her for days, only leaving her side when Emma had come over. It was probably the longest period of time that they had ever spent in the same room together.

Except of course he'd known that he was not the parent she wanted to see. Lulu remembered how she'd kept asking the same question of her father, the doctors—in fact, anyone who came into her room. Where was her mother? Why wasn't her mother there? She had repeated the question over and over again. Which only showed how ill she must have been. Because her mother had been in Uganda, and that had meant she might as well have been on another planet. Out of reach.

Lulu slowly uncurled her hair back over her ear.

No. She didn't need a diary to remind her of where her mother had worked and what she had been doing all those years ago. It was staring her in the face every day.

A series of playful barks on the other side of the patio door made her smile.

Poor Belle had been neglected. Time to make amends.

This was her life now. And it was up to her to make the best of it.

Kyle Munroe swung the Range Rover slowly around the bend from the narrow lane, his eyes scanning from side to side until he spotted a small hand-painted sign attached to a stone pillar. Taylor House. This was it. He had come to the right place.

Thanks to the satellite navigation system on Mike's car, and a very helpful lady walking a dog, he had found it.

The four-wheel-drive car slowed, and he pulled

up on the wide gravel drive which circled around
the front entrance of an imposing Georgian stone
house, complete with narrow, square windows
and a fine collection of chimneys. A decorative
stone porch was lit up with bright pots of pink cy-
clamens and a pair of bay trees, either side of a
very solid-looking wooden door painted in an
elegant shade of dark navy.

His smart boots crunched into the gravel as
he swung down from the leather seat and
slowly uncurled his body into something like a
standing position.

The drive from his father's flat in London had
taken a lot longer than he had expected, and his
body was paying the price. He raised his right arm
above his head to release the tension in his neck.

Fractured vertebrae and strained ligaments and
tendons did not heal overnight. Or at least they
didn't in his case.

Maybe Mike was right. Perhaps he should cut
back on his treks to remote clinics this year and
focus on getting back into shape? His arm was
only the latest of many little accidents he had
laughed off over the years.

It was so frustrating. He wanted to be doing
more aerobic exercise, building his lung capacity.
Not less. He could not let this infection beat him.
Not this time—not ever. He would carry on taking

the antibiotics. He would clear his lungs. Persistent chest infections were a risk in his work. An occupational hazard. But it had certainly put a damper on his plans to extend the vaccine programme.

Kyle pushed his spine out, and looked up through the wide-open branches of the copper beech and oak trees above his head. Blackbirds and robins hopped from dripping branch to dripping branch.

So what if he did miss the English seasons? He sniffed and wrapped his father's scarf tighter around his neck. The people here had never seen the wild rhododendron forests in the Himalayas. Smelt the soil after the summer monsoon.

A grey squirrel scampered across the wet grass at the side of the house to scrabble among the fallen leaves. Kyle smiled. He had forgotten how much he missed such familiar things.

He looked up at the house, with its imposing neat front gardens. Open farmland spread out in all directions, broken by copses of woodland and a distant line of trees where black rooks were calling out to one another.

It was hard to believe that Ruth Taylor Hamilton had grown up and lived here, on the edge of a small country village in the South of England. Suddenly he was struck with a vivid memory of the last time he'd seen Ruth. Jumping into an ambulance just like on any other hot African morning. A quick wave to the local children and she'd been gone, in a cloud of red dust on the dirt road, before he'd even had a chance to speak to her.

And in that moment his life had changed. Yes, they had been working close to a war zone, but nobody could have predicted that only two hours later her ambulance would drive over a land mine on the way to the village clinic.

He shivered, and sniffed once more before crunching his way to the porch.

That had been ten years ago, and a world away from where he was standing now.

He had come to do a job, and part of that job was honouring Ruth—and that was what he intended to do. Her daughter need never know the terrible secret about what had truly happened that morning.

That thought made him stop and pull his hand away from the doorbell. Why had Ruth never told anyone that she had a daughter and a husband back in England? Living in this very house? He could have done something when he'd got back to London. Visited? Tried to appease his guilt in some way?

Of course he had never thought to ask Mike

Baxter about Ruth's family, and he had not kept in contact with the other medical workers when they'd been disbanded to various missions around the world.

Well, it was not too late. And now Lulu was on her own he owed it to Ruth to make sure that her only daughter had everything she needed. It was the least he could do, seeing as he owed Ruth Taylor Hamilton his life.

Just as Kyle stretched out to press the brass doorbell there was a commotion in the direction of the squirrel he had just been looking at, and he turned just in time to see a red setter hurtling through the grass. The playful dog pounced, and pounced again, but her target was already halfway up the oak tree.

Kyle chuckled to himself as he strolled around the side of the house and called out to the dog.

'Hello, there! Not much luck with that one.'

The dog froze for all of two seconds, before bounding towards him and launching herself onto his trousers, yapping and trying to lick him so furiously that Kyle could not resist any longer. He swept the dog up into his arms. Her gangly red limbs and sharp nails scrabbled for purchase, but the muddy dog's muzzle, fur and paws had already done enough damage.

A sharp whistle echoed around the drive, and

the red setter turned into a frantic bag of bones and fur that Kyle struggled to lower to the ground. This bundle of fun was in too much of a hurry, and soon squirmed her way out of his arm-lock to race away around the corner of the house.

With a shake of his head, Kyle shrugged up the collar of his coat and followed her. Perhaps the lady of the house was outside? The gravel crunched under his feet as he turned the corner, hands in his pockets. Then he stopped. Frozen into position by the scene being acted out in front of him.

On the other side of the flowerbeds and neat lawn, the woman he now knew was Lulu Hamilton was leaping from one foot to the other as she held a piece of twig high in the air, playing and pretending to fight off the loving and energetic attentions of the floppy red setter, who was jumping just as high and clearly having just as much fun as the blonde.

Suddenly content to simply watch in silence, Kyle leant on the corner of the house as Lulu threw the stick far across to the tall trees and turned back to an open bonfire.

With a single smooth and practised motion, Lulu lifted a small handsaw and cut through a branch of dry wood. Then again. Small twigs were thrown into a metal fire basket which glowed red and orange as the flames licked upwards, hotter and higher.

But it was Lulu herself who held him spell-bound.

Her arms moved smoothly back and forth, collecting large logs into a crate. The glow from the burning embers shone back from her face in the fading light, and her blond corkscrew curls were scrunched back into a rough ponytail held away from her forehead with a striped bandana.

Her fine high cheekbones glowed pink with spontaneous energy and a sense of natural warmth and fun as she vigorously rubbed the dog's head before throwing another twig. The dull grey suit was gone. Replaced with faded jeans and a padded jacket over what looked like a man's check shirt.

She looked confident, self-sufficient, and totally in control in this space.

The Lulu Hamilton he had met in London had been pretty and intelligent, but also guarded and ill at ease with the grandiose plans that Mike had come up with.

This version of Lulu Hamilton was mesmerising.

She had such a sense of smiling joy in her simple task. She looked like a woman who was accustomed to chopping her own wood, content with the company of a mad dog and a burning fire.

One thing was certain. He had been expecting to meet a pretty blonde in a suit. What he saw instead was a stunningly beautiful woman with a style and body that no man could ignore. Which probably meant trouble.

This was Ruth's daughter, and he had a responsibility—perhaps even an obligation—to make sure that she was cared for.

He could have looked at her all day and not regretted it for one moment. Except the dog had other ideas, spotted him, and decided that it was time for Kyle to join in their game.

Lulu threw the last of the parchment-dry ancient newspapers her father had hoarded onto the fire, brushed down her gloves, and stood back to watch the white-hot flames flare up into the damp air.

This part of her garden looked out over the farmland leading down to Kingsmede, and she could just see the lights from the thatched cottages that were scattered around the old church with its familiar steeple. It was a dreamy scene of soft lights and faint misty air.

She loved this view. This was the only home she had ever known and the only one she ever wanted. Even if it meant renting the house out for a while when she was at art college, it would be here for her to return to.

That truly did make her smile and, picking up one final branch, she turned to see what new garden creature Belle had found to torment.

And stepped back in startled shock and surprise.

The most handsome man she had ever seen in her life was leaning against the wall of her house, only a few feet away from where she was standing. Watching her in silence.

Was she dreaming?

It was Kyle Munroe. The same man whose paperwork she has just been reading. Only this version of Kyle bore no relationship whatsoever to the skinny young medical student in a pop group T-shirt in the colour photos from his book. Her stomach decided to behave like a tumble drier. Skittery did not even come close.

She might have thought that Kyle was attractive that Friday afternoon in London, but this man was from another planet.

The dirty long hair had been expertly cut. Clean shiny brown layers lay flat around his ears, swept away from his cleanshaven face so that the prominent square jawline and the long, straight nose were the first things she saw.

Without his beard the square jaw was so angled it might have been sculpted. But it was his mouth that knocked the air out of her lungs and had her clinging onto the log pile for support. It was a mouth made for smiling, with slight dimples either side.

The corners of those amazing eyes crinkled slightly, and Lulu realised that he had been watching her as his smile widened. Despite the real fire close at hand, the warmth of that smile seemed to heat the air between them. It was so full of genuine charm and delight that she knew, no matter what, that this was the smile that would stay with her whenever she thought of Kyle.

Only now, at this moment, the smile was for *her*. Her heart leapt. More than a little. And just enough for her to recognise that the blush of heat racing through her neck and face were not only due to the flames warming her back.

At this distance in the fading light, his eyes were dark, scrunched up by the deep crease of his smile as he strolled across the grass towards her, Belle scampering around his legs. She knew that those eyes were mostly hazel brown, with flakes of forest-green, but for now all she could see were a pair of heavy dark eyebrows.

If she had ever imagined that Kyle Munroe could not possibly be more attractive than the

photo on the cover of his book, then she had been
wrong. The top two buttons of his pale blue shirt
stretched open as the fabric strained to cover a
broad chest, revealing a hit of deeply tanned skin
and more than a few dark chest hairs.

He was stunning.

Oh, no. Do not stare at his chest. Just don't.

The pounding of her heart was simply because
she had been taken by surprise—that was all.
Trying desperately to regain some kind of control
over feelings that were new and raw, Lulu was
suddenly aware that she was standing there with
a tree branch still in her hand, and casually she
moved forward to throw it onto the fire before returning his smile and turning to meet him.

Luckily he spoke first, his voice low and husky
in the quiet garden as he smiled and reached out
his hand. Lulu shucked off her glove and felt
long, cold fingers clasp hers for only a few
seconds before she released him. The callused
surfaces of his fingers rasped against the skin on
the back of her hand. Gentle, but firm. And surprisingly very different from the handshake they
had shared in the London taxi cab only a week
earlier. Now his fingers seemed to linger and slide
over hers, as though they wanted to maintain
contact for as long as possible.

No complaints from her end on that point.

'Miss Hamilton. Sorry if I startled you. I tried the front door, but your burglar alarm found me first.' He nodded towards Belle, who was snuffling around their feet. 'Apologies for being so late. Not used to the traffic. But it's great to be here at last. Do you mind if I make use of your fire?'

In the fraction of a second it took Kyle to stroll over to the fire and stretch out his hands towards the flames, inappropriate and totally crazy thoughts about the effect those same fingers could have on other parts of her body flitted through Lulu's mind.

No need for flames on this side of the fire. *Oh, dear*.

Lulu inhaled deeply, straightened her back, and managed to find her voice at last as she smiled back at him. 'Please do. It *is* feeling chilly. Mike warned me that your timing was flexible, so no problem. And please call me Lulu.'

Belle sidled up to Kyle and tried to push her nose into the side pocket of his trousers.

Lulu laughed out loud. 'You'll have to excuse Belle. She is totally spoiled and has already worked out that pockets are designed to hold treats.' To prove the point, she reached into her own jacket pocket and pulled out a dog biscuit, which Belle pounced on. 'Let's get inside before she notices we're gone. How does hot coffee sound?'

'It sounds wonderful. I've left something in the car. Back in a moment.'

Kyle jogged back to the Range Rover, scooped up the bakery bag and got back just in time to follow Lulu onto a wide stone patio with garden furniture which led to a dark green door at the back of the house.

Lulu turned the handle and swung the door wide as she shucked off her boots in the long porch. 'Please go through. Welcome to Taylor House.'

CHAPTER FIVE

KYLE walked past Lulu into what would have passed for an art gallery rather than a kitchen.

The riot of bright colours was so totally unexpected he almost recoiled at the sensory overload. The contrast between the cold grey garden and the exotic chaos of colour was shocking, and he turned back to his hostess with an expression of awe.

'Wow! This is like no other kitchen I've ever been in. Are you the artist?'

Lulu smiled across at him as she unbuttoned her jacket. 'Not guilty. My father spent a lot of time working on abstracts. He loved colour and hated change.' She shrugged her shoulders before filling the kettle, determined to settle her jangled nerves with the familiar world of her kitchen. 'I could have painted over it, I suppose, but it is distinctive.'

Lulu watched Kyle step slowly around the

kitchen, grinning and peering closer at the images on the walls, before picking up a purple pottery pig dotted with bright splodges of yellow and red. Long, delicate surgeon's fingers moved over the model, lovingly caressing the little pig, and Lulu gulped down something very close to jealousy.

When he finally looked up at her his face was alive with delight, and an energy so totally unexpected that she almost dropped the cups she was holding when he spoke.

'Please don't paint over it. It reminds me of Nepal. Brilliant! I love it.' He stepped away to loll against the wall, so that he faced Lulu as she busied herself with cups and coffee. 'I can see now how you came to the art world. No orchids, though. Do you have a special room for those? I had been wondering if you forge them yourself or have someone else do it for you?'

'Orchids?' Thank heavens for a change in the subject. 'Oh, of course—the gallery! Yes, I confess, I forge them myself. I'm surprised you remembered that.'

'Yellow orchids. How could I forget? Please— let me help you with that.'

Kyle took the tray from Lulu's hands before she could protest, and carried it over to the old pine kitchen table where she had been sorting through family photographs.

'Are you sure you can manage? I see the plaster cast is missing. How is your wrist?'

A rapid shake and flex of his strapped-up arm was his answer. 'It still needs work. Luckily Mike has an automatic car I can borrow for the week, so I am mobile—but thank you for the thought.'

He flashed her a half-smile, his wide mouth creaking into a lady-killer grin, practised over the years to ensure any female within his target radius would melt into radioactive decay in seconds.

Something strange happened to Lulu's stomach and her legs felt a little wobbly. No lunch. That was it. And the warmth spreading from her neck to her face was just the natural result of being taken by surprise. She tried to hide it by gathering together the photographs as Kyle continued.

'Speaking of Mike—I come bearing gifts from a certain patisserie which apparently you are fond of.'

'Gifts?' she asked, trying not to sound too keen, despite the bag of hares that had started kickboxing inside her stomach.

'Chocolate cake. As some form of compensation for the terrible mess my paperwork must be in.'

He held the bag out towards her, and a scrumptious smell wafted into the kitchen.

'I can assure you that your paperwork cannot be any worse than Mike's—but he does know my weaknesses.'

Lulu pursed her lips and gracefully accepted the bag from Kyle's fingers before bowing slightly in his direction. She could take a bribe now and again. And it gave her something to do with her hands, which were starting to crease the photographs with their pressure.

'That was very thoughtful. Won't you sit?'

She stepped back and flicked on lights as Kyle followed her to the table.

'Thank you,' he replied with a shrug, 'but my old bones need to stretch. Not used to sitting in one place for very long. This really is a lovely room. Oh, I'm sorry. I'm obviously disturbing your paperwork.'

Still spread out across the pine table was the rest of the jumble of old photographs, mostly black and white, and several storage boxes.

Lulu glanced back towards him from under her eyelashes as she unwrapped the deep, dense dark chocolate ganache cake. 'I was looking for a few family photographs you could use in the book. I always intended to put them into albums, but somehow never got around to it.'

'Well, I know that feeling. My dad has crates of my stuff stashed in his apartment. It took me the best part of an hour to find what I had saved from Uganda.'

Aware that Kyle was leaning one handed against the dresser, she gestured towards the kitchen table.

'Some cake, perhaps, to go with your coffee?'

'Thanks, but the cake is for you. I'm not used to rich food.'

She watched as he perched on the edge of the table, only a few feet away from her, so that his long legs inside smart jeans could stretch out in front of him. He looked so at home. Casual. Relaxed. And clearly oblivious to the fact that his taut thigh muscles were straining against the fabric of the trousers.

Lulu felt herself blushing, the heat starting around her neck as she turned away to pour the coffee. It was certainly time to deflect this conversation. By moving back to her chair at the table, she was able to cradle her mug of coffee and divert his attention.

'How do you feel about being back here in Britain, Kyle? Away from the clinic in Nepal?'

He turned so that he could see her side view.

'You must miss them enormously.' Lulu replied. 'Your patients, I mean.' And kicked herself for being so tongue-tied.

How did he do it?

She was not normally so clumsy. She had never, ever felt so awkward and tongue tied and adolescent around a man in her life. And this was *her* kitchen! How was she going to survive two weeks of having Kyle Munroe in her life?

If Kyle had noticed her awkwardness he did not show it as he smiled across at her, raised his coffee with one hand and waved his injured wrist in the air a couple of times. 'Ten weeks ago I was making my way through ice and snow down to the treeline when our ambulance was caught in a rockfall. We all slid out more or less in one piece. Now I'm sitting in this delightful kitchen in warmth and comfort. I consider myself very fortunate to be here. My patients are in excellent hands—but, yes, I do miss the people. Very much.'

Kyle reached forward and picked up one of the photographs from the table. A slim, handsome blond man in brightly coloured clothing was standing next to a large abstract painting, his arms wrapped around the shoulders of two other young men.

All three were laughing into the camera through bearded faces.

'Is this one of your relatives? He certainly has your colouring.'

Lulu casually accepted the photo from Kyle's

hand, as though she had not seen it before. 'Oh, that's my father—Tom Hamilton. There were a couple of exhibitions of his work when he was at art school. Those lads with him in the crazy hippy gear are some of his mates from university. Apparently it was a wild time—and, no, I don't know what they got up to.'

There was a knowing chuckle from across the table.

'Mike told me that he had passed away. I'm very sorry. He must have been fun to live with. Was he a forger, as well?'

Lulu flashed a glance into Kyle's face, anxious to see if there was a hint of irony. Finding a genuine smile in place, she was totally disarmed by it. Of course there was no way that he could possibly know how hard living with Tom Hamilton had been.

'Not at all. Only the genuine article.' She smiled.

She was horrified to see her hand tremble just a little as Kyle focused the full heat of his attention on her. If only he was not dominating this small space! And so close to her. She had to regain control. Time to get down to business. The dining room. She could make sure that there was plenty of space between them in that room.

She lowered her beaker and scooped up the

prints back into the box. 'Do you want to start work tonight?' she asked casually, trying to sound as though it was something she did every day. 'I've tried to collate everything Mike sent me from the official records into some sort of date order, but there are quite a few things where I have no clue. It's all laid out in the next room, any time you are ready.'

He leant his head slightly to one side. 'Absolutely. Although I do need to ask a favour of you before I see exactly what I have got myself into.'

'A favour?' Lulu frowned and half closed her eyes in pretend seriousness. She sat back in her chair. So he had an agenda after all. 'You are welcome to ask. After all, you did bring cake. Please go ahead.'

He turned his body so that he was directly across the table from her now, the full strength and force of his energy and personality focused on her small face. Burning into her skin. Demanding her total attention.

'I admired your mother very much. I meant what I said in my dedication. Stitch was an inspiration to me. Which is why I want this second book to be as much her story as it is mine. And I need your help to do that.'

Kyle gazed across at her and smiled as he

stared into pale blue eyes the colour of a winter sky.

'When Mike introduced us last week I don't think I was very polite. For that I apologise. I could try and blame jet lag, but I always have been a bull in a china shop. I truly had no idea that Ruth had a daughter. So…' He clasped the back of the wooden chair, the knuckles of both hands white with the pressure. 'Here is my problem. I want to be back in Nepal in two weeks. Is there any way I could persuade you to spend more time with me so we can turn this book around in less than ten days? Please? Just tell me what I need to do to convince you, and I'm all yours.'

Lulu sat back in her kitchen chair and stared open mouthed at Kyle, who simply slid his delicious bottom onto the seat of the chair. She had certainly not intended to give this book one hundred percent of her time for the next two weeks. On the other hand, the sooner they finished the work, the sooner Kyle would be out of her life and she could get back to her normal quiet existence again. Which was what she wanted, wasn't it?

Drat this man for making her poor brain spin. Ten days? It might be possible, but there was a lot of material to work through.

'Do you know what you're asking?' she finally managed to blurt out.

Kyle waved one hand and shook his head. 'No clue. Like I said, I am a two-finger typist and proud. I can just about manage e-mails, and a few paragraphs a week, but everything else is hand-written. Pathetic, I know, but that is the truth. Which is why I need your help.'

And then he played his winning card. He turned on his best smouldering smile. Full beam. Maximum strength.

That was it. She couldn't hold it in any longer.

Lulu burst out laughing. 'Do you actually get results with that type of pathetic pleading about being a two-finger typist?'

'Well…yes. I don't find many girls who turn me down.' His face twisted in mock horror. 'Was it truly that bad? I haven't had complaints before.'

She nodded.

'You really thought that I was pathetic?'

She nodded.

Kyle collapsed back against the kitchen chair. 'Crashed and burned. Maybe I *have* been out of this country too long.'

He shrugged and smiled at her apologetically. Suddenly his bravado disappeared in a puff of smoke, along with his playful attitude. The shadows under his eyes and his prominent cheekbones seemed to be even more pronounced without the permanent smile. Or perhaps that was the low-energy lightbulbs that Lulu had fitted to save on the electricity bill?

The change in him was so sudden it was as though someone had turned a light off inside his body. He looked exhausted. And probably was.

She decided to take pity on him and bring that smile back. The room seemed a lot darker without it.

'Don't worry; you haven't lost your touch. Your male ego is still intact, but there are two very good reasons why your plea was doomed from the start.'

Leaning her arms on the table, Lulu leant forward and looked into that beautiful strong and masculine face. His hazel eyes were totally focused on her, and for a second she resisted the urge to look away from the intensity of that gaze. The long dark eyelashes fluttered slightly. She was only inches away from him, and in that small space there was so much unspoken feeling that she almost sensed he knew what she was going to say before the words formed.

'First, I enjoy sorting out other people's paperwork so much that people actually pay me to be their bookkeeper. I like it and I'm good at it. You don't, and apparently you aren't. Fact. You are going to find it hard to keep up with me.'

She let that sink in, and for a moment—just a moment—saw something change in Kyle's face. Perhaps a glimpse of a suppressed smile? As though he was unaccustomed to having someone agree that he did not excel in all areas of his life?

Suddenly she needed an excuse so that she did not have to look at him, and she busied her hands with a completely unnecessary rearrangement of the beakers on the tray as she topped up his coffee. 'Secondly, I already know that you are only doing this book so that your patients can get the vaccines they need. Not for some personal ego trip or to fund your new yacht.' She flicked her eyes up to his. 'You don't have a yacht already, do you?'

Kyle bit his lower lip and shook his head emphatically in reply.

She paused, aware that she had his full attention. 'That's why I had already decided that *if* there is time—' she held up one hand for emphasis '—I *might* be able to help you with any typing you need to finish the book. It has nothing to do with you,' she added quickly. 'Just a sound business decision. The hospice needs those funds as soon as possible.'

He gazed into her face, slack-jawed, and smiled with a sincere warmth she had only glimpsed before. A real smile of genuine feeling that simply took her breath away.

He meant it. For that fraction of a second it was as though she had been given the key to look inside him and see the real Kyle beneath the façade. Outward bravado disguised a man capable of very deep feeling. And it surprised and intrigued her.

This was not the media star she had seen in London. This was more the man whose personality had shone through in his first book. She had misjudged him.

He truly was amazing.

Kyle raised both hands in submission, leant across the table, and with a grin as wide as the kitchen door said, 'Thank you.'

'You are most welcome. But don't thank me quite yet,' Lulu replied as she stood up and tugged down on the hem of her shirt to straighten it. 'You do still have to do the work. Even if it is one paragraph at a time. Using two fingers.' She looked across at him and gestured with her head towards the corridor. 'So, Dr Munroe, since you are in such a hurry to get back to the ice and snow, are you ready to get started?'

'After you. I'll bring my coffee and… Wow!'

Kyle stood at the door to the dining room, his beaker of coffee in one hand and his mouth open as he looked in shock and awe at the boxes and folders spread out across the long table.

'Perhaps we should start this tomorrow,' he whispered, and pretended to slink off back down the corridor on tiptoe to the kitchen.

Lulu shook her head and, throwing caution to the wind, hooked her hand around an elbow and drew him into the narrow room.

'It's okay. Don't panic just yet. Let me show you what I have been working on this last week.'

Lulu pointed towards the first set of folders as Kyle stood next to her, their arms still linked.

'Nine folders. One for each month that you were in Africa.'

Carefully sliding her arm out, with all of the casual *this sort of thing happens every day* nonchalance she could muster, Lulu was free of him. She licked her dry lips and picked up the first dossier.

'Mike Baxter sent over crates of official records. Most of it was a jumble of single pages, but I tried to focus on anything and everything which links to a specific month. I hope that's okay?'

She watched as Kyle flipped open the file and started scanning down the top page before chuckling out loud. 'Okay? It's amazing. You know, I actually remember that.' He looked up into Lulu's face and hit her with that heart-stopping smile. 'We were expecting a delivery of dried mango. Only there was a mix up at the warehouse and we were all eating macaroni for three months. It was wonderful—that pasta probably saved more lives than I did.' With a shrug, and a self-deprecating wistful grin, he looked down the full length of the table before giving a low whistle. 'Did you really do all of this on your own?'

'It wasn't too bad. But I haven't opened your personal rucksack. You will want to do that on your own.'

He winced in reply. 'Do I get any special dispensation at all for the fact that I had just left medical training and was totally green? Did you make *any* sense of it at all?'

'Some. Although there is also a box of memorabilia which you need to sort out. Did you bring your diary with you?'

Kyle patted his jacket pocket. 'I've been reading it on the book tour and trying to join the dots. Not easy. Ruth's diary is going to have to fill in a lot of gaps.'

Lulu stood at head of the table and watched him move down the line, smiling and then more sombre as he picked up one file and then another, before pressing both palms flat against the table and sighing out loud.

'Well, this seemed like a good idea a week ago. I now have ten days to relive all these memories of people and places and create something meaningful. Seeing it all spread out like this makes me realise just what I have got myself into.'

He turned to one side and gave Lulu a short bow. 'You've done a fantastic job. Truly. I would never have been able to do this in the time. The scope is the problem.'

'May I make a suggestion?'

There was a chuckle from the tall man as he ran both hands back from his forehead through his hair in a totally natural and spontaneous gesture, clearly oblivious to how charming he looked. 'Anything. Please. I'm begging you.'

'It might make sense for you to work through one month at a time. Perhaps take one month a day and write up everything you can think of, based on your notes and the background material. That way you can trigger your own memories about each month you were there.'

Lulu picked up an old airline boarding card and waved it around. 'How did you travel there, for example? Mum took a flight, then drove a truck from the city. Could you use that as a way into the diary? How you felt when you arrived at the camp? What the journey was like? Why you chose to go there in the first place? That's what I would be interested in.'

Kyle looked at her in silence for a few seconds, his brow creased with concentration.

'That…is a brilliant idea. Thank you. It would be an excellent place to start. As to why I went there in the first place…' He started to shake his head with a sigh. 'Well, that is a story in itself. Do you really think the readers would be interested? I had my reasons, but they are personal.'

'Of course,' Lulu replied in a gentle voice. 'And that would be your decision. I did get the impression from Mike that they were looking for that personal touch, but if it is painful…and some of it is bound to be painful…then they have to understand that there are boundaries. I know I couldn't write about—well, how my mother died, for example. I just couldn't.'

Her eyes were so fixed on the rug that she hardly noticed that Kyle had come over to her, until he reached out and took her hand, startling her with the gentleness of his touch.

'And I am an idiot for talking about my pathetic problems when you and your family paid a much greater price. I am sorry for being so insensitive.'

The sincerity and affection in his voice was so overpowering that for once Lulu felt like giving in and confessing everything about her confused emotions.

'No need to apologise. I know how this book ends, remember? But I don't know how it begins.' She smiled back at him now, and broke the tension between them as she slid her hands from between his. 'Are you really a two-finger typist?'

He grinned and wiggled his long, slender fingers in the air. 'I lied. Two fingers each hand. If I take my time and use the delete key a lot. Fear not—I won't be disturbing you or your family with ferocious hammering of the keyboard. Speaking of which—' he looked around the room '—when I do I meet the other Hamiltons? Are they out for the evening, or gone into hiding in fear of the wild man from Nepal?'

'The other Hamiltons?' Lulu asked, confused for a second before she realised what he was saying. 'Oh, you mean the rest of the Hamilton family? Well, you have just met them. Belle is a complete flirt, of course, but she doesn't hog the bathroom or leave her laundry on the floor. We get on very well.'

There was silence for a moment before Kyle replied in a low voice. 'You and Belle? That's it? You live in this big house all on your own?'

There was so much concern in his voice that Lulu frowned before replying. 'Yes, that's right. The Taylor family have lived here for generations. And I have no plans to change that.'

A chiming clock on the mantelpiece sounded out the hour, and Lulu turned to it in disbelief. 'Have you seen the time? I am so rude. You must be exhausted. Shall we meet back here at, say, nine tomorrow? That gives you time to get settled in and decide on how you want to work.'

'Nine would be great. Of course I don't want to disturb the rest of your evening.' He hesitated, then drew a piece of paper and a pen from his pocket. 'I shall need directions to the nearest hotel. Can you recommend some place fairly quiet?' He tapped his pen twice on the pad before frowning, which only seemed to increase the depth of the creases around his eyes. 'The media company have been fantastic, but it would be great to have some time to catch up with my sleep and not worry about waking everyone with my coughing in the night.'

Lulu brought her eyebrows together and stepped closer. 'Coughing? I thought you were taking antibiotics?'

He nodded before replying with a sigh. 'This infection likes me too much. The new drugs are helping, but it's going to take a while. Probably about ten days, actually. Strange coincidence that, isn't it?'

'Um…very,' she replied, with a nod of understanding. 'And who said doctors make the worst patients?

'Anyway, I thought you would be staying up with the media execs at Lanston Manor.' Lulu raised her nose high in the air and wagged her fingers in the direction of the front door. 'It's about ten miles closer to London and qualifies as our local stately home hotel. Much more suitable for you celebrity authors.'

Kyle snorted, and replied with a belly laugh that echoed around the quiet high-ceilinged room and was immediately followed by some serious coughing. A dry cough. Rasping, and so alarming that Lulu leant forward in concern as Kyle bent over from the waist for a few seconds before he recovered and pressed one hand to his chest, which he rubbed furiously before shaking his head at her.

'No more jokes like that, please. A stately home? I don't think so. The foundation is paying my hotel bill, not the media people. Every penny I spend on fine dining and fancy beds will be coming out of the Nepal budget. A room above a country pub will be fine.'

Lulu hissed in air between her teeth. 'I see. In that case turn right at the end of the lane and the Feathers is at the end of the village, next to the river. My godmother runs the place and the meals are excellent. But quiet? On a weekend? That could be a problem.'

Kyle nodded and sighed out loud. 'I'm used to late shifts, and it is within walking distance. The Feathers is the place.'

And then he looked straight at her and smiled *that smile*. The kind of smile that bored deep into her body like a laser beam of heat and combustion.

In that life-changing instant her deep frozen heart melted into a pool of warm smooth honey that flowed throughout her body, filling it with the most delicious kind of longing and delight. Fuelled by the presence of this man standing in front of her, her treacherous heart leapt in her chest, yearning, simply yearning for him to touch her and stay with her as long as possible. The sensation felt so sweet and startling that it had to belong to another woman. Not her. Not plain old country girl Lulu Hamilton.

Which was probably why the next words that came out of her mouth were so startling that someone else must have said them.

'There is one other alternative. Would you like to stay here with me? I have plenty of room.'

CHAPTER SIX

KYLE'S eyes widened and his jaw dropped.

That's incredibly generous of you,' he replied, with a touch of disbelief in his voice, 'but I couldn't possibly stay here. What would your boyfriend say? And then there are the neighbours. Kingsmede strikes me as a very small village. Thank you for the offer, but I think I've already caused enough problems for you.'

And that really did make Lulu stare at him.

The idea was not *so* very ridiculous. They could work more effectively, and the house was large enough that they would not be crowding each other. He was the one who wanted the book completed as fast as possible so he could get back to his life.

And he was worried about *her* reputation?

'Well, someone has a very high opinion of themselves! Prepare yourself for a shock. You are not as irresistible as you seem to think you are. Yes. You.' She pointed with one finger as the totally gorgeous man in front of her dramatically reeled back and pretended to be horrified at the revelation. 'And, just to make it clear, I may not have a boyfriend at the moment, but I do have a self-contained ground-floor studio.' Lulu busied herself with knocking the edges of some paperwork into straight lines so that she would not have to look at Kyle. 'My father had a bathroom installed there when he was ill, and I spend most of my time working in the studio anyway.'

Satisfied that the edges of the folders were aligned in parallel rows, she raised one hand towards the ceiling. 'You would have the whole of the first floor and the family bathroom to yourself. And as for the neighbours…'

She looked up and returned Kyle's gentle smile.

'Fifteen years ago there used to be a stream of medics arriving at all times of the day and night for free board and lodging. Plus, you are helping to build a new unit at the hospice. That gives you quite a few bonus points on the respectability scale; so don't worry about my friends in the village. Unless, of course…'

Her voice faltered, and she tilted her head before giving Kyle a cheeky smile.

'Unless? Please continue. I am finding these revelations so informative.'

'I was just going to say…unless you don't think that you will be able to resist my feminine charms for a whole ten days, Dr Munroe. Is that what you are worried about? Or should I expect your girlfriend to arrive any time soon?'

The smirk on his lips told her everything she needed to know.

'No girlfriend. Or wife. Only the press—who have been following me around like bloodhounds for the last week. *They* might find our arrangement a little too cosy to ignore. I can just imagine the headlines.'

'Good point,' she acknowledged. 'Leave that to the Kingsmede Neighbourhood Watch team. They can be a little over-protective. The press won't know what's hit them.'

A giggle escaped from Lulu at the thought of what would happen if city photographers started digging for saucy gossip about her from the lunchtime drinkers in the Feathers. Her godmother had been known to twirl a wicked rolling pin when she had to. Now, *that* would almost be worth seeing.

Kyle still looked uncomfortable, his knuckles white as they pressed against the back of a hard dining chair.

'What do you say, Kyle? Do you want to spend the foundation's budget on tiny bottles of fancy shampoo and a gargantuan buffet breakfast? Or would you like to stay here, where you can enjoy the peace and quiet you need and risk your saintly reputation being ruined for ever? I'll even ask Belle to let you pet her now and again, as part of your relaxation therapy.'

She paused.

'Unless there is another reason why you don't want to stay here? I don't like this quiet thing you do. It worries me. So out with it. I've started to come around to the idea. What's holding you back?'

What was holding him back?

The question echoed around the room and reverberated inside Kyle's mind.

For the last ten years of his life he had pushed himself hard. Very hard. Accepting every mission that Mike Baxter could find, regardless of danger or distance.

Jungle. Desert. High mountain ranges.

Driving himself day after day in a relentless search for something—anything that would prove that he could make a difference to the lives of people whose only hope for healthcare was the foundation.

And he *had* made a difference. He knew that. Time and time again.

So why was it not enough?

In all of those long, exhausting years he had failed to prove to the only person who truly mattered that Ruth Taylor Hamilton had not died that day in vain.

Himself.

He should have been in the ambulance that morning when Ruth had diverted onto a road set with landmines to avoid an army convoy.

He should have died that day. Not Ruth. Not this amazing woman's mother.

And he had been working every hour of every day since to convince himself that fate had not made a terrible mistake.

Except that fate in the form of a publishing contract had decided to play a cruel trick and bring him here. To the last place on the planet that he had ever expected to see. The house and family that Ruth had left behind. So that he could write about the worst—and the best—nine months of his life.

Suddenly aware that he had been staring at his hands, he looked up and locked eyes with this woman he barely knew and who was so full of surprises that he could hardly keep up.

What would she say if she knew the truth?

Would she still be inviting him to stay in her family home?

Or did destiny have another trick up its sleeve? Was Lulu Hamilton the final piece in the puzzle of how he could finally put the past behind him?

He had never walked away from a challenge in his life.

And yet standing now in this quiet room, looking at the thick woollen socks of a girl who had lost her family, he felt as though he was standing on the edge of a precipice looking out over an unknown land.

A land where his heart was in control of his head.

He lifted his head to gaze in silence at the blonde only a few feet away. Both of her hands were pushed hard down onto slim hips. Several corkscrew curls had escaped from her bandana to create an aura of softness against her pink-flushed cheeks and gleaming eyes.

Blue the colour of a winter sky. Fire and ice.

She looked absolutely mesmerising.

He was going to need a guide before he could hope to venture into territory this dangerous and hope to make it through to the other side.

Her eyebrows came together in fierce concentration when he lifted his head to speak, as though she was willing him to reply with some profound and very logical explanation.

'I do have one question before I make my final decision. What are you planning for dinner this evening at Taylor House?'

'This evening?' Lulu replied casually. 'Oh, the usual. Home-made Shepherd's pie and green beans, followed by local cheese and crackers. All washed down with supermarket red wine.'

His eyes fluttered closed, his chest lifted, and his right hand pressed fervently over the place where his heart should lie as his mouth puckered into a contented smile.

'My private fantasy has come true,' he whispered. 'Miss Hamilton, I would he honoured to be your house guest.'

And then he spoilt the enchanting illusion by stepping back, shrugging the tension from his shoulders and rubbing both hands together briskly.

'How soon can we eat?'

Lulu punched her pillow and turned over in the narrow bed. Then turned over again, twisting her duvet around her body, trying to find a comfy spot. And failing. Tugging the pillow over her head in disgust, she was forced to finally admit defeat and throw off the overheated covers.

Even her normally faithful Belle had tired of the constant tossing and turning and headed off to find a quieter spot at some point during the night.

She had slept in the studio many times and never had any trouble getting off to sleep before. What was the matter with her? Or should that be *who* was the matter?

The very idea that a man like Kyle Munroe was sleeping in her spare bedroom only a few yards above her head was enough to keep her head spinning.

How did he do it?

Was this normal?

Did he create chaos and upset wherever he went, like some smiling and benevolent tornado? Because he had certainly worked his magic in this house.

Had she been secretly sending out some kind of subtle message that said, *Please come into my home, which I have been guarding against intruders for the past ten years, and why not bring my pain from the past along with you? And if you wouldn't mind paying me some attention while you are, that would be nice too.*

What had she been thinking?

Sitting at the dinner table the previous evening he had been the perfect house guest, filling her kitchen with laughter and funny stories about his life in Nepal while he relished every mouthful of her food. It had been a pleasure to share his plans for the clinic, fired by his passion for his work and for people he lived with.

Perhaps that was why her dreams had been filled with soft-focus images of the cover photograph of Kyle from his first book blended with the real-live Kyle who had sat on her kitchen floor to play with Belle while she washed the plates?

Of course he was fascinating.

Of course he was handsome and charming and totally worthy of any schoolgirl crush.

Of course she wanted to get to know him better.

And of course her foolish heart should listen to her head. In ten days the cough that had interrupted their meal more than once would be gone, Kyle would be on a flight back to Kathmandu, and the tornado would have moved on, leaving her to clear up the devastation left in its wake.

Throwing her pillow onto the floor in disgust, Lulu slid her legs off the bed and opened her eyes a crack. Early-morning daylight filled the open-plan studio through a gap in the fabric blinds covering the floor-to-ceiling windows.

She sauntered down the hallway to the kitchen, stretching her arms above her head. And stopped, frozen. The kitchen light was on. Lulu swallowed down a fleeting thought of burglars before sighing out loud.

Her house guest. Of course. Kyle must be an early riser.

Groaning inwardly, because she was not prepared to speak to the live version of the man from her dreams, Lulu lifted her chin, inhaled deeply, and strolled into her kitchen as casually as she could.

It was empty, but the back door was slightly ajar, and she stepped outside. Kyle was standing on her patio in bare feet, stretching his right arm high above his head, then his left arm, turning his neck from side as a gentle cough racked his ribcage. He was oblivious to the fact that as he did so the crumpled T-shirt he was wearing had risen up above the waistband of a pair of bottom-hugging jeans, exposing a healthy expanse of tight abdominal muscles.

Lulu had never appreciated the full meaning of the term *'six pack'* before that moment, and it was going to be a long time before she forgot it.

Bells, whistles and several years' worth of unused female hormones sounded off inside her body, and she would have been quite happy standing there for a lot longer with a smirk on her face. The damp, cold morning was a blessing for her burning neck and cheeks. He was edible. Top to toe.

Except that out of the corner of her eyes she

saw a red setter come hurtling around the corner of the house, and within seconds her delicious treat was ruined as the dog jumped up into Kyle's arms and was twirled up into the air, barking and barking in delight as he scrubbed her fur with his hands.

Lulu's heart melted.

He liked Belle. And Belle adored him. She was doomed.

Then Kyle turned around and saw her.

She could only gawp at the tousle-haired man as his eyes widened and shifted a little lower, before he twisted his mouth as though he was biting the inside of his cheek.

Lulu glanced down at what she was wearing and raced back inside the kitchen, her face burning again—now with embarrassment. Flowery flannel capri-length pyjama bottoms combined with a spaghetti strap top which barely covered her chest might be suitable for Belle—but for male house guests? In cold weather?

She had a sudden vision of what she must look like and almost squealed in horror.

Luckily her fleece jacket was hanging behind the door, and she quickly shrugged it on before turning back to face Kyle with a fixed smile as he threw a dog toy for Belle.

'Good morning. Did you sleep well?'

The Greek god covered a yawn with one hand, and then ran his fingers through what passed on him for bed hair. Totally relaxed.

'And good morning to you. I hope I didn't wake you up with my coughing? I had forgotten how hard it is to sneak downstairs in old houses with creaky floorboards.'

'I didn't hear a thing,' she replied truthfully. *Especially since she had not fitted her hearing aid yet.* 'Was Belle a pest?'

'Not at all. She was excellent company.'

It was only when he shuffled into a chair and dropped his head back, eyes closed, that Lulu noticed the dark shadows and pale skin and gasped.

'Have you been up all night?'

He gave her a wry smile as a reply. 'Not *all* night. I managed a few hours' sleep.' He must have noticed the concern in her voice. 'Kingsmede must be having a calming influence on me. I usually get by on a lot less. Why are you shaking your head like that?'

'I distinctly recall Mike Baxter telling you to rest.'

'Advising me to rest,' he replied, then startled her by reaching out and running his long slender fingers through her hair. She froze, unable to move and frightened to speak, until Kyle held up a long white feather with two fingers and waved it in front of her face. 'I think your pillow has sprung a leak.'

She smiled back, the tension broken. 'Old pillow. Old feathers. Thank you.'

'No problem,' he murmured. 'I am available for any kind of personal grooming duty you might have in mind for the next ten days. Just snap your fingers and I'll be there.' And with that he clicked his thumb and third finger together and locked eyes with her at the same time. 'Especially if you wear your hair like that.'

Her hand instinctively moved towards her head, which was a mess of unruly damp-frizzed curls, but he clasped hold of it instead and ran his thumb along the back of her knuckles.

'Don't change a thing.'

Then, releasing her hand, he pushed himself to his feet before she could reply.

'Since you made dinner yesterday, the least I can do is prepare your breakfast. I can see buttered toast and marmalade on the horizon. All you have to is sit where you are, looking gorgeous.' At this point he waggled his eyebrows a couple of times. 'And help me with the one question that has kept me awake in the night.'

Lulu took a breath. A twister had truly hit her little house in Kansas. 'Well, put like that, how can I resist? What would you like to know?'

Kyle had turned to the refrigerator, and she had to strain to hear what he said, but the words penetrated her heart and mind like a bullet.

'You've read your mother's diary and her letters. What did she say about me?'

Lulu sat stunned for a few seconds, and waited until Kyle was cutting bread before focusing on what he was saying.

'Please don't think I'm arrogant, but studying has always come easily to me. Perhaps too easily in many ways. Medical school was hard, but I never felt challenged. When the chance came to go and work for the foundation I thought I was going to change the world. One country at a time.' He waved the breadknife in her direction, as though conducting an orchestra. 'Yes, I know. Young and foolish. Green as grass. All of my life to that point I had been told how clever and gifted I was. And here was my chance to do some good with all of that talent.'

Butter and preserves appeared on the table, then Kyle pressed both palms flat on the pine surface. 'I was an idiot. And it took Uganda to prove just how wrong I was. About everything.' A wry smile creased his mouth. 'I've just spent an hour reading through the records from my first month at the mission, and I am totally embarrassed by how unprepared I was. Ruth and the rest of the crew made sure that the patients didn't suffer, but looking back now it must have been a lot of extra work for them, with precious little gain.'

Lulu tried to focus on the movement of his hands as they set the table, willing him to continue, delaying the inevitable. She dared not look into his face.

'I'm not going to hide any of this. If the media company expect this book to be all about how great I was, then they are going to be disappointed.'

Lulu looked up in concern. 'You are going ahead with the project, aren't you? I've already told the hospice that they can expect a donation.'

His hand stilled, and he stared down at her with pain in his eyes, brows twisted together as he replied in a low voice, 'Of course I'm going ahead with it. I made a commitment to my clinic, the foundation and your charity. I keep my promises. I'll finish the book—it's up to them whether they publish it or not. But it would make a difference if I thought Ruth believed that I had achieved something worthwhile by the end of those nine months.'

She breathed out a sigh of relief as he offered her a plate of crisp toast, but did not speak until he had taken a bite from a thickly buttered and marmaladed heavy crust. Watching his face contort with the simple pleasure of good food made her words seem foolish and pathetic.

'I wish I could answer your question, but there is a problem.' She waited until he was chewing before picking up her own piece of toast. 'You see, I have never read anything she sent home during the last year of her life. Not one word. So I have no clue what she thought about you. Or me. Can you pass the marmalade, please?'

His face paled and his toast hit the plate.

'Please tell me that the papers are not burnt or lost somewhere,' he said, in a decidedly less confident voice.

She shook her head. 'All the documents that came back from the mission are on the table in the dining room. I'm talking about the private letters and diaries. My dad kept everything safe while I was at university. They're all here, bundled up inside an old suitcase in my dad's studio.'

Kyle breathed out loudly, then stared at her. Hard.

'And you have never read them?'

'No.' She swallowed down her toast with a slug of hot tea. 'It was simply too painful after she died, and my dad never discussed it. He knew that I wasn't ready.'

Kyle sat back in his chair and nodded slowly. 'I can understand that. Are you ready now? I *would* like to see her diaries, but it has to be your decision.'

I don't know. And I don't want to read any of it, but I know that I have to. 'As far as I know the diaries from her previous missions had a lot more to do with the day-to-day running of the clinics. That's where we need to start.'

'Are you okay with that?'

Lulu lifted her head and sniffed. She had known this moment was coming for the last week. No surprise. She simply had to face it and do the job she had promised. That was all.

'Yes. Those diaries will be fine. In fact, I can go back to the studio right now and find them for you.'

It was as though Kyle sensed that she had made her decision and they were back on track, and his mood seemed to lift immediately.

'Your studio? Ah. The Kingsmede centre of the art forgery trade.'

'Shush! I thought you said that your lips were sealed.'

She shot him a wide grin, and all the sunlight he had ever wanted was back in the room. Grey gone. This was what he needed. Wanted. This ray of sunshine. Perhaps that was why he heard himself saying, 'I've never been to an artist's studio. Do you mind if I make yours the first?'

Her mouth opened, then closed, before she answered him with a faint smile. 'If you like. There is not much to see at the moment. Come this way.'

Kyle glanced at Lulu as they strolled along the wide staircase side by side. She was clearly oblivious to how tantalising a prospect it was for any man to be walking behind her, and he decided to enjoy the moment for as long as possible.

She glanced sideways at him, as though a hidden sensor had detected that she was being ogled. 'Before I forget, you can look forward to restaurant food for dinner tonight. My godmother has organised a welcoming committee in your honour at the Feathers this evening.'

'Excellent. I look forward to meeting your friends.'

'Before you get too comfortable, I should give you advance warning that Emma is responsible for raising funds for the hospice. I'm sure some cunning scheme has already been launched to make the best use of you while you are staying in Kingsmede. A naked doctors calendar, perhaps? The topless fire crew were very popular last year!'

She stopped outside what looked like a

bedroom door and leant closer. 'Prepare to be dazzled.'

Without waiting for an answer, Lulu gently turned the brass handle, casually swung open the wooden door and stepped through.

It was the complete opposite of what he had been expecting.

Instead of the chaotic blend of startling bright colours that decorated the rest of the house, the walls and ceiling of this space were painted in a brilliant white. Light flooded in from the plain glass windows illuminating one single picture hanging over a large white fireplace. It was a life-size portrait of Ruth Taylor Hamilton, and it was so life-like that the impact of seeing her again knocked Kyle physically backwards.

He was so stunned that it took a few seconds for him to notice that Lulu had already started rummaging around inside a tall cupboard.

'Was this where your father worked?' Kyle asked, gasping in a long breath. He pressed both of his palms flat against the wall behind him, so that he could take in the entire space and regain his control.

'This was his studio for as long as I can remember. I used to play on a battered old sofa that was in the corner there, whilst he painted. In the winter we would light the fire and make toast whenever we felt like it. And sometimes we'd paint together, or just chat. This was always a happy room. He loved working here.'

'You must really miss him.'

Lulu looked into Kyle's face. 'I do. I know it sounds ridiculous, but after he died I used to come in here almost every day and just smell the paints. I only needed a whiff of linseed oil to bring him back to me. There are so many good memories of this place. I had some magical child-hood moments here.'

Kyle Munroe moved closer to gaze at Ruth's portrait for a moment, hands on his hips before leaning forward and staring more closely at the signature.

'T. D. Hamilton? Is that your dad?' he asked, his voice low and business-like.

Lulu came and stood next to him, smiling up at the brightly coloured acrylic portrait of a very pretty young woman dressed in white against a landscape of blues and greens.

Her mother's energy beamed out from the canvas, her warm smile captured for eternity.

'He rarely did portraits. My mum was the ex-ception.' She looked across at him and was sur-prised to find him still staring at the picture. 'Do you like it?'

He nodded. 'Very much. It's so lifelike. Ruth

was a lot older when I met her for the first time, but there is no mistaking who it is.' He paused and turned towards her, so that they were only inches apart. 'There is a lot of love in that painting. He must have been extremely talented. Again, I am very sorry for your loss.'

Lulu looked into his face and saw something so intense that it took her breath away. A raw pain that brought tears pricking into her eyes. Just when she'd thought she had no more tears left to give.

'Are you also thinking of someone close? Lakshmi—that was her name, wasn't it?' she asked, her voice calm, low, as objective as she could make it.

He moved forward and gently wiped away the tear from her cheek.

His fingertips felt textured and rough on her skin. A soft smile lit his face from within. 'It was. But there have been so many. Friends who went to climb mountains and never came back. People I tried to help and couldn't. I get to know my patients as well as any doctor. It always hurts when you get there too late to make a difference—when clean water and a few simple medicines would have…' He swallowed hard. 'You are very intuitive, young lady.'

Then the moment was lost, and the big boyish grin came back like a mask and he closed down.

'You never forget them, you know. The patients who don't make it.' He shook his head. 'Far too many.' And with a final glance at Ruth's portrait, he squeezed Lulu's hand tight before turning to stroll out of the room.

'Kyle. Wait a moment.'

He whirled around to turn back into the room—only she walked faster and their bodies collided softly, surely, linking together so naturally that they seemed destined to be together.

It was pure reaction that drew his hands tight around her waist to steady her—but pure attraction that held them there for a lot longer than necessary. The only thing that he could concentrate on was the depth of the ice blue of her wide eyes and the gentle rise and fall of her chest against his shirt as their breathing became heavier. Hotter. He could have stayed there a lot longer, fuelled by his need to be close to this amazing woman, but Belle started barking outside, and in that instant he glanced over at the portrait over the fireplace.

Ruth. And Lulu was her daughter. What was he doing?

Instantly he relaxed his grip.

'Steady, there. Why did you want me to wait?'

Lulu swallowed down the trembling dizziness that was rapidly taking her down the road to heartbreak. This was only their second day together, and Kyle was already turning out to be far more of a temptation than she ever could have predicted.

Every time he touched her it was becoming more and more difficult to look away and remind herself that he was only here to work. That was all. Except that if she had stayed in his arms one more second there was a very strong possibility that she would have wrapped her arms around his neck and done something very foolish.

And very regrettable.

'The suitcase is on the top shelf. Could you lift it down for me, please? It is rather heavy.' She pointed to the tall cupboard, delighted to have something to distract her from the bulk of him standing so close that she could smell the tang of his body. 'Then it's time to get back to the toast. You're going to need a lot more carbohydrate before you start reading all that.'

Kyle did not hesitate. 'And coffee. *Lots of coffee*. Now, tell me more about the Feathers. What exactly should I expect this evening?'

CHAPTER SEVEN

'I THINK you might have warned me that the entire village were going to turn out to see me last night! The children were a riot.'

'Not the *entire* village,' Lulu replied, as she waved to the occupants of a car as they hooted their way past them down the lane leading from Kingsmede towards Emma's cottage. 'Some of the babies stayed home with their fathers. You have to admit that the junior school had done a wonderful job with the welcome banner over the entrance. And the photographs should go very well with the question-and-answer session you gave in the bar. Especially that one with Emma's nieces in it.'

Much to Belle's disgust, Lulu stopped walking, leant closer, and brushed her hand over a stain on Kyle's jacket. 'I did tell you that Pip and Katy were high on cake and ice cream *before* you hoisted Pip onto your shoulders. I'm sure Emma can get that out.'

'No problem. I did notice one thing in the bar last night.' He pushed both hands deeper into his trouser pockets. 'Everyone I spoke to wanted to know about my clinic in Nepal, and how I was going to raise this money for the hospice, while you stayed in the background. Seeing as you are the reason I am in this village, I'm surprised that Emma didn't make *you* stand on the bar as the star of the show. Any explanation for that?'

Lulu shook her head. 'She knows that I don't like being the centre of attention. That's all. And of course they now have a new celebrity—you were a great hit! And it was your first public outing. They will soon get used to you.'

'I'm not so sure about that. The personal tour of the hotel and restaurant was brilliant. The book signing I could understand. But the autograph hunters? They were… different.'

'Ah…' Lulu hissed, drawing air through her teeth. 'The Bennett sisters. They run the newsagent and sweet shop on the main street. I admit they were a little over-enthusiastic about their new line in celebrity autographs, but when you reach their age any excitement in the village is welcome. Although, to be fair, it was *your* idea to offer to give them each a personal medical exam before you left town.'

Kyle shook his head with a sigh. 'I only want

to make sure that your friends know how hard you've been working on this book. That's all.'

'Thank you for that, but I'm fine.' She paused and stared ahead before she spoke again, in a clear, confident voice. 'I know who I am, Kyle. I have done since I was sixteen. I live my life the way I want to and I'm quite happy to stay in the background.'

He turned and looked at her in silence—really looked at her, as though weighing something up in his mind. Then he startled her by presenting his strapped arm while keeping a tight control of Belle with the other.

'May I have the pleasure of escorting you to the home of Mrs Carmichael on this pleasant afternoon, Miss Hamilton?'

Lulu opened her mouth to give him a snarky reply, glanced at the half-smile on his face, and hesitated for a few seconds before nodding and threading her free hand through the crook of his arm. 'How gallant, Dr Munroe.' She looked up at the sky, where faint sunlight was trying to break through the heavy grey clouds. 'That would be splendid. If you can take the gossip, so can I.'

'Great. Because the cat is well and truly out of the bag. Your secret identity as an orchid painter has been revealed to the world. Forger or not, now you can tell me the truth about that painting you were struggling with in London that day. I want to know all about life as a famous artist.'

And with that he started strolling contentedly down the lane, under the shade of the great beech trees, with Lulu by his side, leaning into his shoulder.

'Famous artist?' She laughed. 'If only that were true and I had the income to show for it. The gallery owner on the South Bank was at art school in London with my dad, and he knows that I love painting flowers. Especially wild flowers.' She stopped walking, pulled back on his arm and gestured to the roadside, where a tiny clump of bright red flowers was almost hidden in the grass.

'Wild red poppies. They look wonderful with Herb Robert—those pink flowers higher up on the bank. Or even pink blackberry blossom and red rosehips.'

She leant in again as they continued walking and Belle became impatient to get going. 'Of course it is autumn now, so I have to rely on photographs that I took in the springtime. Primroses, daffodils. Wonderful spring flowers. I just adore them.'

There was so much joy and pleasure in her voice that it was infectious, and Kyle could only chuckle in reply as he pretended to scan the bushes. 'I don't see any wild yellow orchids! Can you point them out to me?'

She laughed out loud. 'Not down this particular lane.' Then she play-thumped him in the arm. 'It was a commission from a client who wanted a particular shade of yellow. A one-off. My usual work is a lot smaller and more detailed.'

'Why small? Why not just paint the flowers larger?'

'Because I paint life-size. That's why. No delusion. And here we are.'

Kyle felt her slide her arm from his, and the loss had already hit him before she bent down to pet Belle.

'Now, be a good girl for Uncle Kyle. Aunty Emma does not want you in the cottage—you're far too big and boisterous. And make sure that Uncle Kyle tells you a nice story all about his time in sunny Africa. See you back at the house.'

With one final finger wave she took a firmer grip on her cake box and strolled towards the small row of thatched cottages where Emma lived, leaving Kyle holding a dog lead attached to a mad beast who had just spotted ducks on the other side of the river.

Kyle Munroe sauntered slowly down the wet muddy footpath which ran along the riverbank, heading downstream away from Kingsmede, while Belle scampered on ahead. The light drizzle had turned into heavy rain and they were both drenched.

Which was not such a good idea with a chest infection. Right on cue, he choked on that dry cough he had learned to live with over the last few weeks.

Time to face up to his current dilemma. He was going to have to make a decision soon about the last chapter of the book.

The more he came to know Lulu, the more he realised that the pain of the truth would be one more thing for her to carry.

And *he* would be the one piling on the burden. How could he do it? How could he add to her problems? That would be the exact opposite of what he intended. He should be doing everything he could to make life easier for her.

Lulu was not only Ruth's daughter, but also a very special person, with an approach to life he had never seen before. Grounded, certainly. But something else. Something that had intrigued him from the first day when he saw her on that tube train. Lulu possessed an inner serenity, a self-contained calmness which acted like a lure. Drawing him to her.

In a few quiet moments last night in the Feathers, he had noticed the way she smiled at everyone she met without any hint of pretension or false emotion.

This was Lulu with the people who knew and cared about her as a valued member of their extended family, and she clearly cared about them in turn. Was it the village? Or was it Lulu herself?

Kyle looked around him at the picture-postcard thatched cottages that lined the footpath opposite the river. Their lovely gardens were bursting with late roses and apple trees heavy with fruit. Kingsmede and Lulu would always be linked together in his mind—she was just as much part of this village as the square-shaped ancient stone church, the Feathers and the winding river.

Perhaps Lulu's inner peace came from knowing who she was and where she wanted to be? Her sense of place. Was that it? It would certainly explain why he was lacking that perspective on his own life.

An hour later, just as Kyle was about to turn back towards the village, he glanced up and saw the very woman he had been thinking about walking towards him—only this time in heavy weather gear, carrying a golf umbrella.

He started jogging towards her, whistling for Belle as he did so.

She gingerly stepped towards him with a smile.

'Everything okay? I thought you were with Emma?' Kyle spoke calmly, matter of fact, trying desperately to suppress his concern.

She shook her head. 'We are both fine. It's you I'm worried about. I have an extra waterproof here for you, and warm gloves. This rain is getting heavier, and I have no intention of completing your book on my own. You, sir, are soaked.'

With that she pulled a long parka from her bag and passed it to Kyle, who thanked her and shrugged it on over his head.

She looked around. 'What have you done with my foolish dog? Has she run back home on her own without you?'

'Drat—she was here a second ago. You go that way. Meet back here in a few minutes.'

Lulu walked as fast as she could in the pouring rain, but it still took five minutes to reach the footpath that ran down the length of the river.

And there was Belle.

The ducks had been nesting on an island in the middle of the river that was swollen from weeks of autumn rain. The foolish dog had started swimming out to them, barking, only to find that the downstream current was too strong for her.

Lulu watched in absolute horror, calling Belle's name, as her dog was slowly carried down the river by the power of the water. She was a strong dog, but inexperienced. The river widened in a few yards, and would probably be shallow enough for Belle to stand up in as long as she didn't panic.

But, to her horror, Belle started barking, out of control, and fought the current—which meant that she was swimming away from the shallows and into the fast-flowing deep water.

Lulu started to jog along the riverbank, calling to Belle to come to her. Come to the bank and be safe. Belle had been her constant companion since her father died. Nothing could happen to Belle. It simply couldn't. Even the thought of it was starting to give her palpitations.

Suddenly the ducks and swans lifted from the river, and Lulu turned to see what the problem was.

Kyle had started wading out into the water, and the fast-flowing river was already up to his thighs.

Without discussion or argument, Kyle simply crouched down in the water and waited until Belle had been carried to him by the current. He grasped her around the middle and hoisted the sodden animal over his right shoulder into a fireman's lift. His arm held on tight to her scrabbling legs as she wriggled like a fish from the waist.

Slowly, slowly, so as not to drop his precious cargo, Kyle turned around in the river and waded through the water and onto the riverbank.

'Oh, thank goodness. Are you both okay?' Lulu managed to get out, as Kyle bent his knees and allowed Belle to take her weight on her own feet as she slid from his shoulder. Lulu wrapped her arms around Belle, then repeated the process with Kyle.

They were rewarded by a full-body shower as Belle tried to shake herself dry.

'Oh, thanks a lot. Ingrate. Come on you two. *Home*.'

Lulu wandered back into her kitchen, where Kyle was stretched out, half-perched on a kitchen chair, back against the wall, sipping a steaming beaker of tea. His hair was still tousled from the rough drying it had received from the kitchen towel.

'She'll be fine now. Dry, clean and happy. Let that be a warning to us all about the dangers of chasing ducks across a fast flowing river.'

Kyle snorted. 'Looked to me like she was having the time of her life.'

Lulu grinned back, and fluttered his eyelashes at him. 'She was, but thank you all the same. Belle means a lot to me. You are officially our hero. There may be a medal.'

'I don't feel like much of a hero.'

'This is a small village. Standards are low. We'll take what we can get.'

Kyle saluted her with his drink. 'Faint praise,

but I will accept it nevertheless. What made you decide to come looking for us?'

Lulu sat down opposite him. 'Emma and I were concerned when the rain started to get heavier.' She raised both hands in surrender. 'I know that you are the medic around here, but your coughing seems to have improved over these last few days. Of course that was *before* you decided to take a swim in the river . The future of Kingsmede as a spa town depends on your good recovery.'

'Well, I would hate to let the tourist trade down. Did Emma enjoy her cake?'

Lulu sniggered her reply. 'Loved it. Especially the sickly sweet icing, bursting with artificial colours. All washed down with *two* glasses of pink champagne.'

'Is it her birthday?'

'Not exactly. Long story.'

He cocked his head to one side. 'I have nothing else to do this evening except relive trauma in the African bush while Belle is snoring in front of the fire.'

'True.' Lulu sat down opposite Kyle. 'Have you ever heard of the Memory Book Project? It's one of the techniques they use at the hospice, and Emma asked me to help with hers. Basically the person creates a record of the life they have lived, their family history and customs, who their friends and relatives are. Anything they want their family to remember about them when they are gone.'

She smiled up at Kyle, and was humbled by the look of admiration on his face.

'Our generation is used to technology. Photographs, videos, digital images. Not so ladies like Emma. Photographs were expensive before the war. So these memory books can take their place.'

'So, *have* you helped Emma with her memory book?'

Lulu nodded. 'I made some copies of the only photograph Emma has left from her wedding. It was taken outside Kingsmede church. And she started telling me about her wedding day.'

There was a pause as Lulu looked out of her kitchen window at the lashing rain. 'It was a warm sunny morning. The whole family were walking back to the cottage where she still lives today for the wedding breakfast, and they had just reached the river when her new husband, Frank, slipped off his smart shoes and waded into the water with her in his arms, twirling her around and around, laughing and laughing, until they were both dizzy—with happiness and love. So much love.'

Lulu felt tears pricking at the corners of her eyes.

'He died of a brain haemorrhage. He was her soul-mate. Her one and only. They would have been married fifty years today.' She smiled across at Kyle, only he was focusing on the table, his brows tight with concentration.

'And I am babbling. Sorry.'

'You're not babbling. I'm so sorry for Emma's loss. She's a wonderful lady and deserves your love. What's more, you have just given me a clue to what I've been looking for!'

He clutched hold of her fingers, eyes bright, shining with energy and excitement.

'What you are talking about is a kind of scrapbook. A collection of pictures, thoughts, memories. Snapshots from the past that come together to make a complete story. Is that how you see it?'

Lulu simply nodded, bowled over by the change in Kyle. He was transformed. 'Yes. That's exactly right.'

'*That* is how my poor medical brain works. I see those separate parts, but I have a problem putting them all together in a long piece of writing. What if I write the book in that way? Memories. Maps. Photographs. All the separate pieces. I can do that, and I would enjoy it. What do you think? Would it work?'

She blew out, and made the mistake of looking at him—and was instantly swept away with his new-found passion and enthusiasm. A picture began to form in her artist's mind's-eye. 'A bright African collage. Oh, yes, I think it would work. It would work very well.'

'It's brilliant! You are brilliant.' And before Lulu knew what was happening Kyle had leant forward and kissed her heartily on the cheek as he clasped a tighter hold of her hands in his.

She pulled back her hands and smiled, trying to break the tension, but then moved back to rub Kyle's hand.

'Your hand is freezing! How stupid of me. You need a hot shower. I would never forgive myself if you caught a cold. Come on—off with your wet clothes.'

She was rewarded by the kind of seductive grin most girls would melt for.

It worked.

'Well, that's the best offer I've had all day.'

'It's the one and only offer you're going to *get* all day. Here. Let me help you.'

Even with Lulu's help it took five minutes to peel off Kyle's jacket and sweater over the strapping on his left wrist. He was drenched, and Lulu could see him shivering despite her central heating.

She grabbed a thick bath towel and came back into the room just as his shirt hit the floor. She leered, and despite her best intentions she lusted. Then lusted a lot more.

Kyle Munroe had the chest, shoulders and arms of a male model.

Not an ounce of spare flesh covered the well-defined body.

Lulu enjoyed a few more minutes of pleasure as he bent to remove his boots and socks, stretching the spectacular muscles across his broad shoulders, revealing an amazing expanse of taut, smooth skin with a covering of dark hair that was tantalising even before she noticed the waistband of his black underwear.

The reality of his work and life were only too evident from the sharp division lines between the dark brown of his lower arms and neck and the faint tan on the rest of his upper body. He looked as though he had plunged his head and arms into brown dye, and Lulu could not resist laughing out loud at the thought, helping to break up the sensual awkwardness of their situation.

'Well, *someone* has been working out!'

Kyle flexed his right bicep and heaved his boot to his chest in a joky demonstration of his weight-lifting skills, before lowering it back to the tiles.

'You need upper-body strength for the ice

climbing. Not that I've done much of that recently. I've been way too busy at the clinic.'

Lulu gasped with horror as she gently touched one finger to the end of a jagged scar that ran over one shoulder and down his back. Smaller white lines were scattered across both of his arms, and across the bicep of his right.

'Is that what climbing does for you?'

He sniffed, not wanting to break her touch on his sensitive exposed skin. The delicious sensation of that single light fingertip had already set his heart racing and his body pulsing.

'A lifetime of accidents. Usually in the middle of nowhere. Pakistan—now, that was remote. When you have to stitch up your own skin one-handed, you can bet money the wound will be somewhere it's hard to reach.'

'Do you really expect me to believe that?' She looked at Kyle for a moment before exhaling loudly. 'You're *not* joking. Madness!' And then she looked at his strapped wrist. 'Can you manage in the shower?'

She was rewarded by a huge grin. 'Exactly what kind of service are you offering, Miss Hamilton? Do artists receive special training to help in shower emergencies?'

'I was thinking of turning the water on for you, Dr Munroe, and finding you a plastic bag to cover your strapping. Possibly even finding you an extra towel. But of course that would be far too comfortable for a macho hero such as yourself.'

He looked around the room in pretend amazement. 'What did I say?'

'Had your chance. Blew it.' She pointed to the stairs. 'Shower! I'll get your wet clothes into the washing machine, and hope they don't disintegrate with the shock of hot water and detergent.'

'Can you use extra fabric softener?' Kyle asked in a pleading voice. 'I have such sensitive skin.'

Twenty minutes later Kyle walked into the dining room looking far better than any man had the right to, and Lulu's poor treacherous heart performed a double somersault with a twist.

She still had not recovered from the topless incident.

Vigorous use of the coal scuttle and log basket had created a pathetic excuse for her overheated cheeks and burning neck, and the open fire was already burning bright in the fading light, its orange-and-white flames licking up the chimney, creating shadows around the room. A single lamp glowed gently in the corner, and Lulu could hear the sharp crackling from her seasoned apple and beechwood logs.

It was the hair, of course. Any man would look

edible with that length of tousled please-run-your-fingers-through-me curly hair. She could offer him a comb, but on second thoughts she decided she liked him just the way he was. Delicious.

He caught her staring, and glanced down at his clothing with a quizzical look, stroking the fine fabric of his Italian sweater. 'Will I pass?'

'For the moment. Perfect timing. The hot chocolate is almost ready. And help yourself to cookies.'

Kyle bent down to scratch Belle's head a couple of times, before collapsing down onto the sofa, his legs stretched out towards the open fire—where Belle had already dragged her fleecy bed before settling in for a snooze.

'That's better. I feel almost human again, and a lot warmer. That fire is gorgeous. Come and sit next to me and talk about Kingsmede. Anything you like. Tell me more about you and Emma.'

Lulu smiled as he patted the sofa cushion next to him and raised his eyebrows. She filled two beakers with hot chocolate from a saucepan on the hearth, and perched on the end of the sofa as far away from him as possible.

'As you wish, great hero! You drink. I talk. Deal? Was that a nod? Emma is so much more than my godmother. She gave me a refuge when

I needed one. And then she gave me a job and a career! How about that for starters?'

'I need lots more details. Please carry on.'

'Okay. You already know that she has always lived in the village. She was born here. Emma knows everybody.'

Kyle blew on his steaming beaker to cool it marginally before taking a sip. 'So you were actually born here, as well—in Kingsmede? Mmm. This is good. Cinnamon?'

He took another sip as Lulu nodded. 'Cinnamon and a pinch of chilli. And, yes. Apart from a brief spell at university, I have lived in this village all of my life.'

'Wow! I didn't think that was possible any more. I have no idea how many flats and houses I lived in with my folks.'

Kyle frowned, as though trying to estimate how many homes he had used as a hotel over the years, before catching Lulu's eye.

'Please carry on. Emma has lived here all of her life. Got it. What happened to make her your refuge?'

'What happened was the annual arrival of the homeless and usually penniless waifs and strays from whichever far-off land my mother happened to be working in at that time. "Oh, just turn up," she would offer. "Tom will give you a warm welcome and somewhere to stay. Plenty of room in Taylor House.'"

Lulu stopped, and realised that she had been gesticulating with her spoon.

'And so they came. Sometimes we picked them up from the airport; sometimes the docks. And still they came. At first it was the occasional nurse or medic who needed somewhere to rest and recuperate before going to see their family or start their next assignment. Then a few families started to appear. Perhaps a woman and a child who we had to take straight to the nearest hospital. Later whole families. Trying to escape a war zone.'

She stopped as Kyle sipped, his attention totally focused on her face.

'You know what's it like to arrive in a strange country where you don't know the culture. Often you can't speak the language, and the weather is something like today. Or colder.' She shook her head. 'The words *culture shock* do not even come close. But we managed. There was always something we could do, and they truly *did* need our help. And sometimes they carried letters home from remote clinics.'

'So what went wrong?' Kyle asked, still totally focused on her.

'Drink up!' she said, then she nodded. 'Yes, it did go wrong. I remember having a bad day at school.

I was studying hard for my exams. Oh, I loved school, but I had been teased. Again. I just wanted to go home and cry. Only when I got home…'

'You found a house full of strangers?' Kyle filled in the gap.

'The crying and yelling was so loud that I had to shout to ask where my dad was. I followed the loudest of the screaming to my own bedroom, where my dad was sharing out my clothes to the children who were running around him, throwing all my precious books and clothes around the room. My project work for school had been torn and trodden on.'

There was a pause as Lulu played with her cookie.

'I was seventeen years old, and suddenly, at that second, I just stood there, with the chaos and noise all around me, and realised that I wanted a normal life. With two parents and a home I could call my own.'

Lulu's voice dropped an octave as she brushed crumbs from her trousers.

'I know that sounds incredibly selfish, but I just picked up my books and stuffed them into my school rucksack, with the few clothes that I had left, and walked to Emma's cottage.'

Lulu brought the plate of cookies to the sofa, so that Kyle could finish them off, and sat down next to him, her legs under her, both hands wrapped around her beaker.

'I slept there every night for the next fourteen months. In exchange I worked in the hotel kitchens and learnt how to prepare accounts. Oh, I came here to the house every day, and checked that there was food in the cupboards and that the bills were paid and all the practical stuff. I didn't just leave Dad to cope on his own. Then I went to London to art college for a while. Apart from that, I lived with Emma.'

'What changed? What made you go back home? Did he start turning folk away?'

'Oh, no, he would never have done that. Never.'

Lulu sat back against the cushions and suddenly felt queasy at the smell of the hot milk.

'Lulu?'

'My mother died. But you already know all about that.'

She suddenly found the contents of her beaker quite fascinating.

'How did you find out? Did someone phone?'

'Mike Baxter came to see me at the college. All he could tell me was that her ambulance hit a land mine.' She looked up. 'He told me that it would have been very quick, but I always wondered how accurate he was about that.'

Kyle reached out and meshed the fingers of her

left hand with his chocolate-smeared long
fingers.

'It *was* instant. I'm so sorry—it must have been
very hard to hear like that.'

Lulu sat up straight and took a breath. 'I moved
back the day after Mike came to see me. As for
Emma… She had a blood-pressure problem last
year, but the Emma you saw in the Feathers is not
so different from the Emma she has always been.'

'Then I'm glad to have met her. Do you miss
them? Your parents?'

Lulu paused for a moment, before swinging
out her legs.

'I think I've talked far too much for one afternoon. Now, we really should get back to work. At
the moment I am up to month four, and things are
not going too well….'

Then Kyle's hand was on her waist, the gentle
pressure turning her towards him and closer, ever
closer, so that they were looking at one other on
the sofa, their faces only inches apart. His hand
moved to her cheek, his thumb on her jaw as his
eyes scanned her face back and forth.

'Don't lock me out. Please.' His voice was
low, steady. 'Trust me, Lulu. Can you do that?
Trust me?'

CHAPTER EIGHT

BEFORE she could answer, his hand moved to cup her chin, lifting it so that she looked into his eyes as he slowly moved his warm thumb over her soft lips. Side to side. No pressure. Just heat.

She felt his breathing grow heavier, hotter, and her own eyes started to close as she luxuriated in his touch.

Then he snatched his hand away to cover his mouth as a dry cough shook his upper body.

'Sorry. I think I swallowed some of your Kingsmede river water,' he gasped in a hoarse voice. 'Complete with duck feathers.'

He slid to the edge of the sofa and stretched up before reaching for his boots. 'Do you mind working later? Your wonderful crazy hound just cost me five hours.'

Lulu hissed at him as Belle lifted her head and thumped her tail hard against the floor, before settling down again, nose on paws in her comfy dog bed.

'Perhaps you should take the rest of the evening off? Being a hero must be *so* exhausting!'

There was a long sigh before Kyle replied. 'True. We *are* ahead of schedule, and I need to call my family some time today.'

'*Family* business? Now you really *do* have me intrigued.' Lulu rummaged around on the coffee table until she found a familiar book with a distinctive cover, and she waved it in front of Kyle's face before he had a chance to reply.

'I liked your book. But I do remember thinking that there were a few things missing. No mates, no ex-girlfriends—not even an anxious mum waiting at home.' She laughed. 'She must be very proud of what you have achieved.'

She looked up at his face and was taken aback by the sadness he displayed for a few seconds, before the smiling grin went back on.

Lulu broke the silence, her voice low to disguise her thumping heart.

'Sorry. I didn't mean to pry. It really is none of my business. Besides, you might spoil the surprise for the next book, when all will be revealed!'

Kyle answered by reaching out and taking

Lulu's hand in his, startling her. He slowly splayed out each finger as she tried to clench her hand into a fist, and stared down at her palm.

'Long lifeline.' He looked up into her eyes. 'No, Lulu. I didn't leave a broken-hearted mother back in London. In fact, it was more like the other way around. She broke mine. As for girlfriends? Well, nothing serious.'

She didn't dare to breathe or speak at the sadness and regret in this precious man's voice. A sadness that almost overwhelmed her—a sadness that made her want to wrap her arms around him and share every ounce of heat in her body.

'After my parents' divorce my mother remarried and moved to Australia with her new family. There was nothing for me there. I'd finished medical school here in England, so I took off to the most remote part of the world I could find.'

His eyes moved up to hers just long enough to check for understanding.

'Yes. I ran away to Africa to escape my parents' messy divorce. As for being proud of me? Well, I don't know about that. I get the occasional letter, and I know she's read the book. Maybe I'll ask her that question next time I see her?' He beamed a smile out to her. 'That should get the conversation off to a flying start.'

'When did you last meet up in person?'

'In the departure lounge of Singapore Airport,' Kyle whispered. 'About a month before her first minor stroke. She moved back to London soon afterwards with my half-brother, Alex, to start a new life as a twice-divorced woman. The second stroke was two weeks ago.'

Lulu took a sharp intake of breath. 'A stroke? Oh, Kyle. How is she?'

He smiled across at her. 'Recovering. Mother made it clear to Alex that she didn't want me to see her until she had better control of her speech and hand movements. Luckily for me, my half-brother is not someone who follows the rules, and he has been keeping me up to date. She should be discharged from hospital next week.'

'I hope it goes well for you,' Lulu replied, with a sincere sigh of regret.

'Do you believe that there is one person for each of us in this life, Lulu? One soul-mate, like for your Emma? My mother is already on her second divorce. It doesn't bode well for me.'

She looked into his face and saw something she had never seen before. Serious, yes. Concerned, yes. But more. This was fear.

Kyle was looking at her, holding her hand as though his very life depended on it. The flippant answer she had ready died on her lips, and she hesitated before speaking, her fingers moving to mesh with Kyle's, bonding them together.

'Yes, I do believe that. I have seen it.'

He lifted one hand and pushed her hair back from her forehead. 'I have no regrets. Once an adrenaline junkie, always an adrenaline junkie.'

Lulu looked up and raised her eyebrows, let him continue.

Kyle stopped and reached out for the copy of *Medicine Man* Lulu had left on the table.

'Do you see that photograph on the cover? I remember it like yesterday. The biting cold. Brilliant sunshine. I can still smell the smoke from the Buddhist offering to keep us safe on the mountain!' He looked up at Lulu and grinned. 'Those sorts of memories have to be earned. You can't buy them or trade them. You just have to be there, at that moment in time and space. That's special.'

Lulu found something fascinating in the bottom of her cup, then whipped around to face Kyle, her voice trembling.

'I've never understood it. *Never.* People in Kingsmede think that I've somehow come to terms with the danger of what my mother did for a living, but they are so wrong. If it was just adrenaline you wanted there are roller coasters, or any number of things that have thrills. Without the risk of killing yourself. And yet you still chose to climb mountains—by the most dangerous route, no doubt.'

She stretched out her hand towards Kyle as he started to shuffle closer.

'Your parents are probably just grateful that you lived this long and they still have you with them—even if it is for only a few weeks between missions. Sometimes family does have to come first. So don't expect the rest of us to feel grateful that you've lowered yourself to join our mundane existence. And—'

Before Lulu realised what was happening, he had wrapped his hand around the back of her neck, his fingers working into her hair as he pressed his mouth against hers, pushing open her full lips, moving back and forth, his breath fast and heavy on her face.

His mouth was tender—gentle, but firm. As though he was holding back the floodgates of a passion which was on the verge of breaking through and overwhelming them both.

She felt that potential, trembled at the thought of it, and at that moment she knew that she wanted it as much as he did.

Her eyes closed as she wrapped her arms around his back and leant into the kiss, kissing him back, revelling in the sensual heat of Kyle's body as it pressed against hers. Closer, closer, until his arms were taking the weight of her body, enclosing her in his loving sweet embrace. The pure physicality of the man was almost overpowering. The movement of his muscular body pressed against her combined with the heavenly scent that she now knew was unique to him alone and filled her senses with an intensity that she had never felt in the embrace of any other man in her life. He was totally overwhelming. Intoxicating. And totally, totally delicious.

Then, just when Lulu thought that there could be nothing more pleasurable in this world, his kiss deepened. It was as though he wanted to take everything that she was able to give him, and without a second of doubt she surrendered to the hot spice of the taste of his mouth and tongue. Cinnamon and chocolate. And Kyle.

This was the kind of kiss she had never known. The connection between them was part of it, but this went beyond friendship and common interests. This was a kiss to signal the start of something new. The kind of kiss where each of them were opening up their most intimate secrets and deepest feelings for the other person.

The heat, the intensity and the desire of this man were all there, exposed for her to see, when she eventually opened her eyes and broke the connection. Shuddering. Trembling.

He pulled away, the faint stubble on his chin grazing across her mouth as he lifted his face to kiss her eyes, brow and temple.

It took a second before she felt able to open her eyes—only to find Kyle was still looking at her, his forehead still pressed against hers. A smile warmed his face as he moved his hand down to stroke her cheek.

He knew. He knew the effect that his kiss was having on her body. Had to. Her face burned with the heat coming from the point of contact between them. His own heart was racing, just as hers was.

'Is that the way you usually silence women who ask you tough questions?' Lulu asked, trying to keep her voice casual and light as she tried to catch her breath. And failed.

He simply smiled a little wider in reply, one side of his mouth turning up more than the other before he answered in a low whisper, 'I save it for emergencies. And for when I need to know the answer to an important question.'

'Hmm?' He was nuzzling the side of her head now, his lips moving over her brow and into her hair as she spoke. 'Important question?'

Kyle pulled back and looked at her, eye to eye.

'I had to find out if you were holding on to a secret unrequited love. Now I know the answer I can do something about it. So. Would you care to risk being seen out in public again with me?'

Lulu leant back and took another breath, before grinning at Kyle. 'Well, I might.'

He bowed in her direction and pressed his forefinger onto his lips, as though considering his options. 'I happen to know that the Feathers has roast chicken on the menu this evening.' He dropped his hand and pushed it deep into the pocket of her father's best trousers. 'Would you care to join me for dinner, Miss Hamilton? No strings. Or do I have to use my emergency procedure again?'

'Dinner? That's it?' Lulu answered, knowing perfectly well that it was not the only thing he was offering.

'What do you think?' He winked.

And then she made the fatal mistake of looking into those eyes and was lost.

The words that came out of her mouth seemed to have no connection at all with the intentions of her brain. And everything to do with the desire burning in her heart.

'Thank you. I would love to have an evening out. In fact, I was wondering if you would like to be my guest at Emma's birthday party next week,' she said, giving him a polite smile, as though he had not just completely rocked her world. 'We always hold it here, and I'm in need of an escort. Since I'm between boyfriends at the moment, I suppose that you will have to do. If you're available?'

'An escort? Well, how could I resist such a tantalising invitation? I'm available. Assuming that nobody better comes along in the meantime, I presume?'

'Oh, yes.' She nodded and pursed her lips. 'I'd drop you straight away. But don't worry. I could probably pass you off to the Bennett sisters. They don't mind sharing.' A smile widened her mouth. 'I can be ready in ten minutes.'

A few minutes later Kyle was standing in the hallway in his coat, wondering how he'd got there and if he had truly just kissed Lulu Hamilton. Or had he merely dreamed that part of the last hour?

He had not planned to kiss her. Far from it. But the energy and passion of that woman was a flame, and he was the moth.

If ever he had lived for the moment, that had been it.

And, despite everything she had said, and the hurt he had unwittingly caused, when she'd kissed him back the intensity of the woman had made his heart soar.

She had pressed buttons in his body which had not been pressed for quite some time. The sweetness and intensity of that brief kiss had left him reeling—but his brain was still working.

This was no one-night stand. It was too deep, too special. Like her.

She had just told him what she thought about men like him—men who lived for the moment, not caring for the consequences. He had even admitted it himself.

It was true. He knew it, she knew it—and there was precious little he was going to be able to do to change her mind about that.

And yet…she had managed to do something he would have thought impossible. For the first time in years he was actually thinking about having something more. He *wanted* to try and convince her to give him a chance to prove that he was different. That he was going to be the exception to the others. That he would not break her heart when he took off to pastures new. That he was worth her time. Her affection. Her love, even?

And perhaps convince himself at the same time.

It was time to take another of those insane risks. And take an evening off. In the company of the only woman he wanted to be with.

* * *

Kyle stamped his feet on the welcome mat before strolling into the warm, bright and welcoming kitchen, still redolent of the breakfast bacon and tomato sandwiches he had shared with Lulu over several pots of tea while looking at the amazing party invitations Emma had sent out for her birthday celebration that evening.

They had laughed until they'd cried before setting to work for a few hours.

The memory book idea was working. Pictures, memories, facts and extracts from letters and diaries seemed to come together like magic to recreate a real place and time.

The book was going to be everything he wanted it to be and more. It would be a superb tribute to Ruth and the entire team he had worked with all those years ago.

And he could not have done it without Lulu.

The irony of that fact was starting to worry him more than a little. He had just spent the last-half hour by the riverbank, trying to work through the dilemma that would have to be decided in the next few days.

How was he going to end his book? With the truth? Or with the tributes and press statements the foundation had issued? Mike had no idea that there were two versions of the series of events. How could he? The only other person who knew was a paramedic working in Uganda who had probably forgotten all about it.

The more he worked with Lulu, laughed with Lulu, shared his life with Lulu, the more he wanted to be completely open and honest with her—just as she had been with him. She deserved to hear the truth from him, irrespective of whether he wrote about it in the book or not. No more lies and deception. Not with Lulu.

He cared about her far too much for that. Only if he was going to do it, it had better be soon— or not at all. And that was the problem.

Could he risk the relationship they had already built up? He knew that she cared about him. Would the truth destroy any chance they might have of taking things to the next level? Because one thing was for certain. Against the odds, he was falling for Lulu Hamilton.

Belle scampered up to his side with a gentle huff of a woof, as if to say *home at last*, her nails clattering on the polished floorboards either side of the rug before she attacked her food.

A delicious smell of hot coffee and burning logs wafted into the hallway as Kyle slowly raised himself on tiptoe and peeked into the dining room. Not that anyone would have heard him above the din of pop music bellowing out from the open door.

Lulu was standing on the top rung of a tall

stepladder, apparently oblivious to the decibel level. Her hips were gently moving from side to side in line with her shoulders, and she was totally ignoring the swaying of the ladder and the impending doom which might accompany stretching upwards towards a high ceiling with both hands full of tools.

Lulu hummed along to the pop music blasting out from her sound system as she tightened the drill bit with her chuck key. The hammer drill made short work of the brick and plaster, and the plug fitted perfectly. Seconds later the picture hanging screw was in the wall and secure. She stepped down one rung on the ladder to measure the drop from the intricate plaster moulding of the dining room cornice. Exactly the same as the first. Excellent.

The pictures had been crooked for years. It was time.

Lulu was just about to move when she felt something touch the bare section of skin between her jeans and the bottom of her old T-shirt. It was icy cold, and running up and down her ribcage, and it was trying to tickle her under her arms. She squealed out loud.

As she whipped around in shock her left hand grabbed the ladder. At exactly the same time the heavy drill in her right hand swung around with the momentum of the movement. And made contact with Kyle Munroe's head.

'Ouch!' Kyle staggered back to sit on the sofa in a heap.

'Oh, no! I am *so* sorry.'

Lulu scrambled down the ladder and stood next to him as he clutched his head.

'I had no idea you were there.'

'My own fault for creeping up on unsuspecting females, I suppose. I did call out, by the way, but I can see now why you didn't hear me.' He pointed towards the drill, then to the sound system, where loud music was still belting out into the room. 'Having the music that loud can damage your hearing, you know.'

'Oh, really? Thanks for the advice. So can sneaking up on people.'

She moved her hands from her hips to look more closely at the side of his head, where he was rubbing vigorously. She started to reach forward to touch his hair, and pulled back, cautious. 'No sign of blood. How are you feeling?'

'I'll live. And I am the medic around here,' he mumbled under his breath as she tidied away the tools.

'I thought you would be out most of the morning. My dad used to say that a straight picture was a boring one. I don't think my party guests would agree. Sorry again.'

'No problem.' He chuckled. 'Belle disgraced herself with your local swans. They were not impressed, and... Lulu?'

No reaction. Strange. Unless... He snapped his fingers over to his left. Still no reaction.

Her hair was pulled back into a scrunched-up ponytail, and she was wearing her old working clothes again, but she somehow managed to look in control, calm and absolutely stunning. Her inner serenity shone out.

Kyle walked slowly over to Lulu's right side and helped her coil the drill cable before pulling a slip of paper out of his shirt pocket. 'I come with a message from the lovely Emma. The good news is that she has found the curtains you were looking for.' He raised his eyebrows high and gave her a quizzical look before going on. 'The bad news is that they have run out of lemon drizzle cake at the Feathers. So you will have to make do with chocolate muffins.'

'Well, she might have warned me.' Lulu paused. 'How can I possibly hang pictures, fit curtains or type without lemon cake?'

She glanced up and caught him staring at the left hand side of her face, where her hair was barely covering her ears.

He knew.

She smiled and held out the sides of her overalls to create a skirt before bobbing him a short curtsey.

'Ah. You've noticed that I have a hearing problem. Well, I am impressed. Most people take a lot longer. So now you know. Stay on my right side and you'll be fine. Stay on my left and you can say whatever you like. There's a good chance I won't hear half of it.'

'Have you always had a problem in that ear?' Kyle asked, his eyes focused on her, intensely interested.

She paused just long enough for him to know that this was not something she talked about very often before she smiled up.

'It might surprise you to know that I have actually been to Africa. My dad and I visited Mum in the summer holiday I turned sixteen. She managed to get a few days' break on the coast at some medical conference or other, and we had a great time.'

Lulu busied herself unpacking Kyle's dictation machine, her head down.

'I came home with a very interesting souvenir—or at least that's what the tropical disease hospital in London called it. Encephalitis? Meningitis? They never did find out exactly what it was. But I was dosed with every antibiotic they could find, plus a few more experimental ones. I recovered with my brain intact and most of my organs doing what they were supposed to. Except one ear. So overall I would say I was very lucky.'

Kyle whistled and shook his head at her calm and matter-of-fact reply. 'I would say you were very, *very* lucky. Your parents must have been terrified.'

Lulu unwrapped the delicious-looking chocolate muffins before answering in a low voice. 'I was too far out of it to notice what was going on, but according to Emma my dad was hysterical.'

Lulu paused and looked up at Kyle with a smile. 'He actually sent a message to my mum and asked her to come home. Now, that was serious. He had never done that before.'

'Did Ruth come home?'

Lulu shook her head. 'There was no point. By the time the message reached the field station I was in recovery. She called from the nearest large town about four days later. I don't know what she said to him, but I know that was my one and only exotic holiday. Shame, really, but there was nothing else he could do. Fact.'

She passed the muffins across the table towards Kyle, skirting the plastic wallets of diary notes. 'I suppose you are well used to those sort of risks?'

He nibbled into the chocolate icing and tried hard to deflect the question. 'Mmm, this is good. And I seem to recall that it was your hearing that we were talking about. Does it still cause you a problem?'

She laughed and shook her head. 'You don't want to hear about that. Far too boring. And I know you have too much to do to chat to me.'

He held up his right hand. 'On the contrary. I do want to know. The work can wait a few minutes. Please. I'm interested.'

Lulu shuffled the paperwork a few seconds longer, but when she spoke, her voice was lower, calmer, slower.

'Okay. I'll start with a question. When you go climbing in the mountains, do you ever stop in the middle of nowhere and just listen? And marvel that you cannot hear anything manmade? Just the sound of the wind, probably your own breathing. No planes. No cars. No radios or anything else from the modern world.'

Kyle nodded, not willing to break the fragile connection held in her voice. 'It's a very special moment.'

Lulu rearranged the folders in front of her. 'That is what I miss. I miss the sound of silence.

And, yes, I have been to specialists in hospitals all over the country, and tried the latest digital aids. They have no idea what caused it, or how to stop the tinnitus I get now and again. So I've learnt to compensate. But I'll probably never hear the sound of silence again.'

She smiled at him with the kind of tilted head, crinkly smile that melted his heart. 'On the plus side, my right ear is fine—so I still hear birds and ocean waves. Telephones. I love listening to music, and if I listen really hard and overcome my fear of calling attention to myself I can still hear a lot of what people say. Even if it is only one or two at a time.'

She glanced away to look out of the long windows at the open fields which stretched beyond the trees. 'So, yes, I would say that it *does* bother me. But it could have been a lot worse. I almost didn't make it.'

Kyle started to rise from his chair—only Lulu whipped back to face him so quickly that he caught her off balance, and he had to grab her around the waist and pull her towards him to steady her.

Lulu pushed down on his shoulders to steady herself, and made the mistake of looking into his face. And was lost, drowning in the deep pools of his eyes which seemed to magically bind her so tight that resistance was futile. She tried to focus on the tanned creased forehead above the mouth that was soft and wide.

Lush.

He already had the slightest hint of stubble at noon, so the rest of his body must be… No, she couldn't think about what was below the chest hairs curling out from the V of his shirt.

Sitting in her chair, she could see his head and throat were only inches from her face. Her bosom was pressed against the fine fabric of his sky-blue shirt. In a fraction of a second Lulu was conscious that his hand had taken a firmer grip around her waist, moving over her old overall as though it was the finest lingerie, so that she could sense the heat of his fingertips on her warm skin below.

She felt something connect in her gut, took a deep breath, and watched words form in that amazing mouth.

'I think we make our own destiny…' Kyle tried to join words together in a sensible sentence.

He gave up, because Lulu had slowly closed the gap between their bodies, drawn towards him by invisible ropes of steel.

'Destiny…?' she whispered.

'Who dares wins. Don't you take chances, Lulu?'

'Only with you…' Lulu replied, but the words

were driven from her mind as Kyle's fingers wound up into her hair. Drawing her closer, he slanted his head so that his warm, soft lips gently glided over hers, then firmer, hotter.

CHAPTER NINE

THE sensation blew away any vague idea that might have been forming in her head that she could resist this man for one second longer. Her eyes closed as heat rushed from her toes to the tips of her ears and everything else in the world was lost in giddy sensation.

She wanted the earth to stop spinning, so that this moment could last for ever.

Before she could change her mind, Lulu Hamilton closed her eyes and kissed Kyle Munroe back, tasting the heat of his mouth, breathing in the heady smell of coffee, chocolate crumbs and a musky aftershave, sensing his resistance melt as he moved deeper into the kiss.

Her own arms lifted to wrap around his neck. She let the pressure of his lips and the scent and sensation of his body against hers warm every cell in her being before she finally pulled her head back.

Kyle looked up at her with those wonderful hazel eyes, his chest responding to his faster breathing, and whispered, 'Here's to taking chances,' before sliding his hand down the whole length of her back and onto her waist, drawing her forward as he moved his head to her neck and throat, kissing her on the collarbone, then in the warm hollow below her ears, his fingers moving in wide circles around her back.

'Oops. Perhaps those curtains can wait.'

Lulu opened her eyes in time to see the back of Emma's coat, and in one single movement she pulled back and smoothed down her overall with one hand as she gathered up her hair which had mysteriously become untied with the other.

'I…er…need to check on a painting. A present. For your mother.' Lulu just about managed to stammer out, and waved her hand towards the hallway. 'Painting. Studio.'

Kyle nodded. 'Great idea. Me too. Photos. Yes, photos. Catch up with you later. Right. Later.'

'Okay, this is new!' Emma stood at the end of Lulu's bed with her arms folded.

'Yes,' Lulu said, still feeling slightly giddy. 'It was a moment of reckless madness. He made the move and I decided to go along with it.'

Emma breathed out with a shake of her head.

'Oh, Lulu. I can see that he is very good-looking, but Kyle is a tourist. He will be gone in a few days. Are you ready for that?'

'Yes. I know,' Lulu said. 'If only he wasn't so amazing.' She closed her eyes and tried to recreate the heat of his mouth, his fingers running up and down her spine, and could not resist grinning like a fool.

'Well,' Emma said, 'you are old enough to make your own decisions, young lady, and if he makes you happy, good luck to you both. In the meantime, I have a party in a few hours. See you later.'

Lulu slid down the duvet and pulled the pillow over her head. She groaned out loud. Emma was only repeating what she already knew in her head. She did know the risks—better than most people.

It would probably be a lot easier if she didn't need him so badly.

Kyle leant back in the hard chair at the dining table, opened a computer file, and tried to focus on his memories of a distant place in a country he had last visited ten years earlier. Pity that all he could think about was Lulu.

He hadn't planned to kiss her, touch her.

She had kissed him back.

Where had that come from?

His eyes squeezed tight with frustration. *When*

had he become such an idiot? Just who was he trying to protect here?

Lulu knew the score, and had been honest with him from day one. If anyone was being selfish, it certainly wasn't Lulu.

In a few short days Lulu had become his closest friend—the person he wanted to be with. Laugh with. Confide in. He had told her things about his past that not even his family would know about until they read the book. How had that happened? Idiot.

Except that when he touched her face... Wow. Lulu was...so right. Beautiful. Hot.

And a lot more than that.

She had invaded his dreams day and night. Dreams of a life away from the stress and pain of the work he had chosen. Work where his only goal was to make a difference to other people's lives. Not his own. That was the legacy that Ruth Taylor Hamilton had left him, and he had to live up to that. Only now Ruth had given him something more—something so precious he was almost afraid to grasp hold of it, in case it fractured like a thin piece of crystal glass between his fingers.

So where did that leave him now?

This was Ruth Taylor Hamilton's daughter. He should go to her right now, tell her about her mother and take the consequences.

Big mistake. He needed to sort this out and do it now. Because what he was feeling was something new. And more terrifying than facing the highest mountain.

Yet he knew in his heart that this was one risk that he needed to take or die trying. Because he would never have this chance again.

His cellphone rang and Kyle casually flipped it open, his mind full of possibilities.

'Kyle Munroe,' he said, and then closed his eyes. 'Alex?'

His half-brother. The man he had only met once in his life.

'Hi, Alex. Sorry to sound so slow. I'm just in the middle of something. Thanks for getting back to me. Please go ahead.' He picked up a pen and started tapping it onto the smooth surface of the table before writing down an address. 'She'll be ready to be discharged from hospital next week? Fantastic. Yes, that would be great. Early afternoon would be fine.'

Kyle lowered the pen and pressed his forefinger and thumb hard into his forehead in fierce concentration before speaking again.

'No. I told you that I would respect her wishes. I'll make sure that I keep out of sight until you tell me she is ready to see me. Okay. See you then. Thanks, mate. Thanks for your help.'

With a great sigh, he leant back and closed his eyes. His mother was going to make a good recovery. That was one more thing to be thankful for.

Kyle was so preoccupied with dates and timings that he barely noticed that someone had come into the dining room and was talking to him.

'Hello, Kyle. Want to keep an old lady company for a few minutes?' Emma laughed and pointed to the window seat. 'It would make my day!'

Kyle leant forward and grinned. 'Show me an old lady and I'll answer your question.'

He raised his eyebrows a couple of times before giving her a suggestive wink.

That really got Emma going, her shoulders moving up and down with laughter as she wriggled down in the cushions. She waved a finger at Kyle as he positioned himself so that he was facing her.

'Lulu warned me about you, young man. You can save your charm for my only goddaughter. Although…'

'Although?' Kyle repeated, cocking his head to one side.

'I'm pleased that you are working on this book together.' Emma nodded her head. 'Ruth was a good friend to me over the years. She would have been proud of Lulu and what she has achieved.

Yes, very proud. You will be working for a very good cause.'

'So you've known the Taylor and Hamilton families a long time?'

Emma narrowed her eyes and looked hard at Kyle. 'I was born in this village. Spent my life here. There aren't many folk I don't know one way or another. But why do you want to know?'

Kyle looked into Emma's face and recognised that she wanted a real answer. 'Well, for one thing, I admired Ruth Taylor Hamilton a very great deal. To do her memory justice, I'd like to know more about the lady before she became a pioneering surgeon.'

Emma sat back in silence, clearly sizing Kyle up.

'I knew Ruth very well. Eccentric, you might say, but bright! Sharp as a knife! And driven. I don't need to tell you that war surgeons like Ruth were not doing it for the wages.'

Kyle nodded. 'Well, that hasn't changed.'

She cocked her head to one side and stared at Kyle through narrow eyes.

'You married, handsome boy? Engaged?'

Kyle drew back and gave Emma a look.

'Me? No, Emma. Nobody is daft enough to have me. Or should that be brave enough?'

Emma blew out a puff of air. 'Daft. Courage is only part of it.'

She leant forward and grabbed Kyle by his right shoulder, looked into his face.

'Want some advice from someone old enough to be your grandmother? Because you are going to get it whether you like it or not. Don't leave the people you love to face the loneliness Tom and Lulu Hamilton had to look forward to every day. Stay single. Although...' she patted his face before sitting back '...there might be a few broken hearts along the way, a good-looking boy like you. Am I right?'

'Not too many, I hope.' He sat back, slightly stunned by the intensity of her words, and fought to change the subject. 'How about you, Emma? From what I see at the Feathers, there is a lot of mischief going on in a village this size.'

She smiled. 'I was lucky. I had some wonderful years. Sometimes it seems like yesterday.'

She looked down, her eyes glistening. 'It doesn't happen like that twice. Now, get yourself to that studio and talk to Lulu. I need my beauty sleep before the party. Remember to save a dance for me.'

'Wouldn't miss it for the world.'

Lulu pulled open the blinds on the studio windows and was dazzled by the sunlight flooding into the long, narrow room. Slipping off her shoes, Lulu slid down the wall to sit cross-legged, facing the windows.

She was exhausted.

Lulu brought her fists down onto her knees. Hard. *Stupid! Stupid girl!*

Had she not learnt anything?

How was Kyle any different from any of the other handsome young medics who had stayed in this house for a few days or even weeks over the years, until boredom set in, the next job came along and they were gone as fast as their legs could carry them?

Every one hooked on the rush. The adrenaline. The excitement. The thrill of exotic locations and hardship.

So what if he is gorgeous looking, charming and caring? When did that become so unusual?

She was stupid to think he was any different from the others.

Stupid to think he was special.

She took a breath. Stupid to think that he might actually come to care about her. Love her. Want to share his life with her.

Lulu dropped her head as tears pricked the corners of her eyes, burning.

Stupid to think that she could trust him to want to be with her instead of his work.

To dream for just a moment that he would

come home and live in this village. Come back and stay.

Her parents had loved each other. But it had not been enough to make her mother want to stay. Ruth Taylor Hamilton had abandoned her husband, just as she had left her daughter behind to face her loneliness.

A tear rolled down her cheek and Lulu choked back others. She had always promised herself she would not cry about things she could not control. And now look at her.

Kyle stood transfixed and gazed in wonder as Lulu dropped her head back against the white walls of the artist's studio, her joy and serene calm acting like a spotlight, so that the entire room seemed to come to life when she was in it. How could he ever get tired of looking at her?

This was the image he would have to store away for those days when the satellite phone and the webcam failed and he was down to a photo—an imprint of a cheeky smile and those stunning whirls of long, blond, corkscrew curls. But all he wanted to do now was throw his rucksack into a corner of this room and tell her that he was not going anywhere. And keep on telling her, over and over again, until she finally believed him.

Perhaps then, at last, she would trust him enough to let him into her heart.

Except of course he might not be able to keep that promise. The TV company had planned to film in Uganda for a week. Fly in, fly out. But he knew precisely what would happen. A few days into the clinic and he would be stuck there until another medic could take over. Where would that leave Lulu?

What could he offer her? A short-term affair would be wonderful, amazing and unforgettable. But then what? A tearful farewell at some airport and six months of misery, during which he would work himself senseless every day to block out the loss?

While Lulu got on with her life in Kingsmede. Alone again, deserted by yet another medic on a mission.

Kyle looked away as he saw her mouth twist into her tears, torn between wanting to be with her and wanting to quell the fire in his belly he felt whenever they were in touching distance.

Emma Carmichael knew what she was talking about. He had a choice to make. Stay single and go back to the work that had been his refuge for the last ten years. Or change his life and find a new direction which was even more terrifying and uncertain.

Because one thing was clear.

He was infatuated with Lulu Hamilton and there was not a thing he could do about it. There was one task, however, he *could* help her with.

Lulu quickly swallowed down her tears when the door opened a little wider and she looked up to see Kyle standing there, leaning against the door-frame, filling the space.

He looked so handsome he must belong to another woman, another country and another life. He could not possibly want to be hers. She had been kidding herself with a silly teenage crush. How pathetic was that?

He shuffled down next to her, so that he could wrap his arm around her shoulders.

Lulu closed her eyes for a second, to luxuriate in the sensation of his hair and his stubbly chin on her skin. The smell of a citrus shampoo. His smell.

She could not help but instinctively snuggle closer, so that she could lean against him as he stretched out his long legs and crossed his ankles.

He drew a folder of papers onto her lap, and the air between them seemed to freeze. It was the folder of her mother's letters and personal documents from the suitcase, which Kyle had put to one side as they went through her diaries.

His arm tightened around her shoulder and his lips pressed against the top of her head.

'I want to thank you for showing me the diaries. You were right—they *were* full of technical details about the mission, but also I found what I was looking for. Apparently Ruth thought that I was doing okay. And that means a lot.'

'I'm pleased,' she managed to squeeze out through a tight throat.

'Now it's your turn to look at some photographs and choose some for the book. It's time.'

She swallowed down hard in pain, aware of his hot breath on the side of her face.

'I'll be right here next to you. We can go through them together. Okay? Here goes.'

And without another word, Kyle turned the package upside down so that the contents spilled out onto their laps.

She could only watch as he casually started rummaging through the jumble of envelopes, single sheets of paper, and something she had not expected.

Her mother had taken photographs. Lots of photographs.

And not just of the stunning countryside and the animals, but of the field hospital itself, and the patients she had treated. In many cases the name of the person had been written on the back, making them even more personal. Smiling men, women and children, some of them clearly very ill or wounded.

And of course she had taken photos of the people he worked with. Paramedics, orderlies, nurses whose names she recognised. There was one of a younger version of Kyle in a white coat, inside a fabric tent. She looked at it for a few seconds before passing it to him with a smile. 'This would be perfect.'

He smiled back and nodded. 'Book cover perfect.' And then he looked down and picked up another. 'How about this for the dedication page?'

It was her mother. The mission leader.

Lulu took the simple crinkly print from his fingers. Centre stage was Ruth Taylor Hamilton, walking with grinning children along a dusty dirt road below a clear blue sky. She was laughing, and she looked so happy as her arms swung wide to lift one of the children up from the ground.

Tears pricked the back of Lulu's eyes and she wiped them away, aware of Kyle's gentle touch.

'I'm sorry this is so hard for you. I truly am.'

Lulu shook her head as she ran her fingertip across the image. 'You don't understand. I'm not crying for Mum. I'm crying because I am so pathetic. Don't you see? I'm jealous. I keep thinking that it should have been *me* in that photograph. *I* should have been the little girl with her, playing and laughing and enjoying life. *I* was her daughter—not these children.'

Her shoulders were heaving with the pain in her chest.

'Can you understand how guilty that makes me feel? How pathetic? These children had suffered so much; they deserved some happiness. I have no right to be envious of that. None at all.'

He was holding her in his arms now, pressing her closer and closer to his chest, drawing her to him. 'Yes, you do. You wanted your mother and she wasn't here for you when you needed her. You deserved happiness as much as they did, Lulu. But you have the rest of your life to look forward to now. And quite a few letters to read. You can do it. I know that you can.'

'Don't do this, Kyle. Please. Don't make this worse than it is.' The quiver in her voice betrayed her and she was forced to stop. To gulp down her panic.

'It's going to be all right now.' His voice was low. Caring. Concerned. Everything she wanted but knew she could never have.

'And, in case you're wondering, you don't get rid of me that easily. Not a chance. You had better get used to that idea. So, now we're clear about that, I would like to hear what's on your mind, Lulu. Tell me why you were crying when I came in. Is it me? Have I been an idiot?'

Lulu tried to shake her head, but found Kyle in the way.

'No. No, it is not you. You have always made it clear that you want to go back to Nepal as soon as you can. Your work is important there. They need you.' Her head dropped forward a little. 'I knew that from day one. I'm the one who made the mistake of hoping that I might change your mind, Kyle. I'm the one who is being ridiculous.'

Lulu lifted Kyle's arm from around her shoulder and turned to face him. Their noses were only inches apart. She placed one of her hands on each side of his face and her eyes looked deep into forest pools reflecting every shade of amber and green as she forced him to look at her.

'I love my life and my work here in the village. I want to share that life with someone special. But that person has to want to be here. It's totally unfair for me to expect that from you. I am selfish. I know that. I want to wake up with the same person every morning. In the same bed. That's why I wanted you to leave, Kyle. Before…'

Kyle leant his head forward so that their brows were touching. 'Before?'

She smiled. 'I was going to say before we make promises and commitments we want to keep but know in ourselves that we can't.'

There was a huge sigh from the man whose lips were moving across her temple. He slowly pulled away and brought his hand up to push back the wisps of hair which had fallen onto her brow. His fingers stroked through the tight curls, revelling in the unique sensation.

'Is this what the quiet life does? Puts a wise head on such pretty young shoulders? In Nepal you would be called a shaman—a *jhankri*. A witch doctor. Someone who is not afraid to recognise the truth, even when it is hard to hear. But even witch doctors can only heal other people, Lulu. Not themselves.'

Kyle stopped messing with her hair and brought his hand down to cup her cheek as he looked into her face.

'Not many people have come to know me like you do. Know me from the inside. Not even my own family. That is a rare gift.'

Her face creased into a wide grin before her head dropped. 'You're so easy to like.' *So easy to love.* She had to change the subject—quick. 'Now that I've chosen your photos, here's something I painted which *your* mother might like as a present.'

Her fingers creased around the edges of a watercolour sketch of spring flowers that looked so lifelike to Kyle he could almost smell their sweet fragrance lifting from the heavy cream paper.

Her forefinger stroked the edge of the paper, and when Lulu spoke her voice was low and sad. 'Dad never liked my flower paintings. They were too small and too commercial for his taste. Not the kind of work a real artist would do. That's why he wanted me to go to art college. So that I could learn to be a true painter and put this amateur stuff behind me.'

'You really mean that, don't you?' Kyle shook his head in amazement. 'You are so talented, and it's obvious that you love what you do. This is wonderful work, and I know my mother would treasure an original painting like this. You're a very special person, Lulu Hamilton.' He touched her forehead with his. 'So very special. And so beautiful.'

'Kyle? About earlier…'

The telephone rang in the hall.

'It's okay. I have an answer-machine.'

'*What* about earlier?' Kyle mumbled. He was caressing her face now, moving down to her neck, nudging open her blouse with his chin, trying to distract her from listening to the telephone—only to hear Emma's voice echo across the empty space.

'Hi, Lulu. Just to let you know that the party goodies should be with you in about half an hour. See you soon!'

'Half an hour!' Lulu shouted in horror, trying to wriggle herself free from Kyle's grip.

'Relax, sweetheart. You would be amazed at what we can get done in half an hour.'

'Did you just call me sweetheart?' Lulu's eyes widened like a schoolgirl's as Kyle nodded, his eyes never breaking their hold on hers. 'You did?'

'I'll call you sweetheart as many times as you like if it makes you look happy. And you *do* look happy. I can only hope I have played some small part in that.'

'Idiot. You have shown me what happiness feels like—I could get addicted to it. Addicted to *you*. Do you have a cure for that, Dr Munroe?'

He answered by kissing her forehead and neck. Luxuriating in the touch of her skin on his. 'And what if I'm addicted to you? Have you thought of that? A pair of hopeless addicts together.'

'A sad case,' she answered, kissing him back at the corners of his mouth as he tried to speak.

His hand came up and pressed against her lips. His voice was intense. Fraught. 'I can't lose you. It's taken me a lifetime to find you, Lulu. I want to be with you. Can you do that? Let me be part of your life?'

She closed her eyes and revelled in the warmth of his sweet embrace, which was so full of love and compassion. He meant it. There was no doubt. He wanted her as much as she wanted him. But did he need her?

'You have such a big heart,' she whispered as her fingertips ran across the muscles of his chest and collarbone to his jawline. 'I know that you mean those words now, at this minute and in this place, but some time soon you are going to take a telephone call, and then I'll be driving you to the airport.'

Kyle sighed and nodded before replying. 'You're right. I've been assigned to Nepal for another month before the winter closes in. Then there is Africa.'

She smiled as she stroked his face. 'I have good reason to know what it feels like to be left behind by the only person you truly care about in the world.'

'What about the person who's leaving their love behind?' He smiled back, his fingers playing with the curls in her hair. 'Do you have any idea how hard it is to smile and wave and know that you are going to miss everything about them? Especially when I have moments like this to remember.'

Her smile faded. 'Yes. I know that it would hard for both of us.'

She looked at Kyle, and there was so much pain in her eyes that he reached out with both arms and she fell into them.

'My mother broke my heart. And the pain was so terrible that I blamed her for it for a very long time. I never want to feel that way about you, Kyle. That wouldn't be fair on you.'

Kyle cuddled her closer, his hands stroking her back in wide circles. 'It doesn't have to be that way with us.'

He pulled back from her just enough so that she could see one side of his face, illuminated by the sunlight streaming into the room. The sculpted curved lines of his cheeks and jaw had not been created by some Renaissance master but through a hard life of years of work. Shame that it made absolutely no difference to how much she wanted to run her fingers along that skin and feel the man beneath.

With the kind of smile that would have saved her a fortune in central heating, Kyle said, 'Now—it is probably time to get back to work. You have a birthday party to organize, and I have to write the last two chapters of my book. Although I do have one request.'

He grinned down at Lulu as he slowly drew her

to her feet. 'Any chance you could dig out that grey suit? As passion killers go, it was a winner. Otherwise there is absolutely no guarantee that I will be able to keep my hands off you.'

CHAPTER TEN

KYLE glanced around the brightly lit hallway of Taylor House and waved as he was recognised by many of the jovial people in the crowd.

Show tunes from Hollywood musicals were playing in the background, just loud enough to be heard against the laughter and contented chatter of the old friends and neighbours around him. He had helped some of the men from the Feathers string fairy lights along the trees leading up to the porch and hallway, and now at seven in the evening, they looked terrific.

He quickly scanned the hallway and sitting room for Lulu. Then he heard her distinctive laughter echo out from the kitchen and slowly made his way towards the source, acknowledging warm greetings from people he had only met a few days earlier, who had taken the time to make him feel welcome. Part of their community.

Lulu was standing at the makeshift bar spread

out on the long pine table, her attention focused on Emma Carmichael, who had taken up residence at one end with her hand firmly clutched around what looked like a champagne bottle. More Christmas lights had been strung around the kitchen windows, but they paled into a dull glow compared to the woman he was looking at.

It could only be Lulu.

Her long, sensitive fingers were stretched out around a wide bottle, pouring golden sparkling liquid into champagne glasses. Her slender wrists jangled and sparkled with rows of gold bracelets. Bright yellow. Some inset with coloured stones.

A pale green and gold top in shining silk fitted her upper body and highlighted her tiny waist, where a band of pale skin was exposed just at the curve of her back. It was only a few inches wide, but it was enough.

Kyle stopped short, trying to record the image.

An elegant green silk sari was wrapped around her body, heavily embroidered with gold flowers and just short enough to reveal thin gold sandals. He could not help but stare at the gold ankle chains decorated with tiny bells that emerged as Lulu stepped forward on the terra cotta tiled flooring to return the champagne to the ice bucket.

Lulu half turned towards Kyle just as he was

about to say hello, and he stalled, stunned by the woman he could not drag his eyes away from.

Three heavy gold necklaces of varying lengths hung below her face, drawing his attention to her fitted bodice and the tantalising curves of what lay beneath.

Then her earrings moved, sparkling in the coloured lights, making him focus on her face. Stunning make-up illuminated her blue eyes, which matched the colour of the silk cloth. Her lips were full, moist, her face radiant.

She had never looked more beautiful. Or more magical.

This was the Lulu he remembered working in her garden the very first time he had come to this house. This was the real Lulu.

The Lulu he had fallen in love with as she sawed wood and played with her dog.

The fact that he had not realised that fact until this moment shocked him so much that he could only stand and stare as she turned and spotted him.

He was in love with Lulu Hamilton. Not Ruth's little girl, but this unique, amazing woman who was grinning at him from across the room.

'Hello, Kyle,' she said, although his brain was telling him that her radiant smile was more than just a simple hello. 'I'm pleased that you could make it. There are lots of people from the hospice team who would love to meet you. The Bennett sisters have even brought their autograph book.'

Her voice, her smiling face. The way her eyes met his without hesitation or excuse. Welcoming. She wanted him to be here, with her.

Kyle swallowed down a lump in his throat. If this was what being in a real home meant, he had been missing out all of his life.

'Wouldn't miss it for the world,' he answered, well aware that he had a stupid teenage-crush grin plastered all over his face as he walked slowly over to her and inhaled her exotic perfume, half closing his eyes at the intensity of the spicy floral scent. Roses, vanilla, sandalwood. And Lulu.

'That perfume is perfect.'

She tilted her head at him so that he could sniff closer to her neck without the rest of the village calling the police. 'A present from Emma. I'm glad you like it.'

'Have I told you yet that you look…' he breathed in and raised his eyebrows '…totally amazing?' He whispered in her right ear, 'And seriously hot. You should never wear grey again.'

She reared back and stared into his face. 'Seriously?'

He nodded, and silently mouthed the word 'hot'

before taking her hand. 'I am now officially on chaperon duty. Because in that outfit you need one.'

Lulu laughed and grabbed his hand. 'How gallant. Oh, and for the record, you don't look too bad yourself. You should wear a dinner jacket more often. Is it one of your dad's?'

She had the great pleasure of seeing Kyle's neck flush red with the truth.

Of course there was no way that she was going to tell him that he looked so gorgeous that she had almost fainted when she saw him strolling like a male model into her kitchen. She might have guessed that Kyle was one of those men who had been born to wear evening dress. The broad shoulders and slim waist were divine.

James Bond did not even come close.

His short hair had been waxed into a shiny mass swept back above a clean-shaven face. The cleft in his broad chin widened as he grinned back at her, revealing the laughter creases around his mouth and at the corners of both eyes. And then there were his eyes. No, she couldn't look into those eyes.

She would drown and not come up for air. And be happy to do it.

She would snatch at this chance to find a little happiness in her life.

To save herself from doing something foolish, like patting his bottom or suggesting they take a tour of the bedrooms, Lulu started walking from group to group, introducing Kyle to those friends and neighbours he was on nodding acquaintance with from the Feathers and his walks.

'Of course there is one thing I haven't tried yet,' Kyle said between half-closed lips, as his hand moved down to wrap itself around the bare skin at Lulu's waist, his fingers lingering just a second too long before moving to her silk skirt as he drew her into the living room.

He turned and looked into her eyes with that special look for the first time that evening. And her heart melted. The intensity, the need, the loneliness were all there.

In that one single look.

'Dancing,' he whispered into her ear, 'is the only way a poor bloke like me can move closer to a lady without getting his face slapped.'

'Oh, don't be so sure of that,' Lulu said. 'The night is still young.' And with a beaming smile, she raised her left hand to his shoulder.

In seconds his hand was splayed out on her bare waist, pulling her to his body as the music changed to a big orchestra sound.

'Ready to strut your funky stuff?' he asked. 'With a poor wounded medic? I shall try not to step on your dainty toes. Are you willing to risk it?'

Lulu looked into his grinning face.

Daring to risk it, more like! Daring to be pressed against his chest. With her flat sandals she only came up to his chin. How ridiculous was that? How amazing. How…wonderful.

A second later and Kyle had swept her into the room, and he had yet another skill at which he excelled.

'Not bad. Not bad at all,' Lulu reported, as they completed a tour of the room in harmony with the music and each other.

To her eternal embarrassment, at that precise moment she looked over Kyle's shoulder just in time to see Emma staring at them. If that was not bad enough, Emma gave her a knowing nod as she raised one thumb. With a wink. As subtle as ever.

Well aware that her face was warming the room, as well as her neck, Lulu leant forward to get out of eyeshot and found herself peering into Kyle's black bow tie, sensing the masculinity of the man who was holding her in his arms. *Oh, boy*.

'Not too much for you, is it? Want to take a break and catch your breath?'

His hand moved up an inch from the waistband

of her silk skirt until it was resting on bare skin, the rough fingertips light and tender. As she looked up into his face the music and chatter in the room faded away, until she felt that they were alone in a private room.

A room dedicated to just the two of them.

Lulu resisted the urge to close her eyes and succumb to the luxury of the moment.

Suddenly she lurched forward as a pair of small arms wrapped around her leg and tried to drag her away to the open French windows.

'Aunty Lulu, Aunty Lulu—Belle ran away, Aunty Lulu. Come quick. Come quick.'

Lulu glanced up at Kyle with a mischievous look before answering. 'It's okay, Pip. Uncle Kyle is going to find her for you. Aren't you, Uncle Kyle?'

Uncle Kyle said something under his breath about a certain dog that was not suitable for the ears of small persons and released Lulu with a heavy sigh.

Pip immediately grabbed his right hand and dragged him out of the room. Kyle could only manage one half glance back towards Lulu, with a shrug of his shoulders, before he disappeared into the night.

That dog had an agenda. She had thought so before, but now she was sure of it. Lulu stared after Kyle for a few seconds, before the local grocer tapped her on the shoulder and she was off dancing once more.

It was a party.

Why not let her hair down and have some fun for once in her life?

Lulu stood in the front porch of her house and waved as the last of the guests staggered away down the lane towards the village, guided by the lovely fairy lights.

Thank goodness most of them lived within walking distance. Despite the gusting wind, the clear, dry weather had lasted. Unlike her bar. Although nobody seemed to have noticed that she had run out of everything except fruit juice almost an hour ago, when Kyle had taken over from Emma as head barman.

Emma's party was over. And this time next year Lulu would be a student at art school. She would have to rent out the house to pay for it, of course. This truly was the end of an era.

Stars were appearing between the light clouds above the trees as she looked out across the garden. Despite the cold, and her silk sari, Lulu stepped out onto the patio and walked slowly around to the main French windows which led into the living room.

Only to find that she had one guest still in place.

Kyle was stretched out on the sofa by the fireplace. She could just see his face in the glow from the dying fire. Music from Emma's favourite musicals still played softly from the incongruous ghetto blaster borrowed from one of her nephews who worked as a disc jockey at the Feathers, the sound amplified by the silence of the night air so that Lulu could just make out the individual song lyrics.

She stood at the patio door and watched him for a moment. His eyes were closed and his long legs were stretched out over the arm of the sofa, ankles crossed, so that his trousers had ridden up, revealing a tantalising strip of muscular leg above his smart black socks. It would be so very, very tempting to tiptoe across in her sandals and run her fingers up and down that skin and find out if he was ticklish or not.

And then do the same with other areas of his body. Such as the wonderful chest she had seen a few days earlier after his soaking in the river. That was one image had been seared into her brain.

A broad, open-mouthed grin of delight popped across her face as she tried to imagine what her father would have said if he had strolled into this room to find an adrenaline junkie dozing on his sofa. The very thought made her want to giggle, and she pressed her hand across her mouth to stop herself waking Kyle.

Because she wanted this moment to last as long as possible.

She wanted to remember what these little bubbles of happiness felt like when she looked into that tanned stubbly face above those spectacular broad shoulders and… Oh, she would have no problem remembering the touch of his hand on her waist as they danced together. No problem at all.

There went another little bubble of joy.

Making her grin again.

The scar on his upper lip was more pronounced this evening. Dark eyelashes fluttered below heavy eyebrows.

This man had pressed buttons she hadn't known that she even had. He had shown her what being in love could be truly like. She tilted her head so that she could look more closely at the movement of his chest rising and falling.

She was willing to take that risk with this man.

Watching him lying there, his face relaxed, warm, handsome, she knew it would be so easy to be seduced by the sweet and tender kisses of the man she loved.

Tonight had swept away any lingering unspoken doubts she might have had.

This was what she had been frightened of—what she had always feared would happen when she gave her heart. And she *had* truly given her heart. No doubt about it. They had become attached with bonds you could not cut with a sharp tongue or a kitchen knife.

How was she going to walk away from this man? When she wanted him so much? She knew that she was setting herself up for loneliness and pain if she walked down that road.

Kyle stirred slightly and she grinned at him. 'You did a wonderful job with the lights. It was a super idea, Kyle. Thank you for that.'

The hazel eyes remained tight shut as he replied. 'You are most welcome. Remind me not to volunteer to be barman again, would you? Those people can drink.'

There was a sigh from the sofa, and Lulu turned her back to the room and wandered out onto the patio so that he could rest.

In the clear, crisp air, the faint streetlights from the village gave a background glow as one by one the familiar lights from the farmhouses on the other side of the fields blinked out, leaving the garden dark in the cool breeze that moved the trees.

One of the family of barn owls which roosted in the next copse sounded out, ready to begin its night flight.

There was a faint rustling noise from the room behind her, and Lulu felt soft, warm cloth being draped around her shoulders. Kyle's jacket.

'Is that better?'

Lulu could only manage a nod, and wrapped her arms together across her body to stop the shivers running down her spine.

Only this was not the cold. It was Kyle's body pressed against her back.

She could feel the warmth of his chest through her clothing, and without thinking or hesitating she leant backwards, daring to test the comfort she knew she would find there. His left arm draped around her waist and Kyle rested his head gently on top of hers as he looked out into the garden, then skywards.

'Do you know that the people I work with still follow a calendar controlled by the moon and the stars?' Kyle pointed over to the far right, where a thin silver disc had appeared above the horizon. 'Do you see that new moon? In Nepal it marks the start of a new beginning. A time for festivals. Processions with dancing and singing. It is great fun.'

'You must really miss your life in Nepal. Your

patients,' Lulu answered, without moving position.

Kyle hesitated for a moment before answering. 'The people. That's who I miss. The work is the same no matter where I go, whether it is London or Nepal, but the people are special.'

She slowly twisted her body around so that there were only inches between them, so close she could sense the pounding of his heart in tune with her own.

Kyle raised his hand and stroked her cheek with the knuckles, from temple to neck and then back again, forcing her to look into his eyes.

'They love celebrations for a new beginning. A new start. You have chosen a very auspicious day to hold a party for the birthday girl.'

'And what about you? Are you looking for a new start, Kyle? A new beginning?'

Lulu looked up into Kyle's face as he gently stroked hers before replying.

'Maybe I am. Maybe we all are. Would you like to have one last dance to celebrate, pretty girl?' He pressed her fingers to his lips, his eyes never leaving hers.

Lulu leant into his broad shoulder, cuddling into his warmth, sensing and hearing the pounding of his heart as she slid her own arms around his neck.

She had no need of hearing.

No need of sight.

Just the smell of his body. His own unique aroma.

She closed her eyes and revelled in the sensation of his hand on the bare skin at her waist, pressing her even closer to his chest as he moved to the music, his hard-muscled body swaying to the beat.

Her head moved closer, so that she could touch her face against his. Content.

She sensed his arm moving away, then slowly, slowly, he stepped back so that his hand could take hold of hers, their fingers intermeshing.

She opened her eyes to focus on the man so close, so very close to her body. And felt the power of that rush of heat. Kyle was breathing heavily, its pace matching her own, his eyes darting all over her face.

It was Lulu who had the courage to say the words. 'Can you stay a little longer?'

His reply was a long exhale, followed by a hoarse whisper. 'I'm not going anywhere tonight. But there is something I need to tell you. It can't wait until morning.'

His hands closed around her cool, slender fingers and he led her slowly back into the dining room, the warmth of his smile hotter than the log fire burning in the grate.

She could only grin back in return as he released her hand so that she could wrap it around his waist and press her head into his shoulder.

'Now you really have me intrigued. What is it? What do you have to tell me?'

Kyle slowly turned her around, so that they were facing each other, and suddenly Lulu felt the air between them grow cold. The look on his face told her everything she needed to know. This was not going to be good news.

'Please? I would like to know what is going on.'

He nodded. 'I've decided to leave early. I'll be going in the morning.'

Lulu stared out of the French windows, her eyes fixed on the movement of the wind in the trees she could just make out in the light from the house and the drive. The gentle waving of branches to and fro in the breeze was no match to the tornado spinning inside her head.

It felt as though she had been strapped onto a horse on a childhood nightmare of a merry-go-round which had started whirling faster and faster, until all she could do was hang on for dear life, knowing that if she even tried to get off she would be seriously hurt.

Only to be slammed to a crushing stop into a large solid object called life.

He was leaving. Just as her mother had, and then her father. She had always known that this was a temporary arrangement. A few weeks out of her life. It wasn't meant to be so hard to say goodbye. She just wanted him to stay so badly.

Kyle snuggled next to her in silence, so that the left side of his body was pressed against her right. Leg to leg, hip to hip, arm to arm. Her body instinctively yearned to lean closer, so that her head could rest against that broad shoulder, but she fought the delicious sensation.

She had to.

It was almost a physical pain when the fingers of his left hand started to slowly unclench the fist she had not even realised was there. Slowly, slowly, she looked up into the most amazing hazel eyes she had ever seen. The dark flecks of cinnamon and forest-green seemed warmer tonight, in the soft light, but in that moment she could see there was something more. Something she had never seen before. Something different. His unsmiling eyes scanned her face for a few minutes, as though searching for an answer to some unasked question he had not the words to speak.

Uncertainty. Concern. Regret, even.

It was all there in the hard lines of his remarkable face, the shadows and planes highlighted by the flickering firelight. His fingertips clenched around hers just tight enough to draw her attention away from his darkening eyes—only their bodies were so close that she could feel the beat of his heart through the thin fabric of his shirt against her blouse. Her breathing seemed to increase, to match the pace of his, and as she looked up his lips parted so he could take in a deep, shuddering breath.

Was it possible that Kyle was hurting as much as she was?

The voice that came from his lips was low, harsh and barely above a whisper. Trembling. Uncertain. 'There is one final request. I would like you to read the last few pages of my diary before I leave.'

His right hand came up and gently lifted a coil of her hair behind her ear in a gesture so tender and loving that she closed her eyes in the pleasure of it.

'It's not going to be easy for you. For one thing the handwriting is even worse than usual, but I do have a feeble excuse.' The sides of his mouth twisted for a second, but there was no laughter. 'I wrote them in the back of the ancient truck sent to evacuate us from the clinic. It was the first time I'd had a chance to sit down for days, and somehow it seemed right to—well, to try and make some sense of the mess we were in after Ruth's death.'

His fingers started teasing out individual coils of hair, as though that was the most important thing in the world to do at that moment.

Lulu's heart fluttered. This was it. There was some terrible truth about her mother's death and he didn't know how to tell her. He was trying to be gentle.

She tried desperately to remind herself of all of the terrible options she had imagined and dreamt up over the years. Surely nothing he could tell her now would come close to the horror of those nightmares?

Lulu clasped her fingers around his.

'Kyle? Are you telling me that you saw her at the clinic on the day she was killed?'

He nodded, once, and then his head dropped for a second before he looked up and stared directly into her startled blue eyes.

'I was probably the last person to see her alive.'

CHAPTER ELEVEN

'THEN I don't want to read what happened in the pages of your diary or this new book. I want you to tell me in person. Now. To my face. What happened, Kyle? You are the only one who can tell me the truth. Can you do that?'

The powerful legs shifted, and he released her to run his fingers through his hair and walk slowly back to the table spread with papers. He slowly reached out and lifted up the photograph of her mother standing with the local children. One finger traced across the image in silence.

'It had been a hard couple of weeks. We were all exhausted.'

He lowered the photograph to the table and rested his hands, palms down, on the flat surface. But he turned slightly, so that there was no doubt that Lulu could hear precisely what he was saying.

'Ruth had promised the local chiefs that we

would get to the village medical stations once a week. So we'd agreed a timetable. No matter what happened, I would go out in the ambulance every Tuesday morning and Ruth would stay at the hospital.'

After one sideways glance at her, he focused back on the photograph and gave a small shrug.

'You know what she was like—once she had made a promise there was no compromise. It actually seemed to work for a couple of months, but then the fighting started to get closer, and fresh casualties were coming in almost every day. Every bed in the clinic was taken and we had patients in corridors. It was relentless.'

He paused and suddenly found something quite fascinating to look at on the table.

'Go on,' she whispered under her breath. 'It was relentless and you were all exhausted?'

'Lulu, I...'

With one smooth movement, she took a few faltering steps closer, so that she could press the palms of both hands flat against his chest. The fast, hard beating of the heart that lay beneath told her everything she needed to know.

'It's okay,' she murmured, her eyes locked onto his. 'You can do this. I know you can. Just close your eyes and say the words and it will be over. I'm not afraid. I trust you.'

A shuddering long breath blew across her skin, and her eyes scanned his face in concern until his shoulders relaxed a little.

'It was a nightmare. You know how green I was. They don't teach you how to deal with situations like that in medical school. They can't. The wounded were being carried in by their families on carts and donkeys. All day and then all night. It seemed never-ending. The paramedics did amazing work, but Ruth and I were the only two surgeons, so we both had to work flat out, taking turns to catch a few hours' sleep whenever we could.'

He raised one hand and slid his fingers through her hair until he found the base of her neck. Drawing her closer, he lowered his forehead to hers so that each hot breath fanned her face with its intensity.

'The fighting was getting closer, and we had been working thirty-six hours non-stop. I came out of surgery just before dawn, and Ruth insisted I get some sleep before I dropped.'

He paused and raised his head away from her, to look at the ceiling. When he lowered it to look at her there were tears glinting in the corners.

'I came out of my tent just in time to see Ruth jump into our rackety old ambulance. I shouted out for her to wait for me, but she just gave me a wave and took off down the track in a cloud of red dust.' His voice faltered, and the Adam's apple in his throat twisted hard as he swallowed down the tears and the grief that threatened to engulf them both. 'It was the last time I saw her. '

'Oh, Kyle.' The words closed her throat, and she dropped her head to the comfort and safety and warmth of his broad chest, unable to speak.

How long they stayed like that she didn't know, but it was Kyle who broke the silence, his lips pressed into her hair as he spoke.

'Don't feel sorry for me, Lulu. I am not telling you what happened because I want you to feel sorry for me. *You* are the one who deserves sympathy. You and your father were the ones she left behind. If only she had waited a few more minutes. You have no idea how guilty I feel every time I think about it.'

A cold shiver seemed to wave across Lulu's shoulders.

'Guilty? Why should you feel guilty? What difference would a few minutes have made? She was doing the work she loved.'

Kyle's hand pressed harder to the back of her head, as though getting ready to cushion her from the blow to come.

'You don't understand, Lulu. It was a *Tuesday*

morning. *I* should have been the one in that ambulance. Not your mother. *I* should have been the one who was killed that day.'

Lulu pushed away from Kyle and staggered towards the table.

'Lulu? Talk to me. Let me explain.'

She held up one hand as she forced air down into her frozen lungs, a maelstrom of emotions welling up inside her chest and threatening to explode.

'*It was a Tuesday*. It was *your* turn to go out in the ambulance. Is that what you are telling me?'

The voice that came out of her mouth sounded like that of another woman. A woman who had just flung open the doors behind which every nightmare she had ever had were stored and hidden.

'Yes. It was my turn. Ruth told the nurse not to wake me and she took my place that day. Oh, Lulu, I am so sorry.'

Kyle reached out to take Lulu's hands, but she lifted them up and away from him.

'Don't do this, Lulu. Give me your worst— because nothing could be as bad as the guilt I feel every time I even think about that morning. Have you any idea how many times I have asked myself, *What if?* What if I hadn't been so exhausted and fallen asleep that morning? What if Ruth had waited another ten minutes? Or not been so stubborn? Or here's a good one. What if we had called the army to check whether they knew about the landmines on that road?'

'Stop. Stop it, Kyle. I don't want to hear any more.' Lulu wrapped her arms around her body to try and control the violent shivering. 'Is that the real reason why you are here right now? Why you agreed to write this book when it is obviously the very last thing that you want to do? It is, isn't it? You feel that you have to make amends for dodging a land mine? Was that how Mike blackmailed you to come here? By using your guilt that you survived?'

'Far from it. You see, Mike doesn't know that it should have been me who died that day. You are the only person I have ever told. The only person I ever would tell.'

'Me?' She stared at him for a few seconds, wide-eyed, before nodding her head.

'Of course. I see it now. That is why you agreed to come to this house instead of working in London. You are trying to compensate for your own guilt by being nice to me. Taking care of me. Is that it, Kyle? You think that you have some obligation to look out for me because you survived and she didn't?'

She was shouting now and she didn't care. Fists clenched, she strode up to him and stared into his shocked and pale face.

'How much do you like *me*? Or are you only interested in Ruth Taylor Hamilton's daughter? Please—I'd like to know the answer to that question before I throw you out.'

'So what if I do feel obligated?' Kyle snatched up the photograph of her mother laughing under the hot African sun. 'I owe her my life and I had no idea that she had a child. What is so wrong with my wanting to make sure that you have everything you need?'

He moved forward to clasp hold of both of her forearms, only she stepped away and crossed her arms tight, blocking any contact at all.

'But that was two weeks ago. Since then everything has changed. I had no way of knowing how much I would come to care about you. Want to be with you. And, no, *not* as Ruth's little girl. You are an amazing woman in your own right, Lulu Hamilton. You have to know that. Ruth would have been so proud.'

'Thank you for answering my question,' Lulu replied in a calmer voice, her eyes fixed on something fascinating on the carpet. 'But she's gone. And there is not one thing either of us can do to bring her back.'

She slowly raised her head and locked eyes with Kyle through her blurred tears.

'She took the decision to leave you behind that

day—just as she took the decision to leave me behind every time she walked out of the door en route to some airport—any airport.' Lulu raised one hand. 'That was her choice. She was head of the clinic and she had a job to do. It was her decision to go out that day. Not yours. And certainly not mine.' She shook her head before stepping back. 'I've had to live with those decisions all my life. Now it's your turn. So if that is the reason you are here, you can consider yourself officially off the hook. Duty done.'

'What are you saying?'

'My part in this project is over. I've done everything I promised.' She waved one hand towards the boxes of paperwork. 'You can have the diaries and letters. Whatever you want. Just take them and go back to Nepal, or wherever it is you have to go back to so urgently. And allow me to get back to my life.'

'Lulu—please. Let's talk this through. I don't want to leave you like this.'

She looked hard at Kyle, lifted her head, and spoke in a clear, distinct voice.

'I don't want to talk about it. I want you to leave now. Please close the door behind you on the way out.'

And with that, she turned her back on him and walked with as much control as she could to the

French windows. It was only when the curtains were almost closed that she saw the headlights of his car swing out of the drive and head off down the lane.

Dropping her hands away from the cords, she collapsed down on the window seat and put her head in her hands, let the shock take over. How long she sat there sobbing she did not know, but the air grew cold around her and she did not care.

Slowly, she became aware that a red-brown shape was standing patiently by her side, and as she sat up Belle gently laid her head on Lulu's lap and sat quietly, her deep brown eyes looking up at her. She wrapped her arms around the dog's head and let the tears stream down her face and into the dog's fur.

'Looks like it's back to just you and me, Belle. On our own again. Just you and me.'

Early the next morning over a half-hearted breakfast, Emma rubbed Lulu's shoulder as she dropped her head onto her outstretched arms.

'You knew it was going to be hard. But you can do this.' She dragged Lulu to her feet. 'Right? Right. Come on, girl, I'll make the coffee and you get back to work. Those paintings won't paint themselves. It will help.'

Lulu shrugged an ancient sweater over her

overalls. Emma was right. She needed to work on something—anything—to focus her mind and control the turmoil that raged inside her.

She had to get back to her old life.

The past two weeks working with Kyle had been a disaster for her painting projects. The gallery had already called to find out how many watercolours of local wild flowers she could provide. They were always in demand as Christmas gifts and hand-painted greeting cards—she was going to have to work fast if she had any chance of making the Christmas deadline now that the book project was behind her.

Over and done with.

Finished.

I don't want it to be over, she thought. *I don't want to be without him in my life.* But she dared not form those words. She had tasted something so wonderful it was hard to imagine life without that flavour again.

How could she have fallen so deeply, so fast?

In another world they might even have had a chance to make a life together. She knew what his world was like without any complicated excuses. They understood one another without having to explain.

Except, of course, he had not been honest with her.

Lulu dropped her shoulders and closed her eyes tight shut for a moment, before slowly twisting around in her chair to look at her mother's portrait.

This was where her father had sat, day after day. Joined for ever to the woman who still had the power to control their lives.

Ten years ago that woman had decided to let her exhausted new surgeon sleep after working through an African night. One single decision, made for the best of reasons. And Kyle had been punishing himself ever since.

'Oh, Mum,' she whispered. 'Look what you did. You gave me someone to love. Thank you for that. Any chance you can find a way to get him back for me?'

With a fast shiver, and a shake of her head for being so ridiculous as to talk to a painting, Lulu turned back to her work and wiped away the salty tears from her eyes.

Her painting was her refuge. Her solace.

And she had never needed that solace more than today.

She quickly pulled out her portfolio and lifted the first drawing onto the table in front of the window. A cluster of spring primroses peeked out from wide, fleshy leaves. It was a pretty still-life, in delicate shades of pale yellow and green that would sell well. There was nothing daring or brave or exciting about it, but it was true to life and simple. Natural and attractive.

Except that as she examined it more closely under natural daylight she saw that the original pencil drawing was too dark for the pale water-colours she had used, not daring to be too bold, and the leaves were out of proportion with the flowers.

The whole symmetry of the piece seemed wrong to her now.

It would take hours of work with layers of paint and tiny brushes to correct the mistakes and give the painting shadow, depth and texture. To make it come alive.

Suddenly the whole piece looked flat, boring, dull and mediocre.

Where was the life? The wonderful rich and vibrant colour and texture she thought she had created? How had she failed so miserably?

No one would notice the flaws from a distance. The actual painting was no bigger than a hardback book, with a huge white border that would be hidden beneath the mount and the picture frame. But *she* knew they were there.

What she been satisfied to accept a few days earlier was no longer good enough.

Which was why Lulu grabbed the top edge of the sheet of heavy paper with both hands and ripped it down the middle with all of the strength in her body, then again and again, until the table was littered with torn fragments of white and coloured paper.

Heart thumping, she stared down at the pieces with a smile on her face as a sense of freedom pulsed through her. *Liberated.*

She didn't want to go to art college and paint botanical drawings—she could already do that. She was going to art college to find out what she was capable of.

In an instant she had swept her watercolour box and portfolio off the table and replaced it with her father's large sketchpad. Twice the size of her own. Well used. And just what she needed.

Lulu could only smile as she flicked through the old sketchpad she remembered from being a girl. The spine was almost broken, and as she flicked to the next clean page a loose piece of paper fluttered out.

Swooping it up, she suddenly took a sharp intake of breath. This was not a sketch or a drawing, but a single sheet of familiar thin airmail paper covered in pale blue ink.

It was her mother's writing.

Her legs threatened to give way and Lulu collapsed at the table. She certainly had not seen this letter before.

She turned the sheet over in her hands. It looked like a page from one of her mum's letters, except their address had been scribbled on the reverse. That was unusual; she'd usually tried to fill both sides of the pages with tiny thin letters, so she could cram as much as possible into the mailing.

Not this time.

The writing was thin and wobbly, disordered, but with a sense of energy and urgency Lulu did not recognise. There was no date or address to indicate where or when it had been written.

Taking a breath, she read through the words, and then read them again.

There are only the four of us left now. We have already moved three times during the night, carrying patients and whatever we could save to higher ground, but they are moving faster than we can. The villagers have fled into the hills.

We're all too exhausted to go any further, so we sit here waiting for the inevitable. Too tired to talk.

I wonder what you are doing in Kingsmede? Working in the garden, perhaps, with Lulu by your side? Or filling the world with colour and light in the happy home I left behind? It must be so pretty now that summer is here.

You told me once that our lives are our greatest treasure, our most precious possession. Far too precious to waste on anything which is not capable of breaking our hearts. How very right you were. As always. I am looking at the photograph you sent me from our little girl's last birthday party and my heart is breaking.

It is too painful, and the crew are looking for me to get them out of this.

I think you are the only person in this world who knows that I could not even try to do what I do, in these hard places, without the knowledge that you are both safe back home.

You are my heart. My foundation. Without my family I would not have the strength to get up every day, to work to make things better for these people, knowing that I will probably fail. You are the ones who make this possible for me. And I know you pay the price.

At the clinic someone had left behind a book of poetry. I wrote down one of the lines: 'If you love somebody, let them go, for if they return, they were always yours. And if they don't, they never were'.

You are strong enough to let me go. Time and time again.

I'm going to leave this note in my medical bag. If anything happens to me, someone might post it. Kiss our little girl for me. I love you both. Never forget that.

There was no signature. No familiar kisses at the bottom. Only a faint mark of the pen as though she had started to write something and been interrupted.

Along the margin, next to the quotation, her dad had written in pencil, 'Quote from Khalil Gibran.'

Lulu slid back against her chair and let the tears flow down her cheeks.

Terrified, Ruth Taylor Hamilton had held this very piece of paper in her own sweaty hand. She had wanted them to know what she was thinking while she waited for the local militia to arrive and execute her, with the crew and the patients.

Was that why her father had taken it from the box of letters and tucked it between the pages of the sketchbook that had never left his side? To remind himself of that great love? A love which was worth breaking his heart over? A love worth that huge risk?

No. *More than that.*

Lulu closed her eyes and inhaled deeply.

Her father had sacrificed his own happiness to make sure that her mother had a stable base to come home to.

He had let her mother go time and time again in the hope that she would return to him.

Knowing that they belonged together.

Knowing that their love was capable of breaking their hearts.

Her father had stayed married to her because that was what her mother had needed. No matter the cost.

'Lulu? What is it?' Emma had come in and was staring down at her, her face anxious and caring. 'What's happened, little girl?'

'She spent so much time away on missions and he was so lonely,' Lulu gulped. 'I always thought that he regretted marrying someone who didn't want to be with us. But I was wrong. I simply never saw it before today.'

Lulu stared down at the page between her fingers, blinking away tears so that she could focus on the faint blue words written so many years ago.

'I've been such a fool. He loved her so much he was willing to let her go. Even if she broke his heart. Their love was so precious. I can see that now.'

'Well, of course it was. They were two sides of the same coin.'

Emma stood back and turned to one side, to gaze up at the portrait of Ruth Taylor Hamilton over the mantel.

'You only have to look at this painting to know how he felt about her. Your father was a clever man, Lulu, and he did love your mother—very much. He knew that Ruth would never be happy with a nine-to-five job in Kingsmede. And he was willing to make the sacrifice so that she could be happy. Every single time she stepped out of that door it broke his heart. But their love kept him going when they were apart. Kept them both going. Because I know that she felt the same way about him. They adored each other.'

Emma looked back with her head tilted and smiled.

'Why am I getting the feeling that this is not just about your parents? Am I right?'

Lulu suddenly sat up straight, blinking away her tears as she stared out of the window into the brightening sky.

'I'm in love with Kyle Munroe and I don't want to lose him. I need him so much, but I know now that I have to let him go. Even if he does break my heart.'

Emma sucked in a sharp breath of air, then grasped Lulu by both arms.

'Then go and tell him how you feel. Or regret it for the rest of your life. Go. As fast as your legs can carry you. I'll lock up here and follow you with Belle. Go! Scoot! You might just be able to catch him in time.'

CHAPTER TWELVE

PLEASE let him still be here. Please. He could not have left yet, could he?

She pedalled faster, and the arms of her old painting overalls puffed out in the cold wind which lifted the chestnut leaves up into loose whirls either side of the lane.

Lulu's heart soared as she saw a flash of dark green in the car park next to the Feathers. *His car was here!*

In one swift movement she swung her legs from her old cycle and leant it against the nearest tree, before running into the reception area, her eyes scanning for Kyle in the lunchtime crowd.

It took Lulu three seconds to bounce up the steps to the bedrooms and stand puffing and panting outside the only closed bedroom door. Emma's best guestroom.

Her hand stretched out towards the door handle. And then she snatched it back.

Eyes closed, she blew out a long deep breath, her head suddenly dizzy with doubt as the blood surged in her veins.

What was she doing here? What if he said thanks, but no thanks? This was crazy.

What had her mother said in her letter? If you love somebody, let them go? She loved this man and yet she was going to let him go free to live his life? Away from her? Mad. Yet she knew deep in her heart that it was absolutely the right thing to do.

She was risking her future happiness on a crazy decision to trust her heart instead of her head.

And what if he said yes? On the one hand she could be committing herself to the life of loneliness that her father had endured—or, on the other, to loving a man who had shown her how to love.

She had to do it now. Or never. Perhaps that was why she felt so naked? Exposed?

After ten seconds of agonised waiting, she straightened her back and prepared to knock—and at the very second she did so there was movement on the other side of the door. The handle turned on its own and cracked open an inch, then wider, braced by a familiar khaki rucksack.

She was stunned into silence as the door opened and her eyes locked onto his. He looked at her with the kind of intensity that seemed to knock the oxygen from her lungs.

Then those eyes smiled, and she took in the full effect of that handsome face. He grinned straight at her with the kind of smile that turned her legs to jelly. No camera could have captured the look on his face at that moment.

She felt as though the air would explode with the electricity in the air between them.

'Hi.' He smiled. 'You look nice. Although you didn't need to dress up to see me off.'

Lulu glanced down at her oldest pair of painting overalls and smiled back at him, desperate to break the tension so that she could put the words together that she needed to say. Wanted to say.

So much had changed.

'Oh, this little old thing?' she managed in half-breaths.

'I was planning to drive up and see you. I've been pretty busy in the last few hours.' He paused. 'Has something happened? Are you okay?' There was so much love and concern in his voice that any doubts Lulu had had about what she had to do next were wiped away.

'I—I found a note from my mother,' she faltered. 'It was inside Dad's old sketchbook. It said that…' Her throat was so choked the words refused to co-operate.

'Hey. Come and sit down.'

He wrapped his arm around her shoulder and shoved the rucksack aside so that he could draw her inside the room, where he lowered her gently on the bed while he sat on the quilt and held her hand.

'Now, talk to me. And take it slow. Tell me what this letter said that was so important you dragged yourself away from your painting to tell me about it.'

'What did it say?' she replied, stroking his hand as her eyes locked onto his, and all the words she had practised on the cycle ride spilled out in a rush. 'It said that I have been a complete fool. I have been so wrong, Kyle. About so many things.'

She reached up and stroked his cheek, her eyes never leaving his.

'I haven't stopped thinking about what you said. And you were right. This is the biggest risk of my life—your life—anyone's life.'

She breathed in, her heart thudding so loudly she suspected that he must hear it from where he was sitting so quietly.

'I know now that I will always love you, Kyle Munroe, and it doesn't matter where you are in the world. And if that means that I have to let you go—to be free to do your work…' She licked her lips. 'Then that is the way it has to be. I want to be with you. Love you. If you still want me to wait for you?'

Kyle sat very still, staring at her, and she bit her lower lip in fear. She might have just made the biggest mistake of her life, but this was the way it had to be.

'I could be away for six or seven months at a time, you know,' he told her gently, his voice low, sensual and intimate.

'Probably longer. But I am going to let you go and do what you have to do—wherever that is. Because just maybe we can get back together one day. I love you, Kyle, and that is not going to change whether you are in Nepal or Uganda or down the road.'

Kyle did not answer, but slid her fingers from his so that he could caress her face, his eyes scanning from her nose to her roughly tied-back, out-of-control hair.

'You love me but you are willing to let me go and do the work which means so much to me? Is that right?'

She nodded, afraid to trust her voice. 'As long as you are somewhere in this world, loving me, then I shall be complete. My heart will be your beacon home to my love.'

'Then there's only one answer to your question. No. I don't want you to wait for me.'

Her heart caught in her throat, but he pressed one finger on her lips and smiled, breaking the terror.

'You see, I'm not as brave as you are. As soon as I left you this morning I knew that I couldn't leave the woman I have fallen in love with without trying to come up with some options.'

He grinned at her and slid forward, so that both his hands were cupped around her face as tears pricked her eyes.

'I love you way too much to let you go. I need you, Lulu. I need you so much. Nothing else comes close. What would you say if I told you that I will be working out of London for the next twelve months?'

She shuddered out a chuckle of delight and relief. 'I would say, yes, please, and then I would ask how you have managed it.'

'They love what we've done, Lulu. Not me. The two of us. It seems that we make a pretty good team. Mike Baxter wants me to finish the book over the winter, then work with the media company on a series of follow-on books and documentaries. The Nepal mission is going to be fully funded for the next five years, and I have a job managing the missions in Africa and Asia any time I want one.'

Kyle grinned back and took her hands in his,

ready and willing to tease out the delicious moment when she heard the surprise he had planned.

'I did insist on one extra condition before they agreed to double their donation to the foundation. I told them that I would only do it if I could bring my fiancée with me to Nepal next May, so that she could paint the rhododendron forests in bloom. She might be at art college, but she'd deserve first-class travel all of the way.'

'Your fiancée…' She breathed out the words, tears pricking her wide eyes, scarcely daring to believe what he was saying.

'You have given me the greatest compliment a man could wish. You've offered me your love and the freedom to live my life. I never imagined I would find a woman who could love me as much as I loved her. I told you last night that I wasn't going anywhere, and I meant it. Not without you.'

Kyle's voice faltered as he pressed his forehead to her flushed brow.

'Last night, when I held you in my arms, I had the unbelievable feeling that I had come home. That this was where I belonged. I have travelled all over the world, Lulu. I might have kidded myself that it was for work, but the truth is hard to accept. I needed to prove to myself that there was some reason why I survived and Ruth perished. To prove that I could make a difference to people's lives. Just as she had done.'

'Oh, Kyle. It was never your fault. Just as it wasn't mine. I know that now. And you *have* made a difference.' She was stroking the hair back from his forehead now, her fingertips moving through the short curls as she stared into the depths of those stunning eyes.

'I have never felt such an overwhelming sense of homecoming than in these last few weeks I have spent with you. I didn't even realise that I was looking for it. Your heart is my beacon home. Wherever you are is where I want to be. Bring me home, Lulu. Bring me home.' He knelt in front of her as he whispered, in a husky, intimate voice that she had only heard before in her dreams, 'I love you and I want you to be part of my life, Lulu. If you'll have me?'

Lulu looked into a face so full of love that her heart broke.

'Have you? Oh, my sweet darling. How can you ask that after last night? You have to know that I love you. I will love you for the rest of my life. You are the centre of my world.'

She choked with emotion as Kyle stood, then swung her up into the air, whirling her around and around until her feet connected with the bedroom lampshade.

In an instant Kyle had lowered her to the floor and grabbed her hand. She had to skip down the stairs to keep up with him as they ran out together into the faint sunshine, laughing and squealing in joy. Oblivious to the people around them.

Emma Carmichael stepped out of her car just in time to see Kyle grab Lulu behind the knees and throw her over his right shoulder.

Kyle was almost in the middle of the river before she managed to wriggle free, and then, holding hands, they pulled and twirled each other round and round, heads back, laughing and shouting in pleasure, water splashing up around them, before collapsing into each other's arms, their heads pressed together into a passionate kiss.

At that moment Belle leapt out of the backseat of Emma's car and charged into the water to dance and play around the happy couple, barking and scampering in the shallows.

Emma turned to the rest of the village, who had crowded in to look over her shoulder, and shooed them back inside the Feathers.

'Those Taylor girls always end up with the best-looking boys! Now, who's ready for a nice glass of champagne? There is far too much excitement around here.'

EPILOGUE

KYLE strolled into the spacious art gallery and looked over the heads of the glamorous patrons to catch a glimpse of the only person he needed to see.

And there she was. The centre of attention, chatting away to friends and buyers as though she attended an exhibition of her own paintings every day of the week.

Incredibly beautiful. Confident. Unique.

Looking at her now, it was hard to imagine that only an hour ago he had been fighting to pin back her corkscrew curls to display the African tribal jewellery that had been her wedding gift from their friends in Uganda.

She looked wonderful.

By some sixth sense, at that precise moment she turned her head towards him and grinned right back across the room. The familiar heat of attraction flashed through his body. He did not want to be apart from the woman he loved for one moment longer than necessary!

Clusters of people were gathered in front of a wall of brilliantly coloured paintings of exotic blooms. Rhododendron bushes in full bloom, magnolia trees and stunning African blossoms shone out from the walls. Glowing and vibrant. Just like the amazing and beautiful woman who had painted them.

He casually wrapped one arm around the waist of her simple aquamarine silk satin shift dress and was rewarded with a tender kiss on the side of his neck as he drew her closer.

'Have I told you this evening that you look stunning, Mrs Munroe?'

'Um… Once or twice. Thank you, anyway—and you clean up pretty well yourself, Dr Munroe.' She reached up and smoothed down the lapel of his black cashmere suit. 'Although I do have a certain preference for khaki green.' Her mouth lifted into a personal smile that still hit him hard.

'Kyle—glad you could make it.' The beaming gallery owner strolled forward to shake his hand. 'Thank you for delaying your plans for a few days. The exhibition has been a huge success, but we couldn't have done it without Lulu being here. When are you flying out this time?'

'We're leaving for Kampala tomorrow, then

Delhi,' Kyle replied, and laughed out loud. 'But don't worry. We shouldn't be gone for more than a few weeks. Unless, of course, my wife decides to take off on yet another botanical expedition of her own. In which case—' he threw his hands up and shrugged in defeat '—who knows where we'll end up? There is no holding this girl back.'

Lulu squeezed his arm as she smiled up into his face. 'Well, there have to be some perks for marrying the director of the foundation responsible for all of Africa and Asia! But then we are going home to Kingsmede. Together. To start the most amazing journey of our lives.'

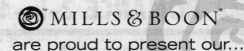

are proud to present our...

Book of the Month

An Officer and a Millionaire
by Maureen Child
from Mills & Boon®
Desire™ 2-in-1

The broad-shouldered military man had no
patience with games. Margie had to go. She'd
been masquerading as his spouse and living in his
house. Now all his skills were focused on payback:
he'd have that "wedding night"!

Enjoy double the romance in this
great-value 2-in-1!
An Officer and a Millionaire by Maureen Child and
Mr Strictly Business by Day Leclaire

Mills & Boon® Desire™ 2-in-1
Available 18th December 2009

Something to say about our
Book of the Month?
Tell us what you think!
millsandboon.co.uk/community

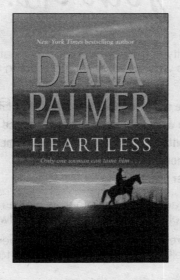

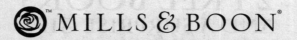

2 FREE BOOKS
AND A SURPRISE GIFT

We would like to take this opportunity to thank you for reading this Mills & Boon® book by offering you the chance to take TWO more specially selected books from the Romance series absolutely FREE! We're also making this offer to introduce you to the benefits of the Mills & Boon® Book Club™—

- **FREE home delivery**
- **FREE gifts and competitions**
- **FREE monthly Newsletter**
- **Exclusive Mills & Boon Book Club offers**
- **Books available before they're in the shops**

Accepting these FREE books and gift places you under no obligation to buy, you may cancel at any time, even after receiving your free shipment. Simply complete your details below and return the entire page to the address below. You don't even need a stamp!

YES Please send me 2 free Romance books and a surprise gift. I understand that unless you hear from me, I will receive 5 superb new stories every month including two 2-in-1 books priced at £4.99 each and a single book priced at £3.19, postage and packing free. I am under no obligation to purchase any books and may cancel my subscription at any time. The free books and gift will be mine to keep in any case.

Ms/Mrs/Miss/Mr_____ Initials _____

Surname _____
Address _____

_____

_____ Postcode _____

Send this whole page to: Mills & Boon Book Club, Free Book Offer, FREEPOST NAT 10298, Richmond, TW9 1BR